"Richard Long intertwined a bag full of genres while creating this intriguing and enchanting story...it's mind-blowing."
— **Stephen King** – *author of Under the Dome*

"Long's prose is deft and clear, transporting the reader from one character's psyche to the next...this tale is a compelling one. A psychological thriller for readers who are bored with run-of-the-mill horror...those who embrace the genre will eagerly anticipate a second installment in the series."
— **Kirkus Reviews**

★ ★ ★ ★ ★ "Intelligent, self-aware, and often amusing, while hitting all the markers for sadistic, salacious, and scary. Written in short cinematic bursts from multiple viewpoints, *The Book of Paul*...weaves in and out of the realm of alchemy, mythology, and ancient arcana. No ordinary writer of horror, Richard Long is doubtless going to build a large and loyal fan base composed of people just like him: literate folks with a bizarre sense of humor who prefer salsa to sugar, red meat to broccoli, and a bucket of blood to a bath filled with rose petals."
— **ForeWord Clarion Reviews**

★ ★ ★ ★ ★ "Totally absorbing! *The Book of Paul* is moving, profound, funny, terrifying and never lets you go. The prose is swift and sharp... at times, even poetic. Masterful storytelling Hats off!"
— **Henry Bean** – *writer/director of The Believer*

★ ★ ★ ★ ★ "*The Book of Paul* is a surreal spellbinding tale of terror and horror destined for bestseller status."
— **RJ Parker** - *author of The Serial Killer Compendium*

★ ★ ★ ★ ★ "Intelligent and compelling. Elegantly written, immensely entertaining and original, Richard Long's *The Book of Paul* is so suspenseful and entertaining that I kept on reading late into the night, wondering what the next chapter would bring. I strongly recommend it."

— James H. Cone, *author of The Cross and the Lynching Tree*

★ ★ ★ ★ ★ "Bloody brilliant peice of work that will keep you on your toes. The characters suck you into their world, digging their nasty hooks (or sickles, as the case may be) into your psyche. There's no turning back, you have to finish it!"

— Millie Burns, *author of Return of the Crown*

★ ★ ★ ★ ★ "Twisted, outrageous, relentless…you won't want to miss it."

— Greg Lichtenberg, *author of Playing Catch with my Mother*

★ ★ ★ ★ ★ "*The Book of Paul* is an astounding achievement with incredible characters of great depth, a body of near-perfect prose, wonderful pacing and a voice that will entice you. In the tradition of Clive Barker, author Richard Long has created a world that is something like we have rarely seen… joining science, magic and religion…he has done something incredible."

— James Garcia, Jr., *author of Dance on Fire*

★ ★ ★ ★ ★ "A beautifully crafted psychological thriller, complete with a love story and relentless action."

— Jeannie Walker, *author of Fighting the Devil*

★ ★ ★ ★ ★ " Kudos for a deliciously dark, wild roller coaster ride…from the beginning to the very end."

— Alexandra Anthony, *author of The Vampire Destiny Series*

★ ★ ★ ★ ★ "Move over Dan Brown! Watch your back Clive Barker!"

— Christa Wick, *author of Texas Curves*

★ ★ ★ ★ ★ "Long's debut novel defies categorization, but that is part of the work's brilliance. Horror, twisted romance, science fiction, mystery—this book quite literarily has it all. A great read and highly recommended!

— **Daniel B. Elish**, *author of The School for the Insanely Gifted*

★ ★ ★ ★ ★ "A twisted, festive, life & death tale dragging us from sunlit rooms into the dark corners of our minds one hammer swing at a time."

— **Kriss Morton**, *CabinGoddess*

★ ★ ★ ★ ★ "An enchanting tale that will leave you spellbound with a mixture of surprise, shock, disgust, laughter, and hope. I can't wait to read more of this series. Hats off to you Richard Long, for creating a truly worthy and delightful read."

— **Nikki McCarver**, *Close Encounters of the Night Kind*

★ ★ ★ ★ ★ "Richard Long is a tremendous and unique storyteller. It will take you on a wild ride…so buckle up!"

— **Shelly Greninger**, *Dive Under the Cover*

★ ★ ★ ★ ★ "You'll just have to read the book to find out how mind-blowing and deceptively rewarding this supernatural, psychological thriller can be."

— **Naomi Leadbeater**, *Naimeless*

★ ★ ★ ★ ★ "Imagine Quentin Tarantino, Brett Easton Ellis and the DaVinci Code, with a liberal sprinkling of the occult and Irish lore and you have the brilliant, powerful, thrilling, page-turner that is *The Book Of Paul*."

— **Ariane Zurcher**, *Emma's Hope Book*

★ ★ ★ ★ ★ "A brilliant masterpiece…I literally could not put it down. Talent like this only comes around every once in a great while and I feel like I have stumbled upon gold. By far the best novel I have read all year."

— **C. Brewer**, *Batty for Books*

THE
BOOK
of
PAUL

a novel

RICHARD
LONG

open
eyes

The Book of Paul
by Richard Long

ISBN-13: 978-0615648644

LCCN: 2012940690

FIRST PAPERBACK EDITION

Cover design: Jason Heuer
Interior design: Colin O'Brien
Author photo: Christian Woods

ACKNOWLEDGEMENTS

First and foremost, my wife and partner Ariane Zurcher, who has supported, encouraged and trudged beside me down a very long road. My wonderful children Nic and Emma who sustain me. John Paine, my editor, who wasn't afraid to cut my favorite parts. Jason Heuer for the striking cover design. Colin O'Brien for making the inside as compelling as the outside. Christian Woods for the baddass author photo. Special thanks to Steve Pagnotta, Henry Bean, Matthew Carnicelli, Adrienne Lombardo and all the early readers seduced by the gleeful villainy of Paul.

Dedicated to
ARIANE

In memory of
NORINE

THE HAMMER

and

THE NAIL

Exercises

He practiced smiling.

Looking in the mirror, Martin pulled up the corners of his mouth, trying to duplicate the expression of the blond-haired man on the TV with the big forehead. Something wasn't right—the eyebrows? His eyes darted back and forth from the mirror to the television, posing, making adjustments here and there…lips down, more teeth…comparing…nope. After a few minutes, his face started to hurt and he gave up.

He did push-ups instead. Push-ups were easy. He did two hundred before he had to stop and change the channel. A show called *The Nanny* had come on and he leapt up like a cat as soon as he heard her whiny voice. He pressed the remote button with blinding speed—*click, click, click, click, click*—until he found an old black-and-white movie. Good. He liked those. He went back to his push-ups, his face tilted up so he wouldn't miss a thing.

In the movie there was a woman who was worried that this man didn't love her anymore. She didn't know it, but the man was worried that the woman didn't love him either. They spent all this time (he couldn't even count how many push-ups) trying to make each other jealous, hoping that would make the other one love them again. Martin didn't understand any of it. He looked at them laughing and smiling while they tried to trick and embarrass each other, then went to the mirror and practiced again.

It still didn't look right.

PRETTY

Birds were chirping, dogs were barking. It was a bright, bright beautiful cool crisp day in the neighborhood. Junkies were up with their crackhead cousins, prowling the lanes of Tompkins Square Park, looking for a not quite empty vial to suck on or maybe a john so they could buy one. The gentry joggers were up already, circling the park in huffy, puffy laps, their pounding hoofbeats echoing the *clang-whirl-shwoop-crunch* of the mob-owned garbage trucks.

Ho-hum. Rose slowly fingered the ring on her nipple and wondered why she couldn't get back to sleep. The garbage trucks were the obvious reason. The booms and bangs down below sounded like artillery fire. Still, she usually slept like a pile of cannonballs at Gettysburg. When she went down, she stayed down. At least until noon. She worked nights at the tattoo parlor, happily infecting all the ink-crazed kids with HIV and hepatitis C (if they were lucky). She didn't realize she was doing that. She'd been following the sterilization techniques handed down by her creepy boss. Unfortunately, they weren't any more effective than the jar of clear blue liquid that the barbershop used to sterilize combs. In the time she'd been working, she had already been responsible for the possibly fatal infection of eleven pierced and tattooed members of the "tribal community."

So Rose, blissfully unaware of her crimes against humanity, lay wide awake at nine-fifteen in the morning, twisting and turning her nipple ring. She wasn't sure why she was awake, but now that she was, she knew what she wanted to do about it. As she rubbed the two silver rings that held her clit hostage, she wondered again why she was up so early and why she felt so…horny? Hungry? What?

She knocked off a quick O like she was popping a wine cork, light and charming but nothing special. That's when she realized it wasn't a sex thing. So what was it?

She gripped the rings on both nipples and stretched them upward as far as she could, dragging her small twin mounds along like a pair of stubborn mules. She pulled and pulled until her nipples ached, then held the rings at the Maximum Stretching Point, feeling the pain course through her, then settle back down again. She didn't back off even a millimeter, just took some deep slow breaths for a moment or two and tried to pull them out even farther.

She thought of a dancer doing hamstring stretches, and she figured the technique and level of pain must be fairly equivalent. After slowly yanking them out again, she thought, *I'm in training*, and started giggling so hard she had to let go. *Thwack*. Her tiny tits and sore, swollen nipples bounced back against her chest like a pair of hard rubber balls. *Boing*. Giggle. Hohum. Hmmm. So it wasn't the sex and it wasn't the pain or the sexpain or the painsex. So what was it? She looked out the window at the blue morning sky and the green bushy trees and the squirrel tightrope-walking on the fire escape and the *cling-clang* of the garbage truck and…

She was happy. She was unreasonably, deliriously happy! But why? The "why" brought a tiny frown to her tiny face, but the "happy" was so much stronger that it brushed away the "why" with a single gust of cool fresh air that came blowing through her curtains.

She threw the covers off the bed and let the breeze wash over her until her skin was a textured roadmap of goose bumps, pits, posts, rings and colored ink. She breathed and the ink breathed with her. She sat on the edge of the bed and jingled like Donner and Blitzen. She smiled and she looked out the window and knew something good was coming her way.

Rose stood up and stretched and took a deep breath and yawned and padded into the hallway where her yoga mat was waiting. She spent the next half hour going through her routine, a rare carryover of the training and discipline that dominated her preadolescent life as a competitive gymnast. She could do headstands and handstands and downward-facing dogs like nobody's business. In fact, it took some fairly severe contortions for her to even break a sweat, but by the final lotus pose, a slippery sheen of perspiration coated her arms and chest.

She sniffed her armpits, bowed to the altar at the end of the hall and lit three candles. The candles were nestled between a variety of crystals and minerals, some so brightly colored she often wondered how something that vibrant and wondrous could actually be growing like a plant on the walls of caves in total darkness. Or like her amethyst geode, actually growing inside a rock, like an egg hatching a million-year-old purple crystal baby. Her favorite gemstone was one her mom gave her, a brilliant red crystal she called a bloodstone. Its smooth, squarish surface was easily five inches across and three inches thick, one of the largest of its kind, she'd been told. She rubbed it for good luck like she did almost every day, then pranced into the bathroom for a very long, very hot shower.

She hummed a happy song while she soaped and scrubbed and rubbed and shaved and shaved and shaved. She wasn't sure what the song was or where she'd heard it before. After three more humming choruses, it suddenly came to her and she could see Natalie Wood dancing in that dress shop, looking in the mirror while the other girls scolded her for being so silly. Rose looked in her defogging shower mirror, liked what she saw and sang out right along with them, "I feel pretty…oh, so pretty…"

Monsters

You tell your children not to be afraid. You tell them everything will be all right. You tell them Mommy and Daddy will always be there. You tell them lies.

Paul looked out the filthy window and watched the little girl playing in the filthier street below. Hopscotch. He didn't think kids played hopscotch anymore. Not in this neighborhood. Hip-hopscotch, maybe.

"Hhmph! What do you think about that?"

Paul watched the little black girl toss her pebble or cigarette butt or whatever it was to square number five, then expertly hop, hop, hop her way safely to the square and back. She was dressed in a clean, fresh, red-gingham dress with matching red bows in her neatly braided pigtails. She looked so fresh and clean and happy that he wondered what she was doing on this shithole street.

The girl was playing all by herself. Hop, hop, hop. Hop, hop, hop. She was completely absorbed in her hopping and scotching and Paul was equally absorbed watching every skip and shuffle. No one walked by and only a single taxi ruffled the otherworldly calm.

Paul leaned closer, his keen ears straining to pick up the faint sound of her shiny leather shoes scraping against the grimy concrete. He focused even more intently and heard the even fainter lilt of her soft voice. Was she singing? He pressed his ear against the glass and listened. Sure enough, she was singing. Paul smiled and closed his eyes and let the sound pour into his ear like a rich, fragrant wine.

"One, two, buckle my shoe. Three, four, shut the door..."

He listened with his eyes closed. Her soft sweet voice rose higher and higher until...the singing suddenly stopped. Paul's eyes snapped open. The girl was gone. He craned his neck quickly to the left and saw her being pulled roughly down the street. The puller was a large, light-skinned black man, tugging on her arm every two seconds like he was dragging a dog by its leash. At first, he guessed that the man was her father, a commodity as rare in this part of town as a fresh-scrubbed girl playing hopscotch. Then he wondered if he wasn't her father after all. Maybe he was one of *those* kinds of men, one of those monsters that would take a sweet, pure thing to a dark, dirty place and...

And do whatever a monster like that wanted to do.

Paul pressed his face against the glass and caught a last fleeting glance of the big brown man and the tiny red-checkered girl. He watched the way he yanked on her arm, how he shook his finger, how he stooped down to slap her face and finally concluded that he was indeed her one and only Daddy dear. Who else would dare to act that way in public?

"Kids!" Paul huffed. "The kids these days!"

He laughed loud enough to rattle the windows. Then his face hardened by degrees as he pictured the yanking daddy and the formerly happy girl. Hmmm, maybe he was one of those prowling monsters after all. Paul shuddered at the thought of what a man like that would do. He imagined the scene unfolding step by step, grunting as the vision became more and more precise. "Hhmph!" he snorted after a particularly gruesome imagining. "What kind of a bug could get inside your brain and make you do a thing like that?"

"Monsters! Monsters!" he shouted, rambling back into the wasteland of his labyrinthine apartments, twisting and turning through the maze of lightless hallways as if being led by a seeing-eye dog. He walked and turned and walked some more, comforted as always by the darkness. Finally, he came to a halt and pushed hard against a wall.

His hidden sanctuary opened like Ali Baba's cave, glowing with the treasures it contained. He stepped inside and saw the figure resting (well, not exactly resting) between the flickering candles. At the sound of his footsteps, the body on the altar twitched frantically. Paul moved closer, rubbing a smooth fingertip across the wet, trembling skin and raised it to his lips. It tasted like fear. He gazed down at the man, his eyes moving slowly from his ashen face to the rusty nails holding him so firmly in place.

The warm, dark blood shining on the wooden altar made him think about the red-gingham bunny again.

"Monsters," he said, more softly this time, wishing he weren't so busy. As much as he would enjoy it, there simply wasn't enough time to clean up this mess, prepare for his guests and track her down. Well, not her, precisely. Her angry, tugging dad. Not that Paul had any trouble killing little girls, you understand. It just wasn't his thing. Given a choice, he would much rather kill her father. And make her watch.

LAUNDRY DAY

Martin felt good. So good he would have smiled if he could. Today was laundry day. He'd been awake for hours, doing his exercises (one thousand sit-ups, push-ups and chin-ups, plus an assortment of martial arts routines), reading his favorite periodicals (*Popular Mechanics*, *Soldier of Fortune*, *Lost Treasures*). Even so, he was still able to tinker with his home surveillance system, take his shower at precisely nine a.m., and then *finally*…move on to the laundry.

Martin enjoyed many things in life: hunting, hoarding, watching TV… but he loved doing laundry the most. Every day was a contest between him and hard water. New York had the hardest water, like it had the hardest everything else. It helped with the dishes, breaking down the dried spaghetti sauce on his plate like hot corrosive acid. It helped in the shower too, where he rigged a special high-pressure nozzle that practically ripped the skin from his knotted muscles. He entered the bathroom with great determination, carefully hanging his gym shorts on their special hook, and proceeded to shave every hair on his head, chest, arms, underarms, legs and groin with an electric hair clipper, to a uniform one-eighth-inch length. One less thing to think about. Then he turned on the shower as hot as he could stand it, stepped inside and reveled in the fire hose blast of all that hard, hot water. *Ahhhhhhh.*

Martin was hard too. Looked hard. Felt hard. Yet his one true luxury in life was softness. Soft shirts, pants, underwear…soft sheets, pillows, blankets. Martin cursed the water silently as he washed his hand washables. He had more hand-washables than most people had laundry. How could you trust your personal garments…fabric that came into physical contact with your *skin*…to anyone else? He muttered and fought fiercely against the hard, spiteful water, but just as he felt the clothes in his hands raise a mushy white flag of surrender, he suddenly heard a sound he never heard in all the time he had lived there. The doorbell.

DING-DONG

Martin had one of those spring-button doorbells that almost dislocates your finger when it pops back out, making that "Ding-dong, Avon" sound. He craned his head over to the peephole while keeping his body to the right side of the doorframe in case the Avon person happened to be carrying a shotgun and wanted to punch a window through the door and his newly trimmed belly. He was being extra careful because he was trained that way, not because he was expecting any trouble. Better safe than sorry.

In the peephole's fish-eye distortion he saw the spiky hair of the girl who recently moved in upstairs. He had seen her on a few occasions, but he doubted she had seen him. Curious but ever cautious, he opened the door an inch and peeked outside. She was young, early twenties he guessed, probably five feet two inches. Her hair was also short and jet black. She had big dark eyes, long lashes and a thin gold ring in her nose.

Martin waited, saying nothing. He hated nose-rings and wanted to hand her a Kleenex. She said nothing either, looking at Martin's eye in the door crack. The silence didn't bother Martin in the least. He spent ninety-eight percent of his time waiting and watching. He had the patience of Job. Besides, this was her errand. Whatever she wanted, she would either get around to telling him or she wouldn't.

"You the super?" Rose asked finally.

"No," Martin replied.

"My sink's broke," she grumbled.

Martin said nothing, since he had no idea how to be concerned about her problem.

"You know where he lives?" she asked after three more uncomfortable seconds. She began fidgeting from staring so long at the unblinking eye.

"Yes," Martin said.

Rose paused a second, wondering if this guy was just stoned or an idiot or mean or what. "Well, do you think you could tell me?" she asked finally, tapping her foot.

Martin hated foot-tapping even more than nose-rings and paused even longer while debating whether to tell her. "Next door," he said at last, as Rose was heading back up the stairs.

"Thanks a lot," she said, her voice dripping with the sarcasm distinctive of New York City apartment dwellers.

"You're welcome," Martin said, ignoring her sarcasm and incapable of it himself.

He closed the door and looked through the peephole, catching a glimpse of her hair moving toward the apartment next door. Glad to have concluded the exchange, he was happier still to return to his hand-washables, pulling out a bottle of Forever New from under the sink where there were six more keeping it company. Then he heard the ding-dong again.

His reaction to the doorbell both startled and confused him. He expected to feel annoyed at being interrupted yet again from one of life's greatest pleasures, but instead he felt a flutter of excitement. Why? He walked to the door and opened it a bit wider this time, shocked at himself for not looking through the peephole first. But it was just the girl, as he expected, still unarmed and grumbling more than ever. "He's not there," she said.

Martin said nothing. The super was in the hospital, where he would remain for the foreseeable future, having slipped in the bathtub after knocking back a fifth of vodka.

Rose stood in the hallway, still expecting some kind of response. Then her eyes widened as she took in the part of Martin's body he had exposed through the six-inch gap. His bare chest was rippling with sinewy muscle and covered with a glaze of short hairs that ran from his chest in a ribbon to his navel and below, disappearing in the loose gray cotton of his gym shorts. Her eyes followed all the way down and she felt an involuntary spasm in her crotch when she saw the big lump in his.

Martin remained silent, watching as her eyes bounced back to his face like a diver on a springboard, hoping she hadn't been caught. Just as quickly, they drifted back down again.

"Know where he is?" Rose blurted out, struggling to maintain eye contact.

"No," he lied, feeling the lump grow bigger from the unaccustomed attention.

"Know how to fix a sink?" she asked with more tension than she intended, partly because of his unwillingness to speak unless spoken to, yet mostly due to a sudden re-emergence of one of her favorite sexual fantasies involving household repairmen.

Something clicked inside Martin's head when she asked that last question. He wasn't sure if it was the question or the way her voice was quivering, but he responded immediately and with some real enthusiasm this time. "Yes," he said. "I do."

THE GOOD STUFF

"My name is Rose," she said to the air in front of her as they climbed the stairs.

Martin said nothing, his senses too occupied with analyzing the changing surroundings to respond even if he had the inclination. When she turned around suddenly to face him, he almost went for the quick kill punch to the Adam's apple he automatically used whenever threatened in close quarters. But he pulled back before she even noticed.

"And what's *your* name?" she asked in the tone you use for a shy three-year-old.

He felt angry at her patronizing tone. He wasn't an idiot for Chrissakes. Yet he was shocked to see his anger melt away under her smiling gaze. "I'm Martin," he replied.

I couldn't believe it! His real name! What was going on here? I wanted to shake him and say, "Hey wake up!" But I wasn't there, not all the way. So I kept my mouth shut.

"Hi, Martin," said Rose, shaking his hand and smiling again. Then she turned with a toss of her short black hair and started up the stairs again.

Martin actually looked at his hand before following her.

As soon as Rose opened her door, Martin's eyes bugged out in wonder. Had he entered some science-fiction teleporter? A time machine? A Moroccan opium den? She couldn't have been living here more than a few months, yet every square inch of the walls was covered in exotic draperies, the intricate patterns almost causing him to hallucinate. His eyes scanned across them and down to the floor, which was layered with what looked like big, white, hairy yak-fur rugs on top of Persian carpets. Resting on the rugs and carpets were giant silk-embroidered pillows, so many he wanted to count them, but his eyes lingered on the low table they surrounded. The table was made of black teak and held over a dozen fat beige candles, all lit and dripping into the red dragon inlays carved into the surface.

Fire hazard, he thought, ever the pragmatist. How she could even think of leaving her apartment with so many candles burning? She could burn the whole building down! He would escape, of course, his acute sense of smell alerting him far in advance, but that didn't mean he shouldn't snuff them out right now for the risk they represented.

"The sink's over here," Rose said brightly, extinguishing his thoughts instead.

She was pointing at a door and he was shocked again to realize that he couldn't match the floor layout with his own apartment. It must be the same or at least a mirror image. That was one of the things he liked most about apartment living, the predictability of the environment. But everything seemed so different.

"Over here," she coaxed in a warm, relaxed voice. When he didn't immediately respond, she took his hand and led him. He looked at her small hand in his and watched in disbelief as his feet started moving, skirting the pillows to follow her. On his way, he paused in front of a thick (couch? mattress? futon?) covered with the silkiest blankets he'd ever seen. Everything seemed so *soft*, including the translucent curtains draped from a central gathering on the ceiling. They surrounded the bed on all sides like a wispy cocoon.

Rose tugged on his hand again, pulling Martin away from the wonderful cocoon.

On their way, they passed in front of her altar. Martin stopped again, mesmerized by the candlelight illuminating all the gems and minerals. He stroked the large red gem much as Rose had done, not for luck, but for the sheer pleasure of the tactile sensation. It was so beautiful. The candles made it look like it was glowing from within, like it was alive and might respond to his touch with an even greater display of brilliance.

"Nice," he said appreciatively, crouching down to gaze at it even more intently.

"It's a bloodstone," Rose bragged, elated that he was enjoying it as much as she did.

"Rhodochrosite," Martin corrected her. "Probably from the Sweet Home mine in Alma, Colorado. It's a fine specimen," he added, standing up again, "best I've ever seen."

"Thanks." She beamed, his admiration erasing her frown from his previous comment.

They silently stared at each other for a moment that stretched out far too long until she couldn't take it anymore and pulled on his hand again. *Yes*, Martin thought, feeling the same discomfort and needing to get back on firmer ground. *The sink*.

When they passed through the door, Martin landed with a w*hump* back on the planet. It was like he was in his own apartment again—sink over here, cabinets there, just a normal kitchen—no candles, no rugs, no softness, no nothing! He wanted to run back into that other world...the world on *that* side of the door. But he stood there dumbly, his mouth open, his head swiveling back and forth between the two rooms.

"I'm not finished," she said, not sure why she was acting so apologetic. "I blew all my money fixing up the other room."

Money? All you need is money? Martin thought, not sure why he felt so angry and disappointed. Then he looked at her pretty face and turned his attention back to the sink, grateful for something to do. "It's not broken, it's clogged," he said with characteristic bluntness. "Don't you have a plunger?"

"I tried." Rose said with a shrug, holding up the still-dripping implement. Then she added with a wince, "Macaroni and cheese."

Cute, Martin thought, an unfamiliar warmth invading his chest.

He grabbed the plunger and pounded the drain like a pneumatic drill. The clog was obliterated in eighteen seconds and his anger had almost vanished too, when a fresh new horror caught his eyes.

"Woolite? You use this shit?"

Rose didn't understand the appalled expression on Martin's face, wasn't even quite sure she heard him right. Did he really just make a disparaging remark about her *fabric softener?* She didn't have time to ask. He was already out the door, grunting, "I'll be back," like you-know-who.

Martin flew down the stairs, unlatched the seven pick-proof locks and the cold-rolled-steel dead bolt and threw the door open so hard the frame almost splintered. He grabbed a jug from his special stock and bounded back up the stairs. Rose was waiting right where he left her. There was something about seeing her lean against that sink that made his cock inflate like a meat balloon. The hard-on was a real surprise for him. Even so, he didn't pay any attention to it, as usual.

She did. Martin had a really big one. Figures. Why should someone who couldn't care less if he used it or not get a really big one? The head of his cock pushed its way out the leg of his gym shorts and was still growing down his thigh. Rose knew her mouth had to be open as she watched its progress, but she couldn't do anything about it. When she looked back at his face, she was even more shocked to see he was completely oblivious to what was happening. Instead, he turned to the sink and thumped down the big plastic jug.

"Here, use this," he said proudly, handing her the bottle. "This is the good stuff."

Rose couldn't decide which was a bigger turn-on…the man standing there with his big huge cock hanging out his shorts like a fat log, or the fact that he was so blissfully unaffected by it. She reached down, grabbed the big fucker in both hands, looked him straight in the eye and said, "No. This is the good stuff."

Preparations

Paul wiped the blood from his hands before lifting the heavy book and placing it gently on the lectern. "That wasn't too smart, you droppin' by unannounced," he chuckled. The body offered no argument. There wouldn't have been one even if he were still conscious. "So much to do, so little time," Paul sighed, pulling out the other nails, hog-tying his ankles to his neck, stuffing the body in a burlap sack and hefting it over his shoulder as easily as a bag of flour. He patted the sack on the rump and stomped out of the room, winding through the black corridors before depositing his burden with a thud on the filthy floor of another dark room.

"Have a nice nappy-poo. I'll be back in time for supper!" he shouted, waving to the still-silent lump as he tromped back through the hallways to his candlelit sanctuary.

He sealed the door behind him and walked to the lectern slowly, deliberately, reaching under his shirt to extract the key dangling from a chain around his neck. He unlocked the wide leather strap binding the massive tome and felt the power course through his veins as soon as he opened the ancient leather binding.

He rubbed his hands gleefully. There was so much fun in store. New friends to meet. Old bonds to renew. Paul relished every encounter. One more than all the rest.

Which isn't to say that no one else mattered. No, you couldn't say that. But nothing mattered more than him.

No one was more important than Martin.

INTO THE SOFTNESS

She dropped to her knees right there and took him in her mouth. It was a tight fit.

"Wow," he said. She looked up at him and would have smiled if her lips weren't stretched so thin.

Martin didn't have many experiences to compare this to, but he guessed that she was very good at this. She was. She had amazing technique and knew all kinds of special tricks, but she didn't need any of that now. She was in a higher state of need and she sucked him hard and loud and sloppy. Martin groaned from the intensity of it...of her.

Her tongue was pierced with a stainless-steel barbell she was rubbing on the soft-hard tube of his urethra. He got scared because he knew she must have something in her mouth doing this to him, but he couldn't imagine what it was or how she got it in there without him seeing it. But he didn't stay scared. He got harder and he knew he had to do something, something more...but not in here. He needed to do it in there...in that room.

In the softness.

Martin picked her up and carried her in. She thought she might pass out from the excitement. He slammed the door behind them and Rose's heart slammed in her chest.

He paused once they were inside and let the dark lost world wash over them, waiting until the candles and smells and the absolute quiet erased any memory of anything that had ever happened before. Then he gently set her down on the bed and stepped back to watch her sink into the billowy fabric.

Rose looked at him standing there, so still, his hands slightly out to his sides like he was trying to keep his balance. She was afraid for a moment that he might be too tender, but when she saw the heat in his eyes, she relaxed and smiled at him. He looked like he was going to smile back, but his features evened out, smooth and unknowable. She looked down and saw his cock was harder than ever, his gym shorts in a pile around his feet.

She unbuttoned the black fabric buttons on the front of her tiny dress and pulled it apart so she could show him her small breasts and the other rings he hadn't seen yet.

Martin came to her like a big cat, low and lumbering, rolling his shoulders as he crawled on top of her. He moaned as he straddled her naked chest, the softness caressing him, coming from everywhere at once. He paused for a moment on top of her, staring at the rings in her nipples and the long golden chain winding between them like a lazy river. At the end of the chain, a small shiny key drew his attention even more than the nipple rings. He felt his heart tighten with dread, but when he looked closer he saw it wasn't the same. Still, it looked so familiar. Hadn't he seen it somewhere before? He tried to remember, but his eyes kept moving, scanning her creamy skin and the crescent moon tattoo and finally resting on her face again. Her smiling face.

When she smiled he felt something move inside his chest. It was more intense than the warmth he felt before, like congestion…but rumbly …louder. As he leaned over to kiss her smiling lips, he noticed a little drop of water had fallen on her chest. On the key. He looked to the ceiling to see if there was some kind of leak, but the angle wasn't right. The rumble in his chest grew louder when he realized the drop had fallen from his eye.

Narrator Intrusion

Call me William. I remember everything. It's what I do.

I didn't plan on entering the story so soon, but I just couldn't take that last scene. Why? Why should it matter to me if they fucked each other's brains out? I thought you'd never ask.

All these things happened once upon a time in the East Village, when outlaws still roamed, junkies copped and squatters squatted. I lived there too, before gentrification and the unusual events you're about to witness swept all of us away.

I have a true photographic memory, the kind that guarantees a perfect score in any test, the kind that easily passes itself off as high, perhaps genius intelligence, even if there are no other outward indications that this is the case.

I sit. I watch. I listen. I record. I see all these people, but they don't see me. I wish things were different. I'm lonely too, like they are. At least I can admit it.

Some of them are better than they seem at first. Some of them are worse, much worse. Sometimes I think evil is just loneliness with nowhere else to go.

Take me for example. All my life I've struggled to do the right thing. Well, most of it anyway. I've fought hard and long against the darker urges, sometimes successfully, sometimes not. It's easy to lay the blame on genetics, or on Paul and The Striker. I could even blame Rose if I wanted. But as I watched her and Martin through my closed eyes, as I heard her scream a cry of pleasure I had never heard, seen, felt, or even imagined, something clicked inside my head.

I wish I didn't see so much. I hate this gift sometimes. When I was younger, I thought everybody had it. I guess I was about six or seven when I mentioned "the eyelid movies" to Mother. She dropped her cup of tea. "You get them too?"

She told me she had them all the time when she was younger and so did her sister. Her sister went a little crazy because of it, she said. That was the most I ever heard Mother talk about her past. She did tell me more about the eyelid movies though. She called them her visions. She said they were really strong when she was younger, then they came less and less frequently. Sometimes they showed the future and the past, but most of the time they were about other people, what they were doing or thinking in the present. It was more like that with me, I learned. Mine never faded away. They got stronger and stronger and stronger. After a while, I didn't have to close my eyes, though it helped cut out the clutter of whatever else I was looking at. Mirrors and ponds are good too, but I like clear blue skies the best. It feels like I'm looking into another dimension. I suppose that's true.

Sometimes I can't see anything. Sometimes the visions are so clear, it's like I'm in the same room. They were much too clear that fateful morning. I could see everything. I could feel everything too. Their hearts beating. Pounding. My head pounding in a queasy echo. And right before I ran to the bathroom to heave up all the hate churning in my guts, I saw something else.

I wasn't the only one watching.

THE BOOK

The Book was everything. As his blunt fingertips skimmed the crinkled pages, old memories flickered through his mind like the stroboscopic sputtering of a hand-cranked nickelodeon. Paul breathed in deeply, savoring the poignant rhythms of a story that had been told and retold at numberless firesides for countless centuries until it was finally, faithfully recorded in this, the only volume of its kind in existence.

He rifled through the yellowed leaves faster and faster, the words and images cascading in a blinding flurry, pages turning and yes, the Great Wheel turning with them, faster first, then slower and slower, so slowly until...

Paul stopped at the center of the book. He stared at the two blank pages. They had remained forever unmarked, but showed him everything he'd ever known or would ever need to know. His eyes rolled backwards into his head until only the whites were showing. No, not the whites. His vein-etched orbs were the color of coffee-stained teeth. They matched the ancient vellum leaves almost perfectly.

He stared at the pages with iris-less eyes and he saw. Saw Martin in bed with the girl. *That* girl. They'd been circling each other day after day, passing each other on the staircase, shopping in the same deli, flitting to and fro like moths circling a lightbulb, far more oblivious to each other's existence, to their significance, than he. And now, she was here, driven by the will of her scum-sucking sire, her very presence heralding the prophecy. They had found each other. They had rutted. And even though neither of them had an inkling of what had passed between them, of what it meant or how deeply their connection was ingrained and yes, foretold, they would eventually arrive at the truth of it, and with that truth they would fully awaken. To each other. They would *know*.

He would never allow that to happen. Measures had been taken.

He gazed at the metal-studded face of the girl, oblivious to anything except the man lying next to her, the man she inexplicably adored, the man she would destroy by the strength of her compassion, if she could not be stopped. He saw the mark on her chest, the crescent she concealed with her first tattoo. He saw the mark on Martin's chest, the ring encircling his solar plexus. It was the sign he knew would appear this cycle.

The training, as always, had been long and arduous. But the boy exceeded all his expectations. Her fingers toyed with the ridges of Martin's scar as if she knew the story it told. The long, sad story. He thought back to the early days. The very early days. There was so much hope then. Now everything was stained and faded. So much promise. So much loss.

The only consolation to his sadness, rage and loathing was that he was not alone in the witnessing, or his suffering. Right before he closed the Book, he saw one last, and not too startling, vision. It was me. Staring right back at him.

THE COLLECTOR

Before I met Rose, before all the darker roads it led to, I had always been a collector. Being a collector is a lifelong adventure, an endless treasure hunt. If you're a collector, you know exactly what I mean. If you're not, you'll probably never get it. Being a collector means that there's always somewhere to go, always something to do, always the possibility of excitement, of discovery…of *eureka!*

It's little wonder why I love it so much. Collecting is the great obsession and distraction for the terminally lonely. The greater the obsession, the more compelling the need to seek and acquire, to escape that gaping hole. I needed all the help I could get.

I never actually thought about becoming a collector. I already was one from as far back as I can remember. Most kids play with toys. I collected them. I would line them up in rows just to look at them. I didn't really define any of this as "collecting" until they came out with those monster movie models you would assemble with that wonderfully stinky, toxic, brain cell-eating glue that millions of children are now deprived of.

My collecting got out of hand gradually, by degrees. Always drawn to the morbid, I branched out from my monster toy collection to monster magazines and movie stills. I read every horror novel ever written. As I grew older, I began to lose interest in horror books. The monsters and ghosts and ghouls had gradually lost their main appeal, which was their ability to genuinely frighten me. They just weren't real enough.

I turned to the occult. Once again, I studied everything I could get my hands on—Gnosticism, Hermeticism, Luciferianism, Satanism, Pythagoreanism, Rosicrucianism, Paganism, Kabala, ancient legends and obscure myths, witchcraft, pagan festivals—the Druids. It didn't stop with books. I learned about divination. Numerology, the I Ching, and the tarot. And guess what? I suddenly discovered that my little "gift" wasn't limited to visions of the *here* and *now*—I could see the *then* too. Well, some of the time. Those visions were always murky by comparison, distorted like a funhouse mirror. Even so, it was enough to interest girls at a party. Keep the bullies off my back.

I loved the tarot and started collecting old decks I found at flea markets or in musty, dusty antique shops and secondhand junk stores. One time I found a hand-painted deck that was so old I couldn't believe it. The dealer only wanted forty bucks for it, which I haggled down to thirty. Any good collector is a good haggler. I recently had it appraised for several thousand dollars, though I'd never think of parting with it.

See? That's what it's like to be a collector. Treasures mean so much more than money.

I never told Mother about any of my occult wanderings, but I'm pretty sure she saw anyway. One day out of the blue she said, "Never use your gift for personal gain. And stay away from the darkness."

Oops. Too late.

I left Mother as soon as I turned eighteen. I couldn't wait to get as far away as I could, applying to East Coast Ivy Leaguers. My SATs and GPA were in the top two percent nationally. Got a scholarship to Harvard. Impressed? You needn't be. I was expelled after the first semester for selling acid in my dorm. Oh, well. I didn't fit in with the pink Lacoste polo shirt crowd anyway. My asshole preppy roommate ratted me out. I never should have had a roommate. Never had one since.

I fled Boston for New York, far away from Mother's outpost in Berkeley, moving into a small, cheap apartment between Avenues A and B. With only a high school diploma and minimal job skills, my career prospects were fairly grim. Even if I stuck it out at Harvard, I still wouldn't be catnip for any headhunters, unless there's a greater demand than I'm aware of for graduates with a major in evolutionary biology and a minor in anthropology.

Guess what I did to make a living? Fortune telling. I put an ad in the *Village Voice*. The headline read: Scientific Readings. The "scientific" part mainly consisted of combining the numerology interpretations with the zodiac designations of the minor arcana cards in their readings. Translation: I could pick the dates when shit would happen. The accuracy of my readings was a surprise even for me. I had a very strong repeat business, which financed what I really wanted to do: collect stuff.

At first it was more of the things I'd already been collecting. Tarot decks, Ouija boards, amulets, talismans and books. Lots and lots of old books, particularly books of spells, incantations and invocations. Grimoires. *The Testament of Solomon*, the *Clavicula Salomonis*, *The Black Pullet*, *The Book of Simon the Magician*, *The Book of Enoch*, *The Sworn Book of Honorius*, *The Pseudomonarchia Daemonum*. Blah dee blah blah.

We're talking ritual magic here. Alchemy. I learned Latin, Greek, Coptic, Arabic and Aramaic just so I could read the original texts and come to my own conclusions about the proper translations. I spent every dime I made when the opportunity arose to possess one of the (hopefully) authentic manuscripts. The culmination of my efforts—and the beginning of my degradation—occurred after visiting a very old man in a very old bookstore in London. He claimed to have in his possession (and was offering *for sale!*), a slim volume with a white leather binding and yellow vellum pages, written in Greek. He said it was the *Corpus Hermeticum* written by Hermes Trismegistus.

Depending on who you ask (if you actually know anyone who's heard that name), Hermes Trismegistus was either: a) the Greek god Hermes; b) the Egyptian god Thoth; c) a combo Hermes/Thoth god; d) the human/god grandson of Hermes; e) a spiritual figure, maybe a god, maybe not, who reincarnates throughout history teaching his secret doctrine to worthy initiates; or f) Moses.

I was fascinated with the various legends surrounding Trismegistus, so I jumped in with both feet, reading everything I could find, sorting through all the contradictory suppositions. My research began, as one should, I suppose, with the gods. Thoth was the god of wisdom who invented writing. Hermes was a herald, messenger and inventor. HT was thought to be all of that and more—a great sorcerer, the first alchemist—and a very prolific writer, composing thousands of texts, most of which eventually found their way to the Great Library of Alexandria. Only a handful of manuscripts survived the heretical purges of the newly Christian Roman Empire.

Whether HT was a demi-god, a great sage or even a real person, all scholars agree that a rich legacy of esoteric teachings sprang from the Hermetic tradition. The surviving books attributed to Trismegistus or his followers were usually written in the third person, even though Hermes/Thoth is usually the main character—a kind, patient, wise teacher. Basically, he's the answer man. The answers are usually veiled in cryptic dialogs between himself and some thickheaded apprentice, or one of his equally dense sons, Asclepius and Tat.

The most legendary Hermetic work is the *Emerald Tablet*, which is said to contain the secrets of (drumroll, please) creation. The sacred text was carved into a big green crystal or maybe the world's largest emerald. Composed of only fourteen verses in most translations, the *Emerald Tablet* became the basis of alchemy—the cookbook of creation. There are probably as many legends surrounding the origin of the *Emerald Tablet* as there are tales of its disappearance, discovery (and subsequent disappearances and rediscoveries). One thing I know for certain, it's not on display in any museum.

The *Corpus Hermeticum* is Hermes/Thoth's greatest hits compilation. It contains most of the extant writings. So when this really old guy told me he had a really old copy of the *Corpus Hermeticum* written by the Great Master himself, I knew it had to be utter horseshit. Yet even if it was a legitimate Greek transcription I could interpret myself, it would be worth whatever he wanted.

He wanted $11,100. "Interesting. How'd you come up with that price?"

"That's the number," he replied grumpily in an unexpectedly rustic American accent, turning his head away, waving his arm like he was shooing a gnat. I thought he was being cute or ridiculous, equating the price with Hermes III, but I didn't ruffle his feathers about it. I was too anxious to get my hands on it to get into a pissing match with the old geezer about something so petty, even though I was already haggling with him in my head.

When he opened his small safe, put on his white gloves and pulled it out, my heart was beating like a bongo. He made me wear gloves too, which wasn't surprising, even though my fingertips were itching to come in direct contact with the ancient vellum. Vellum is skin, by the way, usually lambskin, but I'm getting ahead of myself.

My first reaction was complete elation. I'd seen enough volumes like this to know that the binding and vellum could possibly come from the same time period associated with most of Hermes/Thoth's writings— around 300 CE—the key transitional period from papyrus scrolls to parchment codices, driven by the emerging power of Christianity. The Greek hand-lettering was also consistent with other ancient manuscripts from the same period I'd seen in various metropolitan libraries. Best of all, just from reading the first few pages I knew that the material was truly the *Corpus Hermeticum.* Reading it in Greek immediately highlighted some discrepancies in the Latin and English translations I'd previously seen.

Boy, this is going to be fun!

Then I saw it. There on the spine, like a turd on a lotus flower. Someone had written "Hermes Trismegistus" in black ink block letters.

"What is this shit?" I shouted, my booming pissed-off voice startling even me in the cramped quarters of his tiny office.

"Don't know who did it, don't really care. Just wanna get it outta here. Been nothin' but trouble for me. That's why I'm sellin' so cheap. You know I'm sellin' cheap, dontcha?"

I did. Despite the blasphemous desecration, it was still worth much more than the asking price, unless it was an extremely well-executed forgery. That was a risk, but one I was willing to take. "I'll give you ten thousand," I said. That was a hell of a lot of tarot readings.

"The price is the price," he muttered, crossing his arms across his birdlike ribcage.

I paid. Cash. When I finally held it in my hands, skin to skin, I got such a rush I thought it really might be magical. I couldn't wait to get back to my room and dig in. But he had another jack-in-the-box he was dying to spring on me.

"Ever hear of anthropodermic bibliopegy?" he whispered as I made for the door.

"Yeah," I said, a shudder tinkling the ivories of my backbone. "Books bound in human skin."

"Ever seen one? Held one?" he asked almost tauntingly, displaying his yellow teeth in a quivering grin for the first time that day.

"No," I said. But I knew I'd be holding one soon.

He strained to reach the shelf above my head, pulling a book down, handing it to me. No gloves this time. No, you wouldn't want gloves for this. The cover felt...I guess *crinkly* would be the best way to describe it. Stiff and *crinkly*. The inside cover was smooth as suede. There was an inscription on the first page, written in an elegant hand that made it even more macabre: *"The bynding of this booke is all that remains of my deare friende Malachi Firth, flayed alive by Connor O'Ceallaigh on the First Day of November, 1238."*

"I have more," he said with a deranged spastic eagerness. He certainly did. Lots more. Mostly courtroom accounts of murder trials, covered in the skins of the condemned, a fairly common practice according to my new buddy, the Crypt Keeper. Once he saw how much I was enjoying myself, he figured I was a kindred spirit so he brought out the heavy artillery. "These ain't for sale," he whispered. "But I thought you'd like to see."

He opened a blue velvet curtain that hung floor to ceiling, concealing a doorway and the contents within. It was a narrow room, almost like a closet, with a creepy icon of some saint against an otherwise bare wall at the back. It was surrounded by bookcases containing many shelves holding many, many volumes, all with the same creamy tan bindings I was becoming way too familiar with.

"Wow," I said, honestly impressed. "That's a lot of books."

"No, no..." he groaned, like I was some idiot totally missing the point. "Read one!"

I picked one out at random and started thumbing through it, my eyes getting wider and wider with every page. "Is this what I think it is?"

"Read another, pick any one," he cackled, so excited I thought he would crap himself.

Holy Mother of God. They were diaries. Written by murderers. Notice the plural. Perhaps ten or twelve small volumes would be written in one hand with a similar binding style. Then there would be an equal number, or in some cases up to thirty or even fifty, written by another sicko, each and every one of them covered with the skin of their victims.

"Where the hell did you get these?" I asked, my head spinning as I grabbed one after the other, thumbing through quickly. The gruesome descriptions were beyond anything I had read in a hundred horror novels or even the nightmares I had afterwards.

"Can't say, can't say," he repeated in a mumbling chorus, shaking his head, the gleam in his eyes snuffed out instantly by my prying question. "Have to close now, anyhow. Good day to you, sir," he grumbled, suddenly as surly as when I came in.

Crazy old coot. I was pissed at him for giving me the bum's rush, but I had my treasure to ease the sting. I went back to my hotel and stayed up all night reading and writing. Had some revelations that bordered on the sublime, but my mind kept erasing those visions of a divine realm bathed in ethereal light and replacing it with the sight of a cramped closet filled with hatred, torture and sadistic glee.

I went back the next day. The store was closed. I cursed. Even stomped my feet. My plane was leaving in a few hours. I took the flight, figuring I'd come back again soon and get another dose of that horror of horrors. But I kept putting it off and putting it off. When I finally returned three years later, the store was empty of everything but cobwebs.

I couldn't get that sick scrawling script out of my head. I was so pre-occupied with what I'd seen that I started reading books about serial killers. Suddenly, they were much more interesting than all the horror books or the occult mumbo jumbo. Scarier too. Ted Bundy, Ed Gein, Jeffrey Dahmer. The real monsters. Monsters like I saw in the Skin Library. I learned a lot about them. What they did. How they did it. Where they lived. It was the last category that really got me into trouble.

One day while I was wandering around my favorite flea market, I saw a painting of a clown. The seller had no idea who the artist was—I could tell by the price tag and his complete lack of interest when I forked over three dollars for it. But I knew. Oh, yes, indeed. John Wayne Gacy. After I went home and proudly hung it on the wall, I began to wonder: What if you could get your hands on some of the *real* collectibles from serial killers? The things *they* collected?

A few days later, that crazy bug of an idea shaped itself into a plan. I would go on a road trip. Stop by some of the homes and haunting grounds of these real-life monsters. Maybe visit some of the police precincts where they were captured and see what I could find. See what might be available. At this point, I suppose it wouldn't surprise you that I was quite successful in my quest. I'm quite sure that certain people would do almost anything for a peek at my collection.

Who could blame them for their curiosity? I mean everybody knows about the severed heads that Jeffrey Dahmer kept in his refrigerator. But who do you know that has one?

THE AFTERGLOW, PART I

Rose felt wonderful. She stayed in bed long after Martin had left, feeling the steam drift from her body in little clouds. Her whole body sighed with satisfaction, a deep, relaxed "now I know what everybody's been talking about" contentment that everybody wants, but nobody seems to get. She hugged her chest with a pillow and sighed again with another feeling she couldn't comprehend, a deeper, more elemental emotion...a feeling like... no, not love.

It couldn't be love.

She shook her head to clear away the schmaltzy cobwebs and stared at the table. There was a big leather pouch lying between the candles. She looked at it for a long time, torn between curiosity and the comfort of her bed. Curiosity won out, as always, pulling her to the table. The pouch was heavy, about ten pounds she guessed. She opened the drawstring and peeked inside. Holy shit. It was gold. Tiny ingots, fat round coins. She spilled the contents onto the table, the falling chunks ignited by the flickering candlelight. Some of them fell in puddles of milky wax, melting them all over again, painting them gold, painting everything gold, the deep dark corners of the room now gold, a gold disco ball of rays on the ceiling.

Martin pointed at the bag and the ugly barren kitchen before he left. His last words echoed in her mind. "Finish it," he said.

She stood there naked, sweating gold, knowing what he wanted, wanting it as much. Yes, she would finish it and make a golden nest for them. For *them?*

"Let's not get carried away. He's just a guy with a big dick and a bag of gold." Then she picked up a one-ounce ingot and added, "Well, that's not too bad for starters."

THE AFTERGLOW, PART II

Martin felt terrible. He felt cold and he felt hot. Was he sick? He never got sick. He sat on his favorite park bench, rubbing the worn wood under his palm, willing it to heal him, to cure the chill of confusion sweeping over him like a fever.

What happened to him? What was he going to do? Panic came in waves, but between the crushing tides, he felt something different, something struggling to come to the surface. It was a feeling for the girl, a feeling like...

Suddenly, he looked up. He was here. He knew it.

Martin looked in every direction. Nothing. He tried to relax and rubbed the wood. Words floated by in his head, calming him like a nursery rhyme...over and over and over. He closed his eyes and willed the world to go away. As soon as he calmed himself, the waves came back, propelled by an image of Rose smiling at him.

He snapped his eyes open. There he was. Over by the fountain. Martin watched as he came toward him in slow motion, his long black overcoat rippling in the sun, his stringy white-blond hair blowing from his shoulders. He smelled the stale alcohol on his skin as he lowered his beefy bulk next to him. Then he looked into those blue-gray eyes, watched that mustache curl into a smile, and felt the oldest fear he had ever known.

"Hello, Martin," the big man said.

Martin took a long, slow breath and answered, "Hello, Paul."

Paul didn't say anything. Neither did Martin. He just looked into Paul's cold eyes and wondered what he wanted. Whatever it was, he knew it was going to hurt.

THE HOUSE OF PAIN

Rose did tattoos and she did them well. *Rat-tat-tat-tat.* Wipe off blood. *Rat-tat-tat-tat.* She did piercings too and liked them even more. She had gained quite a reputation for doing what were known as technical piercings. "Technical" because they represented a level of difficulty requiring an equally demanding level of skill. Uvula piercings, for example. If you've ever seen a Warner Brother's cartoon you know what a uvula is. It's that quivering punching bag blob of flesh dangling at the opening of your throat. The one that wobbles like a bowl of pudding whenever Elmer screams at Bugs.

Why would someone want it pierced? Don't ask me. The challenges are significant, not the least of which includes the ability to hold your mouth open a really long time without moving even a teeny, weeny bit because someone is trying to lance that squirming sucker with a six-inch-long needle. And that's just the pier*cee*. The pier*cer* has to take that needle and…well, it gets pretty hard to describe without pictures.

Technical, very technical.

Rose had become skilled at even more challenging body modifications, involving grafts and implants. She was the one to install the row of eleven stainless-steel wedges into the shaved skull of Jim "Stegosaurus" Robbins.

In most countries, you would need seven or eight years of intensive medical training to perform this type of surgery on another human being, or at least a well-forged diploma. But God Bless America, all you need here is a reasonably steady hand and a compulsive desire to carve and mutilate the flesh of your fellow tribal community members.

Anesthesia isn't a problem. Nobody wants it. Pain is more than a fetish in this neck of the woods, it's a badge of honor. The more you can take, the greater your standing in the ink and metal clique.

Rose was no slouch either. Pain and pleasure had become so entwined in her brain that she would give herself a new piercing just to take the edge off a rainy afternoon. She had fifteen earrings, three nose rings (which she would alternate, being one to frown on ostentation), two nipple rings and dumbbell combos, one tongue ball, five labial rings on either side and two clitoral rings (just because the first one felt so good).

Needless to say, airport check-ins were a nightmare.

Rose, still in bed, flicked her clit rings back and forth, debating whether to skip work altogether or stop in for a quick tongue job scheduled for the early afternoon.

She looked at the bag of gold and looked at the kitchen. She thought about the tongue job and how much she loved her work. She thought about Martin and his big horse cock and fingered her clit so furiously it sounded like the phone was ringing.

If she jumped out of bed right now and didn't shower (as if she would shower and wash off the smell of him!), she could do the tongue job, sell the gold and still make it downtown to the fabric shop before closing time. She didn't like to rush but she couldn't bear to wait. She wanted it all: the warm blood, the cold cash and most of all, she wanted what every New York City woman wants, whether she's a manicured, pedicured Upper East Side, Hampton Jitney JAP or a downtown magenta-haired bone-through-the-nose juke joint junkie.

She wanted to shop.

An Invitation

"You look troubled," Paul said. "What would a big strong man, a great fine animal like yourself be troubled with on such a lovely day as this?"

Martin hadn't seen him since…he couldn't remember. It seemed like no time had passed from the way Paul was acting. He spoke in that showy way of his, that Irish brogue managing to sound happy, sad and angry all at once. He waved his arms broadly for emphasis, scaring away the ambling pigeons. Scaring the old couple on the next bench. Scaring Martin too.

"Ahhhh…it's a woman isn't it?" Paul asked, shaking his head. "It's always a woman that brings out the worst in a fine young lad…shaking up the quiet sureness, the certainty, the solid *knowing* that is the very core and center of a man."

Martin listened in amazement, transfixed as always in his presence, wondering once again how Paul always knew exactly what was bothering him. Had he been spying on him? No. He just knew. If it had anything to with pain, he knew.

"You want it back, don't you?" Paul continued with a wink. "You want to know again for certain what is what and which way to go and how to get there. You want to take away all that gray and get back to good clean old black and white again. Don't you, boy?"

The word "boy" cut into Martin like a knife. He gulped on it, and the big back slap that punctuated Paul's question, but he couldn't help but answer.

"Yes," he said, surprising himself by how much he meant it.

Paul sighed a great big Paul sigh. Endlessly tired and endlessly amused at the folly of it all. "Come back," he whispered, his tongue darting out to lick the chapped corner of his lips. "Come back and make the world the way it used to be."

Martin looked away. Silent. Numb. Aching. He ached for the lost blankness within himself. He ached for…

Paul cut him off before his thoughts could trace the echoes of Rose's smiling face. "Are ya comin' or not boy? I don't have all day," he grunted, standing up slowly.

Martin closed his eyes, grateful for the sunshine and the red warmth of his glowing closed eyelids. Then an image of Rose elbowed its way back into his brain and with it came another cascade of raw unfiltered emotions: joy, hope, lust, anger, fear and finally…panic. He opened his eyes. Paul was standing directly in front of him, blocking the sun from his face.

Martin shivered inside the long dark shadow. He closed his eyes one last time and the silence in his head told him what he had to do, what he had to learn all over again, from the man who taught him how.

How to stop feeling.

ROSE GOES SHOPPING

Rose was standing in front of a sign that screamed WE BUY GOLD! in foot-tall red letters. *Good.* She certainly wanted to sell some. She couldn't wait to go shopping, but first she needed to unload the loot she'd been lugging around in her backpack.

"Feels like a pair of bricks," she groaned, hitching the strap higher on her shoulder, adjusting the weight as she stared at the sign. The sign was in the window of one of those WE BUY GOLD! jewelry stores on 47th Street in the so-called diamond district.

Diamond district, flower district, transvestite hooker meat-packing district. How strange and stupid it seemed, all these little stores, clustered together on the same street, fighting toe to toe in some kind of crazy medieval marketplace. They all looked the same. How were you supposed to pick one out? What criteria did you use? The size of the sign? "Fuck it," she said, opening the door, "I need to get to the fabric district."

It took about twenty minutes to conclude the transaction. She had come prepared. She knew the current price of gold ($393.75 per troy ounce as of 4/4/96) and weighed the bag to the milligram on a scale one of her co-workers used for selling crystal methedrine (3807.065 grams). The jeweler's scale was a bit off and she calmly informed him of his error. "You're light," she said. A big racket ensued, but when the dust settled she left with $48,195 dollars and 23 cents.

I watched it all from the sidewalk. When she left the store, I followed behind from a safe distance until she ducked into the Rockefeller Center subway entrance. As I saw her bobbing head disappear, I picked up the pace, running down the stairs after her like I was chasing Alice down the rabbit hole.

Rose adjusted her backpack, practically skipping down the stairs. Cash was so much lighter than gold. She looked at her watch and smiled. There was plenty of time to make it downtown before the fabric stores closed.

I got into the same crowded car with her, at the other end but still within eyesight.

Just when I thought this was getting too easy, she looked right at me. I avoided the direct eye contact, letting my eyes drift around the passengers near her instead. I saw her do the same, her mind visibly busy, trying to figure out where she had seen me before.

Bitch! Sure my hair was longer and I had a three-day growth of stubble, but still! Even so, I didn't actually want her to recognize me, not yet anyway. I got more and more nervous, until I watched her shrug and go back to the typical zombie state of all subway riders, reading Dr. Zizmore's ad for dermabrasion.

I was so preoccupied I almost lost Rose as she exited at Broadway. I trudged up the stairs after her, not so enthusiastic anymore. As I emerged on the street, the afternoon glow had settled in, the sky bathed in silky golds and blue velvets. My eyes found a solitary bird hovering between the old brick towers. I glanced back down and saw Rose moving away at a fast clip toward the dingy storefronts below Canal Street. I knew I had to catch up fast, but first I had to steal one last look at that lonely bird.

My eyes searched and searched, but I couldn't find it.

MARTIN GOES TO HELL

Hell is a lot like death, not at all what you're expecting, always much worse because it's real. You can smell Hell before you see it. It smells like rotten meat left on the kitchen counter for a week. Like a rat that died inside the walls. Like a toilet that hasn't been flushed in a week. It smells like Paul's apartment.

When Martin opened the door, the first thing he noticed was the stench. He once read that the sense of smell was more effective at triggering memories than any of the other senses. Martin had tested it out on his various belongings and discovered this hypothesis was so consistently correct that he promptly scrubbed, soaked, washed and practically sandblasted everything he owned until the scents were blessedly neutralized.

He closed the door behind him and wrinkled his nose, the scent instantly transporting him back to his first visit here. He could picture it perfectly, walking up the stairs behind Paul, waiting as he pushed the door open. And then…that smell.

Martin tried to shake off the memory. Paul smiled and put his hand on Martin's shoulder. He hugged him warmly, then led him down another hallway away from the big bright room.

It got darker and darker as they walked.

Paul occupied the whole top floor of the old condemned building. None of the other squatters living there made much of a fuss when he took it all for himself. Understandably. He had restructured many of the inside walls so the interior was a giant rambling maze of gloom. Well, someone had done it. Martin found it difficult to imagine Paul doing any real physical labor, although he could clearly picture him gleefully smashing through the drywall with a sledgehammer.

They kept walking, making a few turns here and there, until the sight of a dim light ahead triggered another memory of a previous journey through the pitch-black maze. He was alone. Walking in total darkness.

Suddenly, there was a light up ahead, leading to a door, no, not a door, a wall that opened like a door into a room filled with candles and…

Martin was jarred from his memory by the grip of Paul's hand on his shoulder. The light they were approaching came from a normal-sized door, only a few more steps ahead. Paul squeezed his hand more tightly and led him into a small room, lit by a single dim bulb hanging naked from the ceiling at the end of a long black cord. The bulb hovered weakly over a round wooden table, unadorned except for a carpenter's hammer and a thick steel nail about six inches long. "Let's make ourselves comfortable," Paul said, waving his hand at two large oak chairs. "Getting hungry?"

"Yes," Martin said, his eyes drifting to the hammer.

Paul's face turned to stone the instant Martin broke eye contact with him. Martin waited for the explosion, but none came. Instead, Paul's face brightened and he rubbed his hands together shouting, "Me too! I could eat a horse!"

Martin heard some thumping noises and a muffled rustle directly behind his chair. He kept looking into the smiling face across the table, the light above casting long shadows into the sockets of his twinkling eyes. He wasn't about to turn away again to see where the thumping came from.

Paul stood. His face was changing again…to the dead mask. Martin called it the "dead mask" the first time he saw it. He never said it to Paul's face, but even if he had, Paul probably would have liked it, so apt was the description. It was a true mask, perfect in its utter emptiness, a mask you can't argue with or plead with for mercy, because there was nothing behind it.

So pure. So empty. So dead.

Paul wore the dead mask like he was floating in heaven. He looked at Martin for a long time, enjoying the stillness around them. When he spoke, it was in a dull whisper that tolled like an old church bell. "What has become of you, Martin? Are you like other men?"

"No," Martin said.

"Other men don't have the power you have. The fierce clarity. The absolute commitment. The unshakable will. Do they, boy?"

"No," Martin said.

"Other men get all bogged down with feelings…love and fear and pain clouding their proper judgment, sapping away their strength. You don't have feelings like they do. You don't whine and cry every time a little pain gets in the way. *Do you, boy?*"

"No," Martin said.

"Why, I could nail your hand to this table and you wouldn't budge an inch, would you, my brave, strong lad?"

"No," Martin gulped.

And so he did.

MOMMA

There wasn't much blood on the table, just enough to create soft little red pools in the cracks and gouges. Martin breathed deeply and tasted copper in the air. He breathed again and caught a whiff of ozone mingling with the smell of his own sweet life.

Time was moving slow. Tick-tock. The pain was phenomenal, even for Martin. He breathed slower and less deeply, taking shallow gulps as he struggled to lower his heart rate and move to the place where Paul had brought him so many times, a place where everything was equal and pain was just another word, another sound in his head fighting for attention.

They sat across from each other for what seemed like an eternity, neither one making a sound. Martin battled within himself, fighting to stop fighting, to sink like a stone to the bottom of the sea. Bit by bit, he drifted down, losing form and substance until the voice of pain began to whisper instead of scream. The pain was still there but it wasn't "pain" anymore. It was just another nameless feeling he didn't understand or have to obey. Down, down, down, he floated, further into himself where all the pulses and demands of skin and flesh and bone became a single chorus, until at last he settled on the ocean floor.

He rested there, breathing slowly, deeply. He was safe now, if only for a moment. Then he began to remember.

Rats. Martin shivered in bed all night thinking about them. As soon as the sun came up, he would be going hunting for the first time in his young life. He was seven years old. The big man living with him and Momma for the past few months had been talking about it all week, telling Martin how much fun they were going to have.

They weren't going to the cool green forest across the wheat field behind the house. They were going to the town dump. To shoot rats. Martin was terrified.

The man was tall and thickly built with deep blue eyes. Momma made Martin call him Daddy as soon as he moved in. It bothered him at first, but after a while he began to like it. The man was nice and would smile at Martin and give him hugs and tell him what a big strong boy he was. Martin didn't know where Momma met him or what his real name was because she always called him Daddy too.

They lived on a farm somewhere, but Martin wasn't sure where. They didn't do any farming at the farm and there were big rusty machines sitting behind the house and in the broken-down barn. They never had company, except for the other men that came before, none of them staying as long as this one. He could see other houses that were far, far away, but he wasn't allowed to go near them or talk to any people who came to the door, though no one ever did except salesmen. "Don't talk to strangers," Momma said. Everyone was a stranger.

Martin had never played with another child. He knew he was missing something, but he wasn't sure what it was. He only knew there was a big hole inside and he felt sad almost all the time. But Martin wasn't allowed to cry. Every time he cried, even a little, Momma always said the same thing: "I'll give you something to cry about!"

Then she did. Each time the "something" got worse. He hardly ever cried anymore.

Momma didn't have any women friends he knew about except for Norine, who was really Momma's sister. Norine wasn't allowed to come to the house because, Momma said, "She's a nosy bitch and I don't want her snoopin' around!"

Martin went to stay with her once in a while when Momma had to "take a rest" from him. She lived on the same big farm in another house down the dirt road and it only took a few minutes to rumble over there in Momma's old truck and drop him off. Every time Momma came back to get him he wanted to cry, but he knew things would be even worse if he did.

Most of the times Momma went out, he didn't get to go to Norine's. When he was smaller, Momma just put him in his crib. The crib was a five-foot-tall box of raw plywood with splinters everywhere. Martin would just sit there in the lump of his worn-out blankee and stare at the knots in the wood till Momma came home again. Sometimes she didn't come home for a long, long time. If Martin went to the bathroom, Momma would be extra mad so he tried as hard as he could not to do a number two. But sometimes she would leave for two days or more, and he would have all that time to think about what was going to happen when she came home and saw the mess he made.

When he was old enough to climb out of the crib, Momma locked him in the cellar until she came back, leaving a jug of water and some cold cuts and bread. There was a bucket in the corner for him to "empty himself," but he tried not to because the smell got so bad. He hated the cellar more than anything. It was where she took him when she said he'd been really bad, even though he wasn't sure what he did to make her mad. He tried so hard to be good all the time, but no matter how good he was, he wasn't good enough for Momma. He needed to be punished. He needed it all the time.

"If you ever tell Norine, I'll find out and lock you down here for the rest of your life. You'll never, ever see her again."

He never, ever thought about telling Norine. Or any of the men that came to visit.

When the big, blue-eyed man came to stay, Momma didn't hit Martin or say the bad things for a little while. But soon she started up again, bit by bit, like she was slowly sticking her toes into a steamy bathtub to make sure the water wasn't too hot. One day while he was roughhousing with Daddy, Momma started laughing really loud. "He's such a little shrimp!" Momma yelled. "You could throw him across the room like a bundle of dirty laundry!"

Martin got really scared when she said that. But the man didn't seem scared at all. Instead, he looked at Momma like he'd never seen any other Daddy look at her. He looked at her like he was mad.

The Thing About Rats

The old pickup truck bumped and rattled down the dirt road like a circus ride. They turned onto a smooth black highway that seemed to stretch out forever in a straight line. After a while they turned onto another dirt road.

The smell hit them about a minute before the mountains of stinking oil cans, rotten food and battered refrigerators came into view. The truck screeched to a halt and it only took a few seconds before signs of life started to appear. The rats were bold and big as possums. Fat, greasy rats, shiny with the stink of old meat. One even stopped and stared right at him. Martin would have jumped back into the truck if hadn't been for the voice calling out to him, "Hey, little man, gimme a hand with this gear!"

He was in the back of the pickup making lots of clunking noises. Martin darted over in a flash, eager for his noisy bulk and fearlessness. Daddy put his arm around Martin in a hug that was the nicest thing Martin had ever felt from anyone besides Norine.

"Don't you worry about dem filthy, stinkin' rats, m'boy. You'll be seeing in just a teeny weeny bit that they're no match for a big strong lad like yerself." He squatted down until his big blond head was only inches away from Martin's tiny face. Martin smelled something sour on his breath, but compared to the dump it smelled like sweet perfume. "After today, you're not gonna be afraid of anything, anymore, ever. Doesn't that sound good?"

Martin smiled a great big smile that was as honest as it was happy. "Yes!" he cried.

Daddy smiled back and began his lesson:

"The thing…*blam!*…about rats…*blam!*…you see…*blam!*…is that rats…*blam!*…are a whole lot better at runnin'…*blam!*…than they are at fightin'."

Blam-blam-blam-blam-blam! Each *blam!* punctuated the explosion of a cat-sized rat. They were frantically scurrying everywhere, torn between the fear of the cannon-loud shots and the hunger for all the newly fresh meat of their fallen brethren. The *blam!* generators were a pair of brushed silver, .48 magnum revolvers that were actually shooting out two-foot long flames from their barrels with each blast. The kick was so great that the pistols practically hit the man in the forehead each time he fired. It was incredible to Martin that he could control each one with a single hand.

"The other thing about rats…*blam!*…is that they're such hateful… *blam!*…dirty…*blam!*…filthy…*blam!*…creatures…*blam!*…that killin' the little bastards…*blam!*…feels good right down to the marrow of your bones!" *Blam-blam-blam-blam-blam!* Rat guts, bones and clumps of fur painted the side of an old washing machine like a vintage Pollock. "So what do you think, buddy boy? Ready to give it a try?"

Martin shook his head and turned his face to the ground, expecting the sharp blow that always came when he said no to Momma. He didn't want to see it coming from a hand this big. To his complete amazement, the hand came down and gently lifted his chin so he could see the big man leaning over to kiss his forehead.

"Don't you worry, now. You don't have to do anything 'til you're good and ready."

Martin stood up straight and beamed at the man with such a smile that he couldn't resist picking up the tiny weight of the boy and giving him a growling bear hug. "You're a very special boy, Martin," said the man softly. "A very special boy, indeed."

Martin was bursting with joy. He wished and wished with all his might that this one would never ever leave. "Will you be my for real daddy?" he asked shyly, turning his head away again, bracing himself for an even bigger blow. But the big man didn't say the words he expected…the push-away words that hurt even worse than the slaps and shoves and names Momma called him. What he said was this:

"Yes, I'll be your daddy. I'll be your daddy for ever and ever and ever."

FIRST KILL

Daddy pointed at the cargo in the truck bed and Martin shouted, "Wow!"

"You bet your ass 'Wow!' little buddy!"

Martin stared at the green metal footlocker. There was a rifle with a really long barrel that had holes drilled in the side and made a loud *ca-chunk* sound when Daddy showed him how it worked. "Special forces riot shotgun," he said dryly. "Semi-automatic with a twenty-four-round chamber of armor-piercing titanium slugs."

"Uh-huh," Martin nodded, pretending he understood. And there were more: a dozen pistols in all shapes and sizes, resting snugly inside gray plastic cases with foam rubber cut to the exact shape of each shiny weapon. More rifles and shotguns too. They were the most beautiful things he'd ever seen. There was one that made him gasp out loud. It had a black matte finish and looked like a cross between the pistols and the rifles.

"Excellent taste," Daddy said approvingly. "Sawed-off, pistol grip, twenty gauge, side-by-side shotgun. Easily concealed for close-quarter fighting and convenience store stickups."

"I want that one!" Martin shouted with a grin too wide for his face.

"Welllll…I don't want to discourage such noble instincts, but I'm afraid it would rip your little chicken wing right out of its socket."

Martin pouted and scuffed his sneakers on the dusty ground.

"Hey, I've got an idea," Daddy smiled. "Let's do it together. Put your hand under the barrels like this," he said, curling Martin's fingers beneath the twin pipes. It was a stretch, but the span of his palm finally managed to contain them.

"Good," said the big man eagerly. "Now put your other hand here," he instructed, wrapping Martin's small fingers around the pistol grip.

"Now listen carefully," Daddy said slowly, his head resting on his shoulder. Martin could feel his blond mustache grazing his cheek. "A shotgun isn't a rifle. It's a clumsy, brutal weapon. All you have to do is point it in the general vicinity and ahead, always *ahead* of the way the dirty beast is runnin'."

"But how do I point if I don't look down the barrel?" Martin asked, more uncertain than ever. It was probably the most words he'd said to anyone but Norine.

"You move your arms…" Daddy answered, steering their joined hands on the shotgun toward a particularly plump specimen waddling between a box of laundry detergent and a Big Wheel tricycle, "…and you point with your eyes…(Martin followed the slinking rat with more intensity than he thought he was capable of)…and when it feels just right…(just a little more to the right)…and you get a tingle in your stomach…(almost there, just a little more)…and a little voice whispers in your ear…(yes, that's it!)… then slowly squeeze the trigger…(now! now! now!)…and…*BLAM!*

"Wow!" Martin yelled, watching the rat explode with so much force that its guts made a hula-hoop around the Big Wheel's handlebars. "Wow! Wow! Wow! Wow!"

Martin jumped up and down like he might have done on Christmas morning if he ever had the chance. It didn't matter that Daddy had helped him point it or even that he squeezed Martin's finger on top of the trigger. It didn't matter! He had done it too! He had killed the rat. *Killed* it! Wow! It felt strange and confusing and powerful and exciting and…yes…there was no doubt about it…it felt good.

It felt really, really good.

Stigmata

Martin opened his eyes and stared at the nail in his hand. Then his gaze drifted upward to Paul's unblinking eyes. He was still wearing the dead mask, showing him nothing—a shark with his eyes rolled backwards. But as Martin surfaced, Paul came back to life and put on his warm friendly mask, congratulating him on his victory.

"Ahhhh…good boy," he said, with genuine admiration. He started to get up, but then sat back down and placed his hand on top of Martin's crucified one. Paul had no fingernails. He closed his eyes and breathed in slowly through his nose, savoring the moment, feeling the trembling wreckage inside Martin's hand. He had evaded all the bones, tendons and major blood vessels with a surgeon's skill, knowing that Martin would need full use of his hand very soon, but not quite yet. Paul breathed in deeply again, looking into Martin's tortured eyes, smiling sweeter than Martin had ever seen. Then he grabbed Martin's hand and gave it a quick sharp tug toward him.

Nothing in the world could have stopped the scream that bellowed from Martin's throat. Paul threw back his head and screamed along with him, two mad dogs baying to a stone-deaf savior that would never, ever come. Suddenly, Paul stopped, cooing to Martin like he was just a baby, "Shhh…shhhh. Yes, that's a good, brave lad." He said the soothing words over and over until Martin's breathing returned to short, sharp gasps.

Paul rose again from his chair and Martin couldn't stop himself from groaning in relief. At the sound, Paul froze in place, hovering over him.

"Be a man," he sneered, then corrected himself: "Be like Christ."

THE SWITCH

They started with pins. Tiny needles that looked like the ones in Norine's sewing kit. It scared Martin just to look at them. Daddy used the needles slowly. Push. Stop. Push. Stop. Then a little bit more, right to the point where Martin could barely stand it. Daddy talked all the time in a voice so calm it felt like a warm, soft towel: "Pain is nothing. One day you'll grow so big and strong that no one will ever be able to hurt you again. You want to be a big strong man like daddy, don't you?"

Martin would nod and fight back the tears and Daddy would push in the needle again. Push. Stop. Push. Stop. "Feel the needle, Martin. Feel it… don't fight it. Feel the core of the pain. It's sharp, but it's soft inside. Feel the soft part in the middle and go in there, dive into it like a cool summer pond. It's not so bad now, is it?"

It was. But the more they did it, all day long sometimes, the more he could feel the soft part…the cool pond…and the deeper he would sink. Down. Down. Down. No words. No voice. No "Ouch!" Just the switch. There it is, right over there. Push. Stop. Push. Stop. Click. Now the pain was something else. It wasn't good, but it wasn't bad either. It just *was*. There was nothing you could say about it, and no more reason to cry.

The first time Martin didn't want to pull his hand away was the proudest moment of his short young life, even better than his first kill. There was no hurt. No pain. No tears. No fear. Well, some fear, but even that must have its own cool pond. Its own switch. Martin looked up at the man with the sharp needle and asked, "Daddy…what's your real name?"

Daddy looked at him with an expression he couldn't understand, then answered in a whisper so faint he had to lean in to hear it.

"Son, my name is Paul."

STORYTELLER

"Tell me a story," Martin said with a smile half as big as his face. They were in the wheat field again, sitting in the worn wooden flatbed of a broken-down pickup truck.

"What kind of story?" Daddy asked, already knowing the answer.

"Tell me about the angel!" Martin cried in a high-pitched voice.

"Again?" he asked, feigning astonishment. "I have many stories to tell."

"No, tell me about the angel!" Martin yelled gleefully.

The stories had become a ritual for them, every day after his lessons. Now that Martin was controlling the needle, he pushed it in even harder and deeper than Daddy, wanting him to be proud, yes, but also wanting to finish quicker so they could get to the stories. Daddy (he still couldn't call him Paul, no matter how hard he tried) would sigh as Martin drove the needles in farther and farther, sometimes in one side and out again. When he finally said, "Aye, that's a good lad," it was time for the stories. Or story. All his tales seemed connected, like they were part of one big story that didn't have a beginning or an end. Martin liked the story about the angel most of all. It seemed like Daddy did too.

"Please, please, please!" Martin begged, knowing he didn't need to.

"Okay, you little rascal," Daddy smirked, giving him a scorching noogie.

"Once upon a time…such a long, long time ago…there was a very special boy," Daddy began, shaking his long blond hair back from his sunbaked face like a waking lion. "What made him so special?" he asked, giving Martin a wink.

"He had special powers…and a mark on his chest, like this!" Martin yelled, pulling up his dirty T-shirt to reveal a ring-shaped discoloration on his solar plexus. Unlike most birthmarks, it was lighter than the surrounding skin, like a halo. The first time Daddy saw it, he didn't seem surprised. He said it was an omen. It meant he was destined for greatness, like the boy in the story.

"See, I have one too," Daddy said, opening his shirt. In stark contrast to his own scrawny ribcage, Daddy's was thick with muscles. The mark was even more intimidating. It was dark, dark red—so dark it looked completely black except at the edges. It started with a circle in the center of his breastbone, then radiated outward in inky snakes like the twisted blades of some of his knives. They looked like the rays of the sun—if the sun was black. Martin couldn't help but stare. It felt like the black sun was pulling him inside.

"Yes, the boy was very special," Daddy continued, breaking the spell. "So special that he had a very special friend watching over him. His special friend came from another world that was not at all like the world we live in. There was no sun and moon, because everything had its own inner light. The luminous beings in the other world were made of pure energy, so they could never die. But they could never really live either. Not like we do. Some called them gods or daimons, but over time most people came to know them by another name...."

"Angels!" Martin cried with joy.

"Aye, angels," Paul nodded, smiling just as brightly.

"On the day of his birth, the boy's special angel was watching, peering through a gateway connecting their worlds, a portal to his heavenly realm the angel could see through, but was shielded from humans except when they dreamed, or if they had the gift of the *seer*.

"When the angel saw the birthmark on the boy's chest he was delighted. From that moment on, the angel watched and waited for the boy to manifest some remarkable ability that would prove beyond any doubt he was *An Té atá Tofa*."

"The one who has been chosen," Martin whispered worshipfully.

"Aye," Daddy said, suddenly very serious. *"An Té atá Tofa,"* he repeated. Martin had to recite it over and over until he got the pronunciation right. When Daddy was finally satisfied, he continued the story.

"The angel was certain the omen would soon arrive. When it did, and the boy came of age many years later—years that would pass like the flicker of a candle for the ageless angel—then and only then would he offer his magnificent gift to the boy, honoring him with the most profound knowledge ever bestowed upon any human."

"Tell me, Daddy! Tell me what the angel told the boy!" Martin begged.

"The boy wasn't ready." Daddy frowned, shaking his head solemnly. "The omen had not yet arrived. When it did, *if* it did, the boy would have to make an unbreakable vow of loyalty and secrecy. The gift of the angel was so monumental that it could never be allowed to fall into the hands of the unworthy. You see, the angel and all his kind possessed powers far beyond human understanding. They could transform thought into matter and change matter into any form they chose. They possessed all knowledge—the mysteries of life and death, time and space, past and future—the secrets of immortality. They could see far into the future and knew a day would come when our universe and theirs would face the threat of utter destruction. Only *An Té atá Tofa* could avert that apocalypse and bring salvation to all beings. If the omen came and the boy proved worthy, all the powers of the all the angels would be granted to him, if he vowed to guard their sacred knowledge until the time of his anointing. Until the *Becoming*."

"Daddy, what's 'the *Becoming*'?"

"You know full well I can't tell you...until I see an omen about *you*."

"When will the omen come? When will I be ready?" Martin pouted.

"Someday not too long from now, yet not so close either. But don't fret, lad. I know it will arrive, just as the angel knew the boy was blessed.

"For him, the omen came on a cloudless day, as omens often do. The boy was still a tiny infant, lying peacefully in the shade while his mother bathed in a nearby stream. When the angel gazed through his portal to look at the boy, what should he see but the boy gazing right back. He was smiling. Waving! The boy could *see* through the portal, not in his dreams, but awake. And he was only a baby! Not only did he have the mark—he was a *seer!* The boy must truly be *An Té atá Tofa!*"

Suddenly, Daddy's expression changed from elation to sorrow.

"But at the very moment when the boy revealed his true nature, something horrible happened. While his mother was still bathing, a mean, ugly crone snatched up his cradle and stole him away to her filthy hovel made of sticks and mud in the deepest, darkest depths of the forest. She treated the poor child worse than a mongrel dog. When he was old enough to walk, she tethered him to the biggest tree outside, his ankle tied to a rope just long enough to fetch wood for the fire and water from the well. She never spoke to him except to bark commands and barely fed him enough to keep his ribs from poking through his skin…"

"Then one day…" Martin cut in, anxious to get past this part of the story.

"Yes, then one day…" Daddy grinned, goading Martin along.

"He stole a knife from the cutting board and cut the rope and he was finally *free!*" Martin shouted, his smile shining like the sun coming out from a bank of thunderclouds.

"Aren't you leaving something out?" Daddy pressed.

The clouds passed over Martin's face again, eclipsing his eager smile.

"He had to do the bad thing first," Martin replied, his chin sagging to his chest.

"Was it really such a bad thing?" Daddy asked, planting an ogre-sized hand on his tiny shoulder. "Is it a bad thing when you shoot all those greasy, filthy rats in the dump?"

"I guess not," Martin mumbled, glancing back up into Daddy's stern, yet kind eyes.

"So what did the boy do after he cut the rope on his ankle?"

"He tip-toed up to her while she was sleeping and stabbed her in the chest over and over until she wasn't breathing anymore," Martin said, his face pale and queasy.

"And then?" Paul smiled.

"Then he was *free!*" Martin shouted, beaming again.

"Yes, he was *FREE!*" Paul shouted even louder, slapping his skinny back with pride. "He ran all night along the riverbed, his skin glowing under the moon. Yet all the while he sensed a presence chasing after him, a dark shadow overhead. Could it be the old hag, back from the dead and seeking her revenge? Still running, he looked into the clear night sky to see what flew above him, but it was only the shadows of the moon as he ran through the trees. Alas, when he turned his head, he tripped over his feet, stumbling into the water and sinking like a stone into a deep, dark pool.

"He floated down, down, down, deeper and deeper. He knew he was drowning and all was lost, but his life had been so miserable it didn't matter anymore. A wonderful sense of calm and fearlessness came over him as the darkness swallowed him completely. And so he closed his eyes, surrendering to his fate.

"But when he closed his eyes he saw the most miraculous sight. Instead of blackness, he was suddenly bathed in a shimmering bluish-white light, like the moon was shining before he fell. Only this light was so much brighter! It felt warm as it approached, engulfing him completely like the deep, black pool. He opened his eyes, certain he would see only darkness around him again, but the light was even brighter and warmer, taking the form of a miraculous creature. It was easily three time his size, a human shape, neither male nor female, with a face more beautiful than any he could have imagined."

"It was the angel," Martin whispered, his voice filled with awe, his eyes closed tightly. The image was so clear in his mind it seemed to be floating right in front of him.

"Yes, the angel," Paul whispered, stroking Martin's white-blond hair. "It floated wordlessly above him and the boy wondered if they were still in the water or flying in the air. As soon as he thought about flying, the angel transformed itself into a handsome man with long white hair and enormous, white-feathered wings that beat soundlessly in the radiant light.

"'Come with me,' the angel said, reaching for the boy's hand. His voice was so kind and loving that the boy felt like crying, so touched was he after so many years of neglect and abuse. When the boy grasped the angel's hand, he was shocked to discover his grip was as solid as his own. The angel was real! A surge of power flowed into him through the angel's hand. It was so formidable he felt like he could do anything! Grow wings! Fly all by himself! His heart pounded with excitement as they floated together, the angel's radiance shining so intensely it transformed the entire world around them.

"What a magnificent world it was! Even more incredible than the luminous being who shepherded him onward. They were flying over an island more lush and splendid than the green isle of his birth, more beautiful than anything he'd seen in his most fantastic dreams. There were palaces and temples everywhere he looked, bathed in a warm, golden light that came from within. The beautiful buildings were surrounded by waterfalls and green gardens with flowers of every color, and ripe succulent fruit that weighed down every branch. Some of the palaces floated like smaller islands in the sky. Some rose atop mountains in a mist. On the terraces of every building were more amazing creatures like the one who guided him. Some had wings—others were still more incredible, changing shapes even as he watched them.

"The angel and the boy soared onward and saw a wondrous city surrounded by tall, thick walls and colossal statues of kings and queens and more fantastic creatures, some with the bodies of men and the heads of falcons and jackals, some great winged beasts with human heads. Everywhere he looked he saw gold: the statues, the domes on every tower, even the giant doors of the palace. They passed between two enormous golden winged creatures, the boy gaping with wonder at the sight of a temple bigger than all the rest combined, with a spiral tower that reached high into the clouds. The entrance to the temple was enormous, its archway supported by the horns of two bull-headed statues, their human bodies bulging with muscles.

"But when they passed through the portal, the temple had vanished. They were in a place even more astounding than the golden kingdom, a great swirling mass of light and darkness, infinite in size and pulsing with unimaginable power.

"'What is this place?' the boy asked in amazement.

"The angel smiled and said, 'This is the source of all creation and destruction, all life and all beings in existence, all that ever was and ever will be. There at the Axis spins the Great Wheel, the wellspring of all that is real…and of all possibilities.'"

"The Maelstrom," Martin whispered, gazing at the swaying wheat, unsure whether his eyes had been closed all this time. "Can we go there, Daddy? Can you take me?" he begged, changing their usual dialog for the first time.

Daddy nodded, a proud smile on his face, like he'd been waiting all along for Martin to ask that simple question. "Yes, I can take you. But there's something we need to do first."

STORM COMIN'

The days with Daddy kept getting better and better. But the nights got worse and worse. Whenever they stayed out all day, Martin could tell that Momma was mad as soon as they walked in the door. But she wouldn't say anything to Daddy. Or even look at him. He didn't say anything either. He just smiled at Martin as they passed her in the kitchen, slapping him hard on the back. Every once in a while he winked at him.

Momma smiled at Martin too. One time, when Daddy left them alone to go to the bathroom, she said, "You just wait," with a really big smile. "You just wait."

Martin wasn't sure exactly what she meant, but he knew it was going to be bad. Momma drank more. Daddy drank with her. He would smile at Martin and nudge him in the ribs when Momma wasn't looking. Martin didn't understand what the nudge meant, but when Momma turned toward them, Daddy's face would flatten into the dead mask. Momma seemed afraid of the mask too. She'd grab Daddy's hand and pull him up the stairs, smiling extra hard, trying to get his face to soften up again. Sometimes it worked. Sometimes the mask stayed on all the way to Momma's bedroom.

Martin would slink up to his room after they left, close the door and jump into bed.

Sometimes he heard a trail of booming laughter behind him. When the laughter finally stopped, the noises in the bedroom would start. They had grown so loud now that even the floppy pillow covering his head couldn't filter them out. Lately, they hadn't been closing the door, so every grunt and squeaking bedspring echoed through the old farmhouse like the rattling chains of a ghost.

One night, he heard Momma talking while the springs creaked up and down. The malice in her puffing voice sounded scarier than her screams. Even though he knew he shouldn't, Martin crept out of bed as quietly as he could and stood in the hallway listening. Their door was halfway open.

He didn't want to look inside, but he couldn't help himself from trying to hear what she was saying. When the garbled sounds finally fit together in his ears like a jigsaw puzzle, he ran as fast as he could back into his room.

She had been talking about him. Martin didn't understand what Momma said, but it scared him so much that he put all his clothes on, thinking how he might run away down one of those long, black roads. But he didn't know how he could find one by himself, especially in the dark. And he was torn between the fear of what she said and the fear of losing Daddy forever.

Martin jumped back into bed and pulled the pillow so tightly over his head that he could barely breathe. He tried to pull the switch and turn his mind and ears off, but it wouldn't work. When the sounds got really bad, he closed his eyes and prayed for the first time in his life, hoping he was special enough to have an angel watching over him too.

"Please take me away from all this...*take me away!*" the trembling boy begged. And as it turned out, someone was listening.

NORINE

"Put some clothes in this bag," Momma said when she woke him up the next morning. "You're going to Norine's for a coupla days."

Martin couldn't believe the words that came from her red, swollen lips. Did the angel make his wish come true? He felt like his heart might literally explode in his chest, but he did a good job of hiding his excitement so Momma didn't change her mind or take him to the cellar. He let out a silent scream of joy instead, pounding his fists on the lumpy mattress. He was going to Norine's! For a "coupla days"! Yes! Yes! *Yes!* Norine would know what to do. She would help him get away! She had to!

Martin loved Norine more than anything in the world. Even more than Daddy. Whenever Martin came to visit, they would sit in the rocking chair for hours and hours. Sometimes she read stories, but mostly they stayed quiet while he sat in her lap and ran the back of his hand across her cheek. So soft. Martin thought Norine's cheeks must be the softest things in the whole world. He would stroke and stroke and stroke that softness until the knot in his stomach was gone and he felt safe again.

Most times when Momma dropped off Martin she would barely speak to Norine. When she did, she always said something mean. Today was worse than usual. She stopped the truck at the end of the dirt driveway and reached across his tiny chest to open the door handle.

"Go on, git!" was all she said. She had more to say to Norine, yelling angrily, "Don't dig in your claws too deep! Just 'cause you lost yours, don't think you got any claim to mine!" Then she floored the accelerator and disappeared in a cloud of dust.

"What did she mean?" Martin asked after he was sure Momma was really gone.

Norine looked down at Martin, wiping her eyes, pretending she had dust in them, debating whether she should tell him, knowing he couldn't possibly understand, if she did.

"Are you scared of Momma?" she asked, her eyes still wet and red.

"Yes," said Martin, swallowing hard.

"I'm going to tell you a secret, baby—I'm scared of her too."

Martin couldn't hold back his tears. He threw his arms around her and they hugged so tightly he thought his little arms would snap.

"Do you want to go away with me? Far away where she can never find us?"

"Yes, yes, please, yes!" Martin cried, forgetting all about Daddy and the Maelstrom and his promise to take him there—crying with such a sad, desperate longing that Norine could only tighten her arms around him in a protective embrace.

"It's okay, sweetie," she said, stroking his head. "We'll get a good night's sleep and leave first thing in the morning."

"*No!*" Martin yelled, tugging at her arms with all his might, pulling her to the rusting sedan in the driveway. "We have to go right now! What if she comes back?"

Norine sank to her knees and showered kisses all over Martin's terrified face. "She's not gonna come back tonight. She never comes back that fast. We're gonna have all the time we need to get away."

Martin stood and cried, shaking his head in despair. But he stopped pulling and pleading when Norine said, "Let's start packing the car now so we're ready."

They came inside and she made peanut butter and jelly sandwiches. Martin said he wasn't hungry. "I thought we were gonna pack the car," he added anxiously.

She nodded, feeling almost as nervous and began packing up boxes and loading the car. When it got dark, she sent him up to bed early, telling him to get a good night's sleep because they were leaving at the crack of dawn. The "crack of dawn" part sounded great, but sleeping was out of the question.

"Are you sure Momma's not coming back tonight?"

She closed her eyes and became still as a statue. Then she shook her head like she'd bitten into a rotten apple and wanted to spit it out.

"No…Momma's not coming," she said, opening her eyes, swaying woozily. "She's…busy."

Norine walked with Martin up the stairs to the spare bedroom. She had decorated it just for him. There were cowboys and horses all over the wallpaper and little toy army men lined up on the dresser. A pair of clean, fresh smelling PJs were folded neatly on the bed. She left the room and he put them on, but kept his underwear on underneath, stacking his clothes up next to the bed so he could jump into them at a moment's notice.

When Norine came back, she tucked him into bed and sat on the covers, opening her well-worn copy of *The Arabian Nights*. She began to read, but the story was about a genie in a golden temple and it made Martin think about Daddy and how much he was going to miss him.

"Can we just talk instead?" Martin asked, hoping he wasn't hurting her feelings.

"Sure, what do you want to talk about?"

"Where are we gonna go?" he asked, excited but even more nervous.

"San Francisco," she answered, her eyes gazing out the window. "I used to live there before my dad died and left all this land to me and your momma. I could get a job teaching like I had before. It's pretty there. There's a big bridge across the harbor called the Golden Gate, even though they painted it red. I think you'd like it there."

She tried to manage a hopeful smile, but her eyes welled up with tears.

"What's wrong, Aunt Norine? Are you thinkin' about what Momma said in the car?"

"Yeah, baby, how did you know?" she sniffled, looking at him strangely.

"I don't know. Can you tell me what she meant now?"

Norine paused for a long moment. The silence was so complete that the noisy crickets outside sounded almost deafening. She had to tell him.

"I had a baby, but he died after he was born. Something was wrong with his heart, they said. When I came back here to the farm, Momma had already moved in and you were just a baby. You were so beautiful, so perfect. She knew I was jealous. That's why she doesn't want me to spend much time with you. When she finds out I've taken you away, she's going to call the police. If they find us, they'll take you back to Momma and they'll lock me up. We'll have to hide. Change our names. It's a big risk, honey, so you need to know what you're getting into. If you don't want to go through with it, I'll start unpacking and we'll act like nothing happened when Momma comes back."

Martin was scared of getting caught by the police and being sent back home to Momma. He was even more afraid of what would happen to Norine.

"If the police knew Momma hurt me, would they still lock you up for taking me?"

There it was. He had crossed the line. Momma said she would know if he ever told anyone what she did to him. Martin didn't understand how that was possible, but he believed her. If it were true, she'd know what he did. Now they *had* to go away.

Norine asked about the things Momma did to him. He told her everything—the crib, the cellar, the cigarette burns, the places she hit him when she made him get naked. He told her what Momma would do if he told anyone—lock him in the cellar and never let him out.

Norine cried while he spoke, her hands on his knees. Martin hardly felt anything. It was like he wasn't even inside his body.

When he finished, she said, "I don't think she'll call the police if we leave. But if I call and tell them what she's been doing to you, she'll deny it. She'll say I'm trying to steal you and they'll probably believe her. We still have to go. We still have to hide from her."

"Did Momma know you used to live in San Francisco?"

She thought about it. "I'm not sure. I don't think I ever told her."

"We have to go somewhere else," Martin said decisively. "I'll bet Daddy knows lots of good places to hide. Maybe he can come with us. Momma's scared of him."

"*Who is Daddy?*" she asked, more shocked by that than anything else he said to her.

Martin spent a long time explaining, trying to cover up the parts about his lessons, but it was like he was made of glass and she could see right inside his head. "He's a very bad man, Martin. A very dangerous man!"

Martin wanted to defend him, but a more sensible voice in his head knew she was probably right. Daddy had a grim darkness inside him—and Martin didn't have the slightest doubt about how dangerous he was.

"You need to get some sleep now, and I need to finish packing," she finally said, after she was convinced Martin understood that "Daddy" was not to be trusted.

"Okay," Martin said. He was tired from all the talking. But he had one last question. "Who is my real daddy?"

Norine paused for a long moment, her eyes sad and red. She cupped his little chin in her soft, soft hand and said, "When I came back here and saw her with you, that was the first thing I asked. She said your daddy was a traveling man. When one of her...friends came and went, I asked if he was the one. She got so mad that I never asked her again. So the God's honest truth is that I don't know who your father is, Martin."

Martin looked at her blankly. Like nothing she said mattered one way or the other. As far as he was concerned, his real daddy was the man who told him stories and taught him how to be brave and strong and turn off all his pain with the switch.

"Your baby that died...who was his daddy?" Martin asked blankly.

How could she tell him? What could she say? "It's getting late, baby. We need to get some sleep so we can leave early."

"It's not a big question," Martin replied, his eyes unwavering.

She thought about lying, about changing the subject, about insisting that he go to bed. Instead she said, "Sometimes men force themselves on women and they have babies."

"Uh-huh." Martin knew about men forcing themselves on women. Momma didn't care what he saw or heard.

"How many?" Martin asked, shocking her once again with his emotionless reaction.

"Three."

"Don't worry, Aunt Norine," he said, resting his hand on her shoulder. "After we get away from Momma, I'll find out who they were and kill them."

"Martin! How could you say that?" she gasped, gripping his shoulders.

"I'm tired," he said, shrugging her hands off, turning away from her, climbing into bed. "You need to finish packing," he said, facing all the cowboys and Indians on the wall.

She wanted to scold him, tell him he should never even think about such things. But how do you explain morality to a boy who's been tortured by his own mother? She stood silently staring at his back, then took his advice and went downstairs to load up the car.

Martin climbed out of bed as soon as she closed his door. He sat by the window in the little white chair she made for him. It looked like all the other chairs in the kitchen, only smaller. And whiter. On the seat of the chair was a little pillow she embroidered. I LOVE MARTIN SOOOOOO MUCH! cried the big, red block letters.

Martin sat and stared out the window into the darkness, watching for any sign of headlights with the same alert patience that served him so well with the squirrels and bunnies. He heard Norine make trip after trip out to the car, stacking boxes on boxes with rattling glass jars inside. He heard her radio playing faintly in the living room. When the trunk slammed shut, he heard the weary sounds of her footsteps climbing the stairs. There was the sound of the light switching off. Then silence.

He sat and watched, the quiet only broken by crickets and the occasional body-wrenching jolt of a screech owl. Martin had heard the owls before and he only jumped a little when the screech ripped through his ears. Still, he watched and waited, listening to the creaks and groans of the house settling around him. As he listened, he heard the words Norine whispered in his ear right after he told her all about Momma and Daddy: "Don't worry, tomorrow will be here before you know it."

She hadn't been right about that. And just before his struggling eyelids finally surrendered, he hoped she wasn't wrong about anything else.

Mrs. Morgy

Norine woke up early. She yawned, but felt surprisingly well rested. Just to be sure, she had already consumed two oversized mugs of double-dip Folger's. The car was packed and all there was left to do was get Martin up, dressed and into the car.

"Wake up, honey," she said, nudging him happily. He had fallen asleep in his little chair.

"No!" Martin screamed, as he felt Norine's hand on his shoulder. In his dream it was Momma's long fingernails, dragging him down the stairs into the cellar again.

"It's okay, sweetie, it's okay," Norine said soothingly, stroking his clammy forehead and pressing his face into her baby powder cheeks. "It was just a bad dream," she cooed.

Martin looked around the room, his senses gradually clearing. He was still here with Norine, not Momma. They were really going to leave this awful place once and for all.

"Yesssss!" Martin cheered as she put him down on the crocheted carpet. "Yesssss!" he chanted again, marching around in circles like a toy tugboat, following the oval path of cord he helped Norine make with his own little crochet hooks.

Norine chuckled for a moment, then closed her eyes and stood motionless. "C'mon, Martin, hurry up and get dressed."

Martin heard the urgency in her voice and the fear there too. He jumped into the clothes by the side of the bed in less time than it would take a fireman.

"Want something to eat? I have some sandwiches in the car," she said as they marched down the stairs.

"Nope," he answered impatiently, much to her relief.

Then he froze on the staircase. "I forgot something," he gulped. He didn't want to go back, but he couldn't leave without it.

"Never mind, baby," Norine said, their previous tug-of-war now reversed, pulling his arm toward the car. "Whatever you forgot, we'll get another one later."

"I forgot Mrs. Morgy!" Martin cried, and before she could remind him that Mrs. Morgy didn't matter so much last night, Martin wriggled out of her grasp and bounded back up the staircase two steps at a time. He flew into the bedroom and grabbed the worn-out stuffed doggie with the long, floppy ears that were almost as soft as Norine's cheeks. He was just about ready to leap back down the stairs when a far-off droning sound began snaking into his ears. The sound of a truck.

Now, wait, dear reader. Don't think I would be so cruel as to suggest that Martin's sentimental heart was the cause of his undoing. That those few short moments spent gathering his most precious possession spelled the difference between salvation and all the suffering to follow. That if he had only obeyed the tug of Norine's fingers on his wrist they might have somehow escaped.

No, I wouldn't do that to you. Martin's date with Mrs. Morgy didn't matter one iota. The truck had already started up the road before he even ran to get her.

OBJECTIONS

Martin rushed to the window, watching the truck. He saw Norine standing outside, desperately turning her head in every direction, to the truck, to the over-packed Chevy, to the window, to his terrified face that mirrored her own. Martin couldn't move. As the truck drew closer, he saw something else. It was Momma's truck, but she wasn't driving. It was Daddy. He was looking at Norine, and he wasn't happy. He wasn't happy at all.

Martin flew down the stairs as the truck came to a lurching halt amid a cloud of ash-dry, swirling dust. "Taking a little trip, are we?" Paul asked happily, elongating the "we" into a high-pitched song that made the blond hairs on Martin's neck rise on a wave of gooseflesh. Martin was watching from behind the screen in the doorway, one hand gripping his little chair, the other clutching Mrs. Morgy.

Paul was leaning against the hood of the truck. "Well, that's a funny thing, you see," he said, cutting Norine off as soon as she opened her mouth to speak. "I was thinking of taking the little feller for a trip this very morning. Can you imagine that?"

"And who, may I ask, are you?" Norine asked, standing her ground by the Chevy, knowing he was the man Martin sickeningly called Daddy.

"My name is Paul, ma'am. I'm a very dear friend of your baby sister," he replied, the smile fading from his hamburger-red face. "She asked me to take the boy out for a drive. Didn't want him cooped up in the house all day."

"She should have told me yesterday," Norine shot back. "We're going for a picnic."

A picnic. Martin knew she was making it up, but it sounded so peaceful. So perfect. Then he looked at Paul's face and his heart sank to his ankles. He wouldn't be going on any picnic. Not now. Not ever. He wouldn't be going anywhere with Norine.

"A picnic, you say!" Paul hooted, clapping his hands loudly, his face flushed again with gleeful animation. "Well, judging from what you've got stuffed into this car, I guess you'll be having that picnic in California…for maybe a year or two!"

Norine looked away. Paul grinned and brushed his bulk past her shoulder. "What have you got there, Martin?" he called to the trembling boy. It was the first time he'd looked in his direction.

Martin wanted to sink back into the shadows of the hallway. Instead, he stood behind the black-mesh screen and sadly answered, "Mrs. Morgy."

"Mrs. Morgy?" Paul grinned. "What a wonderful name for a little stuffed doggy! Do you think I could have a closer peek at her?"

Martin nodded, a tentative smile returning to his face. Paul began walking to him when Norine grabbed his arm. "Just what do you think you're doing here?" she demanded. If she was as scared as Martin, she certainly didn't show it.

"Well, I'll tell you what I'm doing here," Paul said, "I'm taking Martin for a little drive." He said it with the finality of a truck hitting a concrete wall at ninety miles an hour. "Any objections?" he added, his hands hanging at his sides like a gunslinger ready to draw.

Norine looked him up and down, gauging his size, his weight. She peered deeply into the stillness of the dead mask.

Martin felt his tears well up again as Norine's shoulders slumped in resignation. *No! You promised! You promised me we'd get away!*

Paul turned on Martin again, his boots raising clouds of dust as he trudged toward him with the doomed inevitability of a nuclear aftershock.

"Oh, yes, I've got objections!" Norine yelled at him, her voice strangled with emotion. "I object very, very much!"

Paul turned toward her. Martin flew out the door as fast as he could, dropping the chair as he ran to her, hugging her leg, trying to puff his little chest out as far as he could, letting Daddy know he would do anything… *anything*…that would keep him from hurting his beloved Norine.

What Paul did next surprised them both. He looked down at Martin and softly patted him on the head. Then he stared into Norine's eyes and said, "Maybe if you knew what I had planned for the little tyke, you wouldn't be objecting so much."

"What?" Norine asked, completely thrown off track by his mysterious declaration.

"It's a surprise," Paul whispered, nudging his chin in Martin's direction.

Norine knew it was just another ruse to get Martin into the truck without dragging him screaming inside. "What kind of surprise?" she asked nervously, trying to think of a way to get Martin into her car and try to outrun the lumbering truck with her Chevy V-8.

Paul mouthed a "not-in-front-of-the-kid" pantomime and nudged his chin again, this time in the direction of the screen door. "Would you mind stepping inside for a minute so we don't ruin everything for the dear lad?" he whispered into Norine's ear with a cupped hand. He was so close that her nose wrinkled from the smell.

She nodded slightly. Paul smiled and gave her a secret wink. "Martin, I'm going inside to have a word with this man," she said, turning her back on Paul, signaling Martin with her eyes that he needed to get into the car as soon as they were out of sight.

Martin stared at them with the most heartbreakingly hopeful smile she had ever seen.

He still didn't get it. He still thought everything was going to be okay.

Paul smiled broadly. "That's right, Martin. Go have yourself a rest in the truck while me and your auntie have a nice little chat."

"No, go sit in my car, the seats are more comfortable," she said, knowing she was calling the big man's hand. He would have to show his cards now, perhaps forcibly attempt to abduct the boy. Then Martin would see what kind of man he really was, and at least he'd have a chance to run for it while she did whatever she could to slow him down.

What Paul said was just as unforeseen as his earlier actions. "Splendid idea! Those seat springs in the truck are popping all the way through the upholstery. Make yourself nice and cozy in your auntie's car and we'll be back lickety-split!"

Martin practically peed his pants in agreement. Maybe they could all leave together! He walked a few steps to the car while Paul opened the door for Norine with the exaggerated courtliness of a Southern plantation owner. He even gave her a tiny bow as she passed the threshold. When she was out of sight, Paul turned to Martin and gave him a big, warm smile, lifting up his thumb, as if to say, "Don't you worry now. Everything's going to be A-OK."

Martin grinned from ear to ear, glad to have Daddy taking care of everything again. He scampered into Norine's car seat like they were all going out for a double-dip ice cream cone. When Paul raised his finger to his lips, reminding him to stay nice and quiet, Martin kissed his finger and let out a long conspiratorial "shush" in response.

Martin sat on the fat vinyl cushion and smiled through the dirty windshield. He watched happily as Paul disappeared into the shadows and closed the door. He waited and rubbed Mrs. Morgy's ears against his cheek. They were so soft. But they would never feel as soft as Norine's cheeks. Nothing would ever feel that soft and good to him again.

BYE-BYE

Paul was inside with Norine for a long time. When the door opened, he came out alone. He picked up the little white chair, then walked over to Norine's overstuffed trunk and grabbed Martin's bag of clothes, shouting, "C'mon, little buddy. Your auntie said we should go ahead and she'll catch up with us in a few shakes. She wants to put together her own little surprise for you, so we can all join in the fun together!"

Martin grinned and leapt out of the car, clutching Mrs. Morgy as he scampered over to the truck behind Paul's quickly moving legs. Paul gently placed his belongings in the back of the truck, then hopped into the cab and started the clunky motor without saying another word. Martin jumped into the seat next to him and Paul reached over and rubbed his mop of hair. He threw the gearshift into reverse and stepped on the gas so hard that dust flew up in every direction. He was shifting back into first gear when Martin grabbed his arm as tightly as he could.

"Where's Aunt Norine?" he asked, looking nervously at the motionless screen door. "You said she was coming right behind us."

Paul slammed on the brakes. A cloud of dust cascaded over the windshield like a brown waterfall. "No, Martin, I said she'd be coming a little later." His smile was unwavering and unfathomable.

"When?"

"If I told you that, it would ruin the surprise, wouldn't it?"

"What surprise?" asked Martin, fully attentive.

"It isn't a surprise if you tell. You know that, don't you?"

Martin frowned, mulling it over. Then he grabbed Paul's arm again. "I don't want the surprise. I want Aunt Norine to come with us now."

"That's what you say, but you don't know what the surprise is! Why do you think I drove here so early in the morning? It must be something pretty special, eh?"

Martin had to think about that. Paul said it with such tantalizing allure that Martin's brain momentarily disengaged from the problem of "No Norine" to ponder the dangling promise of the mysterious surprise. He was bursting with curiosity, but his true-blue heart pulled him back like a slingshot to the door on the porch.

"Why didn't she come out to say good-bye?"

"Because she's getting ready, that's why," Paul said glibly.

"Ready for what?"

"For the surprise, Martin...the surprise!" Paul shouted, patting him on the head and jamming the shift down so hard that the grinding gears sounded like the chains of a castle drawbridge. Before Martin had time to say anything else, they were barreling down the dusty driveway. He turned quickly backwards, pressing his face into the rear window.

She had to be coming! She *had* to! But no matter how hard he tried to believe it, he couldn't ignore the feeling in his chest as he searched window after window for any sign of movement.

Why didn't she wave? Why didn't she look out the window and wave?

SURPRISE!

Martin stared at the bare blazing bulb overhead, then down at the nail emerging from the flesh of his hand. As bad as this was, it was a million times better than what he'd been seeing in his head.

Curtains drawn, just in time.

He was glad his memory didn't work like it should anymore. It was more like the switch now, only he didn't have much control over when it turned off and on. That was okay. Some part of him knew when to use it and always seemed to spare him the very worst parts. Most of the time. But not this time. This time he saw too much.

He was in the truck with Daddy. His head turned back every few seconds to look at the dust-blurred speck of Norine's receding house. When they reached the end of the driveway and took a sharp left, his body stiffened. They were headed back home.

"No!" Martin cried. "Don't take me back there! Please, Daddy, please!"

Paul's smile never wavered. "Don't you worry, little man," he shouted back. "Everything is going to be fine and dandy."

Martin's shoulders slumped to his chest. He stared at Daddy's smiling face, knowing there was no use in arguing with him, knowing with equal certainty that nothing was going to be fine, or dandy, or any other word that sounded happy. It was going to be bad. Really, really bad.

"*SURPRISE!*" Paul yelled, throwing open the door to the dining room.

The table was lined with party hats and toys and balloons of every color. More balloons hung from the ceiling with ribbons that reached all the way to the floor. There was a white cake in the middle of the table. It was shaped like a heart with little red candy hearts running along the outside edge like the trim on a lace doily. Eight glowing candles flickered with every gasp of his breath. As he read the script spelled out in gooey red letters, Paul's voice shouted along with him, *"Happy birthday, Martin!"*

Martin didn't even know today was his birthday. Momma never told him. The table was set for three, with name cards in front of each chair spelled out in big block letters in what looked like Momma's red lipstick: MOMMA. DADDY. MARTIN. Three cards. Not four. He looked at the cards and the cake and back at Daddy. He wanted to ask why Norine wasn't coming, but Daddy was pointing at the door on the other end of the room. His sad eyes told him something awful was coming.

Martin's eyes followed past the cake and the balloons. Past the cards and the napkins. Past the toys and the shining wrapped presents. The door opened slowly and Momma walked inside. She had a look in her eyes he'd never seen, even in the cellar. She was all made up, blue eye shadow and bright red lipstick, her hair brushed down, soft and blond, wisping against her naked shoulders.

Her smile was scary. So was the look in her eyes. But that wasn't what made him want to run. It wasn't just her shoulders that were naked. Momma wasn't wearing anything at all.

She came toward him slowly, leering and swaying her wide hips.

"Look at her, Martin!" Paul leered with his arms stretched open, as if his naked mother were the icing on the cake. "Just look at your dear sweet Momma!"

Momma smiled crookedly and cupped her breasts in both hands. Martin turned to run out the wide French doors on the other side of the room, but let out a scream when he saw they'd been locked. "Where you goin', honey?" Momma asked, still walking toward him. "Don't you want to play with me?"

Martin sat and cried, trying to turn his head away, not being able to. Her hair was dark down there, almost black. Even in his blind panic he couldn't help but wonder why it didn't match the brassy blond hair on her head.

She came closer. Her breasts wobbled as she walked.

Martin looked at the doors and at Paul with an expression that could only be a called a prayer. Please. Please help me, Daddy.

Daddy was wearing the dead mask.

The mask didn't change when she squatted down, resting her hand on Martin's leg, moving it slowly up his thigh. It wasn't until she put Martin's hand on her breast that Daddy's face came alive.

"Would you look at that, Martin!" Paul shouted, his eyes wild and savage, his smile sliding up and down like a see-saw. "Would you look at that evil skank of a whore cunt!"

Momma shot up like her legs were spring-loaded. "You bastard!" she shrieked, so humiliated by his unforeseen betrayal that she didn't know whether to scramble for her clothes or attack. She attacked, rushing at Paul with her nails poised like talons, ready to rip the sneer from his face. Paul pushed her backwards on the floor with the one-handed ease of a farmer tipping over a sack of grain.

"*Me* a bastard?" he asked in a gurgling laugh that sounded like a toilet flushing. "That's pretty cheeky comin' from a kiddie-raping cunt like you!" He walked over, plucking up Martin's easy weight and cradling him in a single arm, their heads side by side. Together, they stared into the blast furnace of Momma's hate. "Look at her, Martin…just look at her!"

Martin couldn't. He buried his face in Paul's thick neck as Momma tried to cover herself with an ugly throw rug by the door.

"I'll cut your balls off, you fucking ape!" she growled, regaining her footing.

"Well, isn't that exactly what I'm talking about, eh?" Paul mocked, turning Martin's chin out, forcing him to watch her. "Do you know what she wanted to do?" Paul asked sadly. Martin's stomach tightened with dread.

"*Stop it!*" Momma shrieked, rushing in for another attack.

Paul pushed her against the wall with a head-thumping thwack. Her eyes rolled in a lazy orbit that made Martin wonder if he'd killed her. Paul began talking again as if nothing had happened. "Not only did she want to foul your proud virgin member, but she wanted *me*, your own dear daddy, to take me big willy here and…well, I can't even bring myself to say it."

Martin couldn't hold it back anymore. He screamed with a horror so complete that it washed all his senses into the abyss. "*NOOOOOOO!*"

Paul had to turn his head to protect his eardrum from the sickening wail. He watched happily as Momma's eyes slowly focused. Now they were coated with a wet film of fear. She tried to scoot toward the door, but her legs weren't working right. Paul set Martin on the floor. Martin looked at Momma's naked, squirming body and felt sad and angry and sick to his stomach. When he saw the bloodstain on the back of the wall where her head made the loud noise, he almost threw up.

Paul opened his brisket-thick hand in front of Martin's face. Resting on his palm was the most beautiful pistol he had ever seen, a .22-caliber Beretta with a silver-plated grip. It had been custom engraved in Spain. There was a blue ribbon wrapped around the barrel.

"Happy birthday, Martin," Paul said and kissed him on the forehead.

Martin sobbed uncontrollably. Paul rubbed Martin's head, soothing him with one hand, holding the pistol in the other. "Shhh-shhh, dear boy. I'm sorry it had to be like this, but it's the only way. You had to see for yourself that there isn't a bone in her filthy body worth caring about before you do what needs to be done…just like the boy in the story."

Martin cried on the floor, as confused as he was horrified. He looked at Momma and the pistol. It was the perfect size for a little boy. When Martin curled his hand around the grip, it felt like part of his own flesh.

"Mahtinnn…" Momma groaned, "Pweeasse…"

There was something wrong with her mouth. The left side was smiling, but the other side seemed to sag a little.

Paul knelt down and whispered to him, cold as ice, "I know you don't like knives, so I got you this lovely little pistol. Just pull the trigger nice and slow like I taught you, son."

"I can't!" Martin sobbed, still clinging to some ancient trace of love for the crumpled body below him, her fluttering eyes darting back and forth between them.

"Kill her now!" Paul demanded. "Don't feel, boy, just act!"

"Doan, bibby, please," Momma begged, blood leaking from her lips. She was slurring so badly that Martin could barely understand her.

"Ees da one…" she hissed, wagging a limp finger at Paul, the other arm hanging lifeless by her side. "Ass im abud Noeene."

"What…?" Martin croaked, trying to decode her garbled moaning.

Paul's combat boot crushed the part of her face that was still working. Momma tried to make her tongue move, but the gap between the place in her brain that made the words and the place where the words come out was quickly filling with sticky clumps of blood.

"Norine…she's talking about Norine!" Paul shouted. "Do you know why she hated her so much? She was jealous. Jealous of you and Norine!"

Martin nodded. Hatred rose through his neck, weaving into every crevice of his mind.

Squeeze.

"Remember when she came to pick you up and saw you dancing with Norine?"

Squeeze.

"Remember what she did to you that night…*in the cellar?*"

That was it. All the years of torment erupted like vomit from the depths of his soul. From the cellar. "I hate you! I hate you! *I HATE YOU!*" Martin screamed at her, feeling more powerful with each repetition.

"Shoot her, Martin!" Paul hissed, pointing at the place between her breasts. "Shoot her right through her cold black heart!"

Momma begged him with her eyes one last time. Mercy, son. Mercy.

He couldn't do it…he couldn't. But his finger squeezed the trigger without his head's permission. A long, slow, steady squeeze, just like Paul taught him. The *bang* was deafening in the small room, the kick nearly enough to throw the pistol from his hand. But his aim was true. The lead whizzed out like a rocket ship, not at her heart but at the smooth dead center of her forehead. A dimple of red, just a drop really, appeared above her eyes like a shiny red *bindi*. Momma didn't move. Martin thought he must have done something wrong and began to squeeze the trigger again. Then he saw her eyes. They were changing from a sweat-soaked stare of horror to a milky glaze of utter confusion.

The tiny .22-caliber bullet was ricocheting inside her skull like a pinball, lighting up old memories of love and cruelty as it whipped the spidery gray filaments of her brain into a six-egg omelet. When the lump of lead finished its final twists and turns, there was nothing left of life inside her but the last few twitches of jangling nerves and pulsing capillaries. The same look of bewilderment remained painted on her face as her body slowly crumpled beneath her.

"Yessss!" Paul shouted at the top of his lungs, sweeping the little boy up in his arms. *"You did it! You did it! YOU DID IT!"*

Martin's face lit up in a rainbow of triumph and vindication...his smile beaming from ear to ear and back again. Yet, as he watched the drops of blood ooze slowly from his mother's nostrils he felt an emptiness rising from his toes and burrowing into his chest. The switch clicked again, so hard he could almost hear it. All the feelings he had ever known...love, sadness, hurt, longing...all of them folded up inside his head, tucking themselves away into old wooden cupboards and dark, musty closets where they could never be found again. One by one, the doors closed like an endless hotel corridor. When the final door slammed shut, everything that could have called itself Martin had been silently locked away. And the smile on his face vanished like a wisp of smoke.

SOB STORY

Sad, wasn't it? I almost hated telling you, but I figured you'd want to know. Everybody wants the backstory. Everyone wants to know how people "got that way." Personally, I don't think explanations help very much.

They certainly didn't help with me. I went to therapy for years, digging up all the worms and green goop that were supposed to free me from my demons. The results were less than liberating. I'm not saying I had it worse than Martin, but it was quite horrible in its own way...in its own special way. I won't go into it now; you've already been through enough. Let's just say it was bad. Take my word for it.

Sometimes I feel sorry for myself. I suppose everybody does now and then, some more than others. But whenever I feel really sad about my lot in life, all the terrible things that happened, all the wonderful things that didn't, I start to feel really icky about the self-pity too. I guess feeling sorry for myself makes me feel weak. Then I feel ashamed. So instead of just feeling bad about how shitty my life is, I feel bad about my *feelings* about how shitty my life is. All in all, it's not worth it. Better to hop off the pity-pot and find something else to do.

Actually, that was how this all started. I was feeling sorry for myself. And I was feeling bored with feeling sorry for myself. So I went on the web.

THE WEB

It seems so long ago now, but when I first discovered the website I thought it had to be a joke. I was just prowling around, looking for...well, looking for the stuff I always look for, when I clicked on a link and...*boom!*...there I was, staring face to face with an angry young man, dementedly sticking his tongue out. Not very startling, except for the fact that his tongue was split in two. My immediate appraisal of the blurry low-res image was to guess that it was a Photoshop alteration, poorly done. It was the *poorly done* aspect that captured my attention, drawing me in for a closer investigation that made my stomach churn and tighten. I know a thing or two about Photoshop and if I wanted to make a forked tongue look like it belonged to some Heavy-Metal-Demon-Snake-God, I'd make it long, tapered, slithery, curly, mobile. Not these twin fat lumpy wads of tissue that looked like your pal Jimmy just clipped your tongue in half with a pair of pruning shears. So in the space of a second, the dim light in my head turned on and I realized it had to be real. What the fuck? Why the fuck? Yet there it was. Wag. Wag. The loose flaps of disassociated tongue meat wobbled and flapped in my face, computer animated, moving in crude jerks and flickers. I could have hit the back button and returned to the comparatively warm and fuzzy world of rose tattoo ankle bracelets and diamond stud nose jewelry. I could have shut down the computer, taken a deep breath and walked outside. But I didn't. I couldn't. I had to see more. My fist gripped the mouse in a cold, sweaty squeeze that should have popped the little track ball inside. I guided it over the picture and squeezed the clicker on his tortured stubby tongue flap and...*boom*...I was instantly transported to a very innocuous, nicely designed e-zine.

There was a picture of a young girl who looked about nineteen and would have been called pretty by anyone, regardless of all the rings and posts in her face. Still, it was nothing particularly outrageous, certainly not on the level of Snake-Boy, just your usual assortment of eyebrow, lip, nose and ear piercings. There were a variety of articles that also seemed pretty tame, mostly on tattoos and piercings and personal ads where people with a lot of holes could go meet each other and fill them with metal objects. Then way off in the corner was another title that made my arm hairs crinkle up the moment I read it: "Extreme Body Modification."

Some saner part of me tugged my shoulder and said, "Hey, let's beat it." Of course, I ignored my inner wisdom again. Looking back, I would have done anything to prevent myself from clicking on that link. I won't tell you the name of the URL…it's real, and it's still there…but you'll have to find it for yourself. Nevertheless, I hope you think twice before going there. For most people it wouldn't be a very big deal, you'd look at one or two pics, puke and go have a good stiff drink. But if you're like me…

I suppose I've always had a morbid fascination with gore. When I was a kid, I used to read *Famous Monsters of Filmland.* The magazine had a glossy color cover and cheap black-and-white newsprint inside. I'd leaf through the pages, checking out pictures of vampires and werewolves and what I loved most…the black-and-white shots of the Famous Monster's victims. Black blood. I liked it better that way. It was much more frightening. The color photos with their fake blood and fake shiny guts and fake hanging eyeballs looked…fake. The black-and-white pictures looked real…like *news.*

In the early sixties, television was mostly black and white (or maybe mother was too cheap to buy a color set…I'm not quite sure, I was only a boy then). So when people were shot and they grabbed their guts in all those cop shows and westerns, you'd see a trickle of black oozing out from their vests. Black blood. *The Daily News* used to sell gore on the covers too. The body fallen from the seventh-floor window, the bullet-in-the-back-of-the-head mob murder—it was there on the front page for all to see, in glorious black and white.

I've never really lost that fascination. On the contrary, it's increased quite dramatically over the years. I looked at the picture of the girl with the rings, studs and barbells all over her pretty face and thought that it couldn't be that bad inside. So I braced myself, clicked the Extreme Body Modification link and…*boom*…I had to fill out a credit card application because this part of the site was for members only. I filled out the application and without a single *boom*, I was greeted with the most shocking, mind-numbing horrors in a lifetime of horror seeking.

Pause. Breathe. Gulp. I couldn't decide which was more disgusting, the full color images of the actual "feats" accomplished (now that's real, that's news!), or the bland Matter O' Fact pseudo-medical descriptions of the techniques themselves: scalpel piercings, uvula piercings, scrotal implants, transdermal implants, urethral stretching, subincision, *meatonomy!*

What's a subincision? You don't want to know. What's a meatonomy? You don't want to know. And it got worse and worse. Grafts and implants. Fingernail removal (temporary and permanent). Urethral relocation. Penis bifurcation. Voluntary amputation. *Nullification!* What's nullification? Take a guess. From the verb *to nullify*: destroy, abolish, ruin, dispose of, put an end to, get rid of…cut off. Cut off what? You guessed it. Your thingees. *All* your thingees.

I stopped and rested and got my guts to settle down and I definitely should have left then, but I couldn't and I moved my hand and pressed the mouse and *click*…I saw the shots of the man with a meat cleaver standing next to a butcher block.

Fuck. You know, I almost always call a dick a cock. I just think the word makes more sense when we're talking about one in use. But when you're talking about an *ex*-cock, I guess you'd have to call it a dick.

Try it yourself:

"He cut his own cock off." or "He cut his own dick off."

See what I mean?

THE SCREAM

Michael Bean was a skinny blond rat who wanted to think he was brave. He wasn't. He was a very scared young man who would have been called pretty if he didn't try so hard to pass himself off as a Street Trash Artist Radical, which he was only in the sense that he slept in an abandoned building on Avenue D, panhandled on Avenue A, threw rocks at the police (from the very rear of the crowd) on Avenue B and occasionally read really bad poetry, really badly in a really bad poetry cafe on Avenue C.

And of course, he did his best to cultivate the right look. The Street Trash Artist Radical look in its latest incarnation consisted of greasy dreadlocks, sparse (so sparse you can count the hairs) beard, multiple facial piercings (eyebrow, ear, nose and tongue), dirty white-and-black horizontal striped T-shirt, dirty orange-and-blue sneakers, and very dirty, very baggy olive corduroy pants.

It looked like he wore the same clothes every day. He did. He was wearing them now as he sat on his filthy mattress, staring at the ceiling, listening to the awful scream coming from upstairs. It wasn't the first time he'd heard a scream like that coming from the top floor. He'd heard them so often that he would have called the police if he weren't a Street Trash Artist Radical and didn't live in an illegal condemned building and didn't just hate those fucking cops, man. So instead, he listened to someone screaming like they were being disemboweled every few days, jamming a pillow over his head to filter out the sounds, always failing miserably. He rarely heard such screams during the day. And he'd never heard one that was quite so...

"Intense," he said to the cracked plaster ceiling over his head, hoping the sound of his own voice would shatter the panic rising in his guts. He wanted it to *stop*...wanted to explain it away like he always did, but the scream went on and on, swelling like a choir inside a volcano. *What if someone's dying? I have to do something! I have to do something now!*

Just as the last rays of sunlight disappeared, the screaming stopped. He stared at the ceiling for a very long time—like he was waiting for an answer. The question was whether or not he should go upstairs and find out what happened. Michael stared and stared, but the ceiling didn't say a thing.

Well, maybe everything's okay. But as many times as he'd been able to tell himself that in the past, this time it wasn't working.

Michael wanted to be brave. But more than anything, he didn't want to go up and knock on that door. He'd never seen the man on the top floor. No one in the building would even talk about him, except for the nut on the first floor with the hair down to his ass who said he knew the guy and that he was, "Amazing, man."

When Michael stood up and walked to the door, he couldn't believe he summoned the will to move. Now that the sun had set, it was as dark in the lightless hallway as it was outside. Maybe darker. But the strange compulsion propelling him gave another push and with more courage than he ever expected to feel, Michael started up the stairs.

It didn't make it any easier that they creaked when he walked.

FREEDOM

Paul yanked the nail from Martin's hand without warning. Martin didn't scream this time, swallowing it back through firmly clenched teeth.

Paul said nothing, looking for any further signs of weakness. Martin tightened his focus like a rusty bolt and drew on everything he had left inside to remain erect and still.

After many long seconds of scrutiny, Paul relaxed his gaze, revealing the hint of a proud smile before sucking it back like a soda straw under the dead mask. He lifted a plastic milk crate next to Martin's chair and rolled out a clean, white cotton tablecloth. The cloth was almost dazzling in its brightness. Paul sat on the crate beside him.

In his dazed state, Martin wondered if they were having a picnic. Then he realized it was Paul's version of a first aid kit. Paul began arranging the other contents of his bundle on the table in front of Martin. Clean bandages, a bottle of hydrogen peroxide, a tube of antibiotic ointment, and a long, thick, curved needle.

"Sutures," Martin said, unable to keep the dawning realization from escaping his lips. When Paul nodded in agreement with a twinkling smile, Martin realized something else.

It wasn't over yet.

KNOCK, KNOCK

Paul was finishing up when they heard a soft, distant rapping at the front door. It sounded more like a *nick* than a knock. Paul stabbed in the final suture, tied it off, nipped the excess string with his yellow teeth and rose in a single motion. It should have hurt, but Martin barely noticed.

Paul quickly vanished and the smile he flashed at Martin right before he turned on his heels seemed to linger in the air like a freshly baked meatloaf. Or was it pot roast? Then it suddenly dawned on Martin that he was sniffing more than a simile.

"What's he cooking?" Martin wondered as the earthy smell penetrated the stench of the back rooms. His belly grumbled in response.

He felt like himself again. Or more accurately, he felt his familiar lack of self. Good. That's why he came here. His mind almost sighed with relief, but collided instead with the image of a dark-haired pixie with a turned-up nose. Rose. There she was, still inside his head…beckoning with a curved index finger.

His heart ached even more than his hand. All this for nothing. She was still there. Paul, with all his powers, couldn't drive her away. At first, all Martin felt was despair. *Nothing can stop this feeling from growing.* Even Paul can't stop it. Then slowly, very slowly, his despair faded as two dawning realizations echoed in his pain-puffed brain. The first was that his feelings for Rose felt good. Very good. The second was even sweeter and he spoke aloud what he only dared to think before.

"Paul can't do anything to stop it."

LUCKY CHARM

Ting-a-ling-a-ling. The bell made the same sound when Rose left as when she entered. The only difference was the accompanying *thump* her shopping bag made when it banged against the doorframe as she struggled to exit. The bag was enormous, overflowing with bolts of fabric. She couldn't wait to unroll them all over her bare kitchen floor.

"He's gonna love this!" she squealed, trudging toward the curb. She tried hailing a cab, but it was swing shift and they were all off duty. She began walking, looking over her shoulder every few steps in the hope of snatching a taxi, but after three blocks, she resigned herself to the long schlep home, groaning as she shifted the bag from one hand to the other every two blocks.

She wished she were back home right now. She would knock on Martin's door and shout, "Ta-da!" proudly displaying her wares. Or better yet, she imagined him here with her, carrying the bag so they could make another stop at Pearl Paint along the way. He would cheer her on and tell her to buy more of this and more of that and...

No. He definitely wasn't the shopping type. Damn. What type was he? *The good fucking type.* She managed a grin, but it felt hollow and empty, like she was whistling in a dark alley. Rose looked around. While not an alley, it was definitely a whole lot darker and spookier now that she'd crossed Rivington Street.

The sky grew black and the bag grew heavier and she grew more apprehensive. Why? She didn't see me following her, but I wondered if some part of her knew.

She fingered the key on her necklace, cursing herself for being so superstitious, whispering a prayer in spite of herself. The polished chain felt good around her neck, the key felt even better resting against her chest. She remembered how she used to play with it when she sat in her mother's lap, listening to her gentle voice. It felt warm and heavy. It felt safe.

"Wear this and no harm will ever come to you," her father said as he placed the necklace around her head after her mother's funeral.

"That's not true," she cried. "Mommy wore it all the time and…"

"She wasn't wearing it. She gave it to me. She wanted me to keep it safe for you. She shouldn't have done that," he tried to explain, his eyes tired and red.

"You shouldn't have let her!" she yelled, beating her little fists on his chest.

"I know," he said, letting her pound him as much and as hard as she could, until she finally collapsed in his arms.

If it weren't for the photos she kept in her shoebox, she wouldn't be able to remember what he looked like anymore. He probably didn't look like those pictures now anyway, or the ones in the newspapers. The infamous Johnny Turner (aka Johnny Bones) had been in a mental asylum for fifteen years, since he was twenty-seven-years old. Since Rose was a little girl.

"I'm so sorry," he whispered before they led him away. "Don't come visit me in there. I don't want you to see me in a cage."

She came anyway, as often as she could, always wearing her special necklace. Her new foster parents brought her to the creepy, castle-like fortress by train, but after the first three years, and a particularly unpleasant encounter with her father, they refused to make the long journey upstate again. Soon afterward, they moved east to Boston, enrolling her in a private school and cramming her after-school schedule with music, dancing and gymnastic lessons. That was fine with her. It took her mind off everything that had happened, just as her faux folks intended. She loved gymnastics. She made friends easily. She had a life again.

For a long time after they moved, her father wrote her every week. She wrote him back less frequently. After a few years, his letters became so paranoid and disjointed she stopped writing at all. He said someone wanted to kill her. He told her to wear the necklace all the time. He said a lot of other things that sounded even crazier.

"Remember the story. It's all coming true. You have to be ready."

The story. Her mother used to tell her a story every night before she went to bed. She never read from a book or acted like she was making it up as she went along. There were no hesitant pauses or distant gazes out her bedroom window. The story was long enough to fill a dozen books, yet she knew it so well it seemed like her brain was a tape recorder in playback mode. It made her think of Scheherazade and the *One Thousand and One Nights*. Some parts of it even took place in exotic Arabian palaces, Egyptian tombs—Solomon's Temple in Jerusalem. Other parts were set on faraway islands with stone circles like Stonehenge and underground caverns ruled by a Fairy Queen. All of it was utterly amazing.

"Mommy, you should write it all down. It would make such a wonderful book," Rose said one night after she had finished the story all the way through for the third time. It was becoming so familiar to her that she joined in from time to time, shouting out her favorite lines or whispering in the scary parts. There were lots of scary parts.

Mommy smiled weakly and shook her head, tucking her snugly beneath the covers with the saddest look on her face she'd ever seen. She leaned over and kissed her on the forehead and said, "This story is only for telling and remembering. Don't ever write it down or tell anyone except your own children. It's a secret family story." She whispered, trying to sound playful with that sad, sad look still on her face.

Rose never asked her about making a book again. She never had much of a chance. Mommy died a few weeks later. Daddy tried to take over the storytelling a few nights after the funeral, but it made her so sad she just cried until she fell asleep. Then the police came and took him away. For good.

When the letters from her dad came and he talked about the story, Rose felt as sad as she did on the day Mommy died. She cried till her whole face was wet. She felt angry too.

"Why did you do it?" she yelled into her pillow after tearing the letter to shreds.

Because he was crazy. That's why he was in a nuthouse instead of a prison. She hadn't spoken or written to him in almost ten years. He never wrote anymore either, but sometimes she heard his voice in her head like he was standing right next to her. His voice never sounded crazy, or angry or impatient. It sounded like he used to sound when he carried her on his shoulders. Kind. Warm. Filled with love.

Crazy or not, she missed him horribly. He was only a forty-minute train ride away. Maybe she should buy a ticket in the morning and see if he was okay. See if he was still…

Shit. Of course, he was still crazy. He wasn't even close to being the same person he was when Mommy was alive. Even so…even if he did everything they said he did, she still loved him. *I must be a total idiot,* she thought, using her free hand to wipe the tears away.

Rose shivered and tucked the key under her shirt, even more frightened than before. Was it the blurry image of her father's wounded face as they led him away in shackles? The blackened sky? The angry young men leering at her as they passed her on the sidewalk, their shoulders hunched against the cooling twilight air? No. Her deepest dread sprang from a source more palpable and no less immediate than the shadowy threats around her.

Is he thinking about me? She instantly regretting the query. If Martin was like most guys, he was probably thinking of anything else. She looked down at all her treasures and suddenly felt sad and foolish. Then she shook her head and picked up the pace, fending off her deepest insecurities with the greatest source of reassurance she could cling to.

He just gave you a big ass bag of gold, sweetheart. He'll be back.

Once More into the Breach

I didn't go back to the website for a long time. Well, what I consider a long time…two weeks. It felt like forever. I thought about them all the time. The pictures. The horror. I could see them in my mind, perfectly clear…soft and red and wicked.

I knew I shouldn't go. If I were covered with tattoos and had titty rings and all that shit it might have made sense for me to investigate the "advanced class." But go back there just to look? Like a voyeur at a medieval torture session? That was just crazy. Sick. So I kept telling myself no, fighting the urges. Day after day after day passed and the first thing I thought about from the moment I opened my eyes was going over to my desk and starting up the computer and logging on and clicking that mouse and…*boom*…I had to do it I had to do it I couldn't wait another day, another second!

But I did. Every morning I brushed my teeth and went out for coffee and the paper and sat in the park and waited and waited for the itch to go away. Gradually, bit-by-bit, it did. I went on with my life, uncluttered as it was. I would find a new obsession to distract me, or an old familiar addiction, and put my time gladly in its hands. Every morning got easier until one day…I got up, made a pot of coffee and sat at my desk to fill in some journal entries. And wouldn't you know it, without a thought or a word or a care in the world, I logged on.

I looked at the web page and I looked at my hands and wondered aloud, but softly, "How did I get here?" The answer didn't matter anymore. I was here and I had done it. Somehow I had done it, all by myself, but without my permission. I noticed how odd that was and I noticed that I didn't really care. I noticed something else too, a sign Dante left for me, marking the entrance to the place I would soon call home:

ABANDON ALL HOPE, YE WHO ENTER HERE.

THE SPIDER AND THE FLY

Michael breathed out a huge sigh of relief. He tried, didn't he? Granted, it wasn't very loud, but it was, undeniably, a knock. Two of them, actually. Knock. Knock. He was about to sneak gratefully back down the stairs when he heard the reply.

"Whooo's there?" came a sweet, singsong voice.

Bean almost ran down the stairs, but he somehow managed to stand his ground and utter a barely audible "Uh…" in response.

"Uh…who?"

"Michael Bean," said Michael Bean, his voice stiff with fear.

"The door's open, Mr. Uh…Bean."

It sounded like a dare. The uneasy challenge was compounded by the fact that the man behind the door made no move to open it. Bean reached for the worn brass doorknob. The door didn't look anything like his, or any other door in the crumbling ruin of a building. It was a huge, teak slab with intricately detailed paneling, an ornately carved cross in the center and a fluted doorknob that looked like it came from another century.

"Welllll…" came the singsong voice again, sweeter than before, though now it seemed laced with something else. A threat? Michael turned toward the stairs, but the voice froze him in place. "You're the boy from downstairs, aren't you?" it purred.

Bean's head snapped forward like a compass needle. How the fuck did he know that? He looked for any sign of a peephole, but all he could see was the cross. He stood and stared and felt his legs tremble below him, until finally he reached out his hand to open the door.

"Come in, come in!" Paul warmly greeted him as Michael crossed the threshold. He was so enthralled with the big blond's hearty laugh and easy manner that it took awhile for the smell to hit him. Paul nodded empathetically when Michael crinkled his nose in disgust. "Squatter's rights!" he yelled to the ceiling, then lowered his lips to Michael's ear and whispered conspiratorially, "But you don't get the right to decent plumbing, eh?"

He laughed too hard at his own joke and slapped Bean even harder on the back. Michael felt another pinprick of fear as the sound of Paul's laugh echoed down the tomb-quiet hallway. He felt it again as he measured the strength in the meaty hand still resting on his shoulder, stroking it now, soothing it. *Guy's a fag!* Michael thought, panicking with the deeply ingrained homophobia shared by so many post-adolescent, girlishly attractive, self-professed heterosexual males. *A great big crazy fag!*

Paul gazed into his eyes with the most lifeless stare he had ever seen, savoring every squirm. After a few uncomfortable seconds, he asked, "So what brings you here for a visit?"

Michael shook his head to clear it. For a moment, he couldn't remember where he was or what he was doing here, "I heard screaming," he said dully.

"You heard screaming, did you?" asked Paul with a trace of skepticism, cupping his hand to his ear and scanning the apartment like a radar dish. "Do you hear any now?"

Michael was about to answer when Paul raised his finger to his lips. They listened again together, hard and long. All was silent at first, then as he strained his ears, Bean thought he could hear a low moaning in the distance. "Someone's hurt," he said.

"Aye." Paul nodded. "Someone's always hurt. That's the nature of things, the very hard and coarse nature of the world we live in."

"Someone's hurt in there!" Michael shouted, pointing down the blackened corridor.

"Where?" Paul asked innocently, his hand snaking behind Michael's neck. Bean was about to point again, but he had already crumpled to the floor.

TWO PLACES AT ONCE

Michael was dreaming. He saw a room filled with candles. There was a big wooden table in the middle of the room and something was on it. Something that was moving. He took a few timid steps toward the quivering shape before he realized it was a man. He took a few more steps before he realized *he* was the man and that his hands and feet were firmly nailed down on an altar. He would have taken a few steps back, but he couldn't move. He was looking up from the altar now, those long nails holding him down. All he could see was the blurry head of a man leaning over him. The man chuckled softly.

Bean opened his eyes and screamed.

Paul was hovering over him, in the exact position of the blurry shape in his dream. But Michael wasn't on an altar. He was lying on a dirty couch, staring at a lightbulb that illuminated Paul's long blond-white hair from behind like a halo.

"What the fuck is going on here?" he shouted, almost in tears.

Paul laughed louder as he saw the look of disorientation flood Michael's face.

"Where the hell am I?" Bean pleaded. "And who the hell are you?"

"My name is Paul," he said inside the dead mask. "And this, my son... is home."

PREMONITION

They say you shouldn't do tarot card readings for yourself too often. If you do it all the time, nothing makes sense anymore. The same can be said for other obsessions. Porn. Hobbies. The website. I spent so much time there. Even more hours clicking through to other related sites, to get a sense of what else was out there and who was the best at doing what they did. Tattoos. Implants. Electrolysis. Other…stuff.

Since I worked at home, it wasn't a problem. Soon I found myself working less and less, scheduling half as many tarot appointments as usual. Whenever I took a break, I found myself thumbing through the books I'd collected, then doing readings for myself. I'm not sure what I was looking for. Permission? If that was the case, most of my readings were not encouraging. I kept getting the Wheel of Fortune, which implied a change in destiny—good or bad—almost always followed by a trump card. Occasionally, it would be something optimistic, like The Star or The Sun. More often, it was a scary one like Death, The Hanged Man, The Tower. The Moon.

Did you know that the card called The Moon in the tarot deck doesn't represent the planet? Pisces, the murkiest of zodiac signs ruled by the water, has that dubious honor. The Priestess is the card that actually represents the planet. One day, between quests for tattoo artists I did yet another reading where I got the Wheel, this time followed by The Priestess. As soon as I turned the card over, the doorbell rang.

It was my next appointment. When I opened the door, I knew Fortuna was smiling. She was beautiful, her pale skin glowing like the moon…and covered in tattoos.

"Welcome," I said, meaning it for the first time in months. "Let's get started."

HOME

"How did I get here?" Michael asked with a mixture of rage and timidity as unfamiliar as his surroundings. "I was pointing down the hallway and…"

"It's not important," Paul said wearily. "You blacked out. You lost some time."

"How could I have blacked out when I haven't had anything to…"

Paul glanced down at Michael's hand and cut off his train of thought like a carving knife.

A tumbler with a finger's width of brown liquor swirled in Michael's sweaty grip as he looked down in astonishment. "What the fuck!" he gasped, more to himself than Paul. He sat up on the couch, his head filled with fog and something that made his tongue feel thick and metallic.

"Old Bushmills," Paul said proudly, as if that explained everything. "Sixteen-year-old, single malt Irish whiskey. If there's a more satisfying beverage to be found anywhere on this good green earth, I'm certainly not aware of it. Here, have some more."

This dude is crazy! You have got to go NOW!

"Uh, no thanks," Michael said as calmly as he could. "I've got to get going anyway."

"So soooon?" Paul asked in that singsong voice again.

Bean stuffed both hands into his baggy trouser pockets, shrugging lamely. "Yeah, you know, I got some stuff I gotta do later."

"Yeah, I know," Paul echoed, his thick fingers toying with the strands of his mustache. "But later's later…right? You should at least stay for supper."

"Nah, I'm not hungry. I've got some friends waitin' for me in the park."

"No, you don't," Paul said flatly, turning his head to the window, his sudden disinterest drawing Michael back like a magnet. "You don't have any friends," he continued in a sad, soft voice, barely above a whisper. "You see the same people every day. The drifters. The squatter scum. But you just nod and grunt 'What's happenin?' because what else would there be to say? You kill time at the comic bookstore looking at the dirty ones. You wish you had the nerve to talk to the waitress in the coffee shop, but you wouldn't know where to take her even if she wanted to go out. You can't hold down a job and you only make enough money panhandling to buy a slice of pizza and a beer twice a day. You're jealous of the junkies. They look so numb and fearless. But you're afraid to try it yourself because you don't know where you'd get the money if you liked it half as much as you imagine you would."

Michael didn't even bother defending himself. Paul said it with such absolute certainty that there wasn't any point in arguing.

"But go ahead, shoo little fly," Paul said, waving Michael away from the couch, his brogue thicker than the Lucky Charms leprechaun. "Don't let me be keepin' you. I'm sure there's a much better world waitin' for you out there than anything I could offer."

Michael didn't move. "Offer?"

"Something to fill your belly with, for starters. And perhaps something besides this glorious whiskey to feed your hungry mind."

"Like...?" Michael asked, settling back on the couch without even thinking about it.

"What if..." Paul began, relishing the performance as much as the effect it had on his audience. "What if I knew what you wanted more than anything else in the world?"

Michael said nothing. But his whole body answered, *I'm listening.*

"Well, it's very simple, really," Paul said, waving grandly. "What you want more than anything else in the world...is to be a tough guy."

Michael's face flushed instantly. How could this guy know so much about him?

"It's not a bad thing, Michael," Paul said reassuringly. "There's no shame in it."

Michael nodded. Then why did he feel so embarrassed?

"Most people live their whole lives in fear and never do a thing about it. In fact, just about every man you you've ever met, some of them acting like great big, tough guys…are just as frightened as you. Maybe even more. Most of those so-called tough guys don't even have the courage to admit they're afraid."

"What about you?" Bean asked, feeling slightly better. "You don't seem afraid."

"That is correct," Paul said, without a trace of arrogance. "When I was your age, I wanted the same thing as you. To be strong. Unafraid. Invulnerable. What young man doesn't? It's just the way we're built. The trouble is, hardly anyone knows how to be tough, not just act like it. But some people…some people do."

Michael Bean looked at the hallway. Then he slowly turned to Paul, his eyes wide and hopeful. "How do you know all this stuff?"

"Let's have another drink before supper and I'll fill you in on the basics," Paul said, grinning slyly as he lifted the whiskey bottle. "Then there's someone I want you to meet. One look at him and you'll understand the power and freedom that could be yours."

Michael felt a cloud of jealousy pass over his head. "Who is he?"

"His name is Martin," Paul replied, savoring his envy, "and he'll be joining us soon."

SHOCK

Martin counted to ten, breathing as deeply as he could. Inhale. Exhale. He could still see Momma's empty eyes, the tiny dot of red on her forehead, but he was back in the room, staring at the bare lightbulb overhead, his heart pounding like a sledgehammer.

There were voices in the distance. Paul. Someone else. He slowly rose from the chair, then gently lowered himself back down. *Shit, this is rough.*

Shock. The medical condition, not the reaction. Martin had trained his whole life to conquer almost unimaginable levels of pain and suffering. Yet even though he had managed to disconnect his mind from the most torturous physical sensations and emotional trauma possible, his body still betrayed him by going into shock. Damn. He sat and waited it out, having been through this many times before. In the years after Paul took him away, Martin had been shot three times, stabbed twice, slashed once with a box cutter and had broken twelve bones (three of them twice). Always handy with the gauze, splints and sutures, Paul would merely shrug and say the same thing: "It goes with the job."

But he was "retired" now. "Resting on my laurels," as Paul put it. Then why had he set foot in here again? *Oh, yeah,* he thought, staring at his bandaged hand. *Rose.* Martin took another deep breath and tried to relax, nodding slowly in time with the beat of his heart. Looking back over the continuous mayhem that had accompanied his travels with Paul, he did a quick mental calculation, comparing his current level of shock with the trauma from previous injuries.

On a scale of ten, I'd give it a six. He sat and waited, counting down the time it would take to resume full mobility. He sniffed the air again, trying to isolate the food odors from the cacophony of stench surrounding them. "Lamb or ham?"

Whump. Whump. Whump.

"Almost forgot about you," Martin said, his body relaxed and motionless. He craned his neck only slightly in the direction of the thumping noises in the shadows behind him. He had no intention of squandering even a single calorie of energy on behalf of whoever so frantically craved his attention. "Two minutes and eight seconds," he calculated, focusing instead on his internal post-trauma recovery clock.

Whump. Whump. Whump.

Martin peered deeper into the shadows and willed his irises to open to their maximum capacity, a self-taught biofeedback exercise he'd perfected over the years. Paul would have been proud. Martin guessed that the increased aperture allowed in additional light waves that were roughly equivalent to one-fifth of the average house cat's night-vision capability. On the whole, it would have to do. It was certainly sufficient to make out the thumping burlap bag in the corner of the room.

Whump. Whump. Whump.

Martin guessed from the bag's size, shape and movement that the occupant was male, late-thirties, gagged, hogtied and in the early stages of starvation. "One minute and twenty-two seconds," he recalculated, ping-ponging back and forth between the analysis of his mystery companion and the far more important business of his own physical recovery.

Martin sniffed the air more deeply, trying to isolate the food scents from those of his newfound roommate. He still couldn't make out what kind of meat was cooking but he felt fairly certain that the man in the bag had been stewing in his own piss and shit for a while.

Whump. The bagman started losing steam about the same time Martin's inner clock ticked its way to blastoff. He stood in a single motion. If someone had been watching, they would have been awed at his acrobatic grace. The bagman, sensing Martin's movement, redoubled his efforts. *Whump. Whump. Whump.*

Martin looked at the bag and listened for sounds in the hallway. He only heard a trace of mumbling from a distance that seemed too far away. He sniffed again and cataloged the scent against all the game he had ever cooked or eaten and came to a not so surprising conclusion, given his whereabouts. "Oh, well" he shrugged, "food's food."

He was about to track down the source of the aroma when his curiosity got the best of him. He walked slowly into the corner and stooped to untie the writhing sack at his feet. "Yep, late-thirties," Martin said with a trace of pride, looking past the terror-soaked face that greeted him to the slight shadow of crow's feet braiding his sunken, hollow eyes.

"Mmmpph, mmmpph," came the duct tape muffled plea. Martin pulled the tape off against his better judgment, unwilling to postpone his quest for nourishment for more than a few seconds. "Ih...ih...afe?" the crazy-eyed man gurgled wildly, his eyes darting back and forth from Martin to the hope of freedom offered by the open doorway and Paul's absence.

Martin noted his physical condition. What was left of it, anyway. He was clearly a goner. Then he looked deeper into those desperate orbs and felt his heart tighten with recognition. "I thought you were dead," Martin said with even less passion than he felt.

"Uh ill ih ooo ont…"

It was really impossible to shout, "Help me!" without a tongue, so the bagman started *whumping* again, begging for Martin's assistance as best he could.

Martin was lost in thought, wondering why Paul had deposited his old adversary so derisively in his presence. Was it a message? An insult? Another invitation like the one he'd extended earlier today in the park? "Come back…come back…"

Were there more "loose ends" Paul intended to tie up from their blood-drenched past? Why did he bother with the duct tape after he cut out his tongue? To keep him from grunting out something, obviously…but what? Martin pondered that and many other things, like how the bagman had survived the wounds Martin had inflicted on him so many years ago, and how he had the balls to beg for mercy after trying to slit his throat with more eagerness than he was expressing his desire to escape. Martin would have stayed to try and answer some of those puzzling questions, if he weren't so hungry, if the man's tongue weren't missing, if he didn't already know from the other absent body parts and blood loss that he had only a short while left to live. Even so, Martin was still thinking about his first garbled question as he put the duct tape back on his mouth and walked into the dark hallway.

"It's never safe," he answered.

SELF-MADE MAN

"Men never talk much about being men. I think that's a shame," Paul intoned, clinking his glass against Michael's. "And I don't mean that crap where some businessmen go off on a weekend retreat, beating drums by the fire in their undies."

Michael tried to chuckle but gulped when Paul elbowed him in the ribs. He was having a hard time maintaining eye contact, glancing between the whiskey he was bravely trying to sip without coughing and the waving arms of the crazy man next to him.

"It should have been your father's job to guide you through the rigors of manhood, but if you're like most boys, he probably wasn't much help at all," Paul said sadly.

Michael nodded with a wince, grappling with unwanted flashbacks to his single-mom parenting. His mother's name was Sarah, which she made him call her instead of "Mom." She worked all the time, trying to "keep a roof over our heads," as she said every time he complained about being carted off to a well-meaning neighbor while she worked another double shift. Neighbors, daycare, then school, after-school…and finally the latchkey. He had a lot of time to think about that roof over his head. To stare at it, alone.

Every time he asked Sarah to tell him about his dad, she said something like, "He was really…funny," and changed the subject. When Michael was a teenager, he finally got her to admit they were never married. When he kept nagging her, she said he died in a car accident while she was still pregnant. She cried when she said it, but there was something about her tone that made him wonder if she was lying. He was never able to get her to talk more about his dad, because *she* died in a car accident the next week. With Michael driving. On angel dust. He slammed into a telephone pole at sixty miles an hour. He barely had a scratch on him. His mother wasn't so lucky.

When Michael looked over, her chin was slumped against her chest. "Mom?" he cried out for the first time in years. "Mom?"

When he lifted her head, it was easy to see why she hadn't answered. Her neck was broken so cleanly that her head fell backwards…and backwards…until it finally came to rest between her shoulder blades. Michael stared at his mother's dead open eyes as she stared upside down at the seat behind her.

He ran. And never stopped. He thought he was running from the cops, that he would have been thrown in jail for murdering his own mother, for driving into that fucking pole while he was so fucked up. He needn't have worried. They wouldn't have found any booze on his breath, let alone any angel dust in his bloodstream. They wouldn't have even tested him for it. But Michael ran and ran, stealing food out of trashcans, hiding from a non-existent manhunt, sleeping under trees, collecting emergency food stamps and trading them for cash at fifty cents on the dollar. Alone. Always alone.

Paul watched the young man's eyes glaze, waiting for them to refocus before asking, "What's the matter, son? Did I strike a nerve? Did your dear old daddy let you down?"

"I never knew him," Michael sniffled, turning away. "My mom died last year."

"An *orphan*…" Paul gasped. "Oh, you poor dear lad. That's just awful."

"Yeah," Michael nodded, oblivious to Paul's sarcastic overtones. "It totally sucks."

"Bet it makes you angry too."

"Yeah, I guess it does," Bean replied, the old memories nudged aside from the elbow and the surging anger that accompanied Paul's question.

"It should," Paul shouted, slapping him on the back, happy to be back on track again. "Anger is the best emotion for focusing your awareness. Considering our topic today, I can't think of a better way for us to begin your lessons."

"Huh?" What had they been talking about?

"Being a man. A tough guy. That's our theme! What do you think being a man is all about, Michael?"

Bean looked at Paul's face blankly, unable to get his brain engaged enough to even think about an answer. He squirmed instead and shook his head dumbly.

"Courage," Paul said softly. "That's what separates the boys from the men. Isn't that why you came here, lad? Isn't that what you wanted to learn?"

Michael moved his head silently again, this time up and down.

"Good. Then we're ready to begin. Like all good lessons, the first one begins with a question: Do you notice anything unusual about my hands?"

Holy shit! He hadn't even noticed them before. "You don't have any fingernails," Michael stammered, looking at the huge mitts Paul was holding in front of his face.

Paul grinned so widely that it looked like his cheeks might split in half. "Can you imagine how painful it would be to have someone pull out all your fingernails?"

It wasn't a rhetorical question. Paul really wanted him to think about it.

"No," Bean blurted out, much too quickly for Paul's taste.

He breathed a long, heavy sigh to give Michael more time to fully consider the horror of what he was seeing. "Would you like to?" Paul asked after a twenty-second pause.

"No!" Michael shouted, squirming in fear.

"Ha! I can't imagine that you would, my boy. But let me tell you two little secrets...."

He paused and the grin fell from his face like a blanket of snow swiped off a windshield. "Once you've experienced that level of pain, it changes you forever. You'll never be afraid again...at least not in the same way you've always experienced fear. That's the first secret."

"What's the other one?" Michael asked, the perfect straight man.

Paul smiled and said, "It hurts a little less when you do it yourself."

The Wood Made Flesh

I started with my back. I was still a little tentative in those days, so if I really couldn't stand to look at it afterwards, I wouldn't have to.

It's hard for me to remember how scary it was at the time. Now it makes me laugh just to think about it. Of course, the fear couldn't begin to contend with my newfound enthusiasm. I was so inspired by everything I'd seen. Those pictures. Those people. Real people. Not being tortured or forced in any way. People with the courage and daring to do it themselves.

Now it was my turn. I knew where I'd be going for my tattoos, but first I had to find a decent enough electrolysis person to get the hair out of my back. Where does that hair come from? On your shoulders, for Chrissakes! Anyway, it all had to go.

The pain from the electrolysis was a good warm-up for all the fun that followed.

When that big fat Russian woman bent over to zap the first wiry cocksucker out of my life, I smiled. I'm not a pain freak, mind you. Not exactly. I definitely wasn't back then. But I was proud that I could endure so *much* of it.

Then there's The Zing, that corkscrew windup like all your senses are turning inside out. Where your body screams from the attack and another part screams back even louder. And in between each poke and stab and burn, I said my little prayer:

I am the Hammer and the Nail.

The Hammer and the Nail!

And I am something more than both.

I am the Wood.

THE SECRET TO BEING A TOUGH GUY

"Ouch!" Michael cried.

"Ouch?" Paul sneered incredulously while Michael's face turned red with shame. "Is that how you squeal at the tattoo parlor while everybody's watching?"

Paul was giving a demonstration in what he called "temporary piercings." As usual, his lesson began with a speech: "The secret to being a tough guy... is to be really tough. Being proficient in the deadly art of combat helps ensure your safety and builds your confidence—and it's always a comfort to know that if you get in a little scrap, you're the one who walks out of the bar with the greatest number of teeth in your head. But the real secret to being tough, being a *man*, lies more in your ability to *receive* pain than inflict it. Any punk can sneak up behind you and pull a trigger. But only a real man can take the shot, turn around without a whimper or a sniffle, rip the pistol from his hand and beat him over the head with it until his brains spill onto the sidewalk in a wrinkled pile of pink slush. You get my point?"

Michael laughed. He did. This guy was totally wacko...but was he cool or what?

Paul laughed with him, then cut it short. "If you want to be a real man, the first enemy you must conquer isn't pain—it's your *fear* of pain. How do you think we do that?"

Michael didn't bother answering. Even the question was scaring him.

"Practice, practice, practice!" Paul shouted, laughing till he coughed. "You've already begun that journey, with all your piercings. It can't feel too good when that needle goes in."

"Fuck no!" Michael said proudly. "But once you get used to it, it's not that bad."

"And the more you practice, the easier it gets, until the pain changes into something that doesn't really hurt."

"Yeah!" Michael chimed in. "Like, when I had my nipples done. It hurt like hell, but it also felt kinda good in a weird way too."

"And when the pain feels good, you feel stronger, until you realize you're not afraid of going back for another poke of the needle—you want to!"

"No doubt, dude," Michael agreed, giggling again. "You really know your shit!"

Paul laughed. He liked this one. What a kook. "So, are you ready for some practice?"

"Uh…okay," Michael sputtered. Then he saw what Paul was holding.

"Go ahead, pick it up," Paul told him. It was a long steel rod, about an eighth of an inch thick at the base, tapering to an extremely sharp point. Michael lifted it and gulped. It was *really* sharp. Paul smiled, took it from his hands and held it an inch from Bean's left eye. Michael turned away involuntarily, but Paul grabbed his chin and yanked it front and center.

God, this fucker is strong! Bean panicked, his warm and fuzzy feelings about his new father figure galloping off down a dusty road. *What's he going to do to me?*

"I'm not going to do anything," Paul said, like he could read his mind. "You are."

"What the fuck?" Michael gasped, unsure if it was a question or an answer.

"Like this," Paul said, spreading his fingers apart. He pointed the metal tip at the web of skin connecting his thumb and index finger. On Paul, it looked like the pocket of a baseball mitt. "You should be good at this," he said. Then he pushed the tip through the web of skin as easily as a hot knife cuts through butter. No hesitation. No groaning. No nothing.

"Whoa, dude!" Michael shouted as Paul kept pushing and then pulling from the other side until the rod came all the way out again. There wasn't even any blood.

"Pretty cool, eh?" Paul said with a wink, relishing the boy's admiration.

"Way cool!" It was like watching Moses on the mountaintop.

"I'm glad you enjoyed it," Paul said with a bow. "Now it's your turn."

"*Ouch!*" Michael shouted on his first attempt. After Paul's response, he did better on the second try. He wasn't able to pull it all the way through, but managed to push it in far enough for Paul to give him a nod of approval. To Michael, it was better than an Oscar. He was about to push it in again when Paul stopped his hand.

"That's enough for now. There's more fun to be had, but first you have a decision to make. You can leave right now, or you can stay. If you stay, you'll do everything I tell you, no matter what, without question or debate. In return, I'll teach you things you never dreamed were even possible...and give you my complete protection."

Michael mouthed the words "complete protection" as he stared at the darkened doorway leading to his dingy room downstairs. Of all the boasts Paul tossed around, this one seemed the most plausible and desired. "I could use some fucking protection," Michael replied, making his second mistake of the day and the biggest one of his life.

"Good!" Paul shouted, shaking Michael's hand way too hard. "Unfortunately, we don't have much time, lad. Normally I'd spend years training a promising lad like yourself, but I'm afraid providence demands a much more abbreviated schedule."

Training? Providence? Schedule? What the fuck was he talking about?

"Let me cut right to the point," Paul said, sweeping his arm like he was erasing a cluttered blackboard. "Have you ever wanted to kill someone?"

Michael's mouth hung open, but nothing came out.

"C'mon, lad. Like I said, we don't have much time, and no time at all for bull crap."

"Yes," Michael said, not believing he admitted it.

"Good boy. That's the only honest answer any man could give, because there's not a single breathing one of us that hasn't thought about killing someone at least once in his life. Now here's the more important question: Why didn't you?"

Michael laughed. He thought Paul was joking. Until he looked in his eyes. "Fuck, dude! Because I don't want to go jail!"

"Of course not!" Paul roared back. He seemed so happy that Michael smiled along with him. "But what if you couldn't be caught? What would stop you then?"

"Because it's wrong, dude! You don't go around killing everybody you're pissed at!"

"I do," Paul said quietly. Then he corrected himself. "Well, not everyone. I'll need a nuclear arsenal for that. Everyone I really want to."

"Dude, I'm out of here," Bean said, jumping from the couch.

Paul slammed him back down to the couch like he was swatting a fly. "Could it be you've abandoned your pledge so quickly? In my clan we take our vows with the utmost solemnity. To break an oath is unthinkable, and those that do suffer the harshest of reprisals, dealt by the very hand of destiny itself."

"But I can't…I don't want to kill anyone," Michael sputtered.

"Of course you do," Paul said with a finality that left no room for further argument. "You just need to give yourself permission. I told you we don't have any time for nonsense, Michael. So sit, listen and learn."

Michael sat, freaked out of his gourd at the direction their conversation had taken—and the vow that loomed over his head like a gleaming guillotine blade. He hadn't thought that one out too carefully, had he?

"Here's another way to look at it…" Paul continued, his smile back in full bloom as he rose from the couch, pacing in long strides as he spoke. "Let's say you were drafted into the army and sent halfway around the world to shoot, stab and drop huge, fiery bombs on people you didn't even know, much less have any grudge against. Worse yet, let's say your virtuous government actually made up a great big pack of lies to justify why it was so necessary for you to risk your life and claim the souls of all those completely innocent victims. Even with all that bullshit, it would still be okay for you to march over there, point your rifle at someone's unlucky head, pull the trigger and blow his brains out, right? And why? Because you're a soldier. You're under orders. It isn't just okay for you to kill those people. It's your duty!"

"Yeah, that's some pretty fucked-up shit," Michael agreed, his smile slowly returning, though much shakier with the reminder of his promise still ringing in his ears.

"Fucked up, indeed. What gives your not-so-freely-elected government the right to tell you when it's your duty to kill someone…and then, using the same false claim of authority, command you to die in the electric chair for having the gall to pick your own battles, to wage wars of your own choosing, against your own enemies, against the people who threaten your life directly, not in some abstract sense, veiled with obscene notions of honor and righteousness—*real* people—who mean *real* harm to yourself, your family, and the noble principles of your own calling. What if you had a new country, with its own rules and regulations, its own mandate of authority? What if you were a soldier in your own war—and not a foot soldier either—a general? Would it be okay for you to take a life in the due course of achieving your own strategic objectives? Or would it be even more than okay? Perhaps it would it be your *divine right*…your duty!"

Michael sat mesmerized, more terrified and excited than he'd ever felt before. What Paul was saying spat in the face of every conventional notion of morality that had been stuffed into his brain since he was old enough to think. Yet it made so much sense!

"Aye, son. Freedom is a terrible responsibility," Paul said kindly. "But don't be afraid. Least not of me. I'm here to help in a way that no one else in this awful world can."

"What are you saying, man?" Michael implored, his anxiety mounting by the second.

"What I'm *saying* is this: The world is a very scary place for all of the sheep. But for the wolves…it's paradise."

Something clicked in Bean's head the instant those words snaked into his ears. He looked at Paul and a change came over him he couldn't have explained in a thousand years. He felt full to the brim with all the seething adolescent rage he'd been suppressing since puberty. He conjured up visions of all the schoolyard bullies who teased him for being too pretty, the girls who hosed him and the stupid teachers who didn't know shit about shit.

Then he imagined what he really wanted to do to them. One of his oldest, darkest, hidden fantasies involved coming in to school for "show and tell" with an AK-47 and demonstrating how efficiently it put holes into all of his mean, shitty, stuck-up classmates' heads. He thought about the shooting in Summerville High School when he was a teenager. He felt sad when he heard the news, but he also felt weird that he didn't feel as sad as everybody else in school seemed to feel. What he mostly felt was jealous. Now here was this man, this crazy man, who admitted he was a stone-cold killer right to his face, looking at him like he was proud of it. *Proud!*

Paul watched Michael's face like a giant leering pumpkin. He could see the gears turning in his head and gave them plenty of time to grind before continuing. "You wouldn't know it to look at me now, Michael, but once upon a time I was a shy, skinny, frightened boy…no bigger or braver than yourself."

"No way," Michael said emphatically, shaking his head.

"Yes way," Paul nodded just as vigorously. "But I had an advantage you didn't."

"What's that?" Michael asked, trying to imagine Paul as a shy, skinny kid.

"I had a father," Paul replied softly.

Michael felt the tears well up. It was so unexpected that he was as shocked as he was ashamed. He covered his sobbing red face with both his hands and hung his head.

"There, there, dear boy," said Paul, scooping up his chin with those blunt fingers. "There's no shame in crying. Once. Go ahead and let all the pain out, so you can fill that old aching hole with your newfound gift."

"What gift?" Michael blubbered, trying to hide his tears from Paul's unwavering gaze.

"*You're not alone anymore. And you'll never be alone again.*"

It was more than just music to Michael's ears—it was a symphony. He wanted it to go on and on and on…until he could actually believe it. Always one to go on and on, Paul was happy to accommodate him—at least until Martin arrived.

"My own dear dad was a very cruel man," Paul continued, without any emotion that Michael could identify. "I don't blame him for it. In fact, it turned out to be a gift in its own way, though I certainly didn't think so at the time. I learned to be tough. Hard. And fight back too. I can safely say that on the day my dear daddy died, he was most assuredly impressed with the progress I'd made. Now I can offer you the same gesture, but without the harshness that marked my father's teachings. I've learned much since then, and while pain is still an indispensable ingredient in claiming your freedom, what's even more essential for your growth and development is knowing there will always be a firm, strong hand by your side. To help. To guide you. To give you the advice and encouragement you've always craved and sadly done without, all these long, lonely years."

Michael nodded eagerly. The tears were gone and replaced with a look of admiration that could only make sense to someone who suffered from his condition: dadlessness. He would never admit it, but he'd been waiting for this moment all of his life.

Paul saw the change in Michael's expression and felt the desperate need behind it. Michael didn't know it, but Paul had been waiting for this moment too, not for all his life—for all of Michael's. Michael didn't know that, or a lot of other things. Like why the really tall, really creepy guy that did his scrotum implants told him there was a place to crash in an abandoned building between C and D. Or why he bothered to walk him over and make sure he got settled in. Or why there was already a bed and a dresser inside. Or why he was the only one in the building with a lock on his door. He never questioned the strange twists of fate that were guiding and protecting him. He never questioned why he was never robbed or beaten up by the Puerto Ricans who teased and taunted all the other white kids in the neighborhood, but always looked the other way when he walked by. He never wondered why he'd never seen the man on the floor above him until today. Or why he, of all people, had been singled out for the gift of the big man's wicked patronage.

Paul, of course, knew exactly what he was doing and why. He

congratulated himself on his patience and restraint. He had been saving the boy like a birthday present, to be opened at this precise instant, once all the players had been set in motion. All the pawns. If he had rushed things, if he started too early like he did with Martin, would he be sitting where he was right now, bathed in such complete adulation? No. He had earned this. It was his due. Even more importantly, it was right on schedule.

Everything was going exactly as planned.

Martin Takes a Left

Martin walked through the twists and turns of the darkened corridor, guided primarily by his sense of smell. The wafting food aromas grew stronger with each step. Finally, he saw a light ahead and immediately stopped. The light was coming from his left.

Martin had a touch of OCD, fueled in part by genetics and more, in all likelihood, from the years he spent in training with Paul. After his mind and heart had hardened to a certain degree, his remaining instinctive needs for comfort distilled themselves into a craving for particular physical sensations, like his fetish for softness and his affinity for certain habits and routines. Like most obsessive-compulsives, Martin loved his routines. As a hunter, he recognized that his peculiar, ritualized patterns would have to be undetectable to anyone else as routines, so he relegated most of them to his cleaning and bathing habits, or the way he buckled his belt (left-handed for odd days, right for evens).

He was also extremely superstitious. His biggest phobias involved certain rules he'd created for the direction of his movement, usually while walking. Whenever he felt in danger, he *hated* turning to the left. More than hated it—he physically loathed it. He would go to almost any lengths to avoid left-hand turns, unless his alternative route placed him in even more certain danger.

He looked at the glimmer of light coming from the corridor on his left and pondered his next move. Then he heard the voices. He looked at the light and the left-hand turn and thought about all the good and bad luck he had already experienced today.

"What the fuck," he said, turning left without another thought. "What's the worst that could happen?"

Rose Takes a Right

Rose looked over her shoulder again as she trudged down the sidewalk of Avenue B. Darkness had settled in. Shadows from the glowing streetlights snaked between the trees and crumpled garbage cans like a nest of vipers. She felt a chill of fear and something else (a premonition?) that made her want to run the rest of the way home. She forced her legs to keep walking in a slow, steady gait, but her mind raced ahead, around the next corner, up the stairs and behind the locked door of her apartment.

As she turned right on Eighth Street, she felt the nagging sensation that someone was following her again.

I smiled and crossed the street behind her, pulling my jacket tighter to brace myself against the chilly evening air, ducking into the shadows of an abandoned storefront as she climbed the stairs of her stoop, opened the door and went inside.

As soon as she entered her apartment, Rose turned on some music to chase away her jitters. When she was calm enough to think, she thought about Martin and how nice it would be to see him again. She almost ran downstairs and ding-donged his bell, then remembered why he gave her all that gold in the first place. "I'll make some curtains first," she decided, just to show him how nice everything would look when it was all…finished.

I stared up at her window and watched her dance with a cascade of unrolled fabric bunched around her waist like a party dress. She pranced and reveled like she was the luckiest girl in the world. She looked so ridiculous. All I could think about was how foolish she was to feel even the least bit excited about seeing Martin again and how infinitely better her luck would have been if she never met him in the first place. Or me for that matter.

"Lucky," I snorted derisively. "The luck of the Irish."

My Suitcase

My suitcase is full of dreams. I take it out whenever I need to go far away. It weighs a lot. I saw it in a thrift store in San Francisco. It was a big, old-fashioned suitcase from the thirties or forties, the kind some dandy would take on a cruise ship, beige and tan with shiny brass hinges. At first, I used it to keep my journals inside. Soon there were so many I had to keep them somewhere else. I needed more room for my other treasures. My collection.

Sometimes I wonder what might have happened if I'd never found all that stuff. Or bought it. Or stole it. I guess I'll never know, because I did. Still, maybe even that wouldn't have been so bad. Everyone has a hobby. No, like most people, my biggest mistake wasn't what I'd done. It was telling somebody about it.

"Hi, Rose," I said to the spiky black hair on the back of her head when I walked into the St. Mark's Tattoo Parlor. As usual, I was right on time for my appointment, unlike Rose, who was half an hour late for her tarot card reading. Punctuality wasn't one of her virtues. Neither was facial recognition.

"Heyyyy…" she replied, forgetting my name when she finally turned to look at me. She wiped the blood off the back of some dude who was so skinny his shoulder blades looked like amputated wings. I got so excited watching her that I could barely wait for her to finish and start on me.

"I liked the card reading. It was a little creepy though. What was all that shit with the Wheel of Fortune and The Devil?"

"You might get obsessed with someone who tempts your darker urges."

"My darker urges. Yeah…now I remember. Is it someone I already know?" she asked, looking at me like I couldn't possibly be a worthy candidate.

"I don't think so," I said, hoping I was wrong. "Remember the man and woman chained to the Devil's throne? This is someone who knows all your fears and desires. You could become a prisoner of your own compulsions."

"Sounds kinky…I hope he's cute," she said, turning her attention back to her bony customer. She wiped up the last red droplets from his back. He eased off the table and into the changing room/toilet. After he vacated the chair, she adjusted it so I could lean forward with my back exposed.

"Let's get started," she announced. It was the same thing I said to her before her card reading, which felt a lot eerier than I let on. The reading took almost as long as our first tattoo session, about an hour and a half. That's where the similarities ended. When she finished Phase One of her ink work, my teeth hurt from clenching them so much. When I finished her tarot reading, we had a nice glass of Zinfandel on a cozy, overstuffed couch.

During her reading we talked a lot about her work. I *saw* her poking and drilling into all that voluntarily exposed flesh before I even turned over the first card. I hate to admit it, but I got a huge hard-on almost instantly. Was it because she was so pretty? So sexy? Or was it because my vision of her was so clear, and so clearly a vision of someone at play, not work? She loved it, loved it, loved it! And I loved her, so sadly, at first sight.

Am I an idiot? A complete and utter idiot? Without a doubt. Has there ever been anyone in the history of creation who claimed to fall in love at first sight that didn't lay an exponentially greater claim to mental derangement? My tested and frequently retested I.Q. ranges between 162 and 165, depending on my pre-quiz caffeine intake. Yet once Rose Turner walked into my tidy, bookshelf-crammed apartment, I was dumber than a hand puppet.

I justified my lunacy, like any good, non-God-fearing, divination practitioner would. Fate was my profession. Being a big (so big you'd have to call it religious) believer in synchronicity, I absolutely, positively *knew* Rose had been sent to me and me alone by all the interconnected, romantically scheming powers of the universe. She was an angel, my very own spiky-haired angel. I could hardly wait until I flipped over the last card so I could stop talking about her and tell her how I had been searching high and low for precisely the right person to execute (poor choice of words?) my epic tattoo/body-mod scheme. And gee whiz, guess what? That extra-special, perfectly perfect person simply has to be you, Rose!

Sigh. The wine helped a lot. It calmed me down and loosened me up enough so I was able to behave like a reasonably intelligent person with reasonably interesting things to say. If she sensed my desperate heart-thumping attraction, she didn't act like it. I'm sure she was used to guys falling head over heels for her. I'm equally certain she was kind enough not to squish my teeny heart like a bug if she caught a whiff of my wafting pheromones. My mind-reading radar dish was tuned to Planck wavelengths, yet the only thing I sensed in the two hours and twenty-two minutes we spent together was that she genuinely, happily enjoyed my company. She liked me. And that, dear reader, was more than enough.

When I told her about the tattoo I designed to cover my entire back, she sat up like a fox sniffing blood. When she saw the sketches I'd made, she was more than enthusiastic. She was blown away. "What is all this stuff? All these lines and slash marks?"

"That's Ogham," I said proudly. "This variation is a cipher script I invented, but Ogham was created by the Celts. Irish legends say Fénius Farsaid went to the Tower of Babel and made Ogham from the best of all the confused languages when the tower fell. Personally, I think it was invented by Irish druids trying to keep their secrets hidden from Christian missionaries."

"Cool," she said, amazingly not rolling her eyes like I was a pompous, asshole geek. "I've got some Celtic tattoos from a book my dad gave me. He said they were the marks of a druid priestess and they would protect me."

Her mood darkened, but only for a moment. She pulled up her pant legs and showed me the intricate spiral patterns etched into golden bands around both ankles. "See?" she said, her face beaming, clearly delighted to show off her tats. Her legs were fantastic.

"Nice work," I said, genuinely impressed. "It's in the La Tene style."

"That's right! I learned about that stuff 'cause so many people want Celtic tattoos now. My mom had them too. I guess that's how I got into tats in the first place. Hers were amazing. She was doing it years before everyone thought it was cool. Mom was from the O'Neil Clan. They go all the way back to this king called Niall of the Nine Hostages. My dad gave me a book about him. Said he kidnapped Saint Patrick when he was a kid, during a raid he led on Britain. Twenty-six of his descendants were High Kings of Ireland."

I laughed. Irish people are soooooo into their genealogy. "My mom was Irish too," I said, flexing my pedigree. "I'm not sure about my dad."

"You said *was*," she pointed out, catching it like I did when she said it.

"Yeah. Is your mom dead too?"

"Yeah." She nodded. That single syllable hung uncomfortably in the air for a few silent seconds—then she abruptly reached for her coat. "Make sure to bring those drawings when you come by the parlor."

I came the next day. We worked together for months. Even after we finished, we would still get together, making modifications and additions. Most of that later work was done in my apartment. We'd drink some wine. Talk about Celtic lore. But whenever I spoke too much about the occult, she'd cut me off, saying something like, "My dad was way too into that shit. It freaks me out a little."

It didn't freak her out so much that she didn't want more card readings. Every time she came over she'd ask for one. I always put a positive spin on the gloomy stuff. There was lot to hide. There was a lot of incredible stuff too—so incredible I thought she must be either the luckiest or unluckiest person in the universe. It would shift back and forth between positive and negative poles almost every reading, like God kept flipping a coin that landed heads one day, tails the next. I began to think I was losing my touch, or that she had some really weird surprises in store. Looking back, I'm still shocked by how lightly I took it.

When she told me she did palm readings, I wasn't very surprised. "But never for money," she added. Was that a dig at me? If it was, she didn't keep digging.

"Wow!" she shouted, gaping at my left palm.

"Good wow or bad wow?" I asked, wondering if she was going to give me the censored version like I'd been giving her.

"It's your lifeline…"

"If it's short, don't tell me," I interrupted.

"No, it's the longest one I've ever seen. I guess you're going to live for a very long time."

"Great. Does it say if I ever get happy?"

She laughed. I laughed. We had fun. Strangely, I never had a single vision when I was with her, like that part of me was sealed inside a genie bottle. I didn't care, hardly noticed. It was so nice just to be in the same room with her and bask in the pleasure of her company. I'd never been with anyone else who really *got* me like she did. I even thought we might have ended up in bed together, if only I hadn't grown so trusting.

Trust? How could trust be my downfall?

It happened one night after too many glasses of wine. I knew this was going to be the night something happened between us. Too bad I didn't *see* what. She'd always been enthralled by my book collection, at least the parts of it on display. The more it felt okay to show her, the more I wanted her to see. So I showed her one of my "skin books"—the trial transcript of a hanged horse thief covered with his skin.

She thought it was cool. Said she loved that morbid side of me. Said she had her own dark side. Sure she did. She was a Goth chick. Anyway, I was drunk and a voice in my head that didn't even sound like mine kept nagging me to go all the way, telling me I was *really* safe with her, saying I could completely open up and show her who I was.

So I asked: "Want to see something *really* cool?"

"Sure," she said, a little drunk too.

Then I made the biggest mistake of my life. I took out the suitcase and showed her. She didn't run, or curse me or call the police. But she gave me *that look*. And she never came back, or even talked to me again.

Yes, I was in love. I guess I still am. So you can understand how I felt when I saw her and Martin together. When I thought about Paul and what he wanted me to do. I know you're not going to like it, but I'll tell you anyway. I had some very mixed feelings. Part of me wanted to help her. And part of me wanted to end all that pain.

SUPPER

"Make yourself comfortable," Paul said, ushering Michael to a large oak chair at the end of a long table that consisted of two sheets of raw plywood supported by sawhorses.

Michael stared at the two half-globes of roasted meat in the middle of the table and the paper plates and long bowie knives sitting in front of the four big chairs and realized how loudly his stomach was grumbling. He looked from his plate to Paul, wondering how he could broach the topic of his vegetarianism.

Paul was staring coldly at the doorway. Michael followed Paul's stare. A tall figure stood motionless in the shadows. Paul said nothing, but the look he gave Michael made him want to run away again.

"You're late," said Paul.

"Who's he?" asked Martin.

"This is Michael Bean," Paul said casually, directing his statement more to the roast than Martin. He then began carving it up with all the agility and speed of a surgeon trying to squeak in the front nine at the country club before rush hour. Martin said nothing, sizing up the kid with a single, sidelong, top-to-bottom glance. He summarized his findings with one unspoken word: *Chump.*

"Michael, this is Martin," Paul said, mildly irritated. Martin remained silent, taking a chair at the opposite end of the table, glaring at the interloper as Paul plopped a slab of mystery meat onto his reused paper plate.

Paul returned to his chair in the middle of the table and kept carving. "I would apologize for Martin's lack of table manners, but I never apologize. Though he lacks in the social graces, he more than compensates for those shortcomings in other areas."

Michael looked at Martin with a blend of envy, wariness and unabashed curiosity. Martin looked at the steak Paul slapped on his plate and abandoned all interest in the kid.

Paul looked at both of them with barely repressed glee.

"Uh, is there anything else to eat?" Michael asked cautiously, staring at the bloody hunk of meat on his otherwise empty plate. Martin and Paul looked at him like he was crazy and went back to gulping down the meat in huge swallows, keeping all chewing activities to a bare minimum. Michael stared at his steak, his stomach growling again. "Oh, what the hell. It's not like I never ate meat before." That was true enough. He'd only been a vegetarian for the last three months—after the waitress he had the hots for told him she was a vegan.

Michael picked up his big knife daintily, but once he cut off a chunk and pushed it between his lips, he was shocked by how juicy and flavorful it was, and how much he missed the taste of meat. "What ish this?" he asked, still chewing, the meat squirting with every bite.

Paul set down his utensils and wiped his mustache with the sleeve of his overcoat. "Roast rump. Tasty, isn't it?"

"Yessh," Michael replied, between enthusiastic mouthfuls. "Isshh really good."

Martin rolled his eyes, still not looking up from his plate.

"So, how many piercings do you have there, Michael?" Paul asked, reluctant to change the topic so quickly, but wanting to recapture Martin's attention.

"Eleven," Michael answered, looking from Paul to the expressionless face of Martin, who nonetheless managed to convey acres of contempt. "Got the three brow rings," he said, nervously pointing out each placement with his index finger. "Four earrings, the nose, tongue, both nips and…another one," pointing under the table in a swizzle stick motion.

"You poked your pee-pee?" asked Paul with an exaggerated wince.

"Not my pee…er, my, uh, something else," Michael replied, becoming increasingly uncomfortable, squirming in his chair as if the concealed piercing might be infected.

Martin shook his head with disgust. Another pinhead. The neighborhood was lousy with them. What was he doing here? How did he know Paul?

"Michael lives below me," Paul said, stomping on the floor to accentuate his unexpected reply to Martin's unasked questions. "The poor lad heard you screaming…and like any concerned citizen he came up to offer his kindly assistance."

"That was you…screaming like that?" Michael blurted out with a stupid grin.

Martin's face turned beet red. Paul grinned broadly, relishing the shame and rage transforming his features, stifling the phlegm-laced chortles that threatened to erupt in lava plumes all over his plate. "Indeed, it was," he cut in. "Martin just had his own piercing!"

Martin's stomach tightened and he slowly put down his fork, staring at Paul and the kid. Why would Paul discuss their session with a stranger? He stared blankly at the boy, trying to determine his age. Nineteen? Eighteen? Younger? He could tell from the kid's confused and eager expression that he couldn't have known Paul very long. No one looked like that after they'd known Paul very long. So what was he up to?

Paul gave Michael a wink that felt more like a nudge in the ribs. "Go on," the wink said. "Ask him about it."

"So whatcha get pierced?" Michael asked nervously, his shaky grin teetering between fear and a budding boldness, encouraged by the wink.

Martin remained silent, glancing at his bandaged hand.

"Oh…" Michael nodded, staring at the cloud of red in the middle of the coarse white fabric and the fresh scar in the web of his own hand. "Temporary piercings."

"Temporary piercings," Martin muttered with total contempt. His shoulders relaxed. The kid was just another filthy, tattooed squatter—another toy for Paul to bat around between his mitts like a squeaky mouse until he tired of him.

Michael didn't know what else to say next. Martin stared into his eyes for a long uncomfortable moment, then returned to his meal, eager to conclude this encounter.

"Martin is in a class all by himself," Paul interjected suddenly, with a flattering intonation that caught his tablemates by surprise. "Or maybe I should say he's in a very select class. The master class. As you can see, he doesn't bother with all that fancy jewelry. I'm sure those titty rings feel nice when you're soaping up in the shower, but Martin here is a purist. Like all warriors, he knows that pain has its own virtues…and rewards. He's learned to control unimaginable levels of suffering, and even though he's been known to indulge himself in a girlish scream from time to time, it still can't tarnish his ample achievements."

Michael could plainly hear the admiration in Paul's voice…and his disdain. Now it was his turn to frown with shame.

Despite the "girlish" dig, Martin felt a surge of pride, like he'd been exonerated of the most hideous crime imaginable: vulnerability. But when he looked at Paul's twinkling eyes and saw how determined he was to undermine the kid's confidence as well as his own, he felt another surge of apprehension. Paul was definitely up to something.

"What's your opinion, Martin?" Paul asked, ignoring his wary gaze. "I'd venture to guess you feel nothing but contempt for this new generation and all their showy ornamentation."

Martin nodded halfheartedly.

"Our Martin is a man of very few words," Paul whispered to Michael.

Martin squinted at Paul, then returned to the much more important business of refueling his depleted reserves. Halfway done, he calculated. About twelve more bites.

Paul grinned at Michael like the wolf in Little Red Riding Hood. Michael stared at the grin and Martin's bandaged hand and tugged nervously on an earring. The silence, interrupted only by the sounds of sawing blades and slobbery chewing, hung over the table like organ music in a funeral parlor. Michael ate along with them, until he felt a nagging itch that someone was watching him. When he lifted his eyes up, Martin was staring right back at him with unconcealed malice. *What's going on here? Who are these people?* Michael thought in a complete panic. When Paul had told him about Martin, he thought he was going to be attending some kind of seminar— *How To Be an Action Hero in Ten Easy Steps*—or some shit like that. But not only was this buzz-cut cowboy tight as a clam; not only was he unmistakably, palpably dangerous; not only did he look like Dirty Harry minus the wavy hair and with only half the squint; not only was this lean, mean clearly-pissed-off-for-no-good-reason fuckhead making him feel as squirmy as a baby in a bucket of eels…but to top it off, he acted like he wanted to kill him!

Bean couldn't hold Martin's baleful gaze and immediately shifted his eyes back to his plate and the growing pool of red juice leaking out from his steak. Martin stared at him across the expanse of weathered wood and looked at the knife in his hand.

Paul raised his head from his plate and cleared his throat again. "Martin," he gurgled between swallows of meat, "I don't suppose you'd like to share a story"—(gulp, *slurp*, chew)—"of our exploits together"—(gnaw, *crunch*, gulp)—"with our young guest here."

Martin said nothing, gripping his knife tighter.

"Well, I have an amusing anecdote, now that I think about it," he sighed, leaning on the edge of the plywood table. "I remember a time when you were just a bit younger than Michael here and we were traveling through the redwoods of Northern California."

Martin couldn't believe it. Paul was going to tell *this* story to a seedy little punk like Bean? Who *was* this guy? What the hell was Paul doing?

Paul ignored Martin's bug-eyed stare and turned to face Bean, twisting his chair around to the side. "We were stopping by to visit a very old acquaintance of mine," Paul said blandly. "A man by the name of Firth. Even though we dropped by unannounced, I'll be damned if he didn't act like he was expecting us. We barely made it halfway up the long gravel road in our old pickup truck, when I heard the first shot."

Outlaws, Michael thought. *Cool.*

Paul plowed ahead with his story. "Now you may not guess that a beefy old fella like meself would be the agile sort, but I can move at quite a clip when I feel the urge—and young Martin had a knack for the most amazing acrobatics. So when we heard that big loud *bang!* neither of us wasted any time getting out of the way." Paul punctuated the *bang!* by clapping his hands so loudly that Michael jumped in his seat. Paul grinned and went on with his story.

"Martin bailed out the passenger door like he was parachuting from a plane during takeoff. Meanwhile, I ducked down so quickly in the vacant seat he provided that the whizzing blob of lead missed me with a few milliseconds to spare." He paused to take another slug of whiskey and rose from his chair, waving his arms enthusiastically as he spoke. "The truck crashed into the massive iron gates, and we took the fight to Firth, scrambling through the trees, guns blazing. The house was a castle, really, and his soldiers were shooting at us from the high towers on the left and right. Martin, with his keen, youthful eye and dead-calm trigger finger, knocked out two of them, at a good hundred yards, no less…while on the run! I contented meself with some well-timed shotgun blasts to the stones around Firth. I knew it was him in the highest turret, on account of his cowardly fondness for sniper rifles. I kept him pinned down until Martin blew open the front door with his trusty sawed-off twenty gauge."

Paul paused to take another slug of whiskey. "Hmmm. I wonder if Martin could be persuaded to pick up the tale at this point…"

Martin glared at Paul, then stared blankly at his nearly empty plate like it contained the answer to the riddle of why he'd come back again.

"No? Oh, well. I guess I'll stumble along on my own as best I can. Now where was I? Oh, yes, we went inside and rounded up Firth, his family, servants and soldiers. The soldiers were summarily executed, the servants locked in the pantry and Firth and his offspring, fraternal twins of either sex, were held at gunpoint in the library, until I got what I came for."

"What did you come for?" Michael asked, right on cue.

"Firth had taken a book from me, a very special book," Paul said, his face flattening out again. His answer was so unexpected that Michael almost interrupted again, but Paul filled in the dark, brooding pause himself. "He knew this was the reason I'd come for him, but he'd be damned if he was going to part with it so easily, even though it wasn't his to begin with, though for some odd reason he kept insisting that it was. Now it's hard to imagine a work of literature inspiring such passion, but Firth was willing to bargain with all he had, if Martin and I would leave him and the precious tome in peace."

"Why was the book so important?" Michael asked.

Paul considered for a moment, then spoke with a dismissive wave. "For you it would just be marks on a page. For me it was very special. Let's say it had a sentimental value. Like a family heirloom. Of course, I turned down Firth's offer cold flat, but he was a quick thinker. He proposed an alternative I couldn't refuse, given my highly competitive instincts. He called for a duel!"

"He wanted to fight you?" Michael asked, astonished.

Paul laughed so loud it shook the table. "Me? No, Firth was nobody's fool. He challenged young Martin against his son, winner take all. The book…and all their lives. I asked him why he was betting all his chips on his very big boy, who had more than a foot on Martin, by the way, and looked every bit as crafty as his dad and twice as mean.

"So Firth looks at me funny, well, not that funny, then turns his eyes to his son, as if to ask if he's truly up to the task. The son in turn sizes up Martin who was still a little lad for his age—didn't have that big growth spurt till two years later—and nods back to poppa like this'll be a cakewalk.

"Naturally, I keep my poker face on, but I'm chuckling inside, thinking how many men have already paid the price for underestimating little Martin. All the while I'm making funny remarks to his skinny little daughter, who cunna been more than seventeen, wouldn't you say, Martin? Wouldn't you say she cunna been more than seventeen?"

Martin speared his fork in the last piece of meat, raised it and opened his mouth.

"Martin didn't look at her much, if the truth be told," Paul went on, a fresh hunger in his voice as he watched Michael perk up his ears and lean closer towards him. "He never cared much more for the ladies than he did for all the finer things in life, a good belt of rye, a nice, juicy steak…"

Martin chomped down hard, barely pulling the fork out before the tines were clenched in his teeth.

"No, no, no…Martin was much more interested in keeping an eye on me. I suppose he was wondering what I had in store for the lovely lass after the big battle."

Martin pushed back his chair from the table. Paul didn't even look in his direction, keeping his eyes locked on Michael, sizing up every twitch and flinch.

Michael looked from Paul to Martin. Some part of his soul was trying to wake him from this spell he was under, urging him to run as fast as he could. But a new, different voice was calling even louder, "*Stay…* (what happened to the girl?). *Learn…*(who *are* these people?). *Listen!*"

Michael listened.

"The sobbing girl was the least of Martin's worries," Paul continued. "Firth's boy was circling him to the left, not the best direction to approach him from…and even though he's not the best knife man, he had a long, sharp dirk in his boot and…"

FWHHHIIIISHHHH Martin threw his knife down the length of the table, straight at Michael's heart. Martin had moved so quickly, flipping his grip from the haft to the blade and flinging it in one single sidearm motion, that Michael wasn't sure what happened until he saw the glint of steel.

"Fuck!" he yelled, the knife flying at him so quickly he only had time to scream in horror. There was no chance at all to move out of the way. He just wasn't fast enough.

Paul was. He grabbed the knife in midair, only a few feet from Michael's chest. He grabbed it by the blade. Michael clutched his chest, coughing with terror and relief, his eyes glued to Paul and the knife.

Paul wasn't moving. He looked like he was frozen in time and space, his smile unwavering, his arm stock still, his hand tightly gripping the blade. If it weren't for the blood dripping between his fingers onto the plywood table, Michael would have thought he was staring at a photograph or maybe a hologram. He looked unreal. But what was even more inconceivable than the sight of him, still motionless after seemingly endless seconds had passed, even more astonishing than the act of snatching a knife in midair that was traveling at the speed of a flying hockey puck… was the unimaginable yet undeniable fact that Paul *never changed his position* as he stuck out his arm to grab the rocketing knife. He didn't turn to look at Martin, or the knife. Paul was looking at *him* the whole time.

Michael grabbed his chest as the truth of it sank into his brain, so overwhelmed by the patently impossible feat that it took him another few seconds to tear his eyes away from Paul and gasp at Martin with rage and terror, "Why the fuck did you do that?"

Martin rose silently from his chair.

"Nice throw, but I think you've lost a bit off your fastball over the years," Paul drawled, finally moving, but only enough to drop the knife onto the table, the blade sticking into the splintery wood with a loud *thuck* as it wobbled back and forth.

"I guess I need more practice," Martin said, standing fully erect, as indifferent to Paul's acrobatic prowess as he was to Bean's question.

"Indeed, you do!" Paul shouted, wrapping a dirty napkin around the gash in his hand without a glance at the wound itself. "If you'd been as lazy with Firth's poor lad, maybe he'd be having dinner with me tonight instead of you!"

"I'm pretty sure we just had him for dinner," Martin said, his gaze riveted on Bean.

Paul stared at the roast with a wicked grin. "Well, now that you mention it, I'll be damned if he didn't pay me a visit two nights ago. I'm not sure how he survived your blade all those years ago, or how he kept off my radar screen…but he strolled in here just as pretty as you please to make one last play for the book. He was even bigger than I remembered…and armed to the teeth. Put up quite a fight, he did, but in the end…"

"I'm done with this," Martin said, clenching his uninjured fist, relaxing every other muscle in his body, ready to face Paul's full wrath if necessary.

Paul didn't make a move or say another word. For a few seconds.

"Done?" he shouted, laughing almost as loudly. "You're *done?* You leave me to clean up your trash twenty years on, then tell me you're *done?* We have unfinished business, boy!"

"Is that why he's here?" Martin asked, pointing to Bean without looking in his direction. "You want another duel? See if I can finish it?"

"A duel? Between you two lads? I wouldn't dream of it. This fine young fella's never seen a fistfight. What would be the sport of that? A duel, indeed."

"If I really wanted a duel, it would already be over," Martin sneered.

"Oh, I see. You were just showing off then? Puffing out your chest? Illustrating the story, like a kiddie's picture book? Or maybe you were testing me, aye? Maybe you wanted to see how much I care for my newfound friend here? How far I'm willing to extend myself? Well, now you know, don't you, lad?"

Martin stopped walking, more perplexed than ever at Paul's declaration. Even so, he didn't want to stay another minute asking the questions Bean was much too frightened to pose or even think about: What was he doing here? Why did Paul tell him that story?

Martin didn't say anything. He turned around, walking toward the hallway.

"So that's it, then?" Paul yawned, fingering the knife in the table.

Martin kept walking as if he hadn't heard the question.

"Well, before you prance off on your merry way, there's something else I need to remind you of…"

Martin spun around as quickly as he could. The knife was flying right for his face at twice the speed he'd hurled it earlier. He didn't catch it. But he managed to tilt his neck at a forty-five-degree angle just in time to feel the missile whiz by his temple with enough velocity to bristle the tiny hairs inside his ear canal.

"Hhmmph!" Paul snorted, clapping his hands with delight. "Maybe you've been doing your homework, after all. Even so, you've forgotten the most important lesson of all. Don't ever turn your back on me, boy!"

Michael gasped so loudly that Paul gave another booming laugh, craning his face to the ceiling like he was howling at the moon. Martin remained still for a moment, looking at both of them. Then he walked backwards out of the room facing Paul every step of the way.

Postscript

"What were you guys playing at back there with all that knife throwing shit?" Michael asked nervously, hurrying to catch up with Paul as he stomped to the front windows.

"Exciting, wasn't it?" Paul replied, peering through the dirty glass at the street below.

"Way too exciting," Michael mumbled, clutching his chest again.

"I'll bet you felt alive though. More alive than you've ever felt?"

Michael stopped to think about it. It was true, he guessed, not that he wanted to admit it, or even think about it. His head nodded anyway, as a more urgent question surfaced. "Why was that nutjob so pissed at me? I was totally cool with him and he tried to kill me!"

"Rule number one: never say anything about anyone that you wouldn't have the sack to say straight to their face. Martin is far from a 'nut job' by any standard of assessment. As to his motivation for assaulting you, I'm certain he was much more irritated with me, dear boy. You simply presented him with a more vulnerable target for his frustration. I believe that's called transference. My tale stirred up some uncomfortable memories for the lad, as I expected."

"You were *trying* to piss him off?" Michael asked, his mind spinning.

"If that were my sole intention, I would've taken a more direct approach. As you've probably noticed, bluntness comes naturally to me. My prodding was more of a wakeup call. Martin is a very special man, with a very special destiny. The story I was telling of our encounter with Clan Firth marked a turning point in our relationship. Ever since that day, Martin has been running away from himself, his heritage and, most importantly, his duty. I was simply steering him back on track again, though apparently he doesn't see it that way."

"What happened? How did the story end?" Michael asked, his curiosity in overdrive.

"Stories never end," Paul grunted, "at least not the ones I tell."

"But what happened with the duel?" Bean asked, though he really wanted to know what happened to the girl.

Paul turned to look at him. To look through him. Michael recoiled and Paul turned away, staring down at the street again. When Martin emerged and walked down the steps, Paul's stony expression melted into a smile. "That man down there, who was more boy than man on that fateful day, dispatched with Firth's son in the time it would take me to trim my mustache. We assumed he was dead, not much of a stretch, given the scope of his lacerations. But as you've heard, he lived to fight another day, sadly for him. At any rate, with all the blood gushing from the poor lad, Firth knew all was lost, so he turned on Martin, determined to settle the score."

"Wow," gasped Michael. "What did he do?"

"Martin was always a force to be reckoned with, even back then," Paul said, watching Martin's slow, determined progress up the sidewalk. When he crossed the street, Paul stomped back down the hallway to a large closet with double doors. "Firth never knew what hit him. I pulled Martin off after the first few stabs, so I could relish his final humiliation. Then the girl started screaming and ruined that perfect moment."

Michael stared at him speechless. Paul threw open the closet doors so forcefully that the doorknobs dented the plaster on either side. He bent over and opened a chest filled with every type of weapon imaginable. Michael gawked at the array of handguns, knives and other exotic killing instruments, some weirder than anything he'd seen in the movies.

Paul grinned and asked, "Don't you want to know what happened to the girl?"

"Uh, yeah," Michael muttered, unable to stop staring at the shiny weaponry.

"Martin tried to save her! He pleaded with me, begged me, in fact, to spare the girl…going so far as to forfeit his share of the treasure we'd plundered from old Lord Firth, even all that gold Martin loves so much, if only I'd leave her be."

"The gold?" Michael asked with a greedy shiver.

"Oh, yes. Firth had gobs and gobs of the stuff. Martin was willing to trade it all away for the skinny runt. Well, he wasn't talking sense, now was he? He certainly wasn't being financially prudent. And since he wasn't of legal age, and I was his de facto legal guardian, I needed to make sure he didn't squander all his rightful earnings. So…"

Paul paused and stared at Michael, as if debating whether to continue.

"So…" Michael repeated, goading him on.

"So…" Paul continued with a sigh, "I told Martin that his wish was granted…that the girl could live, and because he'd been so noble, not only could he keep his share of the gold, but he could have all of mine as well. And we all lived happily ever after."

Bean didn't know what to say. He held the gaze of Paul's twinkling eyes far longer than he would have thought possible, before his brain kicked his mouth into motion again.

"Did you get the book?" he asked. It wasn't what he really wanted to know but it felt far safer than asking the other question nagging away at him—about what really happened.

"Hhmph." Paul chuckled. "Now what do you think?"

Michael turned away sheepishly. "I guess you did," he mumbled.

"Very good! I do believe you'll be a full-fledged wizard in no time at all. But here's a secret I don't think you could anticipate so easily: I knew where the book was hidden before we even knocked on Firth's door."

"Then why go through all that stuff with the offers and the duels and all that other shit?" Michael asked, incredulous. "Why didn't you just walk in and take it?"

"Well, my little friend, I can see you have very much to learn indeed. I did 'all that other shit,' as you so eloquently put it…simply for the fun of it!"

VOYEUR

I hid in the shadows by the stoop and peered up at Rose's window for a very long time. God, she was so beautiful…and so unreasonably happy.

Martin. Fucking Martin. It wasn't long before I ceased basking in the warm glow of her beauty and began writhing in the molten lava of my shame, loathing and hatred.

The sound of a broken bottle and loud laughter coming from up the block shook me from my seething contempt like a train whistle. I craned my neck around the stoop and stared into the darkness, trying to make out the shapes under the broken streetlights. A group of five young toughs were on the other side of the street about forty feet ahead, muthafucking this and that as loudly as they could, laughing and swilling malt liquor from the requisite brown paper bags under the sole functioning streetlight. They looked like they were auditioning for an Off-Off-Off Broadway production of *West Side Story*.

I briefly considered a brisk stroll back home to the safety of a more remote viewing location. Then I looked farther up the street and saw the distant silhouette of a tall man walking with confident strides. It was Martin, coming right towards them.

I eagerly receded into the shadows again, hungry for the show to begin. *Now this is going to be interesting. Too bad I didn't bring any popcorn.*

Release the Hounds!

Paul reached carefully into the deep pockets of his coat and felt around for his knife. His pocket-sickle. He had it custom made in Germany, where they still knew a thing or two about craftsmanship and cruelty. The long semicircular blade was hinged in two places and attached to a stainless-steel handle with a 360-degree rotational swivel joint, so he could open it with one swift whip-crack motion, whereupon hidden metal dowels would lock all the hinges in place. It was a scary piece of steel even when it was closed... the razor-sharp edges facing in on each other. You had to be careful just reaching in to grab it because the hair-trigger spring could instantly turn it into a bear trap in your pocket. Ouchy, wowchy.

Paul gingerly patted his pocket from the outside and smiled to himself. Ah, the simple joys of the hunt. He stared at the open chest, looking at all the shiny toys, debating whether there was anything else he wanted to bring. "Hmmm," he murmured, eyeing the Uzi as he twirled his mustache. He was a knife man, rarely used pistols, but it could come in handy for crowd control.

"Uh, could I have a look at that?" Michael asked tentatively, pointing at a nickel-plated Luger Parabellum. It looked like the gun in the old James Bond movies, only cooler. Paul lifted it from its foam-cushioned box and placed it into Bean's grateful palm. Michael's eyes widened in delight as he hefted its sleek weight a few times. "Is it loaded?"

Paul laughed and shouted, "Is the Pope a theocratic despot who only cares about filling the coffers of the Holy Roman Empire while undermining all the fundamental teachings of the Good King Jesus the Christ?"

"Uh, I guess," Michael replied, squeezing the grip of his super-cool pistol.

Paul grabbed Michael by the shoulders and gave him a heartfelt hug. "I like you, boy. And because I'm so curiously fond of you, I'm going to make you a special offer."

"What?" Michael asked, his face suddenly flushed with anticipation.

"If you manage to show me some spine tonight, I'll give you a peek at the greatest treasure in the universe."

"What's that?" Michael asked greedily.

"Why, the Book, of course," Paul said with a strange light in his eyes.

"The Book?" Bean asked, pouting with disappointment. "I thought you said it was like a souvenir or something."

"I lied," Paul said, grinning like a maniac while he strapped the Uzi to a Velcro harness on the inside of his coat. "The Book can give you anything you've ever desired. Power. Wealth. Riches beyond imagining. How does that sound, laddie? Does that make your little pecker go pitter-pat?"

Michael nodded vigorously. "But what do I have to do?"

"We need to move fast, so there's no time for details," Paul continued, hustling down the hallway, Michael trailing behind like a bobbing dinghy in his wake. "Let's just say there's a level of risk proportionate to the rewards."

"Uh, all right," Michael stuttered, his legs struggling to catch up, his nostrils flaring with exhilaration and far less unease than he would have expected.

"Good, good," Paul said, guiding Bean's hand and the pistol it held into the pocket of his beat-up army jacket. "Then saddle up, doggy, we're going for a walk!"

Michael was so excited that he almost wagged his tail.

ALMOST HOME

All Martin wanted to do was go home. He was less than a block away when he saw the crowd of neighborhood punks huddled around the stoop they always used as their drug distribution/intimidation post. There were five of them tonight. Not his favorite number.

Martin had seen them plenty of times before. They never said a word to him or even looked in his direction. Wisely. But tonight Martin knew it would be different. They were predators and would surely sense his weakness. He was hurt, he was tired and he was stupid. He hadn't brought a single weapon into Paul's apartment, because it was forbidden. He also hadn't left one hidden outside. Stupid. Stupid. Stupid.

He thought about crossing the street. But he was so close to them now they'd see his maneuver for exactly what it was—a simple act of cowardice. Not only would they come after him in all probability, but even if they didn't, he'd never be able to live with himself. No, his course was clear. He had to keep walking. Past them.

Yes...just a little farther...a few more steps and...past the stoop...they're behind me now...almost there...almost home...not a fucking peep and...

"Yo, bubblehead!" the leader called out—and Martin stopped dead in his tracks.

HELPLESS

Rose was sizing up the kitchen window curtains when she spotted Martin standing motionless under the streetlight, glowing like her candles. What was he doing? Then she saw the five brutes ambling up behind him, all rolling arm movements, fingers splayed, heads cocked this way and that, like they were in some gangsta-rap monster movie.

"Martin!" she screamed, trying to lift the window. It was painted shut. Her fingers clawed at the frame and her wrists bent with the effort of trying to free it. It wouldn't budge. She slammed her hands against the window in frustration, but even the glass taunted her with weaves of chicken-wire reinforcement.

She sobbed and screamed his name again, hoping he could hear her, hoping he would do *something*. Why was he just standing there? Couldn't he hear them coming up behind him? Why didn't he move? What was wrong with him?

The gang pressed closer. "Move, you son of a bitch! Turn around!" she screamed through the chicken-wire window. "Run, Martin! *Run!*"

DECISIONS, DECISIONS

Martin knew what was happening behind him. Knew they were on the move, knew they would be on him in only a few more seconds. He was so tired. He wanted to go home.

"Yo! Bubblehead!" the leader repeated. "If you a lighthouse, why don't you blink?"

Martin remained perfectly still. The other gang members chimed in raucously, "Yeah, Carlos, make that muthafucka blink!" and "Yo! Fuck *you*, bubblehead!" Carlos silenced them all by calling out to Martin in his flattest, bad-ass voice: "Turn around, punk."

When Martin moved, his only thought was speed. Paul's voice whispered in his mind as he tensed his body for action. One of the first rules he learned from Paul was: "Never, ever get into a fight. Fighting is for sissies— for little boys who need to prove how big and strong they are. Real men don't fight," he said dryly. "They attack, they maim, they murder."

"Cut off the head, and the body dies," he advised on another notable occasion, immediately conducting a practical demonstration by throwing a fifteen-inch Russian military bayonet directly into the drunken heart of the leader of a local biker gang that had surrounded them outside a honky-tonk in rural Tennessee. The "fight" ended quickly.

Martin acquired firsthand knowledge of the wisdom in that saying on many subsequent occasions and was anxious to test its validity again. If he could take out the leader, there was a good chance the others would scatter.

Martin leapt into a flying roundhouse kick straight to Carlos's chin. He missed. His boot sliced through the air directly on course, but two inches below Carlos's stubbly beard. Oops. Nobody laughed at Martin's mistake, least of all Carlos. The strength, poise and authority of his movements were much too impressive for ridicule. However, they didn't start applauding either. They pulled out their guns. Not all five of them. Just Carlos and the bald-shaven, dark-skinned guy on the stoop directly above him to his…left.

Shit.

When Rose saw Martin kick and miss, her knees practically gave out. When she saw the two guys pull out their guns, they instantly straightened up again.

"Fuck this!" Even though she knew it was crazy…that she could be killed…she had to do something. She had to try to save the man she loved.

She *loved?* I couldn't believe it either, but who else even thinks about doing something so reckless? If I'd been with her, *really* with her, I would have tried to talk her out of it. Risk your life…for *Martin?* "Wait a few more seconds," I'd say, "while you still have the view."

Would she have listened? Does anyone listen when they're all pumped up with hormones? Not anyone I know. Certainly not Rose.

She ran down the stairs so fast that her hand got brush-burns from the railing.

STREET FIGHT

"What you gonna do now?" Carlos asked theatrically, waving his pistol in circles.

Good, Carlos was talking instead of shooting. Martin would have kissed the ground in gratitude if he had the time. Unfortunately, like every other variable in the equation, time was against him. He sized up the other gunman on the stoop and saw more cause for optimism. He was scratching his face in the unmistakable manner of someone with an armful of low-grade Mexican heroin. Excellent. He had the itch. If he had the itch, that meant he was moving slow.

Now he was faced with a big decision. He could keep Carlos yakking until he picked the perfect moment to disarm him…or…he could jump to his left, snap the junkie's wrist and hope that Carlos was too slow on the trigger to plug him before he gained control of the other weapon. He knew the latter option was his best bet. But it meant he had to jump to his *left*.

Shit. Shit. Shit.

Martin was still mulling it over as Carlos's face changed into that familiar "Wellllll?" expression every bully gets after he's cornered the school nerd and stuck out his hand for the milk money. It was now or never. Even one more second of indecision would turn the "Wellllll?" into a "Kneel!"

Martin was tensing himself for a fateful leftward leap, hoping the extra jolt of adrenaline pumping in his veins was enough to marshal un-tapped reserves of strength, when suddenly a third contingency emerged he hadn't figured into his calculations…and wouldn't have expected in a million years.

"*MARTIN!*" Rose screamed, running across the street with a nail file in her hand.

Everyone looked. Carlos even stopped his gun-waving histrionics long enough to turn his head in a futile attempt to ward off her subway-brake shrieking. That was all Martin needed. He moved on the junkie with inhuman speed and strength. Dopey's arm cracked like a pretzel log. He didn't even feel any pain until the gun popped out of his backwards-angled arm and into Martin's hand like a piece of toast.

Martin turned to fire on Carlos and Carlos swiveled sideways to do the same. Both of them were blindsided again as Rose vaulted into the air like the teen prodigy gymnast she'd been, landing squarely on Carlos's back.

What a bitch! Martin thought. His reaction was equally appropriate for expressing his unabashed awe, admiration and gratitude for her courageous intervention as well as his utter frustration with her attack plan. Had Rose simply confined her support activities to more of the same ear-splitting screams she previously contributed, he would have already planted three slugs into Carlos's vital organs. Now, as Rose and Carlos twisted together like chicken fight partners in knee-deep guacamole, it was impossible to get a shot off that didn't risk hitting her.

Holding Dopey's writhing bulk between himself and Carlos like a full-body-armor shield, Martin realized they were more or less on equal footing. One pull of the trigger would jeopardize the life of either shooter's partner. Surprisingly, Carlos was the first to abandon all loyalty in favor of pure survival instincts. He started blasting. *Bang-bang-bang-bang-bang!*

Martin had done a terrific job of positioning Dopey's body in such a way that the first three shots were safely absorbed into his upper torso. The fourth shot missed him entirely, ricocheting harmlessly off the concrete steps. The fifth one got him. *ZZZZZZZZmzzzzzzzzt* Martin could hear and even smell the whizzing bullet as it tore into the muscles below his left ribcage. The painful impact, combined with his depleted strength, made it impossible for him to support the junkie's now literally dead weight. Martin collapsed onto the steps, trying to keep the bleeding body draped protectively over him like a lead x-ray blanket.

Martin knew what bullets do when they enter your body and wondered whether he was already dead. For those of you who don't know what happens when a bullet hits a fleshy, bony object—like Martin, for instance—it doesn't necessarily travel in a straight line. More often than not, it twists and turns in the most surprising ways. For example, on one occasion, Paul shot a man in the wrist and the bullet, quite remarkably, made it all the way up his arm and over into his bronchial tubes. Paul called it, "Extra mileage."

Martin paused to determine where his own private missile might have wandered and groaned with relief when he saw a blob of flesh and blood on the cement directly beneath the bullet's entry site. *Good, a nice clean shot.* He'd survived a few of those.

He didn't have time for further celebration. When he looked up, he noticed two remarkable new developments: Carlos had leveled his pistol sight squarely on Martin's forehead, and Rose had her nail file pointed right at his focusing eyes.

Thuck! That might have been the sound Rose made if she stabbed the gleaming tip of her file directly into Carlos's squinting eye. Yet even with Martin's life at stake, she couldn't bring herself to commit an act so basely horrifying. Instead, the sound was more of a *ZZZZZZT* as she raked the filing edge across his exposed corneas just as he was squeezing the trigger.

"Arrrrrrgggh!" Carlos bellowed, raising his pistol-toting hand (much too late) to protect his eyes. *BANG!* The gun fired, but not into Martin's head. The bullet streaked into the air, landing a few seconds later with a harmless plop into the potato salad bowl of a midnight rooftop picnic party one block farther east.

Upon realizing he's been blinded, Carlos became as frantic as he was enraged, indiscriminately emptying the remaining bullets in his magazine while he rotated in circles with the vague hope of hitting Rose or Martin or maybe even one of his useless compadres.

Rose jumped off Carlos's back as soon as she delivered the fateful slash, quickly somersaulting across the pavement as Carlos twirled and fired. All the remaining shots slammed into the brownstone buildings or smog-deadened trees, with the exception of one lonely slug that shattered the shinbone of another of his meathead minions. The poor guy went down hard, breaking all of his front teeth as his face smashed into the curb right next to where Rose was lying. Rose, who liked the sight of blood more than most people, almost heaved as his cracked teeth bounced into the street like a pack of Chiclets.

One of the three surviving goons assumed Rose's former position behind Carlos's back trying to wrestle the pistol away from him, or failing that, at least make sure he was safely behind the firing line. Another hopped behind a row of garbage cans to escape the whizzing bullets. The last thug ran away.

The instant Martin heard the first echoing *click* of Carlos's firing hammer hitting an empty chamber, he stuck his head out from behind his protective cover and started shooting. *Bang! Bang! Bang! Plop. Plop. Plop.* That was it. Three shots, three dead bodies. Rose was shrieking in fear at the sound of even more bullets spraying around her, but when she saw what Martin had done, her mouth shut and her eyes widened.

Fuck! He just killed those guys, she thought, both awed and horrified. *No, we just killed those guys,* she added, even more disturbed. A cascade of raw emotions swirled around her head, pushing each other out of the way, struggling for recognition. Fear. Loathing. Excitement.

Martin watched all those expressions flicker on her face and remembered the smile of a seven-year-old boy shooting his first rat…and an eight-year-old boy holding a smoking Beretta. *Shit,* he thought with a sad shake of pity. Then the switch clicked right on cue.

Good. He'd wasted too much time already. Martin looked at her for one lingering second before he broke the silence.

"Could you get this body off me?"

JUST ONE KISS

Rose groaned with disgust and the effort of pushing the splattered corpse off Martin. After she helped him up, he put his arm around her, looking in all directions for any sign of witnesses. Nothing. *This is weird. After all that shooting, there must be someone.* Then, assuming they were all alone, he did the most unexpected thing. He bent his head down and kissed Rose tenderly on the top of her head.

It was a beautiful sight. Even I had to agree. Tony, the fifth young punk, didn't find it the least bit endearing. As it turned out, he wasn't that big a coward after all. Yes, he ran away, but not very far. He was catching his breath at the far end of the street, tucked under his own shadowy stoop. And surprise, surprise: Tony also had a gun, which he was now pointing squarely at the crown of Martin's lowered, kissing head.

If Martin had known, he might not have waited so long before raising his head again. Even that little movement might have saved his life. Because that little punk Tony had him dead in his sights. And to make matters worse, he was a really good shot.

Tony squeezed the trigger long, slow and even, just like he'd been taught by Carlos, the very man Martin had just delivered from a lifetime of white canes and Braille *Hustler* magazines. His aim was perfect. Martin lingered with his kiss to make it even easier. Nothing in the world should have been able to save Martin from that long, slow squeeze and the speeding bullet that followed.

Nothing at all. Except, just maybe, for a little bit of luck.

CAPTAIN HOOK

Tony couldn't see him. Neither could Rose or Martin.

Paul was coming like a great, shrouded ghost, his long, white hair glowing under the streetlight. He was moving fast, but there wasn't the slightest sound from his footsteps. He snapped the sickle open and it locked into place, its chrome, engraved death's head emblem gleaming under the street lamp. Tony turned around at the sound, knowing it had to be some kind of knife or switchblade, guessing the newcomer must be in league with the tall guy and his rabid girlfriend. As he turned, he continued the slow squeeze of the trigger, his gun thrust out at eye level, gripped tightly in both hands for steady support.

Tony decided he would start firing as soon as he fully turned around. *At this range, any hit will slow him down. Then I'll have time for a follow-up shot.* And that's exactly what Tony would have done. If he still had a head.

One-way Conversation

"C'mere! C'mere! Quick!" Paul hissed at Michael, trying to remain unobserved by Martin and Rose long enough to delight in one of his most treasured indulgences. When Michael didn't move fast enough, he grabbed his hand and dragged him over, under the shadow of a barren tree.

There it was. It could have been mistaken for a half-deflated soccer ball, if it weren't for the ears. "Look!" Paul hooted, practically bouncing with excitement. It was still alive. "Quick! Bend down, there isn't much time," Paul commanded, squatting in front of the…thing. He pulled Michael down with him. Up close and personal. The eyes blinked. Paul raised a finger between them and moved it from side to side. When the eyes followed the movement of Paul's finger, Michael shivered so strongly his head shook.

"Neat, eh?" Paul said, nudging Michael in the ribs. "Go ahead, ask him a question!"

Strangely enough, Michael didn't hesitate. It was as if the question had always been inside him, waiting for the opportunity to be asked. "Did it hurt?"

Michael almost shit himself when the mouth opened horribly, struggling to reply. Thankfully, no sound followed, except a barely audible gurgle accompanied by a pool of black blood spilling onto the asphalt below. Bean took an involuntary step backwards when the mouth moved again, slowly, maybe even calmly, mouthing out the words. Michael was no lip reader, but even he could make out the message.

"Not much," said the head.

"Whoa!" Michael's *Whoa!* seemed to shock the head formerly known as Tony into a state of confusion, or perhaps despair. He closed his eyes and blinked them slowly open again, hoping his intrusive audience had lost interest and gone away. When he saw Michael was still gawking at him, he closed his eyes again. They didn't reopen.

"Well, that's it, kid. Show's over," Paul said happily, slapping Bean on the back, shaking his head with a rapturous sigh of pleasure. "Pretty impressive, eh?"

Michael was so overcome with the madness of the moment that he didn't know whether to nod or faint. Paul understood. It was, after all, his first time. Paul looked down the street to see whether Martin and Rose were out of earshot. He watched as they approached an apartment building more than fifty yards west, and satisfied that he and Michael had some measure of privacy, he picked up the headless body and stuffed it into an empty trash can as easily as he was tossing out an oversize bag of kitty litter. He shoved another plastic bag of garbage from a neighboring can on top to cover the crumpled legs, then pushed down the lid so tightly that the lazy sanitation workers would have to screw it off when they carted the trash away two or three days later.

Michael's legs were so wobbly he almost collapsed in the street. Paul walked over and gave him a hug that almost brought him back to the edge of sanity—then he robbed him of that fleeting equilibrium by picking up the head by its blood-oiled hair, speaking to both the head and Michael like an anatomy professor.

"Here's a little-known fact…little known, that is, to anyone who wasn't around during the Reign of Terror," Paul began, sucking in a huge draft of air while he planted his oak-thick legs a yard apart. He cradled the head gently, then tossed it softly from one hand to the other as he continued. "There's enough oxygen left in the brain after a particularly swift decapitation, let's say from a guillotine during that aforementioned terrible time, or my own modest invention here, that the poor lad's head remains not only conscious for a considerable period, but also acutely aware of his surroundings. You can look into his eyes…and they look back. Better yet, you can even ask him questions, as you've just witnessed yourself."

Paul chuckled, then opened Tony's eyelids with his thumbs. With this latest desecration, Michael felt more giddy than nauseous. He was beginning to acclimate himself to the Dada-esque absurdity of his circumstances.

"And here's another little secret about vacationing heads that I daresay you couldn't learn from any other person on the planet…" Paul paused and Michael's heart might have stopped beating in response. "They almost always answer you."

"Whoa!" said Michael. What else could he say?

"Oh, the things that I could tell you, m'boy," Paul said, shaking his head in wonder. "The things that I have learned!" Then he drop-kicked the head across the street and over a chain-link fence into a vacant lot.

Michael half expected Paul to yell out, *"Goaaal!"* but he casually wiped his bloody hands on his overcoat, wrapped a burly arm around Michael's panicked shoulder and whispered, "And you know something else, Michael?"

"What?" Bean gulped.

"No matter how many times I've been lucky enough to witness that little miracle, I just never get tired of seeing it."

OBLIVIOUS

They say ignorance is bliss. Rose's case was a mixed bag. If she'd known Tony was pointing a gun at Martin's head, she wouldn't have wanted the kiss to linger for quite so long. That would have been a shame. On the other hand, if she'd seen Paul slice off Tony's head with all the aplomb of a master sushi chef, she might have wisely abandoned Martin and his benefactor right on the spot, sparing herself all the suffering to follow.

So, quite oblivious to the danger still surrounding them, and anxious to remove herself and Martin from the crime scene before the police sirens began wailing, Rose wrapped her arm around Martin's waist and led him toward the stairs of their apartment building.

Usually one to forgo any assistance, Martin draped an arm across her shoulder. Surprisingly, he was also unaware of Paul's presence, though for completely different reasons. Part of Martin's lack of awareness could be attributed to all the trauma he had experienced in the last few hours. But the biggest reason for Martin's decline in observational prowess was due to the fact that he was practically deaf from all the close-range shooting.

I, on the other hand, was all too aware of my surroundings. *Okaaaaaay,* I thought after Paul decapitated Tony as happily as someone else might dislodge a champagne cork. I didn't mind being a fly on the wall with Martin and Rose, but I was definitely not in the mood for an encounter with Paul. I put my hands in my pockets and eased down the street as quietly as I could, trying to stay in the shadows until I was cleanly out of sight. As I reached the deli on the corner of Avenue B, I finally dared to sneak a peek over my shoulder...and ducked inside.

Paul was running down the street. And man, that sucker was fast.

Hitting the Brakes

"He's been shot," Paul said to no one, watching Martin struggle to climb the stairs.

Michael thought the comment was intended for him. He was formulating some lame response like, "How can you tell?" when he realized Paul was already gone, zooming ahead in that silent "Ghost Riders in the Sky" gallop. He tried to catch up.

When Paul's voice cut through the muffled numbness in Martin's ears, it sounded more like a songbird than a full throttled yell. "Hey!!!" the voice peeped. Martin turned to see where the "Hey!!!" was coming from. He was only mildly surprised to see it was Paul. What was he doing here? "Following you home," said a little voice on Martin's shoulder. It sounded a lot clearer than Paul's bellowing yell had. "Yeah," he agreed, "but why?"

Who cares? Martin thought, grumbling that he could have used his uninvited company about six minutes earlier. Right now he didn't care much about what Paul wanted. His primary objective was stuffing some gauze into the ragged wound in his back.

Quickly approaching, Paul assessed Martin's injuries ("He'll live," he concluded at fifteen yards and closing). He would have continued at his same hurtling pace nonetheless, were it not for the glare Rose gave him. A glare that asked: "Who the *fuck* are you?"

Paul froze in place, no small feat considering the speed he was traveling, and stared at the young woman, her face gleaming with metal.

Rose was expecting a similar unspoken retort, communicating something like, "No, who the fuck are *you?*" What she never would have expected was the look of recognition she received, followed by a bemused, contemptuous sneer Paul voiced out loud. "Hhmph!"

She wasn't sure how to react. Did this guy know her from someplace? No way. She would have remembered a face like that.

Martin reacted to Paul's look much differently. He couldn't see the recognition in his eyes. Just the hate. Martin had seen that look so many times it wouldn't have registered as even a blip on his radar screen were it not for the fact that he was directing it at Rose.

Unlike Martin, who knew all too well who they were dealing with, Rose was determined not to let the sneer go unanswered, and kept her fuck-you expression locked in place for a few more beats until Michael finally caught up to them. Bean held on to the railing, trying to catch his breath, much to the further disgust of Martin and the added confusion of Rose, who replicated her "who the fuck are you?" look to no avail, because Michael had his head lowered, sucking in lungfuls of air. After a few more anxious seconds, all three of them opened their mouths to speak, but Paul cut them off at the pass.

"Well then, Martin," Paul sighed, completely disregarding everyone else. "Would you be needing a hand with that exit wound?"

TURNING POINT

Martin thought about it. The bigger wound was in his back, not the best place for self-administered care. Paul certainly had his bad points—in fact, almost all his points were bad—but when it came to emergency medical care, no one was more qualified, except perhaps the head of triage at Mt. Sinai. On the other hand, did he want Paul coming inside his home? With that punk? With Rose? With the look he was giving her? Did he want Paul in his life at all anymore? Given his recent experience with the nail and the knife and the kid, he would have to say no. Absolutely not. And yet…

When he saw Paul in the park it felt like an old wound had opened, or maybe his heart. It was hard to tell, they felt so much the same. Pathetic as it was, Paul was the only person besides Norine who ever told him he was special, who thought he mattered at all. Paul taught him how to survive. Protected him. Maybe even loved him. For all those years. When Martin finally left, it was Paul's idea, not his.

They were huddled under an interstate highway overpass where they had taken refuge from a thunderstorm. It rained for hours as they sat shoulder to shoulder in the shelf-like alcove directly below the heavy, green steel beams supporting the crossroad. Their pickup truck had broken down shortly after they stashed their loot from Firth. It began raining almost immediately after the engine seized up, which Paul, of course, interpreted as another omen. An omen about the two of them.

"Talk to me, boy," Paul goaded him after many minutes passed in silence. "I know what's eatin' you."

"I keep thinking about that girl," Martin said softly, unable to erase the image of Firth's daughter from his mind. "Why did you do it?"

"I've told you that before, Martin, and I'm getting tired of repeating myself," Paul said after a heavy sigh. "It goes in one ear and out the other."

"I know what you told me," he replied. "I just don't like what you did."

"I'm quite aware you didn't *like* it. Your complaint was duly noted the first time."

Martin hugged his knees tighter to his sinewy teenage chest, bracing himself against the chill and Paul's icy reply. His next words were much more harsh.

"I think the time has come to dissolve our partnership," Paul said, voicing the words Martin so often ached to say, but still couldn't. "When your heart's not in your work…well, that's when accidents happen…and neither of us wants that."

Martin trembled. Paul was telling him to go? "But you promised to take me to the…"

"All da little birdies have to leave da nest," Paul interrupted. His Irish lilt was still trying to twinkle, but a sadness Martin had never heard in his voice burdened the words that followed. "Even so, a promise is a promise —that's one thing you can always count on from me. We'll meet again another day and take that final journey. But for now, you'll have to make your own bed…and lie in it."

Martin wanted to cry, but he couldn't. He didn't want to leave, but he knew he had to. Paul made it easier. Not the way Martin would have guessed, with a cruel shove into the pouring rain, maybe followed by a gun blast or two if he kept moping, but instead with a warm arm draped across his shoulder. He kept his arm there in silence as the rain dripped and splattered all around them. Martin made no move to discourage him. They sat there together for the better part of an hour, saying nothing. Martin's mind was empty, not in itself an unusual thing, but given the tightness in his chest, he was surprised there weren't at least a few words in his head to accompany it.

When the rain finally stopped, Paul spoke again, pulling his arm back, letting him know it was time. "If you find yourself in the mood to see me, you'll never have far to look," he said gently. "And don't ever forget how special you are."

Martin stared at him blankly, then picked up his backpack,

shouldering the strap over his worn-out denim jacket. The sack bulged with one change of clothes and four-dozen Greyhound locker keys where they had stashed his share of the precious treasure. He rose in a stoop to avoid knocking his head into one of the beams and looked at Paul again. He tried to think of something to say, but nothing came to mind. Paul nodded slowly, for once at a loss for words himself.

Martin didn't look back as he cleared the underpass and straightened up. He didn't look back as he ambled down the grassy slope to the highway below, searching the horizon for oncoming headlights. There were none. He adjusted his backpack and slowly plodded down the road, glancing behind every ten seconds or so to see if a car was coming. He was almost a quarter mile away when he finally thought of something to say, but when he looked up at the underpass, no one was there.

Martin finally let the tears fall. He allowed himself ten full seconds before he turned the switch and snuffled up the snot with his coat sleeve. "G'bye Daddy," he said to the wind.

In the many years since their farewell, Paul popped up from time to time, usually when Martin was thinking about him, seeking guidance, like today. Now here he was again with his hand stretched out, ready and willing to help.

But things have changed, haven't they? he thought, looking at Rose supporting his arm. *And other things haven't,* he realized, feeling the blood flow from his gunshot wounds into his pants. Looking from Rose to Paul, he was more inclined to say no than yes. Then he lifted his shirt to check his back. The blood was coming out fast. Too fast.

"Okay...c'mon up," Martin finally said, his knees ready to buckle.

When he started up the stairs again and saw the way Paul was staring at Rose, his bones ached even more with dread.

SIDETRACKED

I watched Paul trudge up the stoop behind Martin and Rose. Michael trailed behind him with his head bowed and his hands stuffed in his pockets.

Paul never even looked in my direction. Oh well. I let out a blended sigh of relief and disappointment. All he cares about is Martin. Martin. Martin. Martin.

I parted the plastic curtain of the deli's outdoor flower section and strolled back onto the sidewalk, walking at a leisurely pace, wondering what Paul was going to do next, when a hand gripped my arm as tightly as a tourniquet, yanking me down the block as easily as a toy poodle on a choke-chain leash.

When I saw who it was I felt relieved and terrified in nearly equal measure. Relieved that it wasn't Paul. Terrified because I was being pulled along helplessly by the long, bony fingers of The Striker.

Referral

Before I showed Rose my suitcase, as our work together was drawing to an end, I could detect a sadness in her voice that seemed to be about more than the loss of income.

"I'm gonna miss you, William, but there's nothing more I can do," she said with a sweet smile as she finished the final inscription running across my waist like a belt. "For the rest, you'll have to go to The Striker."

I didn't know what I loved more, hearing her say that she would miss me, or hearing her use my name. When I opened my mouth to speak, I didn't make any reference to either observation. At least I'm not that clueless.

"Why do they call him The Striker?" I asked instead, suddenly feeling shy and tongue-tied again. In other words, normal.

"You'll see," she said with an odd grin, wiping the last of my blood away and hanging up the tattoo gun.

Yes, I saw. It was The Striker who set the final gears in motion. After that, all the other pieces fell smoothly into place. Paul, Martin, Rose…and Norine, of course. I've debated it for a while, but now my course seems unavoidable. I'll have to show you the journals.

Just do me a favor, please. Don't tell a soul!

Journal Entry: The Striker

The Striker. With a name like that I was prepared for anything. Anything, except for what happened. When I called to make an appointment, I heard someone pick up the phone and then…nothing. No voice, no hello, just dead air. I waited for a second in the silence and then, feeling incredibly uncomfortable, I spoke first. "Hello?"

Nothing. "Hello?" I tried again. I could hear someone breathing. I was about to hang up, when I felt a prickly urge to say what I would have said if he had bothered to answer.

"I'm William. I'm looking for The Striker. Rose sent me. Is this the right number?"

"Yessssss," his voice slithered into my ear. It was so creepy I wanted to hang up right away, but I hadn't come this far for nothing.

"I'd like to make an appointment," I said, half-hoping he'd say no.

"Did she give you my address?" His voice was so deep, it reminded me of Lurch in *The Addams Family*. When I told him she had, he said, "Come over now."

"Now?" I asked, totally thrown off.

There was no one on the other end to hear me.

The Striker's "office" was a boarded-up storefront on Third between C and D. It was filled with junk and he threw some porno mags off a rickety chair to make room for me to sit.

Again, he didn't say anything. In the silence I heard a skittering sound coming from inside the plywood walls. "What's that?"

"Rats," he said, sitting on a wooden three-legged stool that was full of nail holes.

I was glad he sat down. He was slightly less intimidating. Not only did this guy sound like Lurch, he looked like him too. He was really tall. His head was huge and out of proportion to the rest of his bone-thin body.

His skin was waxy looking, pale with a hint of yellow, like parchment. His head was long and rectangular until it reached the top where his ridiculously high forehead became more domelike. Blue veins snaked up the side of his skull, which was a more apt description than head. He had long, white hair with a three-inch lock of jet-black hair dangling over the side. It looked like a cross between Cruella DeVille and Riff Raff from the *Rocky Horror Picture Show*.

He sat down and adjusted his loincloth. His *loincloth*. He answered the door naked, except for the brown leather rag, which was obviously handmade, but so old and worn maybe the hands were Geronimo's. He didn't have many tattoos. The few he had were simple black patterns around his skinny arms. I wondered whether he was a junkie, because the veins on his arms looked so thick and inviting. I couldn't see any needle marks, though his body was covered with piercings. His nipples, his chest... his throat. Not that many in his face. Except the nails driven into his temples. Yes, the nails.

"I talked to Rose," he said in that Frankenstein-deep voice, yanking my bulging eyes away from the nails. "Why don't you show me the work she did?"

I wanted to correct him and say, "the work *we* did," but I just took off my shirt. He was impressed. He didn't say much, but I could tell. Impressing a guy like this made me feel pretty special. He didn't just give it the quick once-over. He looked. He studied it. "Nice work," he said finally, nodding with half-closed eyelids. It sounded extra flattering in that deep, deep voice of his. "What do you need me for?"

"Implants," I said.

"Rose does implants," he said dismissively.

"Not the kind I want."

He asked for details and I gave them. He nodded as I spoke, When I finished he said, "It'll take a few weeks."

"How much?" I asked.

"Five thousand. In advance." I was expecting more, though not in advance. Could I trust a guy with a loincloth to deliver the goods after he'd been paid?

"That's a lot of money. How about half and half?" I asked, wincing.

"I don't negotiate," he said, standing up, knowing the effect it would have.

"Okay," I said, looking up. Unfortunately, given his height and the angle of my chair I was looking up under his loincloth. Holy shit. I wanted to rub my eyes to make sure I wasn't hallucinating. He noticed my eyes popping and laughed. It sounded like Hell's Bells.

I blushed and leaned back farther so I was looking into his face and attempted a nonchalant segue: "When can we start?"

"When you give me the money," he said, letting me off the hook. He walked over to a dingy refrigerator, picked a wooden box off the top and carried it back to the stool.

He sat down again, but not before I noticed an odd little lamp on the table next to the fridge. The lamp wasn't really that odd, in truth. The lampshade was. I recognized it.

"Is that a Gein?"

"Yes," he said, nodding with the first real enthusiasm I'd seen.

"I have one too." I said, watching his eyelids rise to the point where you could rightfully call them open. "I was thinking about selling it to pay for this work."

I was taking a pretty big risk telling him. I didn't want it getting back to Rose, or anyone else for that matter. I probably wanted to show off a bit and increase my bad-boy status. My biggest motivation though, was working out a barter arrangement.

"Perhaps the man who gave me this would be interested. He's a real... collector."

"What's his name? I might know him." He looked at me suspiciously. I could tell he was about to close the subject so I blurted out, "There's a guy I sell things to that I met on the web. I mail things to a post office box and he mails me the cash."

The Striker kept listening...and watching.

"I've never met him but his cyber name is King of Spades."

The Striker's eyelids rose again, more slowly this time. "Yes, that's the same gentleman. You know, I think you two should meet."

"Why?" I asked, my turn to be suspicious.

"Well…" he began, his voice coolly condescending, "…you obviously share common interests. Aside from that, I think he'd enjoy what you've done here," he said, pointing to my chest.

"Really?" That got my attention.

"I'll see if he's interested," he said, like he was suddenly bored. "Now let's get back to your request." He reached down and opened the lid of his box. "Were you thinking about something like this?" he asked, the light flashing off the metal inside.

Wow. "They're beautiful. I'll see if he wants the lamp."

"Don't bother. Just bring it back here."

"It's worth a lot more than five," I said, nervous again.

"I know. I'll keep it here as collateral until I can arrange a meeting."

"Okay," I said uncertainly, but my heart was soaring. We were ready to start! Then I remembered the question I promised myself to ask from the moment Rose first mentioned his name.

"Why do they call you The Striker?"

His eyelids drooped even lower. Then he spread his legs wide apart, so the fringe of his loincloth draped over the edge of his stool like a theater curtain. "Well I'm a blockhead, for one thing," he said, taking a four-second pause to see if I got it. He could tell I didn't, so he picked up a four-inch-long carpenter's nail from a junk-filled toolbox on the floor. Then he picked up a hammer. He took the nail, pushed the point into his nostril and began pounding away.

"See?" he said, after driving the nail three inches into his face.

"Yep," I grunted, trying to catch my breath.

"I do private performances on occasion. There's even audience participation."

He pulled the loincloth over his thigh and gave me an unvarnished look at what I thought I'd seen before, but didn't think possible. Now I knew where all the holes in the stool came from.

"Go ahead," he said, yanking the nail from his face with the claw of the hammer. He handed them both to me and pointed back down between his legs. "That's a good spot."

Up the Stairs

Clump, clump, clump. Rose was having a hard time. Not only was Martin getting heavier with each step, but her thoughts weighed on her even more as she struggled to make sense of everything that had happened in the last fifteen minutes. She had been in a *gunfight*. Martin had been *shot*. He killed *four people*. She *helped* him. And now they were going up the stairs… not going to the cops…not going to the hospital…going up the stairs…so Martin could get some medical attention for that *exit wound* from this wide-eyed maniac and his scraggly sidekick. What was she *thinking?*

She was weird. No doubt about it. She looked weird, dressed weird, had a weird job, weird friends and a weird sex life. But this other guy was W-E-I-R-D. For one thing, he stank. She didn't know which was worse, the smell of evaporating whiskey wafting off his skin or the moldy perspiration clinging beneath. The way he looked at her was even stranger. Did he know her from somewhere? Did he want to fuck her? Kill her? Both? And what was the deal with him and Martin?

As she struggled to support his increasingly sagging weight, it occurred to her that she didn't know anything more about Martin than she did about his two creepy friends lagging behind, neither one lifting a finger to help or saying a single word to break the uneasy silence. Nothing about Martin made any sense. He was a walking (not talking) contradiction. He was older, late-thirties at least, though his body looked like a Calvin Klein underwear ad. He fought those punks like Bruce Lee, yet acted like a sullen teenager. What did she really know about him? He could fix a sink. He liked soft sheets. He fucked like a starved animal. And he was deadly. Deadly and *experienced*. Anyone capable of killing two armed men with such relative ease must have done something similar at least once before.

Fuck. Martin was a killer, like her father. Was he crazy too?

She thought of her dad again, remembering how people stared at her, whispering when she kissed him one last time before they took him away.

She pictured the screaming headlines and his raving letters…the ones she couldn't bear to open anymore.

Clump. Clump. Clump. Shit. Shit. Shit. She'd been with plenty of bad boys. Now that she had one more flight of stairs to think about it, she wondered if her outlaw fetish had more to do with her father than she could comfortably admit. Bad dad. Bad boys. Bad men, actually. Almost all her boyfriends were quite a bit older and marginally criminal types. Drug dealers. Tattoo freaks. Rockers. Anything that looked good in leather. But the daddy parallel didn't hold up so well when it came to her unfathomable feelings for this strange, childlike lug she was lugging up the stairs…and it didn't give her a clue what to do about the completely insane situation she was embroiled in. Should she make some excuse and run down the stairs as fast as she could? Martin's fucked-up friends would help him, right? She glanced at the smelly guy behind her and quickly looked away when she saw his angry stare. Then she looked at Martin and felt so protective she cursed herself again for being so foolish. She couldn't leave him. Not now. Not with them. He needed her.

Maybe she was letting her imagination run away with her again. Martin wasn't some cold-blooded murderer! He was acting in self-defense! So was she! He was probably an ex-soldier…maybe a marine with that buzz-cut. His big, stinky friend looked like a grizzled 'Nam vet…and the young one was wearing an army coat too.

Rose relaxed her shoulders and tightened her grip on Martin's arm. Then she thought about the way Martin handled himself with those drug dealers again. Even though some of her old beaus seemed very tough indeed, she couldn't imagine any of them doing what Martin had done. At least not with that kind of…flair.

He's like James Bond or something, she thought, recalling how he used that punk's body as a shield while she clawed at the other guy's eyes with her nail file.

I did pretty good myself, she thought with a swell of pride. Then she realized the total insanity of her glorified recollection. *Jesus! What's happening to me?* She searched for an answer but the echoing sound of boot steps on the staircase was all she heard in reply.

When they finally reached the landing, Rose assumed they would be continuing up the next flight of stairs to her own apartment. She began to steer Martin in that direction when he shook his head and nudged his chin toward his own door instead.

Paul wasn't missing a thing, dissecting every nuance of their silent communication like a behavioral psychologist. *She lives upstairs. He's been there before. She hasn't been inside his apartment. Doesn't know what to expect. Interesting. Very interesting.*

Martin saw Paul's gears turning and lowered his head ruefully, wondering how much worse things would get now that Paul knew where she lived.

Michael crept up the stairs behind everyone else, not sure what he was supposed to be doing, trying not to think about it. Looking at Rose made it easier. His eyes were riveted to her tiny ass. As they climbed higher, he deliberately backed off a few more steps so he could sneak a peek up her tight black vinyl skirt. *No undies! Whoa! Check out those piercings!*

He started counting the rings as he followed them up the stairs. One... two...three...

He banged his fist on the railing as they reached the landing and turned the corner.

Martin dug his good hand into his pocket, pulling out the thick ring of keys for his myriad combination of locks. He looked over his shoulder to gauge what Paul was thinking. He returned his glance with a sweaty grin and a leer at the back of Rose's head.

Before he unbolted half the locks, Martin wished he were turning the key in the exact opposite direction. From the other side of the door.

Humpty Dumpty

Rose helped Martin lie down across the clean Formica kitchen table (with the two spare leaves added to give it three extra feet of length). She gingerly removed his shirt and had to cover her mouth to keep the horrified gasp inside. A thick chunk of flesh had been blown out, leaving a large piece of gore flimsily attached to a flap of skin. Blood was leaking out profusely.

Paul wasn't fazed in the least. Martin let out a sigh of relief as he gauged Paul's reaction. Maybe it wasn't such a bad idea having him here after all.

"Where's yer kit?" Paul asked gruffly.

"Under the sink," Martin grunted. "Blood's in the fridge."

Rose's mouth gaped in a "What the fuck?" pantomime.

Paul reached under the sink and pulled out a generic plastic toolbox. Inside was a full array of gauze, scalpels, needles, sutures, field dressings, antibiotics…everything he'd been taught by Paul to keep on hand for any emergency, like self-surgery. There were even four ampoules of morphine should a rare circumstance arise where the only way to keep a steady hand during the procedure was to take the edge off the pain.

Paul scoffed at the sight of it. "You won't be needing this crap, will you, Martin?"

Even though Martin would have vastly preferred a quick shot in the ass, and would have done so himself if he'd been left to his own devices, he knew what the correct response was if he wanted to get the best care possible. "No."

"Glad to hear it." Paul nodded.

"Wait a second!" Rose piped up. "He's in pain!" They were the first words she'd spoken in five minutes. She'd been trying to keep her mouth shut about these guys out of consideration for Martin, assuming that they must be his friends. But what kind of friend doesn't let you take painkillers when you have a bullet hole through your torso?

"Just so's ya know, little girl…Martin knows a lot more about pain than you ever will, even with all those nasty little pins stickin' every which way out of your painted hide!"

Paul breathed hard and leaned over her like the Ghost of Christmas Future, daring her to say anything. She didn't. Satisfied, Paul let out another "Hhmph!" and got back to work. He opened the fridge, took out a pint of whole blood and started slapping Martin's veins below his bicep. Martin remained silent, knowing he needed every ounce of strength for the ordeal to follow. Talking wasn't an option. Neither was screaming, even when Paul jammed the IV tube into a vein with enough force to drive a pencil through a two-by-four.

Paul closed the bullet entry wound with only three stitches. He did it with such quick facility that Martin barely let out a gasp as the needle and thread pulled his skin tautly together. When Paul bit off the excess suture, even Rose remained quiet, much to Martin's added relief, watching the big man's dexterous movements in awe. Being somewhat of a self-taught surgeon herself, she couldn't help feel a kindred admiration when she witnessed someone with such obvious mastery. She also felt a tingle of longing as she saw the curved needle dip into Martin's flesh again and again. As much as she wanted to cling to her protective feelings, it was hard for a pain junkie like herself to get too upset by what Paul was doing. Especially when it started looking good to her.

Martin, like herself, was indeed no stranger to pain, just as Paul had said. He breathed the same way she did when she was pierced (also without anesthesia, of course). She could feel the way he moved into the pain, not away from it. She could also see that he was even better at it than she was. That made her feel a little jealous, but she felt closer to him too.

See, we do have something in common, she thought, adding another lame rationalization to her quickly lengthening list.

Michael was craning his neck to watch the operation with equal enthusiasm. "Cool," he said with a grin, as Paul tugged at the final suture.

Rose looked at Bean oddly for a moment, then noticed how many piercings he had in his face. *Birds of a feather.*

Paul watched the two of them and felt his desire surge even more than it had on the stoop. *I love this new generation.*

"Okay, Martin, let's flip over," he said. Rose and Michael let out involuntary gasps as the flap of skin attached to Martin's wound didn't quite make the turn with him.

"It's liable to get a bit noisy now," Paul declared. "Michael, turn on the TV set. Loud."

Bean zoomed over to the television, turned it on and cranked it up. He zoomed back just as quickly, not wanting to miss a second of this.

Rose was still prepared to make a fuss if Martin wasn't able to cope without medication. At the same time, she found herself wondering how much pain he could take. She also found herself getting aroused, which elicited a wave of shame she hadn't felt since her days at the Catholic school her foster parents made her attend. She stuffed it down quickly and readied herself for the second act.

Paul put on a pair of surgical gloves rather dramatically and poured half a bottle of hydrogen peroxide into the still bleeding wound. He followed with a thick index finger, making sure he worked the fluid into all the nooks and crannies. When the peroxide poured in, Martin felt like his eyeballs were turning inside out. When the finger followed, he almost passed out. But he didn't scream, did he? Martin knew the less he screamed, the less chance there would be for Rose to say something fatally foolish to Paul in his defense.

Rose and Michael's mouths hung open in disbelief when Martin clenched his teeth without uttering a sound. Paul nodded with respect and admiration right along with them. Michael was so impressed he couldn't stop himself from adding some vocal commentary, "Whoa, dude! That is *badass!*"

Paul chuckled. Martin was not amused. For the next ten minutes Paul worked feverishly, suturing or cauterizing every severed blood vessel, one by one. Then he began knitting the flap of flesh back into place with semi-concentric rings of dissolving sutures from the inside out. Martin let out about five low growls, two gasps and one mild shout throughout the whole ordeal. It made his performance with the nail earlier look like a game of touch football. Rose was so turned on with a combination of bloodlust and pride in her man that it was all she could do to not finger herself as the final exterior stitches were anchored in place.

When Paul threw the bloody instruments into the sink, Bean actually applauded. Paul took a slight bow and a bigger swig of whiskey from his silver flask. In the awkward silence that followed, the television sounded deafening by contrast. Martin was so out of it he didn't notice. Paul moved uncomfortably close to Rose, then continued walking toward the TV.

The newscaster said that name: "Captain Hook." Paul hadn't heard it in a long time. He listened to the reporter for as long as he could bear her nasal whine, then turned off the set. The police had found one of his recent dipsty dumpster deposits. On any other night he would have relished all the fuss, but none of that mattered anymore. Time was running out. Not because of the murder, or the perfunctory investigation that would follow. Paul didn't care about any of that. Time was running out because of Martin and the girl and the way they kept looking at each other. Yes, there was no doubt about it. He was losing him.

SPUNK

"So, Martin…how did you meet your little friend here?" Paul asked sweetly.

Martin's eyes narrowed at Paul's none-too-casual inquiry. He was too exhausted to make up a story, but he also didn't want Paul to spend another second contemplating the proximity of their apartments. "We met in the park," he said.

Rose didn't know why Martin was lying, but she was smart enough not to betray his instincts, good or bad. She backed up six feet from the table as Paul came closer.

"You met in the park…well, isn't that sweet," he drawled, smiling at Martin's clumsy lie. "I know how much you love the park, son. And when did this meeting take place?"

"This morning," Martin said, propping himself up on his elbows, hanging his feet over the edge of the table, preparing for what might happen next.

"So you had a nice little chat, did you?" Paul asked Rose, turning his sinister bulk toward her. "What subjects did you cover? Current affairs? The Mideast? *Family matters?*"

"We didn't talk much," Martin cut in, grunting as he sat up squarely.

"Uh-huh." Paul nodded, turning back to him. "Then I guess what puzzles me is why on earth this little darlin' would risk her neck to help you battle a gang of gun-toting junkies, when she only met you this morning and you barely said two words to each other."

"Because she likes me," Martin mumbled childishly, turning his face to the wall.

"Oh, my!" Paul laughed. "Is that the God's honest truth? Does she really *like* you?"

"Yeah, I like him a lot," Rose cut in, stepping forward with a swell of reckless courage fueled by a much more predictable surge of anger. She squeezed Martin's hand, much to his undisguised surprise and Paul's palpable loathing.

"Fair enough, fair enough, he's a likable lad, God knows," Paul chortled, pacing away, then circling back like a shark orbiting two bleeding dolphins. "But what about you, Martin? Frankly, I don't get it. Besides fucking, what on earth do you want with her?"

"Stop it!" Martin yelled, ripping out his IV and leaping off the table. He stood facing Paul in the small bright kitchen, naked from the waist up, muscles rippling, bandaged and bruised and ready. Ready for anything, except the look on Paul's face. It was a look he'd never seen. Shock. Absolute shock. And maybe fear? Martin took a step closer to test that theory, his fists clenched like rocks at his waist. Paul didn't move, didn't twitch, didn't blink. Whatever expression had been on his face was completely erased beneath the dead mask.

"I suggest you relax," Paul said softly. "You're no match for me on a good day."

"Leave him alone!" Rose cried, tugging on Paul's sleeve.

Martin quickly grabbed Rose by the shoulders, yanking her to the side and out of Paul's wheelhouse. But Paul's reaction to that maneuver was even more unexpected than the shock. He didn't swing at Rose, or spit out more invective. He stepped up and hugged him.

"I'm so sorry," Paul said, stroking the stubble on Martin's head. "So you two angels are in *love*, is that it? Maybe you could get married, eh? Make a wedding album with some news clippings from all our adventures."

Martin stiffened. Rose felt beads of sweat accumulate on her upper lip as she watched his silent reaction. Fuck. It was true. He was a criminal. Paul was his cohort, or worse, maybe an Irish mob boss, which seemed plausible from the way he was swinging his dick around. Fuck. Fuck. Fuck.

"And what about you, dearie?" Paul grinned, turning to Rose. "I'll wager Martin isn't the first ruffian that's plundered your grease-hole, but even if you've gang-banged the Hell's Angels clubhouse, you might be a teeny bit over your head with this one. I'm sure you noticed the practiced and quite heartless ease with which he dispatched that riff-raff below. Are a few more thrill-fucks with a cold-blooded killer really worth five to ten in a cramped metal cage with a 250-pound bull dyke sporting a shag carpet between her legs? As you may have read in the papers, murderers have a tendency to get caught and punished, and seeing how careless your hero has been tonight, it would be a far more sensible choice for you to find a good-sized rock to hide under, instead of hunkering down with your gun-slinging beau in this blood-splattered kitchen like Bonnie and Clyde, waiting for the sheriff and his posse to ram down the door."

Rose looked at Martin with absolute panic. She became even more wigged out by the cringing look of acknowledgment Martin returned, a look that stated more potently than the simple words could convey.

He's right.

Paul grinned with delight at their nervous expressions, relaxing his grip on Martin's shoulders, walking to the window, parting the curtain an inch, peering at the street below.

"Ahhhh…just as I predicted. Our little blue friends have arrived. I'm sure they'll be making the neighborhood rounds to see who made that big mess downstairs, so I sorely suggest you abandon your wounded paramour, go upstairs and lock yourself inside. I'm sure you'll be perfectly safe there, like all the other cowardly citizens who don't want to get involved after witnessing such a horrible crime."

Abandon him. Paul had chosen his words wisely. When Martin saw Rose glance reflexively at the door, then back at him, looking first at the escape hatch, he became instantly crestfallen. She was going to leave him.

"He's right. It's not safe. You shouldn't stay here with me," Martin said quickly, his voice croaky, hoping to cut his losses.

"No," she said resolutely, not sure where the resolve came from. Was she really prepared to throw her life away on another murdering crackpot like her dad? Did she really feel what she thought she felt every time she looked at him? Why wasn't she halfway up the stairs already? Had she been hypnotized? Brainwashed? Possessed?

I don't know. I don't care. I have to stay. I have to be with him, she decided, her heart vetoing the urge to throw a few more rationalization logs in the furnace. Instead, her brain synapses ignited like a brushfire, assessing a dozen possible outcomes of the police presence on the street, the possibility of eyewitnesses who may have observed the melee, the likelihood of anyone recognizing them on a street illuminated by only one feeble streetlight, and the even more remote possibility of anyone giving a shit. Who were those punks anyway? Drug dealers. What do drug dealers do? Shoot each other. End of story.

"They won't come up," she said quickly and confidently. "And if they do, we turn off the lights and don't open the door. Those guys were scumbags. The cops don't care. They don't want to do the paperwork. It's all a formality."

Paul stared hard at her. *Johnny really put his dick into it when he made this pistol,* he thought with begrudged admiration. *She's got balls like a bull and thinks fast on her feet.*

"I agree with your assessment," he said with a new formality and respectfulness that had Martin and Rose staring at him in something akin to wonder. "Just the same, I'd like a word alone with Martin to discuss other strategic options should your theory be flawed."

"It's not flawed and it's my idea, so we can all discuss it together," she said defiantly.

Martin saw the veins bulge on Paul's forehead and quickly intervened. "You can go back there for a few minutes," he said, steering her to an open door at the end of the hallway.

"I'm not going anywhere," Rose said, standing her ground on tippy-toes.

"It's okay. It won't take long," Martin said, grabbing her by the hand and pulling her closer to his side as Paul took a measured step toward her.

Rose squeezed Martin's hand a few seconds longer, then with a worried look at him and a suspicious scowl at Paul, she walked down the hallway, Michael slinking in tow.

Martin followed her with his eyes, seriously regretting his decision to let her come upstairs. He wanted to tell her to leave, to get the hell out of here right *now.* He wanted to tell her that it wasn't the police they needed to worry about, it was Paul. He wanted to warn her not to say another word to him. To even look at him. He wanted to, but he couldn't. Not with both of their lives at stake. Not with Paul listening.

Shit. She had no idea who she was dealing with. No idea at all.

Journal Entry: My Patron

Dear Diary, my life is officially over. Why bother saying more? Oh, right —because I'm an asshole. Too bad I didn't remind myself before I went back. Asshole! I'm not sure I'll be able to get all this down the way it happened, so I'd better have a stiff one first.

Okay. The Striker told me to come back as soon as I wanted, so I went back the next day. I brought the lamp. When I knocked at the door, I thought there was no one home. I waited and listened and thought I heard some people talking inside, but when he opened the door he was alone. Still wearing that stupid loincloth too. Jesus. I'd hate to be his drycleaner.

He smiled when he saw the lamp, then put it next to the other one and plugged it in. The sixty-watt bulb cast a warm glow through the skin of the lampshade—made from human skin. I always wondered if Eddie Gein came up with the idea on his own, or whether he was inspired by reading all those books about Nazi atrocities. When you think about the belt he made out of nipples or the shoebox filled with vaginas, it's hard to tell.

Anyway, The Striker looked pleased as hell, and let loose with another of those deep Lurch laughs. Then he led me into a back room where all the windows were painted black. A green, padded table filled up most of the room, and he threw open a big white sheet to cover it. I was surprised at how clean it was. He handed me a towel and told me to take off my shirt and lie on my back. Then he left the room. When he came back he had the wooden box and a fistful of shiny steel tools wrapped in another white sheet. He told me everything was sterile, and if I had any doubts he'd use the autoclave again while I watched. I don't know why, but I trusted him. He asked me if I wanted to do any dope beforehand; he said it was going to hurt like hell and he included it in the price.

I asked him if most of the people he worked on used it. He just laughed that laugh and shook his head, so I shook my head too.

Well, he was right. It hurt like hell, and then some. It still hurts now

179

while I'm writing. I have to say, though, I feel pretty proud of myself. The Striker talked the whole time, I guess to keep my mind off the pain, or maybe because he likes to talk. He's really smart and funny, which took me by surprise. I asked him if he made all his money doing this kind of stuff. He told me he spent a lot of his spare time writing. I asked him what he wrote about and he said, "Porno."

"Does it pay well?" I asked, not knowing what else to say, blushing with embarrassment, trying not to show it.

"It pays well for me," he said, giving me a frown and another extra hard *whack!* with the hammer. "I actually get more satisfaction from the fan mail."

"You get fan mail from porno?" I asked, as shocked as I was from the *whack!*

"Rabid fan mail. Not so unusual, I'm told, for the type of stories I write."

Whack! Clang! I bit down on the leather strap he gave me to keep from screaming. I had to breathe for a few minutes while he wiped up the blood before I could ask the dreaded follow-up question. "What kind of stories do you write?"

"Snuff," he said, as carefree as you please.

I could tell he was daring me. But I didn't know what the dare was. To be outraged? Terrified? Titillated? All of the above? I was more curious than anything, so, as befits my nature, I asked him the next question that came to mind. "Where do you sell your stories?"

"A very private website…and given your taste in furnishings, one you might enjoy." He said it as smoothly as a carnival barker, waiting for me to take the bait.

I wish I had shut my mouth right then, but like the asshole I so clearly am, I asked, "What makes it so unusual?"

"Talking about it would hardly do it justice," he said, putting his instruments down into the bloody tray. "It might be better if you had a little peek."

I assumed from the way he said it that he was finished with my implants for the day. As it turned it out, my implants were the only thing he was finished with. He sprayed me with antiseptic and put on a fresh pair of surgical gloves and rubbed generous dollops of antibiotic ointment around the base of the three implants he'd installed. He dressed the area with a thick layer of gauze bandages. Then I put on a clean white T-shirt that I'd brought along on his instructions and covered it with a second, extra-large one. He told me the blood would probably stop at the first shirt.

I walked with him to an adjoining room that looked like an office. There were two desks inside, facing opposite walls, both with large computer monitors. He sat me down at one desk while he stood over me. Even though the wounds were in my breastbone and ribcage, it hurt like hell when I sat down. He asked me if I wanted a drink. I nodded and before he left, he typed in a domain name so quickly I couldn't read it, then a user name and password at the same blinding speed.

He took his time coming back. I now know it was intentional. He wanted to give me plenty of time to fully absorb the experience. To make sure I got it. I didn't get it right away. Except the obvious part. It was a serial killer site. I'd seen a few before, with essays and photos of the famous killers. This one was different. The porn was one new twist. But it took a few more minutes before I realized just how different it was.

I browsed around, the terrible truth of it still eluding me. Then I heard The Striker's tinkling doorbell in the other room. It sounded like reindeer bells. I heard the door open and close. Hushed voices. Secret laughs. None of that activity interfered with my almost total immersion in the horror before me. The case histories. The pictures! There were at least three-dozen killers in the database, each one categorized more thoroughly than an FBI profile. Yet I didn't recognize any of the names.

That was the final giveaway. I'd been studying serial killers for years. I knew everyone in the field. Yet here were all these people I'd never even heard of. There was only one possible explanation. I didn't know who they were because they hadn't been caught.

I gawked and gaped, unable to fully comprehend it, and all too characteristically, unable to turn away. I tried to read the domain name, but the home page header was just a long list of indecipherable letters, numbers and symbols. It was accessible only through a link from God knows where, followed by a user name and password. For members only.

Why had he shown me? Because of my collection, I assumed. Yet that was so risky. Even though I couldn't tell the police the name of the site, I could tell them it was there. Did he really think I was into this shit? Did he think I was *one of them*?

I had to get out of there fast. I'd play dumb, pretend not to get it, make an appointment for a follow-up session and never show up. Then I realized there was something else I needed to check before he came back. I typed *Striker* into the site's search engine. His list of victims was three pages long. There were even pictures of him—in action. With those droopy eyelids. That loincloth. That hammer. There was a video clip too. He was leaning over a girl, his big iron mallet poised over his head, ready to "strike" again. I say again, because it was hideously clear that the mallet had come down…hard…at least twice before this clip started. I watched in horror as he finished driving two spikes into the screaming young girl's eye sockets.

I tried to stand up, but a big hand pushed me down. It wasn't The Striker's skeletal digits. These looked like they belonged on a catcher's mitt…and they didn't have fingernails. I looked into the face above me and felt something I still can't describe. It was fear, but worse. His eyes were bright and bluish-gray, his hair long and stringy. Blond or maybe white that had yellowed. I couldn't tell how old he was, but if I had to guess, I'd say he was in his sixties. His drooping mustache was dirty and tinged with red. He was dressed all in black, with a long black overcoat. The Striker leaned in the doorway behind him.

I thought I recognized him. That was the thing that frightened me the most. That, and the fact that he definitely recognized me. "Hello there, Billy," he said in a booming voice with an Irish accent. "Oh, yes, I should introduce myself, eh? You'd know me by the handle King of Spades, but you can call me Paul."

I tried to get up again but he held me down and plopped into the chair behind me.

"My dear friend here told me all about you. Not that I needed much new information. I've had a keen interest in you for some time now, Billy, very keen indeed. I'm a collector too. As you can see, I have quite a collection of my own."

"This is your site?" I asked skeptically. He looked like a Bowery bum.

"Why, don't I look like the dotcom type?" he asked, his laugh garbled with phlegm.

"No," I said bluntly. He didn't take offense.

"I can't take that much credit for it, if the truth be told. I merely provide the ways and means. The inspiration came from an entirely different source."

I said nothing but he read the question on my lips.

"Why from *you*, Billy, from you!" he shouted.

My mouth hung open like a drafty cave. Every word that followed etched itself into my memory: "I heard about your collection years ago, almost as soon as you started. I've got lots of friends, Billy. In fact, I made it easier for you to acquire some of your most prized trophies."

I still couldn't speak. I didn't have to. He was far from finished.

"I was so impressed with your dedication, your perseverance…the lengths you went to, the sheer obsessiveness…well, it got me to thinking. I said to meself: I'll bet there are a lot of other young, impressionable people out there, who, with the proper direction and guidance, might develop a similar interest. Juice 'em up with a little S&M, then make it more and more extreme, 'til nothing but a steady diet of snuff will do the trick. Then start charging subscription fees to weed out the less dedicated souls, and take it from there."

"Take it where? What are you trying to do?"

"Hhmph! That's the big question, now isn't it?" He stopped for a deep breath and a gulp from a silver whiskey flask. "This is what you might call a social experiment. Of all the worms you're gawking at, how many do you suppose ever touched a hair on anyone's head before they started watching this filth? Yes, some of them were born to it, or trained for the task at an early age, but so many others found their way here through their own perverted yearnings. Best of all, it was so easy! The longest it took to make one of these monsters straight from scratch was a year and twenty-one days!"

I was glad to be sitting down when he said that. My head was spinning so fast I almost grabbed it. This was unbelievable. He had to be making it up! Then it dawned on me...he *was* making it up! "You guys are cops," I said flatly. "You got me in here to bust me for my collection." I looked around for hidden cameras, shouting, "This is entrapment! I never broke any laws getting that stuff. I've never hurt anyone in my life!"

"We know that, lad," Paul continued, ignoring my other accusations, nudging The Striker in his bony ribs. "The only thing we can't figure out is why. Maybe you can sort out that mystery for us. It's a real brainteaser, that one."

They both laughed so hard I thought their heads might roll off. That's when I knew. They weren't cops. It was all real. I didn't know what to say or ask. Was I in a dream? How was this possible? Self-preservation topped the agenda. I needed a way out. "I gotta get some rest," I said, like I hadn't seen anything. "Do you still want to buy the lamp...or not?"

"I didn't come for the lamp, William," he replied, all life and expression drained from his face. "I came for you."

I almost shit in my boots. I didn't want to know what he meant, but I asked anyway. He answered with a question. "Do you remember the first time we met?"

I related how we met in the AOL "Dahmer" chat room and kept corresponding until the subject of the collection came up. We'd been e-mailing each other for weeks before I felt safe enough to sell him a .44 slug from Son of Sam.

"That wasn't the first time," he said cryptically. "If you can't recall, we'll have to explore that matter at a later date, and since you're so tired and achy, methinks you're wise to follow your own advice. So go home, and while you're napping, maybe you can think about what you've seen here tonight."

I nodded with too much enthusiasm. I thought he was letting me go. Fat chance. He grabbed my arm as soon as I stood. "But first, you need to have a peek at this."

He reached over and scrolled through the list of members until he came to…my name. When he clicked on it we were taken to my very own home page. There I was. Photographs. My face. My back. My chest. All the tattoos. There was a bio, outlining every aspect of my life. They even had pictures of my mother! How did they get all this stuff? I wanted to throw up and almost did. I felt such panic and dread my skin went clammy. But the worst part was still coming.

The Striker pointed his bony finger at another photo at the bottom of the screen. It was a beautiful young girl. Underneath was a caption. The caption was typically brief. It described how I murdered her.

"I've never killed anyone!"

"Yet," said Paul. "Look at the date."

The date of the murder was four months from now, next to the descriptions of how my victim was tortured and finally murdered.

"This is crazy!"

"Isn't it though?" The Striker whispered.

I felt like I was in an episode of *The Twilight Zone*. I looked at their laughing faces and tried to speak, but nothing came out.

"How do you like your nickname?" Paul asked.

Billy, The Kid. I didn't. I leapt from the chair. Paul grabbed my arm in a lockjaw grip and said, "If you ever breathe a word of what you've seen to anyone, anyone at all, those statistics will be exchanged with another one of our members in the database. You will be linked to their crimes and that information will be instantly forwarded to the police. The necessary trophies to corroborate the crimes will be added to your collection while you're under interrogation."

"Why are you doing this to me? What do you want?"

"The *why* I'll reveal in my own sweet time," he said, loosening his fingers. "The *what* is the only thing you need concern yourself with—as in *what* you'll do for me. This murder we've documented…you will make it real."

"Real?" I gasped, trying to think of something else to say, some chip to bargain with.

"*Real* real," Paul nodded, making a pantomime of a noose yanking on his neck.

He guided me toward the door with a soft shove on my rump. "Sweet dreams, Billy," he whispered. "We'll see you again…real soon."

I walked to the door, propelled by the shove, so numb my feet barely made it. As I passed through the door, to what should have been my freedom in the cool night air, I kept wishing and hoping and praying that there was another way out.

THE END OF THE HALL

Martin didn't feel all that comfortable with Rose and Michael going back there unsupervised, but he was grateful not to have her around now that Paul wanted to have an even more candid chat. He wasn't sure what the topic was going to be, but he was certain he didn't want Rose to hear it. As for Bean, he could always kill him later.

Rose walked down the corridor with Bean, looking back at Martin with nervous concern, and at Paul with bold contempt. When she reached the slightly open door, her guts swirled with butterflies. She looked back again. Paul was smiling, but the smile didn't look real. Martin was nodding with encouragement. Something didn't look right about that either.

She pushed the door open and felt a rush of curiosity and foreboding. What was on the other side? A drug laboratory? A hidden arsenal of weapons? A chamber of horrors? With this guy it could be anything. She braced herself as she took the final step…into a very white room.

Everything was white. The walls, the ceiling, the floor, the wooden chair sitting in the middle of the otherwise empty room. The lighting was bright as well, amplifying the effect. What was the effect? Rose tried to get a bead on how she was feeling, other than craving a pair of very dark sunglasses. It was clean. No, more than clean. Sterile. Like a hospital. Or a lunatic asylum. No. It felt safer, warmer. Lived in.

Michael was confused, plain and simple. In a million years, he never would have imagined that the guy out there would sit in a room like this. Everything was so clean and white it was almost invisible…the white chair on the white floor…the more you stared at it, the more it seemed to disappear. He walked over and sat in the chair. "Cool," he said.

"What?" Rose asked, trying to act like she had been in here at least once before. Michael simply stood up and offered her the chair, shaking his head and grinning.

Rose sat down. "Cool," she said. The effect was more than cool. It was completely disorienting. The chair faced a perfectly blank wall that pointed away from the door, so that even in your peripheral vision, all you could see were two more white walls on either side. Even more bizarrely, the corners of the room had been filled with some kind of material that softened the usual right angles into a smooth, seamless transition that made the walls blend in with each other and virtually disappear. The ceiling and floor junctures were treated the same way. When you sat and stared straight ahead, all you could see was white. No top, bottom or sides. Just white. It was like closing your eyes and seeing white instead of black.

I'm in a cloud, Rose thought. *I'm…in heaven.* At least the way heaven is often depicted in contemporary movies, with a big white background and dry ice fog on the floor. She was really impressed…and feeling impressed was really important after everything that had happened. *If there's heaven, there's hope,* she thought, shoring up her confidence.

"So, is this guy your boyfriend?" Michael asked, searching for something to break the silence, unable to stifle the jealousy in his voice.

"Yeah," Rose nodded, hesitantly. Why did she feel like she was lying?

"Nice tat," Michael sidetracked, admiring her inked bicep. "Where do you live?"

"Upstairs," she said, pointing to the ceiling. Was he hitting on her? Who was this kid, anyway? How did he know Martin? Then it finally dawned on her that she could ask him instead. "How do you know Martin?"

"Just met him," Bean admitted. "I guess he's known Paul a while."

"That's his name?" asked Rose.

Michael nodded with a wince. "Just so you know, that guy is totally…" Bean began, then cut himself off when he noticed a strange light pouring from an open door on the wall facing away from the chair. The light came from an open army footlocker in a closet.

Rose's heart practically burst with joy. *I knew it. He's a soldier. Maybe special forces or something.* She pictured Martin in the jungle with camouflage makeup. It was less of a stretch than imagining him sitting in that white chair.

Michael walked to the door. Rose pulled on his jacket, wanting to give him some shit for poking around without Martin here, but the strange glow pulled her like a magnet too. What the hell was it? They stepped inside. When Michael saw what was in the locker, his eyes bugged out like ping-pong balls. Rose had to cover her mouth to keep from shouting.

The locker was filled to the brim with gold.

CLOSET SPACE

When Rose stepped into the closet, she was almost as awestruck by the size of the space as she was by the rays of golden light streaming from the locker. But instead of wondering how Martin came to be in possession of enough gold to ransom a Mayan princess, she became totally preoccupied with trying to figure out why his closet was so much bigger than hers. If she had known anything about carpentry, she could have looked up at the ceiling and seen that a new wall had been created that ran the entire length of one side of the room.

Everyone in Manhattan complains about closet space. Not Martin. When he didn't have enough room to suit his needs he simply made some more. The added wall had the dual advantage of making his "sitting room" perfectly square (ah, symmetry!) while creating ninety-six square feet of extra space. He could fit a lot of stuff in there.

After her initial excitement wore off, Rose became more aware of all that other stuff. There was a clothes rack and a dresser and a small cot next to a tiny table and a lamp. There was a bookshelf above the pillow on the cot and a poster of a painting by Andrew Wyeth called *Christina's World* taped to the ceiling above it.

"Holy shit," she whispered upon realizing that this extremely big closet was actually an extremely small bedroom. "Is this how people who sleep in cardboard boxes feel?"

Then she saw the chair. It was at the foot of the cot facing the wall. It was a little kid's chair with an embroidered pillow and a ratty stuffed dog sitting on top of it. She picked up the pillow and was about to read it when she saw Michael kneel in front of the footlocker.

"Whoa!" he gasped reverently, drawn to the gold like a beaver to wood. It was all he saw and all he ever wanted to see. He dug both hands into the gleaming heap with all the fervor of…well…a drunken pirate. "Yarrrgh!" He didn't say it, but as he dug his hands in deeper and deeper (oh my God it goes all the way to the bottom!) he felt woozy with desire.

"Whoa!" he repeated. Rose set the pillow down without reading it and walked over. The light from the single bulb overhead made the gold sparkle like ocean waves at sunset. It was the most beautiful thing she'd ever seen.

So this is why you always see people throwing coins in the air when they find a treasure chest. It was exactly what she wanted to do and it almost hurt that she couldn't. She couldn't, of course, out of respect for Martin. That, plus a healthy dose of trepidation over what he would do if he saw them in his closet at all, never mind throwing his gold rapturously in the air.

Where did he get all this? Shit. He had stolen it, of course. He really was a criminal. A thief and a killer. *Or maybe a merc!* she thought, still trying to pull a plum out of the pie. Why she thought being a merc was more palatable than a thief or a hit man didn't occur to her; she was just happy to come up with any explanation for the footlocker that didn't imply that Martin was even more dangerous and demented than her father.

Strangely enough, some of Rose's speculations about Martin's career path were correct. He had been a soldier and later, a mercenary, if the assignments were challenging enough. He enlisted in the navy when he was just sixteen, only a few months after leaving Paul, signing up mainly to get as far away as he could from anywhere he had ever been before. He used one of his many fake identities (Dan White was still his favorite) to fool the recruiters, not that they cared much anyway. His drill instructor was so impressed with his already finely-honed combat skills that he was immediately trained as a SEAL.

Martin enjoyed it immensely. He liked swimming underwater in that cool, dark, silent world. He liked blowing things up. He liked it so much that he resigned after his first tour of duty, just so he could enlist in the Army and train as a Green Beret. He enlisted everywhere except NASA… which he still harbored regrets about. The military life was a hard life, but compared to those years with Paul, it was like a trip to Disney World. And along with the rigorous lifestyle, there was a regimental predictability he found extremely comforting. But after a while, he got tired of taking orders from men he respected even less than Paul, so he packed away his uniforms and became a mercenary, only to discover that he hated taking orders from petty despots and contract soldiers even more than his previous commanders.

He bummed around for a while before settling into his current abode. Then one rainy afternoon, while he was leafing through *Soldier of Fortune*, an ad for bounty hunters caught his eye. It sounded perfect. It was, for the first three years. He was his own boss and could pick his own assignments. Nobody to report to. Even better, no one to talk to. He preferred hunting sex offenders, pedophiles in particular. He liked catching them...*dead or alive*, as the saying goes.

However, none of those previous professions in any way accounted for the vast amount of gold Michael and Rose were staring at so intently. Michael had a much more informed deduction about the treasure's origin, not that it mattered to him right now. He only knew one thing. He wanted it. He wanted it bad. His mind went into overdrive trying to figure out how he could possibly wrangle it away from someone as incredibly lethal as Martin.

But he was injured now, wasn't he? Fuckin' A right he was! He sure as shit wasn't at the top of his game now! Maybe Paul would be interested in knowing more about this situation. Maybe he would help him. Maybe they could be partners!

The instant he thought about teaming up with Paul, his euphoria evaporated. Paul didn't seem like the kind of guy you could talk to about partnerships. Definitely not equal partnerships. On the other hand, a finder's fee wouldn't be out of the question, would it?

Shit. He had to have that gold. He had to!

CLEARING THE AIR

Back in the kitchen, Paul was edging uncomfortably close to Martin.

"I'm guessing it's been a while since you had your pipes cleaned, and I can't fault you for feeling some loyalty to this feisty wench for helping you out of that scrape downstairs. But now that you've put the plumbing in, what other good can come from this sordid little tryst? Do you really think you're doing her a favor bringing her into this cramped little lockbox you call a life? If she ever finds out who you really are and what you've done, d'ya reckon she'll keep hangin' around? Trust me, even if you're riding her tall in the saddle, you're certainly no one's idea of Prince Charming. She'll leave you high and dry just like she thought of doing a few minutes back. You saw her looking at the door. You can't trust her. A girl like her is no different from slow-acting poison. You might as well gargle with Drano and spare yourself the wait. So now it's time for you to put all those warm, fuzzy feelings back inside your zipper and wave this bitch a sad farewell!"

"No!" Martin yelled, standing toe to toe with Paul again. "I won't!"

Paul shoved Martin's gasping chest so hard he knocked him back on the table.

"You don't understand me, boy!" he yelled fiercely. "That girl is not for you!"

"What do you mean, she's not for me?" Martin shouted with equal passion, trying to get up from the table while Paul pinned him down by the shoulders.

"She's only going to hurt you more in the end," Paul lied, pressing down harder.

"No!" Martin shouted, not knowing what else to say, or even what he was feeling.

Paul bit his lip, trying not to laugh. But as he felt the depth of loneliness and despair howling from every pore of Martin's being, as he saw the tiny whirlpool rising in the whites of his eyes, he experienced a surge of emotion he didn't think he was still capable of feeling.

"It's…okay," he said haltingly, easing his pressing hands. "It was wrong of me to interfere. This is your life and you're entitled to the pleasures you can take from it. I'll leave you two alone now…and you can sort all this out for yourself."

Martin eyed Paul suspiciously. When he saw the sadness in his face, he felt a glimmer of hope. "Do you mean it?" he asked, his eyes probing for any trace of deceit.

"Yes," Paul answered, shocked to feel a lump in his throat.

Martin slowly rose from the table and gave Paul a hug so strong it hurt his gun wound. Paul hugged him back even harder. They backed up a foot and looked into each other's eyes. Then Paul squeezed the back of his neck between his massive thumb and forefinger and Martin fell to the floor like a tipped cow.

Pow! The sound of the thud reverberated through the walls and floor. Paul knelt over Martin's body and made sure no serious damage was done. When he was certain he was simply unconscious and would remain so for approximately eight more minutes, Paul straightened up and shook his head sadly.

"Martin…will you ever learn?"

A King's Ransom

Rose didn't hear the thud as much as she felt it. Martin had soundproofed the closet, so it was difficult to hear anything above the din of golden nuggets cascading into the locker through Bean's greedy fingers. She hadn't heard the yelling. But the thud? That she felt.

Michael felt it too. He was terrified. They looked at each other and the door leading back to the kitchen. Neither wanted to move. They watched silently, ears pricked up like hound dogs', waiting for the aftershock. When none came, Michael relaxed a little.

Rose was too worried to relax. Martin was out there, alone, with *him*. She wanted to hide, but she couldn't. She had to see if he was okay. So she stood up and walked into the big white room. It was so quiet now. So quiet. Rose took a tiny step toward the door with her tiny left foot, then stopped, wishing she had more courage. She took another step anyway.

I wanted to cheer her on. Tell her how brave she was. Tell her that courage didn't mean you weren't afraid, it meant taking those tiny little steps despite your fears! I thought about giving her a bigger, longer pep talk, but it really wasn't necessary. Before she took another halting step, Paul opened the door.

"Dearie, could you give us a hand?" he asked sweetly. "Martin had himself a little faint and bumped his noggin."

Rose ran past Paul down the hallway so fast she left skid marks on the white floor. Martin was lying a few feet from the kitchen table, a puddle of drool beneath his open lips. "Oh, God!" she shouted, dropping to her knees, cradling his prickly head. "Baby…talk to me!"

"I'm afraid he isn't feeling too chatty," Paul said, leaning over her shoulder. "He's suffering from hypovolemic shock. What he needs now is a good long nap, so if you could give me a hand, let's get him into this nice cushy chair over here."

Paul didn't need any assistance relocating Martin, but he loved group participation. He turned Martin over on his back and hooked his hands under his armpits, asking Rose to help out with Martin's size-twelve feet. Michael entered the kitchen and was quickly recruited to grab another leg. After they eased him into his tan leather Barcalounger, Paul was about to wrap his thumb and forefinger around Rose's neck in thanks for a job well done when Michael began tugging his sleeve like an animated chipmunk. Paul reluctantly withdrew his grip. As Rose leaned down to pat Martin's pasty forehead, Michael whispered into Paul's ear as quietly as he could: "I have to show you something."

"Could you grab an ice pack from the fridge and cool down the dear boy's head?" Paul asked Rose. She glared at him, but Paul knew she wouldn't hesitate to fulfill his request. Rose was in full Florence Nightingale mode and as far as she could tell, Paul was as concerned about Martin's well-being as she was.

She went to the freezer and pulled out a plastic sleeve that was the perfect size for a forehead compress. Shit, was there anything Martin wasn't prepared for?

Actually, yes. He wasn't prepared for Paul's Vulcan nerve pinch and the ill effects it would have on Rose's health if Paul left the building with her in the remaining minutes he would be unconscious. The ice pack wasn't going to help matters either, since it would constrict the local blood vessels even more, thereby lengthening his stay in Neverland.

While Rose had her face in the freezer, Paul and Michael walked down the hallway and into the white room, closing the door behind them. "Hhmph! What do you think about that?" Paul snorted appreciatively. He sat in the white chair and gazed into the blinding vision of nothingness. He kept staring and had the biggest surprise of a very eventful day. The white wall disappeared and he was *seeing* into the hidden realm. *Oh, my! My, my, my! Now this is a room with a view. Looks like I underestimated you once again. It seems you have the gift after all!*

"No!" Michael whispered from the closet, frantically pointing at the locker. "Here!"

Paul was extremely annoyed at the interruption. When he saw the bullion and Michael's reaction, he was more amused than irritated. "Gold? You're all hot and sweaty over a box of *gold?*"

"Duh," Bean wanted to say, but instead he asked, "Isn't this the gold you took from Firth?"

Paul looked inside the box. "Some of it, I suppose. There was much more than this."

"More than this?" Bean asked in a whispered cry. "Are you kidding me?"

"Oh, no, I wouldn't kid about that. Firth had gobs and gobs of the stuff. *Be prepared* was his motto and like a good boy scout—or maybe Chicken Little—he stuffed as much in his mattress as he could for that long rainy day he knew was coming."

Paul paused to savor Michael's greed-widened eyes, before continuing in a whisper, "And as much gold as he had, Lord Firth was far from the only one, laddy. We paid visits to a number of these survivalists over the years, all with the same morbid doomsday preoccupation and a corresponding certainty in the revival of the gold standard. I can't see why, but Martin loves the stuff. Meself, I couldn't care less."

"How could you not care about *that?*" Michael gasped, pointing at the shiny nuggets.

"Shit, boy, you're as silly as he is for hoarding it. Let me tell you something about gold. It's dirty and it's heavy. If you like things that sparkle, consider diamonds instead. Much easier to travel with. And much, much easier to trade on the international market." Then he added with a wink, "But if it's gold that captures your fancy…I suggest you simply take it."

Michael's look of shame was instantly replaced with unvarnished admiration and an even more palpable greed. Paul stared back at him like a game show host pointing to door number three. "But what about them?" Bean asked anxiously.

Paul paused as if deep in thought. "Well, Martin will be coming around soon and I'm sure he wouldn't take kindly to you running off with his precious baubles, now would he?"

Michael shook his head. His knees were shaking too.

"Then I suppose you have no other choice but to kill him while he's napping."

"I couldn't do that!" Michael gasped.

Paul shook his head sadly. "I didn't think so. So put down the lid and let's see how the lad is convalescing."

"You…could do it," Michael suggested hesitantly.

"Oh, no," Paul said, shaking his head vigorously, "I couldn't possibly. Martin's a dear old friend of mine. Still, I'll agree it's the best chance you'll get and I wouldn't stand in the way of someone so ambitious. Yet, I'm afraid you'd be totally on your own with this venture."

Fuck! Bean clutched the Luger in the pocket of his army coat as he stared at the gold again. *Could he do it? Could he really kill him?* "But if I used this…" Michael mumbled desperately, pulling the gun out, "wouldn't that bring the cops up?"

Paul chuckled, breathing in the scent of Michael's rising corruption like a fragrant wine. "So use your hands…a kitchen knife," he said after a long, deep sigh. "Personally, I don't care if you use a candlestick in the ballroom with Professor Plum—all I know is that you better think fast. I can't imagine you'll stand much of a chance with Martin awake."

"What about the girl?" Michael asked, thinking as fast as he could.

Paul looked into Michael's hungry eyes. He knew there wasn't a chance in Hades that Bean could actually pull it off, but it wouldn't hurt to let him try, would it? It wouldn't hurt to give the lad some practice!

"I'll take care of the girl," he said flatly. "The rest is up to you."

EAVESDROPPER

When Rose heard the door close at the end of the hallway, she stopped halfway between the freezer and Martin, the ice pack numbing her fingers. Then she remembered the way Michael had been looking at the gold. *They're going to rob him!* She ran over to Martin's chair. "C'mon, you gotta wake up," she whispered, shaking him hard.

He was out like a log. She looked nervously down the hallway, wondering what they were up to back there. She tiptoed down the hallway and put her ear against the door. At first, she heard mumbling, then Paul's voice, "So use your hands...a kitchen knife..."

Rose gasped involuntarily, covering her mouth with one hand while she leaned against the wall for support. Her knees were buckling. She kept listening anyway. Her ear was pressed so tightly against the wood that she could have been standing on the other side.

She missed the part about Firth. But she heard the worst part, about Martin and...her.

"I'll take care of the girl. The rest is up to you."

She heard their approaching footsteps and ran as quickly and as silently as she could down the hallway. When she reached the kitchen, it looked like a fork in the road. To the right, Martin, still unconscious in his chair, like a football fan passed out from too much beer and pizza. To the left...the doorway. It was crazy to stay. They were going to kill her. Martin too. But when she saw him there, helpless as a sleeping child, she couldn't leave him. So she ran over to Martin and shook him so hard his belt buckle jangled. But dammit, he wouldn't wake up!

THE OMEN

BRRRRAAAAAANNNNGGGG! Michael was turning the doorknob when Martin's buzzer rang. It was incredibly loud, more like a car alarm than an intercom buzzer. Martin had rewired it. He heard buzzers going off in the apartments on all sides of them too, even above and below. *What the fuck was going on?*

Michael timidly stepped through the doorway. Paul gripped his shoulder and pushed him out of the way. He was holding an Uzi in the other hand. Bean fell to the floor. His legs snagged Paul's ankle, tripping him. By the time Paul disentangled himself and clomped down the kitchen hallway, the buzzers had stopped ringing. He turned into the living room and got a surprise more disconcerting than the buzzer concerto. Martin was awake...and he had a shotgun pointed at Paul's face.

"Drop it," said Paul, leveling the Uzi at Rose, who was crouched behind Martin and the Barca. "I'll spray her with a dozen bullets before your slug even tickles my nose."

"Shoot him!" yelled Rose. "He was going to kill us while you were sleeping."

"He wasn't sleeping, dear...he was unconscious," Paul corrected her. "And I had no intention of doing you any harm, lad, though I must confess my young protégé here was thinking of relieving you of all those Spanish doubloons."

"Drop your weapons and walk to the door," Martin said, glaring from Bean to Paul.

Michael dropped his pistol instantly. Paul groaned in disgust, not lowering his weapon an inch. "You know I'm not one to back down from a challenge, boy. Do you really think this is the best time to get into a firefight—with the cops standing right on your doorstep? Or did you think those buzzers were from the Girl Scout cookie drive?"

"I'm giving you a chance to leave," Martin said. "I'll deal with them later...and you too, if that's what you want."

Paul looked at Rose and then at Martin's trigger finger. It was already squeezing.

He could scarcely believe what he was seeing. Martin was awake and had the drop on them to boot. Only an hour earlier, he had rescued Martin at the last possible instant from being gunned down in the street, and now Martin had awakened from his semi-coma just in time to prevent Bean from bushwhacking him. This was incredible. Preposterous! It was destiny.

God is good! he thought, his eyes glued to Martin's trigger. Then he rephrased his mental exaltation more suitably to, *God, he's good!*

Yes, it was time to give credit where credit was due, and not to himself for once, though he felt a swell of pride at all his contributions. But no, this was Martin's victory. He had saved himself. He knew Martin had absolutely no awareness of his accomplishment, or why his buzzer had been pressed so propitiously, but that didn't matter in the least. It all happened anyway, at Martin's silent, cataleptic command—by the power of his *will*.

"Hhmph!" Not even Loren could rival such a synchronistic display. Martin's life had been threatened while he was unconscious and he had done something about it. The final omen had arrived and conveyed with it all his greatest hopes.

Martin was ready. By sunset tomorrow the *Turning* would transform them and...

But what if it wasn't Martin bending the quantum field? What if Johnny was protecting Martin and that little bitch in preparation for their own ascension into glory? Could his power have eroded to the point where such an outcome was possible? No. He refused to accept that. Martin belonged to him.

Rose and Michael stared at Paul like he was crazy, standing there so motionless, squeezing his trigger, his eyes locked on Martin's like a *Star Trek* tractor beam, his red-cheeked grin threatening to split his lips.

"Get moving," Martin said, breaking the spell, still squeezing, every bit as perplexed as the others, but a thousand times more baffled by the look on Paul's face.

Get moving? On any other occasion Paul would have called Martin's bluff, disarmed him, confronted the intruders, and dragged the girl away for a much needed spanking. But not tonight. Not after an omen like this. So hopeful. So threatening. No, he had much bigger fish to fry, and a risky struggle was not on the agenda. Just one stray bullet and…

"Unlock the door," Paul grunted to Michael.

"But what about the gold…?" Michael whined, his voice wimping out even faster than the rest of him when he saw the glare in Martin's eyes and the arc of his shotgun inching in his direction. Bean scuttled over to the door, hiding behind Paul's bulk like a hermit crab. He unlocked five of the seven bolts before Paul spoke again, this time to Martin.

"Where's your emergency exit?" he demanded. "And don't even think about fibbin'."

"Use the roof. It's a short hop down to the building next door."

Paul looked into Martin's eyes, probing him. Satisfied he was telling the truth, he moved backwards through the door Michael had so clumsily opened. Bean was already out the door and sneaking up the staircase. Paul lingered for a moment in the doorway, then spoke with an ache in his voice Martin had never heard before.

"Join me now and all is forgiven. Your fate lies with me…not her."

Martin shook his head almost imperceptibly, his silence more cutting than words. Paul glared back, first at Martin, then at Rose. In the heat of his rage, he almost pulled the trigger. It took every ounce of restraint to remind himself how much was at stake. He paused one more instant, until he heard the sound of buzzers braying from all directions again. Then he shrugged his shoulders, gave a doomsday grin and took the stairs three at a time like an Olympic hurdler.

Journal Entry: The Dead End

The pain in my chest is still incredible, the ache in my heart even more excruciating. Why did I do it? Why did I go back? Because I had to. What were my options? Run away? That was my initial plan, after our first meeting: buy a plane ticket and fly off to Pago Pago. But what would I do there? Lie in the sun with all my beautiful black ink fading into a sickly blue color? With three metal implants nailed into my chest?

Besides, if I ran away, I knew what would be waiting for me if I ever came back—an FBI Most Wanted picture taped to every customs agent counter, complete with a detailed description of my so-called crimes. No, I had to go back. They knew it too. Because…and this is as crazy as crazy gets…they knew I couldn't stand to leave my implants unfinished. That's why they didn't show me the site until the first ones were attached.

As much as I felt compelled to return, every cell in my body was filled with dread. When I finally managed to push myself out the door and made my death march back to The Striker's, I wasn't particularly shocked to see Paul open the door. What did surprise me was the reception I received. When I walked in the door, the two of them welcomed me like one of the family. Given the dearth of those specimens in my life, it felt almost…nice. When we settled in for the main attraction, the attachment of two more implants, Paul was every bit as gleeful as his lanky pal, leaning over the table, his chin nestled in his meaty fist, oohing and aahing and chuckling with every *whack!* and *clang!*

The Striker really put his heart into it today. *Bang!* My chest was getting slammed so hard it felt like I was being resuscitated by a CPR trainee.

"You're crazy as a bedbug for doing this," Paul said, "especially when you could be doing it to someone else and having twice the fun. Even so, it tickles me pink to watch!"

"Glad you're enjoying yourself," I grunted between *clangs*, both annoyed and amused by his jolly commentary. After The Striker finished,

I had to lie down for a long time. When I finally stood up, Paul put his arm around me and said, "Good work."

I felt proud when he said it, which made me cringe. It was confusing. Disturbing. How could I have any positive feelings at all for these psychos? What's the matter with me? I feel sick just writing it down. The only shred of self-respect I can cling to is that I'm still trying to figure out how to fuck them back even harder than they're fucking me. Which is not going to be easy. They're both smart as hell, but I know there has to be a way out of this, if I can only keep them talking. So far that's been surprisingly easy. What a couple of chatter bugs. It seems the only thing they enjoy more than hammering is yammering.

I kept asking questions and they kept answering. After The Striker bandaged me up, we all went online together...so they could, "more effectively illustrate the situation." How can they be so cavalier about the most indictable criminal evidence on the planet? Then again, why not? I had everything to lose. And they, or at least Paul, were untraceable.

The members are divided according to a ranking system. The Striker is in the top tier, along with the Turley Twins, Morris Keifer, Alexander Pate, half a dozen creeps named Kelly, and in a category all by himself...Johnny the Saint. Profiles are scant or nonexistent for the big shots. My profile is lumped in with the peons, all of them trying to outdo each other with video clips of their crimes that go on and on and on. Ick. Notably absent from the site, in any category, is Paul.

"How come you're not on here?" I asked, genuinely baffled by his absence.

"Modesty prevents," Paul answered with a sweeping bow. "The Striker rules this roost, but I offer my support in other less tangible ways. There's no need to give such gullible types as yourself any superfluous information to distract you from the mission at hand."

"The murder mission?" I asked, posing the question that had been burning inside me. "You wouldn't go to all this trouble just for that. This can't be just an experiment."

"Oh, you're a sly fox Billy. Of course it's about more than that. I did all this for The Striker…and you."

"For me?" I was so bowled over by his statement that I had a hard time paying attention to his explanation. Little snippets registered: "…a part of you that's missing…another part of you…still asleep…your love affair with death…when you fully awaken…unimaginable power…help you see your true nature…help in other ways…a loyal army of enforcers…terrorists… sworn allegiance to The Striker…they think he's a daimon…their Lord of Darkness."

"Lord of darkness?" I blurted out, feeling like I was going to faint.

They both looked at me like they didn't know what I was talking about. Like they hadn't been saying any of the shit I heard. Like all of it was coming from inside my head.

"Ahem…as I was saying, they come in quite handy," Paul continued, rolling his eyes. "Let's say we need some help around the house, you know, move the couch a few inches to the right…get a lift to the airport…it's always nice to know there's a helping hand ready to pitch in, without the grumbling you'd expect from someone less burdened with a proper sense of duty. And because our membership includes some rather aggressive personality types, we've found them to be quite useful when any security issues pop up, or if we require a convenient scapegoat. When you're as busy as we are, it helps to keep the wolves far away from your door…forcefully when necessary…and knocking at someone else's."

"So we're all slaves for you," I grumbled.

"Indentured servants would be more apt. But we also provide a valuable service."

"Indeed," The Striker chimed in. "Through the miracle of modern technology, they don't have to suffer in solitude. We even have our own clubhouse…The Dead End. They can have a friendly chat over cocktails, hone their craft, and best of all, get support and encouragement. And after they've submitted proof of their first unassisted murder, we charge no additional membership fees!"

They both doubled over in laughter again. Incredible. Now that I was part of the club it seemed like they were having the time of their lives. Which gave me another opening.

"Your social club, The Dead End...can you take me there?" I asked as casually as I could after putting on my T-shirts. I thought if I knew the location of their serial killer saloon, I could leave an anonymous tip at the nearest police precinct and then...

"Oh, I'm afraid you wouldn't enjoy that field trip very much," Paul chortled. "At least not until you have a firmer grasp on your role in this grand tradition."

Grand tradition? "I'm listening," I said, trying to remain reasonably calm in the face of my mounting anxiety. I had no idea what his response would be, but I remember physically bracing myself against the back of my chair.

His response was extremely anticlimactic.

"I'd prefer a more intimate setting for that discussion," Paul replied dryly, denying my curious prodding for the first time today. Then he turned his back on me and The Striker, and with a tiny wave that looked more like a salute to himself, he bade us both farewell.

WELCOME TO THE CLUB

Forgot all about me, didn't you? Don't feel bad. I'm used to it.

The Striker dragged me down the street in long, swooping strides. I had to take two steps for every one of his to keep up. Not that I had much choice. His fingers gripped my arm with so much strength that I was trotting along just to keep the painful pressure of his squeezing, tugging hand to a tolerable level.

He was wearing a slick 1950s black suit and a white shirt. As we crossed the street and turned up Avenue B, I looked at the shiny fabric and wondered what he was dressed up for, given his more casual, though every bit as eccentric attire on all our previous encounters.

"Where are we going? What's the rush?" I shouted, trying to shake off his iron grip.

"Our little clubhouse," he answered in that deep, hollow voice. "For members only…"

Oh, God. We were going to The Dead End.

The outside looked like a boarded-up saloon, which it was, I soon learned. The plywood was painted black. A rusty gate blocked the entrance. The door was a dark, sickly red. The color of dried blood.

"Open up," The Striker hissed in a raspy whisper. What, no secret password?

A shadow passed in front of a small peephole and the door creaked open. The man who opened it didn't look as creepy as my host, but he was no slouch, with a bristly flat-top, two barely open slits for eyes and a tattoo on his neck with three neat rows of boldface letters, written in the language I'd most recently studied: Gaelic. The man said nothing, but nodded to The Striker with obvious deference. The gate parted with a loud metal screech that made my teeth hurt and before I could slow the pounding of my terrified heart, we were inside.

O'PEN SESAME

On the stoop outside Martin's apartment, O'fficer O'wen O'Donnell folded his arms across his chest after pounding on all the buzzers and waiting almost a full minute for someone to answer the intercom so he could feed them his long-practiced but thus far never uttered line: "Open the door, this is the police!"

All he wanted to do was ask a few people if they'd seen who was firing all the shots outside, and nod his head gravely while they all replied, "No." Then he could wait for the ambulance, have a cup of joe while they shoveled the bodies inside and head back to the precinct with a lot less paperwork staring him in the face. He would have turned around and done exactly that were it not for the faint shouting he heard, coming from the lone window in the building with a light on inside.

Something was wrong. He knew it. He waited another minute for someone to answer the intercom. But nobody did. Nobody did because the only three remaining tenants were Rose, Martin and a stone-deaf old biddy with thirteen cats up on the top floor. All the others had been booted out by their pragmatic landlord, who, having had the foresight to anticipate the inevitable wave of gentrification sweeping the neighborhood, bought up every building on the block, while refusing to renew the leases of every tenant inside them.

After a few more seconds, Owen waved to his partner, Pete, who slowly ambled over. "I think we got some trouble inside," Owen said, puffing his chest out like he was Kojak or something. "I heard some shouts, and no one's answering the buzzers."

Pete glared at Owen like he always did, with a "Who does he think he is...Kojak?" look, then whipped out his pistol and broke the glass of one of the narrow ornamental windows on the side of the door. "Jeez, you'd think we had all day," Pete scolded him, and reached his hand inside to turn the doorknob.

DIVERSION

Martin was watching their every move. As soon as Paul departed, he told Rose to relock the door while he turned on the television. He flicked an A/B switch resting on top of the TV set and suddenly the image changed from the donkey-dumb weatherman promising another sunny, humid day, to a grainy black-and-white image of Owen and Pete standing in the doorway. *Just two of them?* He switched channels to another camera mounted on the building facade and scanned the street in both directions. Except for the lone squad car, the street was eerily vacant.

Martin thought about how easy it would be to kill the new intruders as he followed their progress up the stairs with more hidden cameras he'd installed on every landing. Then he thought of something even better. He grabbed his two-way intercom microphone, held it up to the TV speakers so it would generate plenty of noisy feedback and made a brief announcement: "*Squawk! Crackle! Screech!* Intruders are on the roof! Request immediate back-up! Do you read me? *Squawk! Crackle! Screech!*"

The cops looked frantically in every direction, trying to determine where the sound came from. Then they scrambled up to the roof, where Paul had fled only seconds earlier.

"You have to go now," Martin told Rose as he watched them on his monitor.

"Go where?" Rose asked fearfully.

Martin handed her a wad of hundreds from a cookie jar on the kitchen counter. "Somewhere nice," he said.

Rose thought about the backpack full of cash she left upstairs. "I have lots of money left from the gold. I'll get it."

"No, you need to leave *now*," he insisted. "You can come back here when it's safe."

"I'm staying here with you," she said firmly.

"Not a good idea," Martin argued. He had to settle things with Paul.

If that didn't work out well—an almost certain likelihood—he didn't want Rose anywhere nearby.

"You're gonna let me walk around on the street with all of them still out there?" Rose protested, her arms crossed stubbornly across her chest.

Martin thought about it. "No," he finally said, and walked into his closet.

When he came out, he wasn't carrying another bag of gold. Instead, he was shoving a little pillow and a stuffed dog into a shopping bag.

"Are you coming then?" Rose asked hopefully.

"Yeah," he said, handing her the shopping bag.

"Where are we going?"

"What hotel do you like?" Martin asked, putting on a leather jacket, shoving two semi-automatic pistols in his belt and a small silver-engraved Beretta in his pocket.

"I've always wanted to stay in The Plaza," she said, trying not to focus on the guns. "You said someplace nice, right?"

The Mirror

The Dead End was surprisingly crowded. "How many of them are...?" I whispered, but couldn't finish the question, glancing around nervously at the two-dozen or so patrons.

"Registered users? Only a few. The others...well, I think you have a fairly good idea who the others are by now," The Striker sneered with his whiplash grin, looking ahead into the gigantic mirror behind the bar where we sat. His eyelids started drooping down as usual, and it made me wonder what else he might be seeing beyond its cool, clear reflections.

"I beg yer pardon, m'Lord," said a short, thick ogre of a man directly behind us, his brogue even thicker than his lumbering physique. "I'm dreadful sorry to intrude, but I was hopin' you could introduce me to your guest here. It'd be a real honor for me, sir."

M'Lord? An honor? To meet me?

"Some other time," The Striker said dryly. The man rolled away like a warty tumbleweed, leaving The Striker completely undisturbed as he turned his face back to the mirror again, staring so intently that I soon joined his fixed gaze, past the brightly colored bottles, past the reflections of the men seated on either side of us or milling around in the background, past the walls and up to the roof of Martin's apartment.

ON THE ROOF

When Paul threw open the door to the roof, the first thing he did was look over the edge to the street. *Hhmmph!* The squad car was still there, but he couldn't see the cops. Then he heard the squawking sounds of a police radio in the stairwell. They were coming.

He jumped ten feet down to the roof of the adjoining building as easily as most people walk off a curb. Michael looked down, horrified. "Jump or die," Paul instructed. Some option. He climbed over the edge and hung by his arms until the drop was only a few feet. Paul smacked the back of his head and dragged him by the collar to the fire escape on the courtyard side of the building. There was no courtyard below, only a rubble-filled wasteland. He pushed Michael down the staircase ahead of him, looking over his shoulder every few seconds with the Uzi raised in the air. They had gone down two flights of rusted steel steps when he heard a voice from the rooftop above. A loud voice.

"*Officer responding to request for backup!*" Owen shouted with both hands cupped to his mouth. When no one answered, Pete followed up with the much less official-sounding query: "Where the hell *is* everybody?"

Something was wrong. Both cops leaned over the edge to the street below. They looked at the neighboring rooftops, craning their ears for any sound. Nothing but the wind. "We've been had," Owen whispered. "But by whom?"

"Whom?" Pete growled, unable to stifle his contempt another instant. "*Whom?*"

While Owen tried to make it sound like he was just goofing when he said it, Paul was sneaking up the fire escape again, motioning with the Uzi for Michael to follow. Michael wanted to scream in frustration. He thought about running the rest of the way down by himself, when he calculated how many bullets were housed in the submachine gun's ten-inch clip. Way too many.

When Paul reached the top, he peeked his eyes over the curved tile lip of the building. He saw the arguing cops, their faces lit by the nearby street lamp. Paul had to cover his mouth to keep from laughing. This was too perfect. Heckle and Jeckle. Paul raised the Uzi and prepared to fire when Owen let out another loud yell.

"Hey, you down there!" he shouted, pointing to the street below. "Freeze!"

Before Paul could squeeze the trigger, they ducked out of sight, blocked by the ten-foot wall of Martin's building. Paul ran over to the other side of the building to see what they'd been looking at. Not that he needed to. It was Rose and Martin, limping their way toward Avenue B. *Hhmmph! Could this be possible? Had Martin outwitted him?*

There was no time for regrets or recriminations. Now he was faced with a painful choice: scale the wall, kill the cops, and bolt back down the stairwell, or chase Martin and Rose via the most direct route possible: down the sheer front of the building. He looked over the edge, saw Martin and that bitch cruising away and weighed his options. It wasn't even close.

"Time for a piggyback ride," he said to Michael, who had shuffled over next to him.

He was looking at Paul with utter confusion. Not having a single second to spare for explanations, Paul holstered the Uzi, grabbed Michael's arms and wrapped them around his neck. "Hold on tight!" he shouted, looking over the edge to the sidewalk five floors below.

Michael wrapped his arms so tightly around Paul's neck he would have choked him had he not become weightless in the very next instant. When Paul jumped off the building.

ACTION

Paul would be great in any action movie. He jumped with his back (and Michael's) facing the street, his face only six inches from the coarse red bricks. After they dropped twelve feet, their fall was slightly broken by an ancient flower box hanging ten inches out from a window. It ripped off the wall with a *BANG!* that exploded the window and sent thousands of tiny glass shards falling to the street in a jagged rain shower.

As they continued to fall, Paul grabbed the drainpipe with both hands, which also ripped off the wall and sent them hurtling toward a nearby tree like Siamese-twin pole-vaulters. Michael, too frightened to scream, kept his eyes squinched tight the whole time until he heard the loud *ca-ching!* of Paul whipping open his sickle.

He opened his eyes just in time to see them streaking toward the tree at ninety miles an hour. He would have let go right then if he hadn't also noticed that they were still twenty feet above the pavement. He closed his eyes and braced himself for the worst, praying that Paul's bulky torso would absorb most of the impact. Too bad Michael closed his eyes again. He missed the best part of the ride.

Paul swung the blade as hard as he could at the thickest oncoming branch. *WHHHHAAAAAAANNNNGGGGHH!* the steel and wood screamed. Then came a louder *creeeeaaakkkkksssnapppp*, as the branch broke and tipped downward, still attached to the trunk by a fat bundle of bark and wood fibers. Paul gripped the falling branch like a raggedy fireman's pole and slid all the way down to the ground.

Plop. The eagle had landed.

LONELY GUY

Michael opened his eyes and was ready to let out the biggest *Whoa!* of his life. Then he noticed there was no one around to *Whoa!* to. Paul was already halfway up the next block, running so fast his head looked like a floating white blur above his all-black ensemble. He thought about running after him, then laughed at the absurdity. He looked all around. The street was quiet again. *What am I supposed to do now?*

Then Owen and Pete burst through the door.

Michael clenched his teeth with dread as they galloped down the stoop. They were coming right toward him. *This is it. They're going to arrest me for cutting that guy's head off! I'm going to jail for murder!*

They never gave him a second glance. Owen hopped down the steps after Martin and Rose as fast he could. Pete followed at a less urgent pace, grumbling all the way. When his feet hit the sidewalk, his eyes widened. The guy and girl were gone, but someone else was chasing them. His long white hair was streaming behind him, and something shiny was gleaming in his hand, flashing like a strobe light as his arms pumped up and down under the passing street lamps at a speed even greater than his legs.

Owen was already halfway up the block, his legs and chest heaving to catch up. He could see the shining object much more clearly than Pete. It looked like a...sickle?

What the fuck? Then a blinding flash ricocheted in his head, smacking Pete in the noggin at almost the same time. The morning briefing. The body on 10th and C. The body without the head. The long curved blade. *Holy fuck! It was Captain Fucking Hook!*

Pete picked up the pace. Owen ran harder and faster. Michael watched them huffing and puffing with a nervous grin. *Good luck,* he thought, as Paul tore around the corner at Avenue B like he had rocket fuel in his boots.

So what now? The gold. He looked at the cracked glass by the doorframe. It would be simple enough to get back inside. Then what?

He couldn't get through Martin's door without a bazooka. And he sure didn't want to be inside if he came back.

He felt inside his pockets and found them empty. As usual. The super-cool gun was gone. So was the last of the cash he had traded for with his emergency food stamps. Fuck. He'd have to panhandle just to buy a beer. He should have stolen some of that gold while he had the chance!

He watched the running cops. They were finally approaching the street corner Paul had zoomed around fifteen seconds earlier. Then he turned his head to the other end of the block and thought about Paul's closet full of guns. What else might be hidden inside?

He swiveled his head back and forth one more time, then said two fateful words that should never have entered his brain after all he'd been through tonight: "Go home."

He started walking. Then running. And all the way back, he never once stopped to ask why the voice didn't sound like his own.

TAXI!!!!

When Martin flagged down the cab, he looked back again to see if anyone was coming. Just an old couple shuffling along on the other side of street. When he jumped in the back with Rose, he looked again. Nothing.

"Where ya headed?" the driver asked.

"The Plaza!" Martin yelled. "Step on it!"

"No need to be rude," answered the lazy voice of the driver, pulling away so slowly Martin wanted to jump out and push.

Martin looked back one more time and sighed with relief that no one had followed. Even so, he kept glancing back over his shoulder every few seconds to make sure. He looked over at Rose and clasped her hand as the taxi finally picked up speed and turned the corner on 9th Street. She looked at him and smiled nervously. "We made it, didn't we?"

"Yeah, I think we did." Martin nodded.

It's too bad he didn't take one more backward glance instead. He would have answered her question quite differently.

CHASE SCENE

Owen was the first to sprint around the corner. Pete, unfortunately, wasn't very far behind. *PFFFFT Thump.* Ten seconds later, *PFFFFT Thump.*

Paul stared at the heads lying on the dirty sidewalk. The heads stared back at him.

He glanced at the taxi rumbling three blocks away, then back at their sad, blinking eyes. Paul chuckled, marveling at how closely they had landed to each other—and at just the right angle—they could look at him and each other so easily!

"Sorry, lads," he said, giving them a happy wink. "I'd love to stick around for a little chat, but I'm runnin' behind." They were still staring at him as he streaked away.

Paul couldn't stop smiling. He could see Martin peering through the back window of the cab every ten seconds, but he knew he was safe. He almost wanted Martin to see him for the sheer comic value. Martin was watching every car and taxi. Paul was riding a bike he had stolen from a pizza delivery boy. He stayed far behind, having already memorized the taxi's medallion number in case they were separated, but traffic was slow on Madison Avenue and Paul was able to maintain a fairly leisurely pace while keeping Martin within easy eye shot.

Suddenly, a frown crossed his face. The girl.

"She's the cause of all this trouble…and the antidote," he growled among the honking horns and ambulance sirens. By the time he watched the taxi pull over, his bike-riding glee had almost evaporated. But when Martin climbed out and led Rose by the hand into the lobby of The Plaza Hotel, Paul laughed so hard he had to cover his mouth.

"Looks like my luck's holding up after all!"

JOURNAL ENTRY: HOUSE CALL

He came here today. To my fucking apartment.

"Aren't you going to ask me in?" Paul said, practically filling the doorway. When I stepped aside, he brushed past me and threw his coat over my favorite chair. "I'll have some tea, if you please," he commanded, gazing at the string of lights surrounding my bookcase. "You left your Christmas twinkles up. If you're waiting for Lent to take them down, I'd like to remind you next week is Ash Wednesday."

"They cheer me up," I answered honestly.

"I can see how you'd need cheering up, with all your…hobbies." He smiled, then went off on a mini-lecture about the druids and how the Christian missionaries appropriated their Yule solstice ritual to promote the Savior's birth. He said that you could take any pagan festival and do the same thing. After three or four centuries all that remained were the newly created Christian feast days—All Soul's Day, the Annunciation—and on and on. You name it, they stole it. He continued talking about the druids' oral teaching tradition, how it could take up to twenty years for an apprentice to perfectly remember every verse in the story.

"Nobody knows if it was a story, or poetry, or genealogy. Nobody knows what the druids practiced, because they never wrote anything down," I said, challenging him.

"What if they did?" he replied with a self-satisfied grin.

"They didn't," I said decisively.

"But what if they did? It'd be worth a pretty penny, don't you think? The only extant manuscript of the entire druid teachings?" he said, strutting over to my bookshelf without looking at me, heading straight for my collection of rare books. The white binding of my most treasured volume, the *Corpus Hermeticum* must have called out to him like a homing beacon.

"Excuse me, that's really valuable. Please don't touch it," I said, rushing over.

He ignored my request like he ignored my body trying to block him from the shelf.

"Not as valuable as it would have been if I hadn't labeled the spine," he said dryly. "Let me guess, you picked it up at Weisman's in London, for eleven thousand, one hundred dollars. I wouldn't hang on to it for too long if I were you. This book is cursed, you know."

Who was this guy? My Corpus Hermeticum, my pride and fucking joy, used to be his? He wrote on the spine? It was cursed?

"By whom?" I snickered, trying to sound incredulous and haughty, not coming close to pulling it off. I was so damn curious I would have lit a fire and propped his feet on an ottoman just to keep him talking.

"Long story, longer than the book," he replied disinterestedly, fanning through the pages with a flap of his fat thumb. He put it back daintily after waving it in the air like he had to fumigate it. Meanwhile, the odor wafting from his raised arm was burning my nostrils.

He leaned closer to the shelf, squinting like he couldn't make out the faded words on the spines, then snorted, "Hhmmph! Now what have we here?" Grinning happily, he pulled out another very old, very rare volume, number two on my prized possessions roster.

"How on earth did you come by this?" he asked, with a genuinely warm smile.

"Flea market…in Cape Cod," I said, feeling pretty cool.

"Fama Fraternitatis Roseae Crucis. Do you know what it means?"

"The Fame of the Brotherhood of the Rose Cross," I answered proudly. It was a first edition, printed in 1652.

"Yes, but what does it mean?" he asked, his eyes boring into mine.

I told him what I knew about Christian Rosenkreuz, Rosicrucianism and Masonry. From there, we segued into alchemy. He corrected me every few sentences, giving me the exact dates and titles of manifestos, describing alchemical formulas like he was reciting a recipe book. He knew everything. *Everything.* Every detail, every quote, every historical reference. When he commented on my mistakes, he never lost his patience or made fun of me. The cruel condescension he previously served up nearly every time he opened his mouth was replaced with the tone of a wise, caring teacher. I lost my know-it-all demeanor after the first two minutes. After an hour, I was completely enthralled; after the second hour, I felt like I was under a spell. It was so incredibly exciting to finally talk with someone who was a true scholar of occultism. He seemed even more delighted to share his knowledge.

"What is the most fundamental treatise of alchemy?" he asked, throwing me a softball.

"*The Emerald Tablet* of Hermes Trismegistus," I replied, like it was the Daily Double on *Jeopardy*. When he pressed for a deeper analysis, my fumbling response elicited a groan and a sad shake of his head. Yet for the first time he declined to offer his own interpretation of the mysterious verses. Instead he asked:

"What do Trismegistus, Pythagorus and Plato have in common?"

I ticked off some of the tenets of Hermeticism shared by the Greek masters: the belief in an immortal soul, a connection between the divine realm and the material world, a force Pythagorus called the *Apeiron* that creates and destroys all life, which was guided by a godlike intelligence called the *Nous*. I would have continued, but he cut me off impatiently.

"Yes, yes, but what did all these beings have in common *collectively?*"

"They were all great teachers, with disciples who passed on their teachings. They were part of a learning tradition that stretched over centuries."

He nodded. "They were all *one in spirit*. They all *knew*, passing down the Great Truth only to worthy initiates. And the most important aspect of their collective responsibility was the *line of succession*. Do you know why?"

"They had to pass down knowledge properly, or it would be lost or misinterpreted."

"Theoretically, that is correct, but it didn't work out that way. Power-hungry disciples broke away time and again, corrupting the knowledge at every fork in the road to suit their selfish ends. The old line of succession is of utter importance, because ultimately it was…"

He paused for such a long time I began to feel extremely uncomfortable.

"Ultimately, it was a failure," he finally said, gazing sadly at the books on my shelves like they might crumble into dust as he spoke. "The master/disciple model should have been the most effective medium for the sacred transmission. The culture was celibate, monastic, vegetarian—no distractions or temptations, no bloodshed, nothing to stand in the way of their single-minded dedication to the Great Work and the preservation of the *knowing*."

The Great Work...alchemy. "Tell me about the Philosopher's Stone."

"That is a subject that exceeds the scope of a casual fireside chat," he said with an impatient wave. "Focus on the topic at hand. Why didn't the master/disciple model work?"

I had to think about it, but eventually I came up with a good enough answer to earn me a lung-collapsing slap on the back. "Jealousy and ambition. There's only one master and one successor out of all the disciples, which leaves a lot of pissed off also-rans."

"Indeed! (*slap!*) Hence all the make-my-own-religion separatists."

"So if that system didn't work, what took its place?"

"Your turn again, Billy."

After much grinding of gears, I said, "Okay, it's an enormous responsibility. Requires complete commitment. A fanatical sense of duty. An even stronger appreciation of your heritage and your role in the lineage. So it had to be dynastic...a bloodline succession."

"Ha! I can see you've been taking your vitamins. Blood is thicker than water. The heir is raised from birth knowing where his ultimate duty lies. And should the chosen one lose his footing, there's plenty of kinfolk waiting in the wings to take his place."

"But wait a second, you still have the same problems...jealousy, ambition..."

"...competition..." Paul added happily. "But now the problems aren't problems anymore...they're assets."

"Huh?" I queried astutely.

"Think about it," he said, with less of a scolding tone than I expected. "When disciples are thwarted in their ambitions, their resentment turns into a 'Feck you, Master, I always knew you were a feckin' idiot!' attitude. Then they go rogue and twist all the teachings around so they can put their ego-fueled, 'new, improved' stamp on it. In a monarchal succession, the One Truth is the King's most fiercely guarded treasure. The teachings are sacrosanct. His *knowing* consecrates his divine right to claim the throne of power. Even though many competing factions may vie for supremacy, their thirst for power only strengthens the value of the one, unimpeachable doctrine. Only the Keeper of the Grail can wear the crown. All the wannabes, including other heirs to the royal bloodline, may fight for it, betray each other, duel to the death, but the result is always the same—as it is in every aspect of nature. The strongest, most clever and ambitious candidate will always prevail, regardless if he's the chosen heir. If he can take the scepter, if he has the sack to hold on to it in the face of all opposition, his claim is legitimized. Survival of the fittest. Thus the continuation of the line and the preservation of the Truth is assured with Darwinian certainty."

"But Hermeticism is all about a higher purpose...the Great Work. What you're talking about is just a dog-eat-dog, winner-take-all feudal society where the ultimate prize is the right to sit on the throne. How can that be considered remotely spiritual?"

"I never said it was remotely spiritual. It's practical, pragmatic and necessary. Is it spiritual when a lion fells an antelope? When a praying mantis eats its mate? This is the natural order of things. In the grand scheme the only thing that matters is the ultimate prize—which I can assure you does not involve sitting on any earthly throne."

That threw me for a loop. "And so the ultimate prize is...?"

"A million light years beyond your reach at the moment." Paul laughed. "You'll never understand what I'm saying 'til you make your own commitment —so how about a little entertainment, instead? Let's have a look at your cabinet, Dr. Caligari. Pull out your suitcase. I could use a good laugh."

I didn't bother asking how he knew about the suitcase. I didn't hesitate to pull it out. What the fuck, right? One thing I knew for sure, he wasn't going to run away, no matter what I showed him. If he did, so much the better.

"This is attractive," he said, trying on a necklace of human ears. "How do I look?"

Fucking scary. I didn't say that. I didn't say much of anything as we rummaged through the contents. He laughed louder with every item I displayed. I thought he was going to start rolling on the floor. I have to say it felt really good to share my dirty secrets with someone who would never judge me harshly—because he was so fucking evil that this was all a big joke. His joy was so contagious I started laughing too. Then I discovered the real reason he asked for a presentation. A little box wrapped in gold paper with a red bow. I stopped laughing instantly.

There was a severed toe inside.

"Sorry I missed your birthday, but better late than never."

"Does this belong to anyone I know?"

"In truth, no. But according to a recent update on your Billy the Kid profile page, it belonged to a poor innocent girl you met in a bar last week."

I almost shit myself. It had been so incredibly easy for them to plant this in my apartment, even though I'd barely gone out all week. A perfect gift-wrapped reminder of what will happen to me if I ever cross them. I'm trapped. If I try to fuck with them in any way, there'd be plenty more "evidence" scattered around my apartment or made instantly available to the authorities. I was about to launch into a rant at him, when he made an off-the-wall segue that did an excellent job of shutting my mouth.

"By the by, you missed your cue back there to ask the most important question of our lesson today: What royal family took over the Hermetic succession?"

"And that would be…?"

"Mine, of course," he answered without a trace of his usual smile.

"Let me get this straight: *You*, who has a serial killer website, who is blackmailing me into killing an innocent girl…*you* are the heir to the Hermetic bloodline? *You* are the guardian of the truth?"

"First of all, she's not innocent. None of us are. All your moral quibbles have nothing whatsoever to do with the will of the *Intelligence*. Secondly, I'm not the *heir* to the bloodline. I'm king of the ruling clan…Clan Kelly."

I got such a jolt when he said that, like all my brain synapses ignited trying to make the necessary connections to some part of my memory that refused to yield its secrets. I had never heard him or The Striker mention his last name, but I knew what he was going to say after seeing all the killers named Kelly on his website.

"Clan O'Ceallaigh reaches all the way back to the Milesian kings and farther still…to the dawn," he announced, puffing with pride. "And you, dear boy, share the same noble blood."

"Me?" I asked, my legs suddenly wobbly.

"Do you think I just picked your name out of a hat, or decided your morbid taste in tchotchkes made you a suitable candidate for blackmail? You are a Kelly. As am I."

He gave me a funny look when he said that, like he was trying to draw something out of me. "My name is William Cleary," I said tersely, "sorry to disappoint you."

"You mean *O'Cle'irigh*, don't you?" he replied, using the Gaelic pronunciation. "Are you aware that O'Cleary was the first fixed surname in all of Europe? Written references to the name date back to 850 CE," he announced. "Impressive, aye? For your mommy, not for you. *Your* true surname is Kelly."

"I never knew my father," I said, looking at him with a wince. Please. No. No. No.

"Well I did, and he was a full-fledged cunt, I can tell you that. Nevertheless, we share the same blood and it's blood that will set you free, my boy."

I bent over, sighing with relief. He laughed so loudly it shocked me upright again.

"Well, thanks for the sneaky peek at your sinful collection, Billy," he said, rising from the chair. "It's quite impressive, though I prefer your Hermetica. I know you've been putting off your implants, so I'll be expecting you tomorrow. Don't procrastinate or the police will find another present in your suitcase. In the meantime, you don't mind if I borrow your Rosy Cross for a little bedside reading, do you? I haven't read it in such a long, long time."

CLOSING TIME

I heard a low murmur circulate through the crowd behind me, then a lower, deeper cough. "He don't look like much," the coughing man said in a grating hack that didn't sound much different. "Are you sure he's a Kelly, Loren?"

Loren? The Striker's name was *Loren?* The shock of hearing his real first name was somewhat diluted by the disorienting experience of hearing my true surname uttered aloud for the very first time in public. Kelly. William *Kelly*. I didn't have time to dwell on the matter. The crowd was parting to make way for the cougher as he swaggered closer to me. I kept my eyes fixed on The Striker's reflection, acting as if I didn't hear him, but it wasn't much use. He was right behind us, tall and extremely muscular, with snow-white hair and a neatly trimmed jet-black mustache. He had the look of a military officer, or at least the bearing of one, though he was dressed more like a grunt, with rumpled green trousers and a tight khaki T-shirt that made his overdeveloped pecs bulge like he had stuffed a pair of porterhouse steaks inside. His arms were bulging with sinuous muscles and snaked with veins that were so gross and distended that his biceps looked like a worm farm.

Sniff. Sniff. Oh, God. He actually started sniffing the nape of my neck.

"Wait, what's this?" he gasped, glancing from me to Loren with a malevolent grin. "It's not a 'he' after all! I didn't know the Kellys were raising breeders again after all these years. Did you bring him in here for recreational purposes, Ole Snake Eyes? I know you don't frequent our modest establishment quite so often, now that your schedule is so full, running errands for your glorious Master. Nonetheless, I assume you're still aware this is a *men's* club, not a place for little Nancy boys to sip their Shirley Temples before heading off to the *men's* room for some glory hole action."

I tried to make a break for the door when he clamped his hand on my shoulder so fucking hard I wondered if he dislocated it. Then I looked at his hand. His hand was black. Black as midnight in a cave. It wasn't a tattoo, I could see that right away, and it wasn't a birthmark, because the blackness extended only to his wrist in such an evenly demarcated line that I would have thought he was wearing a glove were it not for the wrinkles on his knuckles.

"Where you going, darlin?" asked the black-hand man, his voice dripping with malice. "I was going to drop a quarter in the jukebox so we can snuggle up for some *slooow* dancing."

I was about to totally lose it when I noticed that the thus-far silent spectators were forming two clench-fisted camps, one group in a ring behind me and The Striker, the other clique queuing up behind Blacky, who seemed as unfazed by all the activity as he was delighted by the clammy look of fear in my eyes.

"Are you fully prepared to place this large a wager?" The Striker cut in dryly, never looking away from the reflection of his own drooping eyes in the mirror. "You must surely be aware that 'the Master,' as you so eloquently phrased it, has entrusted me with his safety. And regardless of my feelings in the matter, which reflect your own sentiments much too closely for the responsibilities I'm obligated to shoulder, I will break every bone in that sadly discolored hand of yours and then happily disembowel you and every other member of your mongrel clan if you don't evacuate the premises in the next fifteen seconds."

Which, quite surprisingly, they wordlessly did…though it only took them thirteen.

"Have another, Mr. Kelly?" the pockmark-ridden bartender asked, pointing at my empty vodka and grapefruit. I was grateful for the question and the refill. No one else said a word to me after Blacky and his crew shuffled out, shooting glares in my direction with every other step, though not one of them dared look at *Loren*. He wasn't talking to me either. Why had we come here? To soak up the atmosphere?

"You don't seem surprised that he took a hike," I asked, breaking the silence. "Does everybody do what you tell them?"

"Just the sensible ones," he said, refusing to make direct eye contact.

"Why are we here?"

"You're feeling trapped, aren't you?" he whispered, finally turning in my direction. "You see so much, but you don't know what to do."

I didn't speak, didn't nod. He was looking inside me.

"The Master has entrusted you with an enormous responsibility, yet he has given you neither the training nor the resources necessary to ensure the required outcome. He knows the power lying dormant within you and the darkness he seeks to awaken. His plan is a sound one. It should have been simple enough—it *still* should be simple enough, and he believes you will come to your true self in time to succeed. But I harbor no such delusions. Without assistance, you will fail. In doing so, you will jeopardize everything we have fought so long to attain. He wants all the pieces to fit together, but he has taken enormous risks in doing so. He is old and his powers are weak."

"Weak? Are you *kidding?"* I asked too loudly. A dozen heads turned.

"Be quiet, you fool," he hissed, glaring at the eavesdroppers with a blood-curdling snarl. They all snapped their heads away at the same time. He went back to staring in the mirror for a long time, then whispered, "You've never witnessed his full capabilities, but I have. Many, many times."

I waited for him to say something more, to get to the point so I could get the fuck out of there, but he kept staring into the mirror. I opened my mouth to ask another question. He shook his head almost imperceptibly, nudging his chin at the smoky glass. I glanced behind, watching all the creeps milling around, talking in whispers. Looking at me like nobody ever looked at me before. With respect. With fear?

I turned my head and gazed with him into the vastness. There was so much to see.

I saw Martin and Rose walk up the steps of The Plaza Hotel. I saw Paul dump his bike on the curb across the street and follow them inside. I saw Martin slip his key card into the door of the honeymoon suite. Saw Rose follow him into the room. I saw it all from my stool, wincing at the dangers neither of them could see. I closed my eyes and saw even more terrible things, but when I opened them, I saw what I knew I'd see from the instant I stepped into the cigarette-stained air of the most aptly named bar in the universe. I saw Paul staring right back at me, his eyes rolled backwards in his head. He was smiling. Beckoning me to join him.

I didn't heed his call. I left that awful place without another word to The Striker, but I knew why he had brought me there. He wanted me to see all the vultures waiting in the wings should the Great King fall. Wanted me to witness the power he held over them, to see the ease with which he could protect me, to know the real truth of my circumstances.

Paul was vulnerable. And Loren could help.

LOVE NEST

The room was more beautiful than Rose had imagined. The sheets were softer than any Martin had felt. Except his own, of course.

"What are you thinking about?" Rose asked, needing to talk. Needing him to talk.

"Luck," Martin said, after another uncomfortable pause.

"Good or bad?" she asked, sitting next to him on the bed.

He looked in her eyes for the first time since the taxi and said, "Good, I think."

"Does that mean we're safe now?" she asked with a guarded hopefulness that hurt Martin more than the nail or the bullet or the sutures.

Pause. "Yeah," he lied, "we're safe."

"Martin, what's going on here?" she asked, her frown rolling in like an undertow. "Who the hell is Paul? What's the story with you two?"

The story. Martin shuddered at the mention of it.

"I can't tell you," he said, turning his head.

"Martin, he wanted to kill us. I deserve to know."

"If he really wanted to kill us, he would have."

"Are you guys mercs…or in some kind of mob? Are you…a hit man?"

"I can't tell you."

"Listen, mister, I took some pretty big risks with you…"

"I know that. That's why I told you to go home. I don't want you to be part of this."

"Part of what? Martin, I need to know. I'm…*with* you."

"You don't need to know. You don't want to know. If you don't know anything, maybe I can protect you. You want me to protect you, right?"

"Yes. I want that very much."

They settled back into silence again.

"So what's the plan?" Rose asked, after another long minute passed.

"Relax. Lay low," he answered, glad to be telling the truth again, or at least part of it.

"Okay." Rose nodded, forcing a smile, placing her hand on his thigh.

Martin nodded back, his cock rising like a movie crane. Rose wanted to feel the lump, but wanted to keep talking even more. "Why do you think we're lucky?" she pressed.

Another pause. "Martin, I need you to talk to me."

Martin let out his own big sigh and finally said, "We're lucky because we're alive."

Rose wanted him to say more. Wanted him to tell her everything—about Paul, about Michael, about the gold and the guns and the stuffed dog and the pillow in his shopping bag. She wanted to ask him about all those things, but his earlier warning and the poignant sadness in his voice made her think about her father, instead…and her mother.

Yes, it was good to be alive. It was good to be here together. Now the quiet between them didn't bother her as much. It felt almost calming. Respectful. The door was less than twenty feet away from this glorious bed. There wasn't any lock on the inside. Nothing was holding her here. Nothing except…

She stopped thinking and kissed Martin softly on the lips, nodding to him with a lump in her throat that matched the one in his pants.

"Yeah, I think you're right," she said, a tear streaking her cheek as she pictured her mother lying on that soft, satin bed in the mortuary. "I think we're lucky too."

BLACK HEART

Martin wasn't as lucky as he thought. Neither was Rose. None of us were.

Paul stormed into the The Plaza's lobby with both fists clenched. One of the porters rushed over to stop the huge, crazy homeless man from going any farther...until he saw his face.

"I'm terribly sorry, sir. I didn't recognize you."

"I can see that," Paul barked without a trace of an accent. "Are my rooms prepared?"

"As always," he said brightly. "Do we have any luggage this evening?"

"*We* don't," Paul hissed, rumbling past him, making sure that he kept the sides of his overcoat closed. "Bring me my key."

"Yes, sir," he said, scrambling over to the registration desk like a Jack Russell terrier. He whispered something to the desk clerk and scampered back to Paul's side.

"Right this way," he said, bowing this time. Paul had already passed him into the elevator. He pressed the penthouse button as soon as he got inside and the porter had to rush to keep from getting caught in the closing doors.

"Beautiful evening," he said, trying to brighten the gloom.

Paul ignored him. "A tall man checked in with a short girl. Lots of metal in her face. See them?"

"Yes," he snickered, eager to please. "Quite a pair, they were."

"Find out what room they're in," he snarled. "Keep me informed: who comes, who goes and when. Use this number," he ordered, scribbling on a slip of paper.

"Certainly, sir," the porter said, forcing a smile. Paul said nothing, snatching the key card from his hand as soon as the elevator door opened.

The porter started to follow, but Paul blocked him. "I'll find my way just fine, son," he said, slipping on the brogue like a pair of well-worn slippers. "Don't let me down, now."

Paul entered the dark room and didn't bother turning on the lights. He sat in his favorite chair by the window and tried to sense where Martin was at this very moment. Was he right below him? Had he changed his mind and checked out again? No, he was here. He could feel it, yet he couldn't *see* him. Very strange. But now his other eyes and ears were open. Martin and the girl might as well be tagged with a radar beacon. The porter would tell him their room number in minutes, if not seconds, and then…

He rubbed his hands together, then took a long deep sniff of his armpit. Ripe. Very ripe. He debated whether to take a shower. Decided against it. Why bother at this point?

He closed his eyes instead and searched for Martin again. Still nothing. Was Johnny blocking him? Raising a cloud of mist, a bubble of safety? If so, the bubble would burst soon enough.

"Martin, Martin, why hast thou forsaken me?" he implored, raising his hands in supplication. Then he laughed so hard he hocked up a green one on the clean, white carpet. He stared out the window into the darkness of Central Park and thought about Martin and all the others that had come before. Now this new boy too. He tried to picture what Michael was doing and was pleased to find their connection still intact.

At least he made it home.

"Every mistake is an opportunity," he reminded himself, wincing at his foolish errors. Then he congratulated himself on the fact that he was here right now…and so were they. All the players were in motion. The *Turning* was upon them. He smiled. Then frowned. Martin had been impeccable tonight. His uncanny displays of providence were even more astounding. Looking at it from one angle, he was magnificent, confirming his most hopeful assumptions about Martin and his power. Never had there been a more worthy candidate. On the other hand, what of his own unforeseen miscalculations?

He thought about Johnny again. In his isolation had he somehow gained in strength? Was it…the girl? Even Michael and those stupid cops seemed to be pitching in, albeit unknowingly. Michael, tripping him up, the cops pressing those buzzers right on cue. Could something else go wrong? Was his power truly waning?

No. Despite all his sins, he was still the one, he had always been the one, he *would* always be the one. The scales were tipped in his favor. Who held the upper hand? He did. They had come to this place—his stronghold, his fortress—of their own accord, like lambs to the knife. Yet who made the decision? Had Martin awakened to his memories? Had he told her all he knew? Were they seeking the portal, to unite and defeat him? Could Martin betray his clan and his vow so completely? And if this destination was her choice, who had lured her? Was the *Intelligence* steering her? Was Johnny springing a trap?

There was too much at stake to rely solely on his intuition or logic or conjecture. He had to know exactly what had occurred and why. It was an incredible risk to take on the eve of battle. It would weaken him greatly. Still, he had to know for certain what had transpired before planning his final moves. He rose and walked to the other room, to the white door. He unlocked the door and turned the handle. Soon afterward, he crossed a second threshold. The crushing force required every ounce of his considerable power to endure, until he reached the Axis and *saw* what had thus far escaped him.

When he returned, he was exhausted, but he *knew*. The girl made the choice to come here. Martin was still asleep. He had told her nothing, still loyal to his vow whether he knew it or not. Johnny was pushing them to travel west, as far away and as fast as they could travel.

Ha! Johnny had failed. Again. And the *Intelligence*? Did it even care? Had it ever cared? The Maelstrom certainly didn't. He had just witnessed that undeniable truth with the same clarity he had seen on every occasion he breached its unquenchably hungry maw. It churned on and on, devouring all, creating all, grinding the gears inexorably forward, shaping, molding, driving to the Singularity, when the *Becoming* would occur despite all their plotting, their misguided loyalty, their quest for participation, despite any aid or resistance from all of them, all the Clans, all the Kings and Masters, all the Knights and Lords and Druids, all thinking their path was the righteous one, their knowledge and wisdom the soundest, their goal the noblest. All of them had made the sacred vow, to guide, to protect the *Intelligence* and its intent, to safeguard the knowledge they had been given. But that knowledge was corrupted at every turn, just as he had been in the end—he the longest to resist those urges, the longest except for Sophia's children. Now only Johnny and his bitch were left. By sundown tomorrow there would be only Johnny, trapped in the prison of his own choosing, free to weep at his leisure for the loss of his final treasure all the years he remained alive. For the loss of love itself. Just as he had done.

Only he knew the Truth. That knowledge was gained with the price of his great sin. He had transgressed the will of the *Intelligence*, betraying his son, his Clan and worst of all, himself, all for his selfish need to survive. To remember. To be the One.

Selfishness. Arrogance. Pride. Without even making a conscious decision he had succumbed to the most corrupting temptation. And what had he discovered? That his sin didn't matter! The Wheel still turned. He grew ever stronger. His lust for vengeance was slaked time and time again without the slightest repercussions. As for the *Intelligence,* he didn't give a shit. The *Intelligence* was in him. It was *his* will that mattered. He had been made for this purpose and this purpose alone. He of all people of all time had been chosen. He was still chosen. Regardless of his betrayal, the interventions that followed, regardless of the Christ, whose failure to set the course straight they would celebrate tomorrow, he had been chosen, as he had chosen Martin. Together they would triumph.

He was so close to the end. The world was a stinking pile of shit. Humans were devolving. Science and its fair-haired son Technology were accelerating exponentially, barreling onward like a runaway train to the Singularity. He was the last man standing. The last true son of Light and Life. Darkness and Death. There would be no more cycles after this. Martin had proven his resilience. The vessel would endure until the prophecy was fulfilled in them. Everything would occur according to the plan—*his* plan—once the girl and Johnny had been defeated. His will *would* be done. His Kingdom come. On Earth as it is in Heaven!

But if…

A tendril of doubt crept into his heart and he felt a surge of apprehension he'd never experienced in his very long life. He crushed it like a cockroach and exploded with another booming laugh. "Just another game of chess. Black defeats white in the end."

With that he went back to work, sorting through every detail, considering how all these loose ends might be straightened out with the right amount of cunning and foresight. It took him less than an hour to concoct the perfect scenario, full of fun and surprises. After the final piece of the puzzle snapped into place, his mind went back to Martin. He pictured the two of them together in the early days. How good it had been. For him. He was surprised by the depth of his feelings.

"He's just a boy, like all the rest," he told himself, like he had so many times before, trying to keep his emotions at bay. But no, this time he wanted them to come. He needed them. His heart would take him exactly where he wanted to go.

His chest rose and fell with the pain of those indelible memories. And in the deep, dark fringes of Paul's black heart, the feelings grew. A little layer cake of sunshine. He could no longer deny it. There was someone in this world he actually loved. He was surprised, maybe even a little shocked, but another part of him had known it all along. Love. Sweet love. He savored the feeling with each big drumbeat in his chest and swirled it like a brandy snifter. It made him feel warm inside. It made him feel happy.

It made him want to kill.

WHITE KNIGHT

Martin was still awake, thinking about luck. The more he thought about it, the less likely it seemed that their escape could be attributed to simple good fortune. He had seen Paul battle countless adversaries. No one had ever raised a finger against him, much less a loaded weapon, and escaped unharmed. How was it possible he was still alive? That *they* were still alive, he corrected himself, watching Rose's sleeping body curled up next to him, making tiny snoring sounds.

He went into the bathroom and put on the complimentary terrycloth robe hanging on the back of the door. He nodded approvingly when he examined the label. "One hundred percent Egyptian combed cotton," he read aloud. It felt so nice when he put it on that he forgot all about Paul for twenty-two seconds.

Where is he right now? Martin wondered, easing himself into the comfortable chair overlooking the dark forests of Central Park. The streetlights sparkled like diamonds between the blue-green-blackness of the trees. It was so beautiful. And they were still alive. But why?

"Come back," Paul said. "Come back and make the world the way it used to be."

Martin nodded, the cobwebs of self-deception slowly clearing away. There could only be one reason why Paul showed up today and why they were still alive. Unfortunately, it didn't have anything to do with luck. He was alive because Paul wanted him back...to finish what they started. But what was that? All he could remember were the endless duels, the clan rivalries, the treasure hunts, the planning. But he couldn't remember *why*.

Martin stared out the hotel window at the dark swaying trees and thought about the other questions Rose had asked him in the taxi. He wanted to tell her, he really did, but he knew what would happen if he ever talked about Paul. What would he say the next time she asked?

"I can't tell you," he said, rehearsing. It would have to do. Even if Paul didn't do all those terrible things to him for telling her, he would do all those things to Rose. "He'll do all those things anyway," a wiser part of him whispered. So why not tell her everything he knew?

"If she knows what you've done, she won't like you anymore," Martin answered. That was one good reason. There was another one too. He couldn't tell her everything, because he still didn't know what was going on. He didn't understand why Paul was so insistent on keeping him away from Rose…or why Paul had turned on him.

"What on earth do you want with her?" he whispered, hearing the echo of Paul's sneering voice. He hadn't known then. He did now. He wanted to be with her. He wanted to stay. Could they run away together? Could he turn his back on Paul forever, escape to a place where he could never, ever find them? No, there wasn't any place like that. If Paul wanted to find them, he would. He watched Rose's chest rise and fall with each tiny breath. He saw her legs twitching in her dreams. Was she running too?

There has to be another way to stop him. Could he kill him? Actually kill him? How many had tried and failed? Warriors much stronger and more adept. Could he even be killed at all?

"The Book. The answer is in the Book," Martin said, not sure where the notion came from or why it sounded so convincing. He breathed in and out, emptying his mind of fear, comforted by the fact that they had managed to flee and Paul didn't seem to want him dead. Not yet, anyway.

"Yes, the Book." Martin nodded, more sure than ever. But what was the connection? He looked out the window and forced his mind to relax. "All I have to do is remember."

"Please, Daddy, tell me what happened to the boy and the angel. Tell me what happened when they went to the Maelstrom!" he cried to Paul in the wheat field.

"That's a secret," Paul whispered, cupping his hand at Martin's tiny ear.

"Please, Daddy, please! I promise I'll never tell anyone ever!" Martin pleaded, grinning widely. He knew Paul would tell him, it was part of their ritual. But only after he promised.

"That's a serious promise," Paul said with a fake frown. "Forever is a long, long time. Are you sure I can trust you with such an important secret, no matter what happens, for as long as either of us shall live?"

"Yes, Daddy, you can trust me! I promise! I promise! Just like the boy in the story!"

Daddy smiled and rubbed Martin's head. Then he resumed the story.

"The angel took the boy deeper and deeper into the Maelstrom, but as they approached the swirling core of light and darkness at the heart of the Axis, the boy began to scream in agony. It felt like the flesh was being ripped from his bones. Like his body was disintegrating into dust. But the pain ended as suddenly as it had begun and when he could see again, he was in a completely different place, a temple with a round stone altar. There was a huge golden bowl embedded in the center, with a great wooden staff running through ring handles on opposite sides of the great cauldron. Two people, wearing robes with hoods that concealed their faces, stood across from each other, gripping the pole and chanting words he didn't understand."

Paul made him repeat the words in the other language, over and over and over until he pronounced them perfectly before continuing the story.

"As they continued chanting, they pushed the pole in a counter-clockwise direction...."

"And the whole altar moved with them, like they were turning a wheel!" Martin cried.

"Yes, just like a wheel," Paul nodded happily. "And when the wheel turned, two secret chambers opened up. One of them had a sword inside with strange marks carved into the blade. The other one had a large, square, red crystal. One of them took the sword and the other took the crystal and they went back to the altar. There was a small metal square at the bottom of the cauldron. The red crystal fit inside it perfectly. They held the sword together over the cauldron, the tip almost touching the crystal. They held it by the blade, not the handle, right where the marks were carved and began chanting the words inscribed in the steel, repeating them as they squeezed the sword. They gripped it so hard their blood ran down the blade, mixing together and flowing onto the red crystal. As their blood covered the crystal it began to glow and soften, almost as if it were made of flesh. Then they drove the sword through the crystal and the caldron, burying it deep into the stone altar.

"After the sword was lodged in the stone, they clutched the wooden staff in their bloody hands and began pushing in a clockwise direction." Paul paused. When he spoke again, his voice trembled with emotion as he closed his eyes and said, "And the Great Wheel turned."

Paul paused again, inhaling deeply. Slowly, he opened his eyes and continued, "When the stone altar turned a second time, the temple was flooded with golden light. The light was so bright the boy couldn't see anything, as if the temple, the people and the whole world had been swallowed up in it. The angel transported him to another place and another and another. He was showing him visions of the past, the present, and the future. The visions changed faster and faster while the angel spoke without opening his lips, telling him why he had been chosen and what he'd been chosen for. The angel took him far into the future and showed him something wonderful that was going to happen, something he was part of, something he would do. Then he showed him another future and another. In each of those futures, the wonderful thing didn't happen. Terrible things happened instead. They were so terrible that the boy became very afraid, but the angel said he would live inside him for all the days of his life and together they would have the strength, wisdom and power to guide their destiny to that wonderful thing. All the boy had to do was make a sacred vow to protect and guide the *Intelligence* until they completed their goal…the *Becoming*.

"'But how can I honor my vow for thousands of years?' the boy asked.

"'First you must make your oath,' the angel commanded.

"The boy nodded. He was ready. Suddenly, they were transported again, to another temple in a faraway land. They were standing on top of an ancient stone altar covered with mysterious markings. The angel wrapped his arms around the boy, hugging him so tightly almost all the air in his lungs was squeezed out. With his last gasping breaths the boy made his vow and spoke the secret words the angel told him to repeat—the magic phrase that would unlock the Maelstrom and all of its secrets.

"When the Maelstrom opened for them, they ventured together to the Axis, where all was calm and beautiful and perfect. There the angel revealed to him the greatest secrets of all—the secrets of life and death, creation and destruction. The secrets were hidden in a story, in many stories that together formed the long, long story I'm telling you now," Paul said, his face gravely serious. "The boy had to remember every word of it, in the same sacred language the people in the temple spoke. But he was a very special boy with a very good memory."

"Like mine!" Martin shouted proudly.

"Aye, like yours." Paul smiled, rubbing his bristly blond crew cut.

The story didn't stop there. In fact, it had only just begun. The story seemed to go on forever. At every twist and turn, there was so much adventure! And better yet, treasure! They went on a quest to hunt it down. The things they found were incredible. So incredible he couldn't believe treasures like that could exist without everybody knowing about them. "That's why it's a secret," Paul told him.

Martin loved the secrecy, loved all the planning. And just as in any good story, there were plenty of bad guys to battle along the way. "Monsters," Paul called them. The monsters were scary, just like monsters should be, but Martin didn't mind. He liked the challenge. The monsters made everything more exciting because they were real. It felt like he was inside the story, acting it out. And winning every time! What could be more fun for a growing boy?

The treasure was real, too. Jewels. Rings. And best of all, gold! Martin loved the gold. He wasn't sure why, but he loved it. When he was little, he loved it so much he wanted to eat it. He even tried once, on a really old coin. His teeth sunk in when he bit it. There were other treasures too, scrolls and statues, staffs, goblets and swords, really old stuff. And the Book. Paul liked the old stuff much more than the gold and he loved the Book more than anything. Martin knew why. The Book told the story. All of it. But why did he like the Book more than the gold when he already knew the story? Paul made fun of him when he asked. He called him stupid. Martin recoiled from the shame. It took him three minutes and eight seconds to remember what he'd been thinking about. Oh, yeah: the story. Martin thought the story was about the treasure, but Paul kept telling him no, he was missing the point.

"The story isn't about the treasure, dummy! It's about…"

Dammit! He was forgetting again! He closed his eyes, moistening them, then gazed at the undulating trees, deeper and deeper into the shadows between the branches, the waving blobs of charcoal gray, navy blue, and deep, dark green. The darkness shifted and swayed, weaving in and out like a living, breathing tapestry. The shadows. The branches. And after he stared with open eyes for a long, long time, he heard Paul shouting at him again:

"The story isn't about the treasure, dummy! It's about…"

That place. That place where Paul took him, when they were standing on the altar, after he made his vow, before Paul killed…No!…don't go there…focus on the story.…

He paused, breathing in deeply, emptying his mind of everything except the image of Paul in the wheat field, his arms waving wildly as he told his tale. He closed his eyes and the image became so clear it felt like he was actually there again, sitting at Paul's feet, listening rapturously. He could hear Paul's booming voice, smell the whiskey on his breath.

The memories came flooding back in a tidal wave: He was remembering everything! Martin tried to stay calm, but couldn't help gasping as all the jigsaw puzzle pieces rearranged themselves and slipped smoothly into place. He could see it all, his heart beating faster and faster…until there was something moving toward him, coming at the end of the train of memories like a lonely caboose.

This wasn't a memory…it was a place…the wonderful place where the angel told the boy all his secrets…the same place Paul took him…the place that finally made sense of all the awful things they'd done together. It was coming toward him now. No, it was here…obscuring all the trees and the buildings and everything…a glorious mass of swirling light that was talking to him without words…pumping a completely formed thought into his brain that was even more vivid than a memory. It sounded like Paul, but no, that wasn't right…it wasn't a thought or a voice, it was a knowing…a certainty that Martin spoke out loud:

"The story has a purpose. We're doing something together…something that will change…"

Fuck! Martin banged his fist on the armchair as the words vanished from his lips, as the swirling waves disappeared with them and washed all the *knowing* away like it had never even happened. It was gone! Every part of it erased in an eye blink.

Martin paced in front of the window. *I need to bring it back!*

He forced himself to calm down. To sit down and try all night if that's what it took. And if that didn't work, there was still another way. The white room. That was why he made it. To show him the world of dreams. To help him remember…and forget.

The white room would bring it all back. He would clear his mind and stare into all that blankness and concentrate on the one image he could still cling to. The swirling shape that gave him everything and took it all away left one solitary clue behind in its wake: an image of the prize Paul valued above all else…and the key to snatching it away from him.

Yes, there it was, only a few feet away, at the end of a long, gilded chain, gently rising and falling on Rose's sleeping chest. It was the key to protecting Rose, the key to everything. He wasn't sure where she got it, but he remembered where he'd seen it before. Even though the one Paul wore around his neck was different, he guessed they both did the same thing.

It was the key. Yes, the key. Now all he needed was the Book.

ABRACADABRA

Bean opened the closet doors slowly. He was glad there was a light in this part of the hallway. Even so, it was still hard to see. He wondered how Paul hooked up his electricity in the long-condemned building. Probably tapped into some live Con Ed lines in the basement. Even more puzzling was why he only had a few functioning lights. Some of the other hallways were so dark you couldn't see more than a few feet ahead. Michael stayed clear of those, retracing his steps back to the big closet the instant he walked in Paul's front door. The closet that was filled with…

It was empty. *What the fuck?* The wood inside was charred. It smelled like a drowned campfire. He closed the doors to see if there were dents in the wall where Paul had slammed the doorknobs. Yep. Could there be more than one closet? He looked around and saw the room with the couch and the windows facing the street. It was only a dozen yards away. This had to be the right closet. So where were the guns? He opened the closet again, even slower than before…and almost screamed in shock.

The burnt smell was gone. The wood was smooth and clean. The chest was there, open and gleaming with all that deadly steel. Instead of comforting him, the sight threw him into an absolute panic. Was he crazy? What the *fuck* was going on here? He almost ran down to the street and probably would have if not for what he saw inside the giant chest of weapons. He saw three golden coins. Three beautiful glowing coins.

They were sitting on top of a very big book.

Puppeteer

Paul watched over the city that never slept and thought about how much they had in common. He wouldn't sleep tonight. I was already dreaming. And I saw him, sitting in that chair. Watching me.

"William…" he whispered.

"What?"

"Are you ready?"

I couldn't answer. He knew I wasn't. He didn't care.

I saw him smile, taunting me. I saw those long, fat fingers drumming on the arms of his chair. Soft, muffled sausages. *Farump. Farump.* I looked at his face and saw a resemblance to mine I'd never noticed before. My dream-self moved in for a closer look and I watched his expression change by infinitesimal degrees. Softening. Flattening.

As it changed, the resemblance grew stronger and stronger, until finally at the end, just as the sky was starting to brighten in the east, it became frighteningly clear:

I could no longer tell the difference.

THE WOOD

PSEUDONYM

I am William's soul. I am writing this Book from a place you can't imagine. I found this story rendered whole, complete. It was there before I started.

I dole it out in drips and drabs. Sometimes he listens. Sometimes not. It doesn't matter. It will all come out eventually. Unraveling, thread by thread.

I am the machine that makes his dreams. I make them fierce and thrilling. Sometimes I tell him things I wish I could take back again. I see the trouble they cause. I watch from my way, way far-off place. I see him try so hard to be good.

I keep talking and he keeps writing. I can't stop it. He can't stop it.

Even if I could...make it nicer...make it happy...make it safe...I still wouldn't. Because I have to tell you...I really like it this way.

WAKE-UP CALL

"Picnic," Rose whispered in Martin's ear early in the morning, before he was even awake, as the sun twisted around the corner of their spacious bedroom suite, poking between the hanging plants, filtering through the gauze-sheer curtains, looking for a bed to warm, a face to paint. It found Martin's stubbly cheek. He hadn't shaved in one whole day, definitely a record. Rose didn't mind. She rubbed her own soft cheek against his bristles—up and down, up and down—like she was exfoliating with a dry loofah sponge. She did one cheek and then the other until her skin was red and sore. Rosy.

Martin opened his eyes and looked at her curiously. She grinned and ducked between his legs to rub her newly flushed cheeks against his morning erection.

Rose loved sucking cock. She loved it like other women love baby showers. Not "giving head," or "going down," or any of those other sanitized euphemisms her girlfriends sometimes used to describe what in her mind was best defined by the act itself.

"Mmmmm," she sighed, grabbing the meaty club in both fists. Martin was fully awake now, scrunching a pillow behind his neck to get a better view. She pressed the fat underbelly of his cock down with both her hands, mashing it against his washboard abs, rocking it back and forth like a rolling pin. Martin did a sit-up crunch to heighten the effect. Rose looked up and gave him a beaming smile, then yawned her mouth open and took him inside.

Martin didn't complain, but what he really wanted to do was fuck. Now that he was getting more practice, he was as excited about fucking as Rose was about sucking. He tried to coax her head away so he could get between her legs. It wasn't easy. Her mouth clung to him so voraciously it felt like he was trying to pull a bowling ball off a swollen finger. Eventually, he succeeded and climbed on top of her. But even someone as emotionally dense as Martin couldn't help notice her sad pout as he began thrusting in and out of her in long, even strokes. He was rushing things. Not good. It didn't take long for him to pump the pout off her face, but it registered nonetheless. So when they finished and she moved back between his legs, he let her do whatever she wanted at her own slow pace.

After twenty-three minutes and nine seconds by Martin's internal clock, she wiped off her face and led him by the hand to the window. They looked out over the sprawling mass of Central Park, both of them thinking it was the most beautiful sight they'd ever seen.

"Can we go for a picnic?" Rose asked, stroking his back. "Do you still think it's safe?"

Picnic. Why did that sound so appealing? And unsettling? He almost heard Norine's voice warning him, but the switch clicked and all he was left with was a deep longing in his heart. *Picnic.* It sounded so good. So necessary. But what about that other word?

"Yeah…it's safe," he said, trying to convince himself, torn between the longing to forget everything that had ever happened before and the job still waiting to be finished.

Paul. The key. The Book. Martin had spent most of the night awake, trying to recreate the vision that slipped between the fingers of his mind. The more he tried to corral those re-erased memories, the faster the switches in his brain locked down, until finally, exhausted and angry, he settled between those soft sheets and wrapped his arms around Rose's even softer body. *Nice.* That was the last word that registered in his mind before sleep carted him away. Waking up with Rose was even nicer. It was the nicest thing that had ever happened to him. He gripped her hand, staring at the same view that seemed so sinister last night. Everything looked so different. So new. He pictured them lying in the sun with some sandwiches. Could he deal with Paul later? Could he do something good, just once?

"It's so nice out, isn't it?" Rose asked in a childlike voice, trying hard to pretend she hadn't noticed the hesitance in Martin's last reply, needing him to affirm her denial.

"Yeah, it's nice," he said. "Everything looks like gold."

HE'S GOT THE WHOLE WORLD IN HIS HANDS

Michael clutched the coin as he looked at the Book in his lap. It was so thick and heavy it practically pinned his legs to the couch. From the instant he held it, he ceased thinking about anything else. Not the weird hallucination with the burnt closet, or the equally surreal incidents preceding it: the beheading, their leap from a five-story building…not even Martin's gold. As soon as he saw it, he knew this was the book Paul had taken from Firth. *Taken* back *from Firth,* he thought, wondering how anyone could take anything from Paul in the first place without losing his head in the process.

"Some things are worth more than treasure," Paul had said.

What did *that* mean? He couldn't begin to guess. Because he couldn't open it up. A wide leather strap with a big brass lock bound it tightly shut. *Fuck!* It was driving him crazy. He'd been up all night trying to pick the brass lock with a rusty old paperclip he found on the floor, but the metal bent like rubber every time he stuck it inside and twisted. He even thought about grabbing one of those gleaming knifes in Paul's "war chest" and slicing through the strap, but he knew what Paul would do to him for mutilating his most precious possession. Michael shuddered at the thought… then he started in with the paperclip again.

After another round of futile poking and twisting, he paced around the room. But like every other time he set the Book down, something felt so wrong about it that he scooted right back to the couch and picked it up again. *Ooof.* When he lifted it this time, the morning sun flashed across the leather surface and he felt the strangest sensation he'd ever experienced. The Book felt like it was pulling him forward, dragging him across the room and into the dark hallway. *What the fuck? Was he tripping?* He followed the tug on his hands for a few steps, then commanded his feet to stop.

There was something up ahead in the hallway. A light? He walked down the corridor, the tug from the Book growing more insistent with every step until suddenly he wasn't afraid of the darkness. What darkness?

The hallway was swirling with light. Where was it coming from? It seemed incredibly bright, but it didn't hurt his eyes. He wanted to go closer. He needed to. The Book helped him, pulling him onward with a force that felt like gravity. This time he stopped resisting, his blinded eyes open, unseeing and seeing at the same time. But after he walked only a dozen yards, the darkness returned all at once and swallowed him up.

Holy shit! He couldn't tell which direction he'd come from or where he was headed. The Book knew. It kept pulling him. Bean tried to slow down, afraid he'd slam into a wall and break his neck. He ran into a wall anyway. As the feeble light coming from his left flickered against the surface, he saw that it wasn't a wall after all. Well, it was and it wasn't. It was the same height as the wall and it was covered with the same filthy wallpaper. But it wasn't a wall. Not really. It was more like a door.

Journal Entry: The Chapel

The Striker finished my implants today. I'm so wiped out. Between the agony of the procedure and the misery that followed, I can barely sit still to write this. It doesn't help that I hardly slept last night. The gift Paul left in my suitcase was one reason. Strangely enough, the threat of arrest is much less disturbing than the panic I've felt since he dropped the Clan Kelly bomb. When he told me that his family—*our* family—co-opted the Hermetic line of succession, I could only conclude he was certifiably insane. What else could I think? Unfortunately, no matter what I thought, how obvious it seemed, how much I wanted, *needed* to believe that he was totally off his fucking rocker—in my guts, in my heart of hearts, I knew he was telling the truth. How crazy is that? Insanity must truly be genetic.

Regardless of his craziness or mine, he had also given me the first solid fact I could use to track him down. I went on the web to see what I could dig up. Kelly is the second most populous Irish surname after Murphy. There are a lot of Paul Kellys out there. I ran down as many as I could who seemed in the right age range, but I couldn't find anyone who fit the bill—a big, burly Irish sociopath with a fondness for collecting ancient occult manuscripts and blackmailing young men into committing unspeakable acts of horror. I wasn't particularly surprised when I came up empty. This obviously wasn't a guy who craved publicity.

So I trudged over to their grisly parlor today, hoping Paul would be as chatty as he'd been yesterday. He was not. In fact, he barely spoke the entire time. When at last The Striker struck his final blow and cleaned off the blood, we all went to the mirror together to check it out. The golden rays snaking from my solar plexus were surrounded by inflamed bloody tissue. It looked horrible. Staring at my raw, red, ravaged skin, I can't believe I ever thought about doing something so insane. As horrified as I felt, Paul seemed exceptionally pleased with the results. "Billy boy, you did such a fine job here that you're due for a reward."

"A reward?" I asked, completely flummoxed.

"Come with me," he said with a sly wink. "There's something I want to show you."

The way he said it made me feel the same excitement I feel when I'm collecting: like an adventure is about to begin. I put on my coat. The Striker nodded and opened the door for us, but remained inside. We headed east, almost to the river. The wave of gentrification hasn't pushed that far and most of the buildings are abandoned. It's really scary at night, so I was grateful there were still a few rays of sunshine left. I'm not sure why I felt so jumpy. Even if it were midnight, I was in no danger of being mugged with Paul stomping beside me.

We walked up the stairs of a dark brick building until we came to an old teak door with an engraved cross. It was definitely a collector's item. There was a strong odor inside I'd smelled many times before. I knew what it was, but considering who I was with, I wasn't shocked. We walked into what I assumed was the living room. The furnishings consisted of a ratty old couch, a rattier chair and a liquor cabinet. He poured us each a glass of whiskey. My stomach churned. I hate brown liquor. The smell of it alone is enough to make me puke.

I asked if he had any vodka. He looked at me like I was the ultimate pussy and put the drink in my hand. "Cheers," he said, laughing when I took a baby sip. My head shook involuntarily. He laughed again. I wanted to run away. He must have sensed it because he put a huge arm around me and led me down a pitch-black hallway. It went on for much longer than it should have, twisting and turning until we finally came to a stop and he pushed against a wall. The whole wall moved, or I should say, a section that was four feet wide. It was a door. A door without a handle.

Inside, I saw the dim flicker of candles. The room was about twenty feet long. At the far end was a large altar with a massive crucifix behind it that went from the floor to the ceiling. It looked extremely old, maybe even medieval. On it hung a life-sized figure carved from wood. It wasn't like any other crucifix I'd seen before. There were nails everywhere, covering his arms, legs, torso…and wings. The wings were long and white and carved from the same worn wood. As I drew closer, it was easier to see the face. It was beautiful and smiling. The hair was long and blond. There was no crown of thorns. No beard. That's when I fully realized the figure wasn't Jesus with wings. It was an angel. A crucified angel.

It was fastened to the cross with at least two hundred nails. They weren't exactly nails either: They were more like those handmade spikes African shamans hammer into their magical totem figures in a similar profusion. The more I looked at the angel on the cross, the more I was reminded of those totems. There were leather pouches hanging from the chest. They looked hand-stitched. There were bones lodged between the spikes. There were small photographs here and there, and small, brightly colored objects that might have been children's toys. Covering all the visible skin was a thick grainy crust that looked like tar. I had a good idea what it was made of.

My eyes were drawn to the middle of its chest. I gasped, staring at the golden rays of metal emanating from his exposed heart in all directions, like the beams of the sun. I opened my shirt and stared at my implants. I looked back at the angel. And back at my chest. The shape and placement of my implants was exactly the same as the rays on the angel's chest. How was this possible? When I went to The Striker for my implants, I'd never even met Paul, let alone visited his sinister sanctuary. I stared at the angel and I felt like I was having a déjà vu or remembering something from the distant past, but it was just out of reach, like the hem of a black tattered robe skittering around a corner.

"Look. Look and learn," Paul said, pointing at the altar.

The altar was also wooden, with tall candles on either side. I stroked my hand across the surface. It was black and sticky with the same residue as the cross. There were holes everywhere, reminding me of The Striker's stool. This was far more gruesome. I followed Paul's finger to the front of the altar. There was a cabinet inside. I knew from the way he was looking at me that I was supposed to open it.

I hesitated, but not for long. After what I'd seen while assembling my collection, I was prepared for anything. I let out a sigh of relief when I opened the cabinet. There were only some thick leather volumes inside. In a glance I could see they were bound with hand-tooled leather. I could also see that the bindings weren't very old—certainly not in the league of any books I expected to see in Paul's collection given our most recent encounter. My somewhat disinterested response seemed to antagonize Paul and he shook his head ruefully like I was an idiot.

"You of all people," he said, but didn't finish the thought.

When I shrugged, he pointed at a small lectern in front of the altar with another book on it. I stepped in front of the lectern, which faced the cross and the angel. I read the inscription: *The Book of William*. It was so creepy I can't find the words to describe it. It was even worse when I opened it. I saw a baby photo of myself looking right back, and a photo of Mother when she was younger, the same photo they posted on the website. A thousand questions swam in my brain. When I turned to Paul, his expression told me I'd get the same one-word answer: "Look." So I turned the pages forward. It was the story of my life, a cross between a scrapbook and a biography. I quickly skimmed through the pages, until I reached the most recent entries—photos of the tattoos and a new one of the implants. I read the note next to a large shot of my face: "He's almost ready."

I went back to the beginning, looking for a clue that showed how I was related to Paul—some genealogical information, a family tree—or better still, a picture of my father ("the cunt," as he put it). There was nothing, which seemed extremely odd considering how thorough the other details were: all the different towns we moved to, all the new schools where I instantly became a target for humiliation. Bully bait. Yet there was nothing connected to Paul, until I read the description of my mother's death. My own journals were much more detailed, but these were astonishingly complete. They talked about the cancer. How it had moved to her brain. It didn't say anything about the double mastectomy, which I thought was odd by omission.

The big shocker came next. He'd written down some of her last words to me. "You're a good boy, son. Don't ever forget it."

"How did you know this?" I blurted out, horrified and furious.

"I told you before. All your answers are in this room. Take your time."

He walked out and sealed the wall behind him. I guess I should have been afraid, being left alone in a place like that. Instead, I felt oddly comfortable. I looked at the walls and all the photos and carvings. I looked at the votive candles, with pieces of paper tucked between the red glass cups and the silver holders. I thought about Mother's death.

I had only talked to her on the phone once or twice the year before she died. She never mentioned the cancer. I still remember how my knees shook when I got "the call."

It's funny. You wait all your life, knowing that one day you're going to get the call. Even so, when it finally comes, you're never ready. I was luckier than most. At least she was making it. "I'm dying. I need to see you."

I flew in, rented a motel room and went to the hospital every day. It was good to see her. It was bad to see how far gone she was. She told me not to be sad. She was ready to die. In the days that followed, we talked about the weather, the news, anything that didn't matter. She always seemed on the verge of saying something important. She would begin with some cryptic phrase, then stop herself, looking around like someone was listening.

On the last day, she was barely coherent. I sat in the corner, knowing she was fading. Suddenly, she lifted her hand to beckon me. "Do you need the nurse?" I asked hopefully. When she shook her head sadly, my knees buckled even more than when I got the call. There was something she wanted to say. Her last words, I thought. I expected them to be about how much we loved each other or how much she would miss me. What she said wasn't anything like that. "You have to find Martin," she whispered. "Use your gift. Be careful."

"Who is Martin?" I asked angrily. My overwhelming thought at the moment was a selfish one. How could she waste her last moments with this crazy talk?

"You're a good boy," she said, trying to calm me. "Don't ever forget it."

Suddenly the sound of whistling came from behind the curtain dividing her room. The woman in the bed next to her was in a coma. The nurse said she'd broken her neck in a diving accident. She moved in the same week Mother died, but never had any visitors until today, a big man whistling Broadway show tunes. Mother was out of it from the morphine when he arrived. I don't remember if he spoke to me. I just remember the sound of his whistling. Mother's eyes grew wide when she heard it. She pulled me to her whispering lips. "Save Martin…and you'll save yourself."

"What do you mean? Help me, Mother. I don't know what to do!"

A sound came from her mouth, but it wasn't an answer. It was an awful hollow rattle, like a gourd filled with stones. When it stopped, her eyes were empty. I let out a terrible scream. I didn't remember it until today, but Mother's death rattle wasn't the very last sound I heard before I screamed. It was the sound of Paul, still whistling.

"Do you remember the first time we met?" he asked me that day with The Striker.

A surge of anger shook me from my recollection. With it came a moment of inspiration. I looked at the other books in the cabinet. They were all the same thickness as the one about me. I pulled the books out one at a time until I found the one I knew would be there. *The Book of Martin*. When I saw the words, I shuddered. I set the Book on the altar and placed *The Book of William* next to it. I started reading them…fast.

When I read about what happened to Martin when he was a little boy, I scanned the opening sections of the other books to see if any of them mentioned the boy's father.

Of course not. The sin of omission. I was such an idiot.

When Paul returned to the chapel, he asked, "Now do you understand?"

"Yeah," I said, feeling like I was about to puke, "you're my father."

I paused and waved my hand across all the volumes at my feet. "You're…*our* father."

"Who art in heaven. So nice to have you back where you belong, son."

I couldn't think of a thing to say. I couldn't cope with the emotions I was feeling in any way whatsoever, so I did what I usually do in any intimate circumstance: I went straight to the intellect. "I thought these were going to be about Clan Kelly and the Hermetic lineage."

"Oh! The Hermetic *lineage!* Is that what you're looking for? The noble bloodline of Clan O'Ceallaigh? We, the proud guardians of the Secret Secretorium!"

He was goading me. But I didn't know what he was goading me toward. I decided to push back. "Maybe it's better if I talk to Martin. I noticed he lives nearby."

"Yer sweet dead mum would love for that to happen. That is not an option for you."

"Why not? Has Martin seen this?"

"He's been in this place. Not much of a reader, that Martin."

"Does he know you're his father?"

"Hard to say. He's always known me to be High King of the Clans, his Lord, mentor and benefactor. In his heart, I've always been his dear swee' Da, but until he set foot in this room, I'd always encouraged him to think I was his adoptive, rather than his biological sire. To be honest, I don't believe he cares a fig whether I actually planted the seed or not, any more than he cares for the knowledge you're so desperate to possess. At any rate, the poor lad has no recollection of our time here together. It seems he's blocked it out, like a great deal of our fun adventures. I believe it's called post-traumatic stress disorder these days. I still prefer shell shock. Yet, even with his lack of ambition and Swiss-cheese memory, of all my boys, he's the cream of my cream, the guardian of our collective heritage."

"How can he guard something he doesn't give a shit about? Why did you bring me here? Am I supposed to be jealous of him?

"Like your forgetful brother, you're still hiding from yourself, even more effectively than he. But I haven't given up on you yet, Billy. Far from it. You have talent, son, and a glorious gift. Still, you haven't tasted blood… and there's no salvation without baptism."

I felt myself responding. Or part of me. It must have been my pride. No one had ever praised me before, except Mother.

"Why are you telling me all this instead of Martin?"

"I didn't tell you anything. I showed you things, but you arrived at the proper understanding on your own. Or at least a small part of it. If you can embrace the entirety of your past, your prize will be even more glorious than Martin's. If he can do the same, it will be the sign I've been waiting for since he first stood with me upon this bloody altar of our ancestors. But if you attempt to contact him directly and reveal the secrets he has hidden from himself, it would be better if you had never been born. Though you probably think that's already true, aye?"

I nodded in honest agreement. I was about to elaborate on that admission when a hazy memory took me by surprise. I closed my eyes and a startlingly clear image appeared…a truck coming up a long dirt road. Two people watching, a woman and a little boy. I'd seen it many times before, in my dreams and in waking. I didn't want to make that final connection. I wanted to keep that last patch of solid ground under my feet. Paul took it all away with a single question: "What was your mother's name?"

"April," I said, my eyes snapping open as I saw Paul get out of the truck. As I watched him go inside with her. As he pulled out the knife.

"That wasn't her name. That's when she changed it! Stop running from yourself. You can *see* it, boy…I know it!"

"No! You're lying! You're doing this to me!"

"You know I'm not! She changed her name and took you as far away from me as she could. Now, she's eight years gone and you're finally ready to receive your legacy."

"You raped my mother!" I shouted, my blood boiling with hate.

"Oh, I didn't just rape her. I cut off her tits. Did a sloppy job of it too, wanted to make sure she didn't do any more breeding in this lifetime. You two were quite enough."

I don't know where I found the balls, but I charged him like a bull. He looked shocked for an instant, then pleased. He pushed me aside like a kid in a playground. When I got to my feet, ready to take another run at him, his last utterance finally registered in my brain.

"*Two?*" I asked, wondering what fresh new horror he would disclose.

"Yes, you and big brother. The heir apparent."

"Martin? How could he be her son?"

"What you just *saw* wasn't her first rape, dear boy. She didn't recognize me on that long ago day, but I don't blame her. On our previous encounter, it was quite dark and we didn't chat all that much. Another reason why rape is my preferred mode of female discourse. There's something about non-compliance that cuts right through the small talk. Once I escorted her from Martin's hopeful eyes, put the knife to her throat and mounted her, it all came flooding back—our previous tête-à-tête in San Francisco—such a romantic city, such narrow dark alleys.

"I knew I'd planted some prime seed in her—and from the way she screamed at the end, I think she knew it too. She must have, since she carried to term, not that I would have let her abort the child. I'd sooner chain her in a dungeon and deliver the baby meself. Sadly, that wasn't necessary.

"When she gave birth to the blessed child, stealing him was the easy part. After Martin was born, we substituted another babe that was horribly mutilated, not a pleasant thing to see, or do, for that matter. Since I'm so fond of ironic twists, I gave baby Martin to your wicked Auntie Mabel, who by some exquisitely timed coincidence had gotten herself knocked up on the very same day I raped yer mommy—by my brother Angus!

"So picture this, and hold on to your ribs, cause it's a real corker— I snuck my wet nurse and Martin into the cellar, then gave the wicked witch of the west some Pitocin to induce labor. She birthed at home about an hour later, her farmhouse being so far from any medical services. After she delivered and took a little nap, I gave her child to the nurse, and sent them on their way back to Angus. Prince Martin was substituted for her bitty baby and the rest, as they say, is history.

"Whew! What a horror that cunt Mabel was! I can't even describe the suffering poor Martin endured until I rode in on my big black horse to rescue him. The tortures of the damned, son. The tortures of the damned!"

I just stared at him in shock. Paul grinned back at me. "What? You're not laughing? Well, there's no accounting for one's taste in humor."

I slumped to the floor and closed my eyes, mourning my mother's death and her life all over again. I looked at the *Book of Martin* and saw how much courage she had, how much she had given of herself, to both of us. Everything she told me on her deathbed made perfect sense now. But nothing in what Paul said made any sense at all.

"Why did you do all this?" I asked, unable to conceive what advantage he could possibly gain from concocting such a sadistically elaborate deceit.

"Excellent question," he said like he actually meant it. "When we spoke last night, what did I say was the most important aspect of our collective responsibility?"

I just sat there, fighting back the tears.

"The line of succession," he answered for me. "Your mother was a very special woman, a hybrid of two bloodlines, both endowed with the gift. I knew she'd yield *An Té atá Tofa*, as she surely did. I was so pleased with her gene pool that I took another dip when the opportunity presented itself, and with our second hate-making session I got another gem from the same mine. You're every bit the treasure Martin is to me, and one day soon you'll fully grasp the truth of that."

He was sucking me in again. I tried to shake him by repeating my question. "Why all the subterfuge? Why kill a little baby?"

"All I will say for now is that unlike many of my cruel urges, there was a very specific reason for every action that was taken. Should you apply yourself to your studies, you will understand. You're not going to beat my blackmail game and you certainly can't kill me, so stop your whining, put a plug in the pity jug and get busy with these books."

I looked at him. At my father. He was right. I'd spent my life wishing I'd never been born, but I'm grateful to be alive now. Not so I can fulfill his twisted dream of my destiny, but to keep the promise I made all those years ago—to my mother, Norine.

The Elephant in the Hotel Room

As much as he wanted to, Martin couldn't keep avoiding the subject. "Where did you get that necklace?" he finally asked, pointing to the key dangling from Rose's neck like a hypnotist's pocket watch.

"My father gave it to me. It used to be my mom's," Rose said brightly. Wow. He was asking a question. They were having a conversation. No, even better: a normal conversation!

"What are your parents' names?" he asked haltingly.

She wanted to avoid answering him—her father's name was more recognizable than David Berkowitz's. "John and Kathy Turner," she said with a weary sigh.

"Johnny Bones," Martin breathed, looking away.

"Turner," Rose said curtly. She felt ashamed. Ashamed of her name, ashamed of her nakedness. She went into the bathroom and put on her complimentary robe. It was so long on her that she looked like a Jawa from *Star Wars*.

Martin sat on the bed. He'd been bracing himself for this, but now that she'd said it, he felt like he'd been kicked in the guts. She was the same little girl he saw wearing that necklace when they led Johnny away in shackles.

"That girl is not for you!" Now he knew why Paul yelled with such vehemence. Why hadn't he come right out and said what he meant? It wasn't like he ever restrained himself from expressing his loathing for Clan O'Neil. There was a lot Martin couldn't remember from their time together, but he always remembered the feuds and duels. Of all the clan chiefs they fought against there was no one Paul regarded as a more hated adversary than Johnny the Saint. And there was absolutely nothing Paul regarded as a bigger betrayal than what Martin had done years after they parted ways. He helped Johnny. Befriended him. Defended him.

Rose came out of the bathroom and watched him sitting there, shaking his head.

"Why are you so bent out of shape?" she scolded, "Look at the people *you* hang out with!"

"No, no, no," Martin sputtered, as shaken by her outburst as he was by her familial lineage. "I'm not…I don't think anything bad about him…."

"Then why are you sitting there, shaking your fucking head?" Rose challenged him, half steaming, half grateful for his stammering attempt at reassurance.

"I knew him…your dad…a long time ago."

Now it was Rose's turn to sit on the bed. "How did you know him?" she asked with a grimace, like she was pulling the trigger in a game of Russian roulette.

"San Francisco," Martin said, stifling a fake yawn, growing more anxious with every word. "Met him in a bookstore. I was looking at an old map. We started talking."

"And…" Rose pressed impatiently.

"We talked a long time. Became friends, I guess."

Martin talked a *long* time? They were *friends*? She was *fucking* her father's *friend*?

"So you knew him when…it happened?"

"Yeah," he said, standing up, putting his robe back on.

"Oh, boy," she said, tightening her lips. A wave of grief washed over her before she could think of anything else to say or ask. Martin looked out the window, thinking about the last time he saw Johnny and the little girl he kissed good-bye. She sure looked different now.

"Johnny's a good man," he mumbled, facing her again.

"For a killer?" Rose shouted. "I guess that doesn't matter, since you're a killer too!" She wasn't sure why she felt so angry with him. She wasn't sure about anything.

"Johnny never killed anyone who didn't deserve it," Martin replied without emotion.

"My mother too? She deserved it?"

"He didn't kill Kathy."

"Yeah, that's what he told me. But he's crazy!"

"He isn't crazy. He never was. And he didn't kill her."

"How do you know that? What did he tell you?"

"He didn't have to tell me," Martin said, still strangely calm.

"Because…?" Rose asked, totally unnerved by his expressionless tone.

Martin turned toward the window again.

"How do you know he didn't kill her?" Rose shouted, going over, pulling his sleeve.

"Because I was there."

Rose staggered backwards, holding her thighs for support. "*You* did it?"

"No…no…not me!" Martin stammered, holding her, easing her back onto the bed.

"Then who?" Rose demanded, almost choking with shock and grief.

"I don't know. But I know it wasn't Johnny. We were together when he found her. I saw…his reaction."

"*Together?* What were you doing? Why didn't you tell the cops? How could you let him go to that awful place? Why didn't you help him?"

"He wanted to go there," Martin replied, avoiding the more troublesome questions.

"He wanted to go to the nuthouse?" Rose spat back.

Martin nodded. "He said it was the only place he'd be safe."

"From *who*?" Rose sniffled, wiping her nose with the sleeve of her terrycloth robe.

Martin turned to the window. He had to stop talking…

"From whoever killed your mother," he whispered, in spite of himself.

"Martin, who killed my mother?" she asked, sounding out each syllable. "You know, don't you? You're lying!"

"I don't know," Martin lied, while a memory tugged at him more urgently than Rose. The memory of Johnny making him promise never to tell his daughter who did it. He couldn't tell her. He swore he wouldn't. He thought about what happened the last time he broke a vow of secrecy, when he told Norine about Momma and the cellar. Momma said she'd know if he ever told anyone—and the next morning Paul came and took him away. If Momma knew what he was saying when she wasn't around, Johnny would too. He didn't know how it was possible, but he knew Johnny could do lots of things that weren't possible.

"It was him, wasn't it?" Rose yelled, "Your buddy! Paul!"

"No," Martin said, shaking his head. "Whoever did it wanted that key. And Paul…" He cut himself off again.

"And Paul…" Rose prodded, waving her arm in circles, begging him to speed it up.

"Paul already has one."

"Oh, he already has one. That makes sense," Rose muttered, collapsing onto the bed. "Martin, what the fuck is going on here? Why would someone kill my parents for this key?"

Martin grunted, turning away.

"Stop holding out on me!" Rose shouted, startled by the strength in her voice.

"Okay…" Martin began, gritting his teeth, pointing to her "lucky charm," amazed he was even remembering all this. "There are two keys. You have one. Paul has the other. He wears it around his neck all the time… like you."

"What is it for?" Rose asked, a chill racing up her spine. "What does it open?"

"A book," Martin whispered, breaking the final taboo of his secrecy oath. "At least, I think it does. I'm not sure if your key fits the same lock… but Paul's key…it opens a book."

"A book," Rose repeated, completely dumbfounded. "Are you saying my mother was murdered and my father is in a lunatic asylum because of a book?"

"Yeah…more or less," Martin replied.

"What kind of fucking book is it?"

"I don't know," Martin answered, his cheeks turning red. "I can't remember. I did for a little while last night…then I forgot again."

"Are you fucking with me? You can't remember any of it?"

"No. But I know the Book is more important to him than anything." *Or anyone,* he wanted to add. "The Book might be our way out of this. If I can find it…take it from him…and your key fits…maybe we could barter with him."

"Barter with *him*? That maniac?"

"It's our best shot. I could try to kill him, but I've seen a lot of people try and they're all dead. He'll probably kill me just for making a grab at it. Anyway, it's a shot," Martin said with a shrug, predictably oblivious to the calamitous effect his matter-of-fact explanation was having on Rose's frantic mind.

"Who *are* you people?"

"Clan Kelly," Martin answered simply, taking her question literally. "Paul's my…"

Martin paused for a moment, so motionless it seemed he'd been frozen in space by a ray gun. Another dim recollection nudged him, prodding his brain like a warm, wet finger.

"Paul is the High King of the clans," Martin continued robotically, flipping the switch, forcing the foggy words and images back into the dark, dank cellar of his subconscious.

"Oh, my god. I'm with a crazy man. Just like my crazy dad. I must be crazy too!" she cried, hanging her face in her hands.

"I'm not crazy. Johnny isn't crazy. And you're not crazy," Martin said, sitting next to her like he actually knew how to comfort someone.

Rose sobbed for almost a minute and Martin managed to hang in there the whole time, stroking her hair. It helped that her hair was so soft.

"Paul…he knows my father, doesn't he?" she managed to say, knowing the answer already, bracing herself for even more terrifying revelations.

"Yeah," Martin said, grimacing. "That's why he's been looking at you that way. He must know you're Johnny's daughter. Johnny is the king of Clan O'Neil…and Paul really hates the O'Neils."

"My dad is the king of Clan O'Neil? This is insane!" Rose screamed, out

of her head with fear. *"This can't be happening!"*

Martin held her by the shoulders, trying to calm her down, saying nothing, taking long, slow breaths until she seemed calm enough for him to continue.

"Do you remember any stories your parents told you? Like a really long story you never heard anywhere else?"

"Yeah," she said, sniffling into her terrycloth robe. "What's that got to do with this?"

"Everything, I think," he said, feeling hopeful for the first time. Maybe he didn't need the white room. Maybe he didn't need the Book. Maybe her story was the same as Paul's. "We better have that picnic. I'll tell you everything I can remember. Maybe your story will help me remember the rest."

"Picnic! You still want to have a picnic? After all the shit you've said?"

"Yeah," Martin said, completely unfazed. "I'm getting hungry and this is going to take awhile. But I have to tell you…some of this stuff is going to sound really weird."

"Weirder than everything else you've been saying?" Rose asked, recalling all her father's insane, ranting letters. "How weird could it be?"

"Weird weird," Martin said, trying to think of a more apt description. "Religious."

Saint Patrick's

Paul bumped his shoulders into as many of the hustle-bustlers choking the aircraft carrier width of Fifth Avenue in front of St. Paddy's as he possibly could. Bump. Wump. It was morning rush hour on the sidewalk, and some of the more pissed-off jostled pedestrians gave him the old "fists clenched like they're really going do something" look. A few of the ballsier women gave him the old "Hey, watch where you're going!" shout of indignation. Once they got a load of Paul, they kept on walking.

Paul looks even scarier than he is, if that's possible. He has that longshoreman, teamster, biker, 'Nam-Vet, might-be-homeless, might-be-crazy, definitely-dangerous look down to such a T that the entire crowd would have collectively walked across the street to avoid him if they had seen him coming. Wump. Bump. Too late.

Paul walked up the cathedral stairs in his big clunky boots, making as much noise as he could with each thudding step. *Whomp. Clomp.* He went out of his way to thud into two more tourists on their way out the massive bronze doors, quickly erasing their "Wow, what a great big fancy place!" grins with twin shakes of their heads that said, "See, it *is* true what they say about these goddamn New Yorkers."

Paul sneered with equal contempt. *People. Can't live with 'em...can't kill all of 'em.*

He paused in the vestibule to soak in the candlelit, incense drenched air and gulped down as much of the musky scent as he could manage. He stuck his bald fingertips into the Holy Water and half-expected to hear it hiss and bubble. It was crowded today, as he expected. The altar was draped in purple. There were flowers everywhere. He made the sign of the cross, gave an inch-deep genuflection and clomped down the center aisle to his regular seat, a pew three rows from the front, on the left-hand side.

Someone was sitting there. Paul took a deep breath and stared down at the small gray-haired lady, with her white lace shawl and black, shiny rosary beads. She didn't seem to notice. Her tightly combed bun and happy-sad, creamy-puffy cheeks were bobbing rhythmically in deep prayer, her lips moving in a whispery quiver, mouthing out the time-honored blur of sound that passes for The Hail Mary in marathon rosary specialists: "HailMaryfullagracetheLordiswitheeblessdrthouamongwomenanblessd isthafruitathywombJesusHolyMaryMothaGodprayforusinnersnowanat-thehourofourdeathamen." Pause. Repeat.

Paul was having none of it. "That's my seat," he rumbled in a low, raspy grunt that only a gawking, T-shirt-clad couple walking down the aisle took any notice of. They quickly rolled their eyes and waddled away, but the little old lady, her eyes seemingly welded shut, showed no sign of acknowledgment whatsoever and wheezed in enough wind to motor her way through another black bead.

Paul stuck a chisel-hard finger in the square of her hunched back and pressed it in like a fleshy harpoon. "Ow!" she said, her eyes fluttering open in fear and dumb surprise.

"That's my seat," Paul repeated.

The poor, sweet, frightened lady was torn between feelings of fear, rage, shock and disbelief. She felt like running, but her fear and proud anger kept her rooted on the spot. "No sir, this is *my* seat," she finally managed to croak with all the courage she could muster, her voice trembling like a butterfly's wings.

"Darlin', you can move now or I'll wait here all day and then follow you home."

She moved. But only enough so Paul could sit next to her.

"Hhmmph!" Paul "hmphed" with more admiration than he cared to admit. He scrunched his beefy bulk up snug against the still-trembling saint and gave her a shy smile and sidelong glance as he humbly lowered his head, knelt down and clasped his hands in pious prayer.

"Dear God," he began, muttering in a barely audible voice. Barely audible that is, to anyone except the shrunken figure next to him, who twitched with fear at the sound of it.

"Dear Gawd," he repeated, louder this time, his brogue more exaggerated than ever, hoping to get another rise out of her. She was steadier this time as he continued:

"Bless da little bunnies in the forest and all da hungry children wit doze great big bellies over dere in Africa dat doan have all dis yummy good food we have over here like da Ray's pizza and da Slim Jims and da tater chips and da big, tick, juicy steaks you can cook up in your nice, warm oven by da fridge. And bless all da kiddies here too, dat be suckin' on da crack pipes all day long. And damn deir dirty feckin' parents all to hell dat send 'em out to live on da streets and fend for demselves while dey sit at home and suck on deir own crack pipes and watch da telly an' tink up more nasty ways dat dey can get more money to neglect dere little babies wit. And bless all da poor Mick cops dat have to put up with all dis stinkin' filth and shit and hopelessness so dat it's no wonder dat dey doan just go out and gun down every last stinkin' one of dem. And most of all…bless poor, dear Martin who's gone and turned away from his lovin' Da, for the sake of a dwarf harlot dat's got him all mixed up in da head so dat now wit da hour of reckonin' near, it seems I've but one last chance to convince him of da error of his ways, else I'll be left with no other choice dan to take him out behind da shed and put him down like a dirty, mongrel dog, amen."

Paul let out a deep, long sigh and slowly opened his eyes, still keeping his head bowed and his hands folded. He looked at the cross and the poor sad Christ with all the beautiful red dripping holes in his hands and feet.

"Tsk. Tsk. Such a shame about that," he sighed, shaking his head. "If only you'd listened, we could have spared you all that misery. And you ours."

He slumped back into his pew and gave his murmuring partner a warm crinkly smile as he listened to her mumbled prayers that were faster and more urgent than ever. He watched her pray for a long time, sitting motionless, smiling while her eyelids fluttered open from time to time to make sure he was still there with her.

"You're a good ole bitch, grandma," Paul said, nudging the old lady in the ribs with an elbow of genuine kinship.

Her eyes snapped open, filled with a little less fear this time. She was about to speak when Paul held a thick, fat finger to her old, wrinkled lips and said, "Shhhhh…don't tax your sweet breath, my darlin', you'll be needin' it for that next round of Hail Marys."

She opened her mouth to speak again, but then her face froze in place when she saw the nail was missing from Paul's still-poised fingertip. "Say a little prayer for me, sweetie," he whispered in his perfect Irish lilt, "and say a great big one for Martin."

Then he pinched her cheek, made the sign of the cross, stood up and walked away.

VIGIL

Michael had seen some weird shit already, but this was ridiculous. The cross. The angel. The altar. *Holy. Fucking. Crap.* He looked around and saw all the pictures and carvings and drawings. Everything looked scary, but the angel frightened him most.

"Man, this is some seriously fucked-up shit here!" he said in the flickering darkness. Part of him was curious about the pictures and the books and the other stuff. But not enough to stay in a creep palace like this. He wanted to stop right there, turn around and run away screaming, but the Book wouldn't let him. It kept pulling him forward, closer to the altar.

As he approached, he noticed a cabinet below. It was empty. The altar wasn't. There was a single gold coin resting on the blood-caked wood. He hesitated before picking it up. He even let out a little laugh. Then he reached out his trembling hand and raised it to his eyes. On one side was an angel with its wings spread out like the one on the cross in front of him. On the other side was the profile of a face. The head was graced with a laurel wreath, like an emperor. It looked a lot like Paul.

He dropped the coin and ran for the door. But the door wasn't there anymore. He couldn't even tell where it had been. Not that it mattered anyway. The shadowy figure blocking his way had a look on his face that said Michael wouldn't be going anywhere.

When he started to speak, Michael understood why.

Don't Make Big Decisions on an Empty Stomach

Martin was getting dressed. Fast.

"Where are you going?" Rose asked, rubbing her tear-stained cheeks.

"Pastrami," he said, as if that were explanation enough.

"Well, I'm coming too," Rose said, shucking off her robe.

"You can't leave now," Martin said, hoisting it up again, "not until it's…"

"Safe?" Rose taunted him, dropping the robe again, tossing it onto a chair. "You've been saying that since we got here. You can't tell me all this shit and then walk out of here like nothing happened. If you're so fucking hungry, call room service!"

He said he'd rather get pastrami from the Carnegie Deli. Rose had another shit fit.

Martin wasn't lying about the pastrami. He craved it every time he was within ten blocks of the place. But what he really wanted was to case the lobby and make sure no one had followed them. Without Rose in eyesight. Or gun sight. "I'll only be a few minutes," he said, putting on his jacket, feeling the twin pistols in his deep side pockets. "Twenty tops."

"You're not going anywhere without me," she said defiantly, "Do you read me?"

Martin grabbed her wrist and plopped the Beretta in her hand. "Listen," he said coldly, "you need to trust me on this. I know what I'm doing. You'll be safe here with this. Don't let anyone in except when you hear this knock.…"

He rapped on the nightstand. *Bop-ba-ba-da-da.*

Rose nodded. The look of determination in Martin's eyes couldn't be argued with. She tried anyway "But why can't I come…?" she pleaded.

"Snipers," Martin said simply. So simply, and with such an air of authority that she paced over to the chair, slumped into the seat and cried.

Martin put his hand on her shoulder, like he'd seen other men do in the movies when they were trying to provide reassurance.

"I'm pretty sure we weren't followed, but I need to look around. You should stay away from the window. It's not Paul's style…he uses knives mostly, but better safe than…"

Rose began crying so hard that it took another five minutes before Martin could make another attempt at leaving. "Maybe you could take a bath or something," he said, stroking her hair, like Norine would have done. He was starting to get the hang of this whole comforting thing. "I'll be right back. Then we can have that picnic. It's a nice day."

"Are you *crazy?*" Rose yelled. "A *nice day?* You think I still want a *picnic?*"

"Well, I do. I've never had one," said Martin with such a hurt expression that Rose didn't know whether to laugh or cry. She managed a smile.

"I need to know what's going on here. Can you understand that?"

"Yeah, but we can talk about that while we eat."

"Let's stay here and talk, okay?"

"I'll be fast," he said convincingly. "Don't worry…everything's going to be fine."

She nodded, surrendering to the inevitable.

Martin took the elevator to the lobby and gave it a thorough sweep before venturing into the throng. It was bustling with activity, people coming and going, checking in and checking out, sitting in the slightly uncomfortable chairs, soaking in the atmosphere, or walking and gawking the length of the cavernous room so they could tell their cousins back in Omaha that they'd been to The Plaza!

Martin was an expert at spotting anyone trying to "act natural" while they were on the prowl. He scanned the room from every angle and was relieved that not a single person in the shuffling tapestry looked like they didn't belong there, except maybe for the two plainclothes security guards that were eyeing the breasts of a porn star on the arm of an ancient codger in a navy blue blazer, complete with brass buttons. He gave the room one final pass, then walked in long strides toward the less trafficked exit at 58th Street. He did a quick 360-degree swivel outside the door and a more detailed building-by-building, window-by-window search from the fountain across from the entrance. If he saw any observers, he would make a beeline straight back to the room and stand guard over Rose.

Finally, convinced no one was watching, Martin looked in the direction of the Carnegie Deli, debating the wisdom of his errand for fatty meat and mustard. His heart was calling him back to the hotel, to Rose's sensible suggestion for room service. His stomach was growling for that pastrami, his mouth watering as he imagined biting down on the thick onion roll and all that succulent meat. His head was pulling him to Paul's apartment, where he could search for the book, or better yet, to his own apartment, where he could sit in the white room, stare into the blankness, and let all those bottled-up memories flood his mind in one-tenth the time it would take Rose to tell him her story, maybe giving him even more effective ammunition or bargaining chips than the Book could provide.

The white room. Still, a quick trip home was out of the question. It would take him twenty minutes each way, not counting how long it took for him to get beyond the dreamy images he always saw in the whiteness or how big a fight his stubborn brain would put up before surrendering those long-guarded memories…memories of where he'd seen Paul with the Book. Candles? A room full of candles…and something really big on the wall?

Fuck! He could almost see it again! Just a few minutes in the room would bring the rest of it back. No, he couldn't leave Rose alone that long. Not with that sad, scared look she gave him. On the other hand, it would only take him twenty minutes or less to run a few blocks, grab the pastrami, run back to Rose and have that goddam picnic.

"Twenty minutes," he said, breaking into a jog. "That's all it'll take."

Just enough time for Paul to do what he came for.

OLD

Paul had left the cathedral only minutes earlier when his beeper went off. He looked at the green screen, and watched the message scroll across: *Elvis has left the building. Alone.*

"God, I hate it when people try to be clever," he grumbled, wump-bumping into even more pedestrians on his way back to the hotel than he had while going to church.

He stared in the mirror while he waited for the hotel elevator, studying the lines around his eyes. The other people waiting gave him an unobstructed view, crowding together in clumps on either side of him at least five feet away.

You're not getting younger, he thought, smiling wider to accentuate the wrinkles—and in sheer anticipatory glee of the encounter awaiting him upstairs.

When the elevator arrived, no one entered the car with him, which gave him another opportunity to admire his reflection in the elevator mirror…and his cunning. These last few months had taken a toll, but here he was in the final stretch with more than enough get-up-and-go to finish his task. Everything was ready.

"Fit as a fiddle," he said, thumping his cast-iron belly, grateful for these few private seconds before the door opened. He pressed his fingers against his face, smoothing out the deeply lined skin until he looked half his age. When the door opened, he gave the mirror a final jolly wink before stepping into the hallway.

"No, you're not getting any younger," he admitted. "We're going to have to do something about that."

ABANDONMENT ISSUES

Rose stared at her key while she listened to the radio. How could she have let Martin go without telling her everything? Everything!

The wafting sounds of the salsa station matched the rhythms of the warm breeze blowing through the open window. It was so beautiful outside. She'd been looking forward to a picnic so much…before Martin started talking. Hell, she'd been looking forward to talking with him so much, but not about this.

She fingered the key, rolling it between her fingers. Her mind drifted back to her mother and the story, to her father, to his letters, to the day he gave her the necklace. She thought of him now. Pictured his kind, loving face. Pictured…the letters. *Words. Phrases. Drifting apart. Recombining. His voice. A memory?* A warning: "If anyone looks at this necklace like they've seen it before, don't trust them. If anyone tries to take it…run!"

It sounded like an actual shout in her head. It scared her so much she peed on the bed. She ran to the window, then stepped backwards. *Snipers,* she thought, almost hysterical.

She cursed herself for staying behind and plopped down on the bed. On the wet spot. "Goddammit!" she yelled, springing back up.

She paced back and forth, far from the window. She looked at the gun Martin left on the nightstand. Would she be able to use it? After reviewing her performance with the street punks, she guessed the answer was probably yes. Probably. But who knew how many of these creeps were out there looking for this key. Looking for her. And where was Paul right now? What did he want to do with her? Kill her, of course. Kill her and take the key. But if he already knew she had it, if he knew who she was and where she lived, why hadn't he taken it already? Why was she still alive?

She cursed her predicament again. She thought about her father's voice in her head. Then she saw the shopping bag with that stuffed dog inside and longed even more for Martin's speedy return. *I can trust him. He told me all this stuff because he cares about me. He wants to protect me, just like he said in the...taxi.*

Shit! What if Martin had left her? Hopped in a cab. What if he was gone for good? *Dammit!* What was the matter with her? She should be on the phone with the police right now. How could she still be waiting for her murdering "boyfriend" to return?

Why did Martin leave me all alone? How could he do this to me?

"Because he's a cold-blooded killer, without a scrap of remorse or compassion?" she offered tearfully. "Oh yeah, that's right," she added, slapping her forehead. "Stupid ole me!"

She closed her eyes, wiping the tears away. She felt so desperate that she actually prayed for her father to help her. Guide her. Protect her. Oddly enough, she got an answer. This time it was more than a voice in her head. It was a feeling in her chest, wordlessly saying:

"I'm here...I'll always be here, but now you have to...*run!*"

"*Ouch!*" Her fingers had pressed against the key so hard that her chest was bleeding. "Shit!" She ran to the bathroom and hung her robe on the hook behind the door. She took off the necklace and hung it on the doorknob. She turned on the shower, leaping behind the plastic curtain before the water warmed up, shrieking from the shock of it. Another round of achy tears joined the water pulsating from the shower massage nozzle, joining the even saltier scarlet stream dripping from the gash on her breastbone, leaking down her trembling legs...washing down the drain. She was about to have a full-blown meltdown when she heard the loud knocking.

Bop-ba-ba-da-da... She leapt from the shower, grabbing her robe off the hook, forgetting all about the necklace swinging from the doorknob, the pistol on the nightstand, rushing blindly to the door, her chest practically collapsing with relief.

Tsk. Tsk. If only Rose had remembered, she might have grabbed the key, or the gun. Because the instant she turned the handle, the knock on the door continued two beats longer than it should have: ...*bop-BOP!*

And in came Paul.

INSTANT REPLAY

Something was wrong. Martin was only a few blocks away, issuing a steady stream of saliva at the prospect of all that juicy pastrami, when he suddenly got a very bad feeling.

"*Go back!*" a voice shouted in his head.

He turned around instantly, running back to her while his mind replayed his exit from the hotel with the efficiency of a digital recorder, revisiting every move he made, searching for possible errors. His memory was perfect with things like this—and he was absolutely correct. There was no one in the lobby that didn't belong there and there was no one watching from outside. Still, something wasn't right. He went through it again, moment by moment. This time he saw it. The porter. It was the way he looked at him when they passed. He looked afraid. That wasn't unusual. Most people looked at him that way. What he failed to notice on the first pass was his clammy-faced attempt at a smile.

People smile all the time, especially porters, he thought, trying to rationalize it. *Not at you,* came a speedy comeback he had a hard time recognizing as himself. "Shit!" Martin cursed, shifting his legs into high gear. "How could I have left her all alone?"

"C'mon, c'mon," Martin muttered, pushing the elevator button over and over. He felt the bulging pockets of his leather coat to check his guns almost as many times.

A frowning mother and her small boy were inside the car with him. They kept looking at him like he was crazy. "Stop pressing the button," the kid said in a canary-high voice.

"Sorry," Martin said, surprised he meant it.

"It's okay," the boy replied, smiling broadly as they exited on the tenth floor. His mother gave him a scolding look and dragged him away.

Martin followed, unsurprisingly, since he'd been pressing the same button repeatedly for the last nine floors. He walked away from them, then sprinted to the stairwell exit when they entered their room. He took the staircase up one more floor, listening for any other footsteps. He opened the stairwell door silently and checked the hallway for any sign of movement. Then he crept up to his room and stood to the side of the door.

Well, this is it. Please be inside.

He drew out the chrome-plated pistol with his left hand and raised his right hand to knock. Then he hesitated. Should he use the key card instead? He told Rose he would be using the special knock and to blow a hole through the door if anybody tried to get in without it. He didn't seriously think she'd do that, but it was possible. But, if he knocked and Paul *was* inside with her, there goes the element of surprise. On the other hand, if Paul was inside, it would be for one of three reasons: She was already dead and he wanted to gloat; or they hadn't had time to leave yet; or Paul *wanted* to wait for him. In any case, he would be holding the stronger hand, and a gun or knife pointing to some vital part of Rose's anatomy. If she was still alive. Was she?

You're wasting time. You'll find the answer soon enough.

Bop–ba–ba–da–da…he knocked, raising his pistol.

And heard nothing in reply.

THE PRISONER

Bop–ba–ba–da–da . . .

Rose was sitting in her robe next to Paul when she heard the special knock again.

Paul told her that if she made any sound at all, under any circumstances, except as a direct reply to a question from him, she would regret it more than anything she could imagine in her worst nightmares. She kept her mouth shut.

Paul walked to the door. He'd been sitting next to her in a matching chair by the window, separated only by a small tea table. On the table were a silver whiskey flask and a bag of Oreos. He picked up the Beretta that had also been resting between them, touched the tip of her nose with the end of the barrel, then shoved it into his pocket.

Bop–ba–ba–da–da… came the knock again. Rose tightened her lips as Paul slowly turned the handle.

It was the porter. "He's downstairs," he told Paul, "back in his room."

Rose's head sank to her robe, the last of her hopes deflated. When she had opened the door for Paul, he whisked her away so quickly that she knew Martin wouldn't make it back from that stupid fucking deli in time to witness her abduction. But when she heard the special knock again— on the door of this gigantic penthouse suite—she thought Martin must have known they were here. He had come to rescue her! Rose was in such despair after seeing it was only the porter that she barely noticed when he began leering at her. It would only occur to her later that "shave and a haircut" was probably not the best secret knock to use with a human life resting in the balance.

The porter began walking inside, but Paul stopped him with a fat hand at the threshold. He gave Paul a knowing smile he assumed all men were supposed to exchange under such circumstances. The knowing part, he guessed, meant knowing that the man on the receiving end was about to have sex with a young, pretty girl due solely to his irresistible powers of seduction, which deserved some special acknowledgment.

"Thank you very much," Paul said without the accent, enjoying Rose's discomfort as the porter ogled her. He gave him a few more seconds to enjoy the view before closing the door in his face. "I'll take it from here," he said, smiling at Rose.

She managed to remain silent during the entire exchange. That was lucky for her. Her luck ran out soon afterward.

"Let's give Martin a little jingle, eh?" Paul said sweetly, picking up the receiver. "He must be worried sick about you." He raised his finger to his lips while the phone rang, reminding Rose of his earlier threat. Or promise.

"We're in the penthouse!" she cried out as soon as Paul smiled into the receiver. He hung up before the second word left her lips.

"That was a mistake," he said, handcuffing her wrists behind her back through the rococo carvings of the wooden chair. "I'll call back in a bit, after I get you quieted down. Then we'll have a little lesson about following instructions. I hope you like pain as much as you think you do, my sweet, little porcupine."

Rose did, of course, like pain. But not nearly as much as Paul.

SACRIFICE

"Lie down, please," said the shadowy face so high above him. "On the altar."

"Why? What are you doing here?" Bean panted, sweat pouring from his forehead.

"Getting you ready for him," the voice said simply, lifting the giant book, setting it on the lectern, flipping the golden coin high in the air, catching it in the palm of his hand.

"For...Paul?" Bean asked, wiping his clammy brow with his dirty shirtsleeve.

"Of course. He'll be joining us momentarily, but I need to prepare you."

Bean gasped as the nearly naked figure walked around the altar, spreading his arms in invitation, the span of his skeletal fingers mirroring the giant winged creature behind him. "Lie down, Mr. Bean. Make yourself comfortable," Loren said softly, lowering his hands behind the altar and raising them again with a hammer and four nails in his grip.

"Fuck you, man!" Bean shouted, backing up against the far wall. "I have Paul's complete protection. Don't even think about touching me!"

"'Complete protection'?" The Striker mimicked with a deep chuckle. "That's an odd way of putting it, though I wouldn't dare to question his phrasing or intent. Considering that I've been summoned here for the express purpose of performing this ritual according to his precise instructions...I can't fathom a guess as to what he might have meant."

"He *meant* that you should keep your fucking hands off me!" Michael bellowed, desperately clawing his fingers into the wallpaper. The opening had to be back here someplace. Where the fuck was it?

"No, I'm quite sure you're mistaken in that regard," The Striker said, swinging the hammer in a pendulum arc as he stepped around the altar, closing the distance between them by more than a yard with each step. "But perhaps he has a deeper grasp of your ability to withstand discomfort than I can discern from your futile attempt to escape your destiny. Perhaps he meant that you have no real need for his generous offer of protection. Perhaps this won't hurt you a bit."

"Get the *fuck* away from me, man!" Bean yelled, circling the room, trying to keep as much distance as possible between them.

"I have neither the time nor the patience for any more of this nonsense," The Striker sighed. "So get on the altar without further ado, or I'll crush your skull with this hammer."

Michael stopped running. His heart sank like a coin in a wishing well. None of his prayers were going to come true. Not now. Not ever.

"Please," Bean begged him in a voice barely louder than a whisper. "Please don't do this."

"Since you asked so nicely, I'll spare you the additional flourishes I had in mind," The Striker purred, gently grasping his hand, leading him to the altar like a groom escorting his bride. "Soon the Master will join us. He has something very special planned for you."

"He's going to kill me, isn't he?" Michael wept, meek as a lamb.

The Striker squeezed the nails in his fist and hissed, "No. Something even better."

TOOLS OF THE TRADE

Rose was bathed in golden sunlight from the window. The sky was so blue she began to cry. The combination of the gorgeous day and the fate clearly awaiting her was too much to bear. Her fate clearly awaited her because of the implements Paul was placing on the table between them. He took his time laying them out in front of her. His sickle was joined by a pair of pliers, a hammer and two knitting needles. Paul removed them from a gigantic fifteenth-century French armoire filled to the brim with even more exotic instruments of torture. Some looked so strange she couldn't imagine what they were used for, which made them all the more terrifying. Even so, they weren't half as scary as the ones he chose, dirty and rusting like they'd been purchased for fifty cents at a garage sale.

"I think this suits you," he said, stuffing her mouth with a black, rubber, penis-shaped gag attached to a leather harness. Then he made the universal thumb and pinkie symbol for a telephone call, silently mouthing, "I'll be back in a minute."

He went into an adjoining room and closed the door. Rose rocked the chair back and forth violently, trying to break one of the rungs binding her handcuffs. It didn't even creak. She gulped frantically, trying to swallow the built-up saliva pooling in her mouth without choking on the cock gag. Her mounting terror amplified the struggle.

She looked away from Paul's torture tools in an attempt to gain some measure of composure, but the sheer splendor of their surroundings was so out of place with Paul's ratty appearance that she became even more frightened. His suite was like a palace. The ceiling was at least thirteen feet high, with ornate moldings, six-foot-wide mirrors and a number of Renaissance paintings. Most of them featured naked women being killed.

TOO LATE

Rose was gone. Martin knew it before he opened the door, even before he knocked the second time. So why were his legs still frozen, staring at the empty room?

The red light on his phone was blinking. That got him moving. He ran to the phone and pressed the button to retrieve his message. An instance of heavy breathing, then Rose's terrified scream, "We're..." *Click.*

Fuck! Fuck! Fuck! Where the *fuck* are they?

The porter. He knows. He ran to the door, then stopped and stared at the phone. What if she called again? Or Paul? "The porter," Martin said aloud. He took another step toward the door...and the phone rang.

"Hello, Martin," Paul said sweetly.

"Where is she? What did you do to her?"

"I haven't done anything of consequence...yet. As to where she is, what does your gut tell you, boy? Can you *see* where she is right now?"

"Tell me!"

"You're not even trying," Paul complained. "If you're so desperate for the little lass, the least you could do is make a decent effort. Perhaps I shouldn't have bothered calling."

"Wait. Don't hang up. Tell me what you want."

"I want you to answer the question," Paul said without emotion.

Martin took a deep breath. Clearing his mind as quickly as he could, he started running calculations. Given the length of his absence, the speed of the elevator, the fact that Rose was dressed in her robe when he left and the difficulties in smuggling an unwilling, undressed hostage through a crowded hotel lobby, he came to the most logical conclusion, which in his experience, was usually the correct one.

"She's still in the hotel. With you."

"Correct," Paul said. "But which room? Can you picture what I'm about to do to her?"

"If you hurt her…" Martin shouted, only to have Paul immediately cut him off.

"Yes, I'm surely in for a terrible time if I so much as pull a single ring from her nose, but if you don't keep your mouth shut and listen, I'll make it even harder on her, okay?"

Martin bit his lip so hard it bled, but refrained from another outburst.

"Good boy," Paul continued after hearing Martin's grunt. "Here's how we'll play it: If you discover where we are in the next…hmmm…let's say thirty minutes, she's yours."

"Why are you doing this?" Martin whispered, his voice shaky with rage and the pain of Paul's betrayal.

"You're wasting time," Paul said dryly. "Don't be feeling so sorry for yourself lad. There's someone here who's having a much worse day than you. The sooner you find her, the more pain she'll be spared…assuming you find her at all. And Martin…"

"Yes?" he asked, praying for any clue that could help him.

"Don't give away my presents again. That Beretta was very special."

Click.

"Wait!" Martin yelled at the dial tone, staring at the nightstand where he'd left the pistol and the ticking clock beside the vacant space. "Rose!" he yelled again, slamming the phone down so hard he cracked the plastic. *What was Paul doing to her right now?*

THE SAFE WORD

"Are you ready to begin?" Paul asked, rubbing his hands together like a Boy Scout building a campfire. Rose shook her head violently in protest.

"Good, good," he said, opening her robe, exposing her pierced and tattooed breasts. "Hmmm," he murmured thoughtfully, examining her manifold piercings. "You've already done so much damage here, I might be gilding the lily." He paced around in slow circles before plopping down in the chair. "Still, I suppose it's as good a place as any to begin."

Rose groaned beneath the gag as Paul leaned in closer, his nose only a few scant inches from the fresh droplet of blood trickling from the key-shaped scar.

"Hhmmph! Now what have we here?" he mused, sniffing the blood like a hound dog, prodding at the purple welt with his callused fingertip. "If I didn't know better, I'd say this bruise is shaped like a key! But the odd thing is, even with all these other shiny barbs stickin' every which way out yer tiny titties...I can't imagine where a mark like this could come from. Might you have been wearing a certain necklace earlier today? About twenty-eight minutes ago, perhaps?"

"Mmphh," Rose grunted, trying to avoid his gaze.

"Oh, yes...you're suffering from a little congestion. Let me give you some air."

Paul loosened the strap on her gag just enough to extract a few inches of the black rubber cock clogging her gullet.

"I gave it to Martin," Rose gurgled. She wanted to say more, but Paul strapped the gag back on again...after brutally shoving it in and out a few times.

"You gave it to Martin, did you?" he chuckled, lowering his face to her harness-strapped head. Rose gagged on the saliva trapped in her mouth as she gazed into Paul's dead eyes with absolute horror. Then she choked again, almost drowning in spit as Paul slowly rolled his eyes...upward...

and upward…and backwards…until only the whites were showing. Paul smiled with those blank eyeballs, laced with a hundred tiny capillaries. Then his irises drifted back down again, locking on to Rose's pupils like a ratchet wrench.

"No, I don't think so. I just spoke to the dear lad…worried sick about you he is, though Gawd only knows why. If he had your little trinket, I'm thinking he might have mentioned it, desperate as he is for anything to barter for your worthless hide.

"By the by, it surely was a mistake for you to have taken off that precious bauble, even for a moment, leaving only this sad shadow in its wake. I'm not sure what Johnny told you about it, and frankly, I don't care, but you might want to know, now that's it's far too late, that that innocent little scrap of metal, in addition to its more practical function, is a very powerful amulet. A protective amulet, if you believe such nonsense. I've heard stories…aye, legends about that key. Even though it can't be proved—certainly not now anyway, with you here all helpless in my evil grip—but some say it's the most powerful amulet that has ever existed. So powerful, in fact, that even a big, strong bully like meself would be hard pressed to injure a teeny hair on your spiky head, were you wise enough to still be wearing it. But sadly, you're not wearing it, dearie…are you?"

"Mmmmmmph," Rose gurgled in blind, absolute panic.

Paul slowly stood up, reaching his arms toward the heavens, and shouted with all his might, "Are you watching, Johnny? I know you are! So keep both eyes open. I wouldn't want you to miss a single second of this! Your little bitch is mine now! All mine!"

Rose stared at Paul's hate-filled screaming face and shuddered with a terror so complete she almost fell over backwards in her chair.

Paul lowered his arms. He was laughing now. "Oh, I do get carried away sometimes. I surely do. Still, you shouldn't be so frightened," he said, stroking her cheek. "Look at all the pain you've already endured, at your very own hands. This shouldn't be much different, d'you think?"

"Mmmpphh!" Rose grunted, her eyes pleading.

"Still, I believe it's customary within your S&M circles to have some kind of 'safe' word—a signal to express your limits regarding the level of pain you're able to endure. However, since this is strictly a disciplinary action as a result of your foolish disobedience, we should think of a word that has a more direct bearing on these unique circumstances.

"Now what should it be?" he mused, picking up the pliers, holding them to his mustache, plucking out a single white hair while he mulled over the possibilities.

"I've got it! It's not really a word, more of a phrase to be accurate, but if the pain gets to be too much, if I go too far, just gurgle out as best you're able, 'Please, Daddy! Save me!'"

Journal Entry: Dust

I've been going to the chapel day after day, equally impelled by my thirst for revenge and my insatiable curiosity about the Clan Kelly mystery. Any knowledge gained, I thought, would be potentially useful in whatever last stand I could muster against the man who had decimated all our lives. Mother. Me. Martin.

Paul never came inside while I was in there. I looked at the pictures stuffed between the candles, the weird inscriptions on the walls, but mostly I read the books. Some sections were easy to read, but a lot of it was written in teensy scribbles, some of it backward, or in Ogham. I knew a little bit about Celtic Genealogy from reading the *Annals of the Four Masters*, but these notations (almost always in the margins), were so pointed, critical and comical I could almost hear Paul reading them aloud.

There were frequent references to the Milesians: Heremon, Heber and Ir and many of the big guns in their lineage; Tormac Mac Art, Ugaine Mor, Crimthann-Niadh-Nar, Eochaidh Dubhlen, Colla da Crioch, Maine Mor, Ceallach (the first reference to "Kelly" I found)…and my personal favorite: William Boy Kelly. Even more interesting was the fact that Paul's marginal commentaries were all written like he personally knew them. For example, in the *Book of Connor*, Paul's fifth son, he wrote, "Sometimes he reminds me so much of Niall, I wonder if he's a Kelly at all." I assume he's referring to Niall Noígíallach, of the nine hostages. It seemed that they were once allies, but something went wrong and the Kellys and O'Neils had been feuding ever since. Which made me think about Rose. Another O'Neil.

The narrative was similar in every volume: the training period, the killings and thefts of ritual objects in "raids" as he calls them—and in most cases, their deaths—at the hands of rival clans, their brothers, another clan member and occasionally Paul himself. The raids are launched to plunder ancient artifacts, like St. Grellan's Crosier—good story there. Even more bizarrely, Paul and his sons (Martin, usually) sojourn on lengthy quests to obtain what they call "the four elementals" which are the four treasures of the Celtic Gods, the Tuatha Dé Danann: The Dagda's Cauldron, The Spear of Lugh, The Stone of Fal and the Sword of Nuada. From what I've read, he claims to have nabbed two of them.

I kept reading and making notes, hoping the books might contain the answer to the question that nagged me most of all: What were they really trying to do? If this was a competition, someone had to win something more valuable than all the loot they were taking, even the elementals. A grand prize? Yet I couldn't find a single reference to any reward other than the gold and artifacts they found, stole and hoarded. Everything else I learned raised even more questions. There were never any explanations, as if everything was written for someone who already knew the story. Every time I asked Paul a direct question, he wouldn't say a word. He'd just smile and point back to the chapel. Yeah, yeah, I know. Look and learn.

It made for great reading. But the more I read, the more frightened I became—not from the content as much as what it implied. The incredible notion that they had somehow maintained an underground Celtic feudal society after God knows how many centuries—complete with kings, lords, nobles and a druid sect—put me right back to square one with my belief that Paul was, in fact, an extremely dangerous paranoid schizophrenic with delusions of grandeur. Correction: with delusions of everything. He had invented his own terrifying little world, I thought. It was as if he and his clan were trapped in a Renaissance Faire that never ended. They had even convinced some Irish genealogy nuts from other families to join the game. Did they get all dressed up too?

I wonder if the first person to discover Henry Darger's hidden collection of several hundred watercolor paintings felt the same way I was feeling. I'm guessing he did, especially if he spent any time reading his 15,145 page, single-spaced manuscript *(The Story of the Vivian Girls, in What is known as the Realms of the Unreal, of the Glandeco-Angelinnian War Storm, Caused by the Child Slave Rebellion)* featuring prepubescent girls with penises fighting off an army of soldiers who routinely hung, strangled and eviscerated them. But I'm sure the person who discovered Darger's stash didn't find a blood-caked altar and a crucified angel in the room, or a website filled with snuff videos.

Still, that didn't mean all the "clansmen" weren't sharing a delusional worldview. Plenty of cults accept ridiculous mythical stories as the gospel truth, some of them so wacky they make Paul's adventures seem downright plausible. Hell, all the big religions do the same thing and there's always more money piling up in the collection plates. Virgin births. Water into wine. Resurrection. Paul and his clansmen were all crazy cultists, tilting at windmills, questing for grails—and murdering each other with apparent immunity. There was no rhyme or reason, no occult or Hermetic references and nothing at all that described the all-important line of succession Paul kept harping on. I was thinking just that when he stomped into the chapel and asked, "Are you beginning to get the big picture?"

"I haven't been able to get through everything," I said, pointing at all the volumes in the cabinet below, "but I think I get the gist of it."

"And the gist of it is?" Paul asked with a dubious expression.

That you're totally fucking crazy, I wanted to say, but I answered, "Well, you rape these women, abandon us as babies, but you keep stalking us, writing these books. Then at some point you show up in our lives and train us to be killers. Well, you train most of us; you haven't done anything with Michael as far as I can tell, and I guess my training's just begun, right?"

"I've taken a different tack with you and Michael. Call it an accelerated learning curve. His training will commence shortly. By the way, you need to pick up the pace, lad. You're falling far below my expectations. Now, what else have you learned?"

"I don't know…some of this other stuff…it just doesn't seem possible."

"Such as…"

"For one thing, most of these books are written in the first person, and the handwriting is different in each one. I don't know how you did it, but some of the writing in here," I said, pointing at the *Book of William*, "it matches my own perfectly."

"Hhmmph! That is quite odd, now that you mention it. What do you make of that?"

"Well…maybe you imagine what it's like to be in our heads, then you forge our handwriting. Either that or…" I tried to think of a tactful way to say it. Nothing came out for a few seconds and then, like I wasn't even in control of my lips and tongue I said, "Or you're totally fucking crazy."

I fully expected him to go ballistic, which he did, but not with rage as I expected. With laughter. It took him almost a minute to settle down enough to speak again.

"You're a real pisser, Billy Boy! So I'm a madman, eh? Delusional psychosis, is that your diagnosis? Well maybe so…that would explain the trouble I have falling asleep at night. But what about you, then? Same problem? Is that why you can see and hear things that aren't humanly possible? Are you crazy too, lad?"

"What are you talking about?" I asked, avoiding his eyes.

"Don't play dumb with me," he said, cold and deadly. "I've seen you use the gift, both in my dreams and my own wakeful visions."

I said nothing, wishing he would stop.

"Close your eyes," he suddenly commanded. I hesitated, looking at the pitch-black hallway beyond the candles, wondering how far I could run before he stopped me. Then, accepting the futility of my situation, I slowly closed my eyes, praying the images wouldn't come. They didn't. I saw nothing but the flicker of candlelight darting across my sealed eyelids. "Keep them closed," I heard Paul say. But his voice sounded different, like it was coming from somewhere else in the room. "Now open them."

I grabbed my chest in shock. I was looking at me, from where Paul was standing. From inside his head. My eyes looked back at me. I saw an almost indescribable intensity in them and I said…I mean my body said, in a voice that will haunt me forever: "Look in my left eye with your left eye."

I did what the voice told me, even though I didn't have a clue who I was or where I was. It felt like a rope was being pulled inside my gut (whose gut?) and…

Wham! I was back inside my body, looking at Paul. I hadn't moved. Nothing had changed, except my perspective. And that was everything. The sensation was beyond amazing. I'd been seeing my visions for so long they didn't seem strange to me anymore. But this was something else. If something like this was possible…

"What isn't?" Paul said, finishing my thought.

"So if you're not crazy, and I'm not crazy…"

"Then everything you've ever known, everything you've ever believed about yourself…about the description of reality you've clung to so stubbornly all your life…all of it…every bit of it…is an illusion. Yes, Billy, you'll be looking at life through a new pair of glasses now. A nice, red, rosy pair."

I swallowed hard. There were a million more questions I wanted to ask, but one burned far brighter than the rest.

"Do the others…can they see things too?"

"Better finish your reading. They, or most of 'em, are long in the grave."

"Not Martin," I argued.

"Ah yes," Paul sighed. "Actually, I've been wondering the same thing meself. I've seen the power in him, glowing like a dormant ember, but never have I witnessed him use it. Since your talents are so…expansive, perhaps you can answer that riddle even better than I."

Was he being serious? Did he mean my "gift" was stronger than his? I wasn't sure what to say or do next, but I didn't have to worry about that. He'd already made plans.

"Let's take a stroll. We have an appointment and we're runnin' late."

"Where are we going?" I asked, happy to get some fresh air.

"Church. I'm going to show you how *not* to run a religion."

Here's a fun fact: Old St Patrick's Cathedral on Mulberry Street is the oldest Catholic church in New York. It was razed by a fire in 1866, but was restored two years later, much as it had been before: simple and unpretentious. I read about it on a flyer in the vestibule. The mass was already in progress. He didn't seem to care, clomping ahead, sitting in the back row of pews.

I slid in next to him and whispered, "What's up?"

"It's Ash Wednesday," he said, pointing to the priest kneeling in front of the altar. God, I hate church.

When it came time for the "ashing", Paul stood up and I followed him into the aisle. What the hell. When it was my turn, I knelt down in front of the priest and watched him dip his thumb in a bowl full of gray ashes. Then he rubbed it on my forehead, making the sign of the cross. While he was doing it, he mumbled something incoherently.

Instead of going back to our pew, Paul stormed out of the church, clearly furious. "What was all that about?" I asked him, after we exited into the drab morning light.

"It was bad enough when they stopped using Latin," he fumed. "But now you can't even understand what they're saying in English!"

I asked him if he was talking about the ash prayer and he shouted, "Yes, Goddammit!"

When I asked him what the priest had said, he told me, "Never mind, it's all ruined now."

Okaaaaay. Paul grumbled and waved for me to follow him home.

We sat on the couch, saying nothing. I guess that was the point. I tried to probe inside him, making sure to keep my eyes open—so he couldn't do that switcheroo thing again. I could feel him blocking me. He took a sip from his flask and walked into the dark hallway without another word.

I twiddled my thumbs for a few minutes, getting pissy, when I was suddenly slammed with an image of Paul inside the chapel, sitting in a huge oak chair. He was inviting me to join him. I resented the sudden intrusion and tried to shut him out. I wasn't sure how to do it and made the initial mistake of closing my eyes to concentrate on pushing him away. Instead, the image became even more vivid, to the point where I could see that he had a golden chalice in his hands. I opened my eyes and I could still see him. I was about to surrender and join him in there, when some part of me, some physical part took over. It started with a tingle in a spot directly below my navel. Then a long grunting *pussssssshhhh!* The only physical sensation I could compare it to is taking a shit. A really difficult shit. I wondered if this was the kind of push that mothers felt in childbirth.

I saw Paul's face begin to fade. *Pussshhh!* And fade. *Pusssssshhhhhhh!* Then he was gone. In a few more seconds the image of him came back and I pushed again. It worked! When he came back a third time, I left to join him in the chapel. I wasn't sure if he knew what I'd been doing, but I didn't want to "push" it any more, until I found out.

When I walked into the chapel, it looked exactly as it had in my vision. Lots of candles. Incense too. And the smell of something else. I looked at the altar and saw a large stone bowl filled with ashes. The chalice Paul was holding was filled with ashes too. There was an empty oak chair about five feet in front of him. I sat down and noticed the kneeling pad in front. When he spoke, he made no reference to the game of tug-of-war we'd been playing. Maybe he couldn't tell what I'd done. He gave me a sermon instead. He even stood for it. I can still remember every word.

"DUST!" he shouted so loudly I thought the ceiling might crack.

"The Bible says God made Adam out of dust and breathed His life inside him. He made him born to die. All things turn to dust in time, they say. All except a few. My children died so I could live, and earn the wisdom of their sacrifice. Now I'll pass it on to you. All of us are killers. Each and every one. We live by eating life. Time has robbed us of this knowing. Time and our shame of the truth. We let others do our killing. We pretend goodness is better than hunger. We fear death and the pain that accompanies it. We pretend they don't exist."

He paused and looked at me. "There once was a spiritual seeker who found a guru on the mountaintop. He couldn't believe his good fortune and so he asked the question that had been burning in his heart: 'Master,' he asked, 'What is the greatest mystery in life?'

"The wise man said, 'The greatest mystery in life is that we see death all around us and we still can't believe it will ever happen to us.'"

"I can see you found that amusing," Paul said, smiling back at me, "but here's a little twist. The wise man wasn't so wise after all. It's no mystery why we hide from death. We hide because we fear it. The greatest mystery of life *is* death. What force engineered this necessity? What is this thing we call 'food'? We eat life, William. We eat *life!* And we eat it every single day!"

He stopped for a moment, then walked to the lectern and put his hands on a giant codex. It looked like it might have been made in the fifth century or even earlier. "When this book was made, people didn't pretend they were above the occasional murder," he intoned, rubbing the thick leather binding like Aladdin rubbing the genie's lamp. "They didn't put their noses up in the air each time someone lost their head. It was all out in the open. People would fill the public squares for a beheading. Torture was a science. An art! The bravest saints would know the rapture that awaited them when their final breath was torn away. There wasn't the slightest pretense we were any better than that. Now we have marches and rock concerts, and petitions to stop it. And slaughterhouses and food factories that hide it. Wrap it up on a Styrofoam dish. Microwave it. We pretend death is everywhere except here." Then he got very quiet. I had to strain my ears to listen. "But death is here. Now. In this very room, watching us. And death has many secrets to share."

I felt the hairs on my neck tickle at my shirt collar. "What secrets?"

Paul looked at me with his head tilted. Probing me. "There are three ways to learn about death. The first is by talking about it, which leads to no real comprehension. The second is by watching it…and I can see by the look on your face you know exactly what I mean. The third and by far most effective route…is…?"

"By causing it," I answered, despair filling me up like a giant test tube.

"Still squeamish, eh? It's hard for me to remember now, but I had misgivings too when I was just a lad. Then I learned the folly of my ways and by hook and crook, I claimed my destiny."

Paul paced around the room, squinting hard at me. "Tsky, tsk. Still wringing your hands, eh? Since I've once again failed to boil your bloodlust, I'll appeal to your spirit of analytic inquiry. Stimulate that big useless gourd on your neck. I'm a scientist, like yerself, Billy, and my particular area of interest is pain…and death. Why does pain exist? Why are we killers? Why does life require life to feed it? What are we making when we reproduce? What story is the DNA telling? What are we struggling to become?"

"And you claim to have the answers?" I asked, a cough hiding my scoff.

"I don't make claims. I make widows and orphans. But if you don't think I have the knowledge you seek, why are you listening so raptly?"

"You are a fucking lunatic," I said, rising from the chair.

He slammed me down again. "I like you, son, a lot more than you like yourself. But you're full of shit. You say you want to know, but you don't. You pretend not to know things you already do, because you're so afraid of losing your most useless character trait!"

He waited for my question. When I refused to ask, he shouted, "Your compassion! You still want to be good. And what good has ever come from it? Has it made you strong? Happy? Has it brought you recognition? Wealth? Love? It isn't you, Billy. Stop trying so hard. There are plenty of people who love life, but yer not one of 'em. You love *death*. If you still have any doubts about what I'm saying, just look in your feckin' suitcase."

I wanted to defend myself. What could I say? He filled my silence easily.

"We all have to eat, Billy. Just try stopping. And that means we all have to kill—even those goddamn vegetarians. The only difference between killing an animal and a plant is that you can't hear an eggplant scream. And the only difference between killing an animal and a human is the conversation you can have while you're doing it. Everything you eat is alive. It's all a sacrifice…and a sacrament. Even if you follow the path of the meek, one day you'll be sacrificed too. To the worms…and to the Maelstrom."

I'd heard that word before. "What's the 'Maelstrom'?"

Paul shook his head like he cursed himself for saying it. "Never mind, boy, the point I'm trying to make is still a simple one. Your compassion is useless. It's in the way. Let it go! It's the only thing that stands between you and true glory!"

"Glory? What the fuck are you talking about? Just tell me!"

"No. Bury your compassion and you will awaken to your true self."

"I won't kill her."

Paul didn't flinch. "Then you will die."

"I'll die anyway," I said with surprisingly little fear.

"There are different ways to die, son," Paul gladly pointed out. "You can go like all the other lemmings we sat with in the pews—robbed of the knowledge of their own divinity by the very church they swear allegiance to, completely ignorant of the buried truth their beloved Christ sacrificed himself to teach them, marked with the cross of mortal slavery on their foreheads. Or you can find another way. With me."

I rose up and he pushed me to my knees on the pad in front of my chair. He held my shoulders down until I stopped struggling, staring up at him with absolute hatred.

"Too bad that worthless priest was mumbling today," he said, sticking his thumb in the chalice and poising it over my forehead. "You would have heard the saddest words in all the liturgy...the prayer of the sheep. Hear it clearly now and ask yourself if you want to be like the rest of them, doomed to a fate you can never escape."

He made a fresh cross on my forehead and shouted, *"Remember, man, that thou art dust! And unto dust thou shall return!"*

He let out another thunderous peal of laughter. I was so full of rage I couldn't speak. "Get up and get moving. Think very hard about what I've said today. There's nothing more I can do to aid you if you won't help yourself. Don't dirty my doorstep again, until you're the one with the answers."

I stood up, wiped the ashes from my brow and stomped to the doorway. "Do you know what your problem is?" I asked, turning around.

"Besides being crazy? Oh, what, pray tell? Enlighten me!"

"You wish you were the Devil."

Paul laughed so hard he had to hold his knees to keep from falling over. I was almost out the door when he stopped laughing and called after me, "It's really been a lovely time, Billy. But I'm afraid you've got it backwards. The Devil is jealous of *me!*"

TORTURE

Paul was impressed. "You know, dear, you'd give Martin a run for his money," he said, patting her head. "Maybe even me."

Rose kept her eyes open. She always did when she was being pierced. It kept her connected to the movement, and the pain. She could travel with it, anticipate it, sometimes even change it. The best she could do now was endure it.

"I can see why he's so taken with you. You're a tough little nut to crack," he chuckled, and began pushing again.

Rose didn't make a sound. Not even a muffled gurgle. All her attention was focused on the pain. *I can do this,* she thought stubbornly. When she began to succeed, she felt a fresh bolt of fear.

What if this only makes him try harder?

"Hhmmph!" Paul snorted, reading her mind. He picked up the pliers. "It's kids like you who take all the fun out of torture. If I'm to get a rise out of you and provide some decent entertainment for your dear papa...I suppose I'll have to do something really vile, won't I?"

"Mmmph," she grunted, choking again, trying to recover from the first onslaught, desperately wishing she could voice the words her eyes were begging: "Have mercy?"

"Sorry," said the dead mask, reading her terrified expression perfectly. "Fresh out."

MARTIN TO THE RESCUE

Martin wasted another sixteen seconds before he abandoned his attempt to determine Paul's location using his queasy gut instincts. He squandered eight additional seconds trying to access his even more unreliable memory.

"The porter," he said finally, bolting to the lobby to wring his toothpick neck. Unfortunately, the porter had already left for the day. Fortunately, an even more practical search tactic popped into his brain. He picked up the house phone and asked in the most civilized voice he could muster, "What's the most expensive room in the hotel?"

"That would be the Ambassador Suite," the snotty receptionist replied.

Martin only hit the elevator button two dozen times on his way up to the penthouse. No one was inside with him to complain this time. When the elevator opened, he saw the big double doors of the Ambassador Suite at the end of a very long hallway. He crept down the hall and waited outside the doors longer than he wanted, listening. Not a sound.

Were they in there? If they were, how was he going to get inside without making a big racket? No one had seen him on the way up, he was sure of it. But he didn't want to take any chances on what might happen to Rose if he suddenly burst in on them by shooting the door handle off, for example.

Where was the maid? He found her in a room at the other end of the long hallway. She had her back turned to him as she changed the bed sheets. He pinched the back of her neck in the way he'd practiced so many times before. "Ouch!" she yelled, whirling around.

Martin clocked her and took the key. He never got the hang of that Mr. Spock thing.

"No, that's not it...down a little farther...now over to the left...*there!*" Paul would shout at him until their subject collapsed. No matter how often they practiced, it would always take Martin three or four tries to get it right. He didn't have time for that now.

He flew back to Paul's suite, his gun drawn. He put his ear to the door one more time. Not hearing anything, he slipped in the key card and slowly turned the handle. Oh, no. Rose was handcuffed to a chair twenty feet away, her eyes like a raccoon's from her tears and mascara. Her head was down and her eyes were closed. He couldn't tell if she was alive or dead.

There was no sign of Paul. Anger flowed through Martin like a torrent of molten lead. He wanted to run to her, but didn't dare until he searched the suite. He went from room to room, his gun pointed in front of him like an extension of his arm. The suite was clear. There was one white door that was locked. He assumed it led to a connecting suite. He put a chair against the knob to brace it, just in case.

He put the pistol in his pocket, ran back to Rose and slowly lifted her face. She was alive. He could feel her breath on his hand. Was she unconscious or comatose? He opened one eyelid and checked her pupil. Unconscious. He searched for a bruise on the back of her neck. There it was. Given her size, the effect would last more than forty minutes.

Good. Let her rest while I take the cuffs off.

He tried to calculate when Paul had left by the color of the bruise. It couldn't have been more than a few minutes earlier. *Fuck. I just missed him.* Then he saw the blood seeping through her robe. *You fucking fuck!*

He gently parted the thick terrycloth and saw what Paul had done to her breasts. He chewed his knuckles, trying to keep his cool while he appraised her injuries. They looked horrible, but the actual wounds were small and would leave only tiny scars with proper treatment. He slowly pulled out the knitting needles, grateful she wasn't feeling them on the way out like she must have felt them on the way in. He ran to the bathroom, searching for a first aid kit. He found one under the sink. He grabbed it and ran back to the sitting room, tenderly daubing the streaks of blood away, covering the small holes with antiseptic and band-aids. When he was finished, he closed her robe and moved behind her to see what he could do about those handcuffs. *Fuck!* He could usually pick handcuff locks faster than he could pick his own teeth, but he had never seen a keyhole that remotely resembled this. Was it magnetic? *Fuck! Fuck! Fuck!* He examined the chair next, calculating how difficult it would be to break apart without causing her any further injuries.

That's when he saw it. The gleaming metal device under her chair. He dropped to his knees, tilting his head sideways like a bomb-squad periscope. Under the chair was a strange contraption attached to all four legs. In the center was a broad round metal plate. In the middle of that was an inch–thick, stainless-steel pole, tapering to a razor-sharp tip. It looked like a spring-triggered device that would engage if any leg was lifted or the weight of Rose's body was removed. When the trap was sprung, it would instantly shoot up through the seat. Through Rose. He almost punched a hole in the wall. He sat down in the chair across from her instead, pondering his next move. As he sat, some paper crinkled under his ass. There was a long note sitting on the cushion. How had he missed it? He snatched it up, marveling at the gorgeous penmanship…until he read the message:

Dear Martin,

If you move this bitch a single inch, I've installed a very interesting device under her chair that will make you wish you hadn't. It has a timer set for 3:15 this afternoon, if you don't help it along by fiddling around, trying to get her out of that chair. Even though you're good with gadgets, there's only one thing in the world that can disarm it: a simple remote control device. If you're able to find where I've hidden it and make it back here in time, then she'll be yours. That shouldn't be much trouble for a resourceful lad like you. And because I feel such compassion for all the suffering I'm causing you, I'll give you a tiny clue: I've hidden it in a very special place, a place you've visited before. All you have to do is remember. Then again, you should have known where she was in the first place, because you've been here before too. Good luck, lad. I wouldn't tarry too long. Even though you have enough time to accomplish your task, I've thrown a few obstacles in the way, just to keep things interesting.

Love and kisses, Paul

Martin looked around the room and felt a sense of dread creep into his bones that he had never experienced. He *had* been here before. He knew it as soon as he read Paul's note. Was he out of his mind? He looked at the old paintings, the draperies and furniture and felt a deepening sense of déjà vu with every painful glance. When had he been here? What had they done? Why couldn't he remember?

He looked back at Rose. Her tearstained eyes. Her punctured breasts. He could have saved her. He had totally blown it. He got down on his knees again and looked under the chair, praying he could figure out how it worked. There was a black plastic disc near the telescoping pole. A button? Maybe it locked the mechanism. Or triggered it. *Fuck!* There was no way of knowing.

Usually a paragon of decisiveness and efficiency, Martin held his head, agonizing over what he should do next. Should he leave right now? Track down Paul and the remote control? Or try to disarm it? If he fucked up, he'd kill her either way. Shit! He had to make a decision now, before Rose regained consciousness. If she saw him and he left again to hunt down Paul, she'd go nuts and spring the trap. "What should I do?" he fretted, never expecting an answer.

"She'll be okay," said an urgent voice in his mind that didn't sound at all like his. "You need to go now, find the remote and…"

Martin didn't recognize the voice or listen to the rest of its instructions. He looked back only once, at Rose's hanging head, then ran to the elevator as fast as his feet could fly.

Mistaken Intentions

"Bye, bye, Martin," I said with a wave down the hallway as I opened the door of the Ambassador Suite. I went inside as soon as Martin left in the elevator. I quietly closed the door and walked over to her, stroking her hanging head. Good. Still unconscious. At least she hadn't heard me bidding Martin a fond farewell. I was going to have my hands full anyway, explaining my presence when she came around.

I opened her robe…to look at her injuries, of course. I'm not some kind of pervert. As you may have guessed, Martin did a bang-up job dressing her wounds. I gently closed the red-stained fabric and read Paul's note, then looked under the chair.

Ooooeey. That was some nasty piece of metal. I saw the button Paul showed me. I pressed it and heard a loud metallic *ching!* A tiny black screen popped out of the metal with a switchblade sound. A line of red digital letters streamed across the black screen like a news ticker in Times Square:

CONGRATULATIONS, BILLY! I KNEW YOU COULD DO IT!

Then the letters disappeared and were replaced by digital numbers…ticking backwards. Son-of-a-*bitch!* I cursed myself and cursed Paul even more vehemently. Yet there was still time to correct what I'd set in motion, if that's what I really wanted. Be a hero. Get the girl.

There's a solution to every puzzle. Sometimes it's a simple one. I got an idea and fiddled around. Then I sat back down and composed myself, waiting for her to awaken.

She opened her eyes slowly. As they focused on my face, I raised my finger to her lips, not so much to quiet her as to warn her against any movement. "It's me," I said stupidly. She remained silent, her eyes soaked with fear. She must have thought I was here to help Paul. Who could blame her?

"I came here to…protect you," I said, settling on "protect" instead of "save." It was less self-serving and slightly more honest.

"How did you know I was here?" she asked, her head clearing, more angry than afraid, moving her shoulders forward, tilting the chair with her. "You know him, don't you?"

"Don't move. There's a trap," I said in the most forbidding voice I could manage.

"I know," she said, glaring at me through her streaked eye makeup. "Your buddy really enjoyed telling me about it before he…" her face took on a puzzled expression before she concluded, "…knocked me out."

"He's not my buddy," I said testily. "Did he tell you how it's triggered?"

"If I move, if I wiggle…if I try to scratch my ass," she said, managing to make her whisper sound like a scream. "And if I don't manage to kill myself…he put a timer on it."

"Did you see anything that looked like a remote control?"

"No," she said, her lips barely moving. She began to cry. I touched her shoulder. She shrugged it away. *Now is all that matters,* I thought, struggling to regain my composure. "I'm here to help," I said.

She raised her head. Not with the same look of contempt. With a flicker of excitement. "My boyfriend! He must be looking for me! Call room 1112. He'll be able to get me out of here! Wait, what am I thinking? Call 911!"

I didn't move.

"Why are you looking at me like that?" Rose cried, clearly upset by my lack of enthusiasm and initiative. "You said you wanted to help! Pick up the phone and call the cops!"

I stared blankly at her until her fear mounted to such a crescendo that it blessedly extinguished her frantic, bossy suggestions. When she finally became still, I spoke again.

"I'm sorry, but the cops won't help you. Paul has a very special relationship with certain members of the police department. Understand?"

Her eyes clouded with suspicion. "So call my boyfriend…"

"Martin," I sighed, looking into my lap, cleaning my nails. When I looked up again, her face was ashy white. I held her gaze a bit longer than I should have, feeling those old familiar resentments before I came to my senses. "We came here together," I lied, forcing a smile, doing my best to reassure her again. "He took those needles out. Cleaned you up."

She looked at the bloody knitting needles on the table, then down her slightly parted robe. Band-aids. She looked confused. Then her cheeks turned red with rage. "How do you know Martin? Where is he?" she hissed. "What did you do to him?"

I had to laugh. Me? Do something to Martin? No. I could see she meant it, though my laughter unnerved her again and she retreated into silence. *Shit.* Things were spinning out of control, so I showed her Paul's note. Explained how Martin left to hunt down Paul and find the remote. How I stayed behind to guard her. How I, not Martin, was her true hero.

"No! Martin wouldn't leave me again! He wouldn't!" Rose said, her face quivering, trying to hold back an impending flood of tears.

"Well, he did. He was kind of stoic about it, actually. He told me to look after you, but he didn't even leave me a gun. I hope he knows what he's doing."

"I don't believe you," she said, quite convincingly. "I don't believe a word you're saying. I want you to call my room right now…in front of me."

I called her room. *Ring. Ring. Ring.* I even left a message. Her reaction was predictable. She started crying again. Begged me to call the cops. Then I had to explain *that* all over again. Why wouldn't she believe me? Yes, I know. Why should she believe me? I was lying. But they were good lies. I spent a lot of time thinking them through.

"You're in this with him! You helped him do this to me!"

I'd been looking forward to seeing her so much, but this wasn't how I imagined things going at all. "If I wanted to hurt you, it wouldn't be too difficult," I said with a yawn.

Her face clouded with a film of pasty fear. "What are you doing here? How do you know Paul…and Martin?"

"You wouldn't believe me if I told you."

Rose thought about her father again…his crazy letters…Martin's even crazier revelations. She glared at me and took a deep breath. I followed her eyes as they traced the absurd splendor of the Ambassador Suite. I watched her point her chin at the armoire and its bizarre contents. I saw her stare at the bloody knitting needles on the table between us. Then she looked back at me, rolled her eyes and said, "Try me."

CONFESSION

I decided to tell Rose everything. How could I not?

"Martin is my brother. Paul is our father. I only found out a few months ago, after we finished the tattoos. He wants to kill you because you're an O'Neil. His clan is at war with yours, so there's no way he's going to let you hook up with Martin."

"Martin would have told me if Paul was his father!" Rose cried, her mind reeling with the horrifying implications of Paul's blood flowing in Martin's veins.

"Martin can't remember fuckall. Paul traumatized him so much as a kid that his memory is in lockdown mode. He thinks Paul is the Clan King and he's one of the stupid knights. You'll understand all this better if I start at the beginning."

"No, start at the end. How did you know I was here? Why didn't you come before…?"

Her stern expression was momentarily wiped away with a cascade of tears. Her sobbing gave me a few seconds to think. In the weeks I spent preparing for our encounter, I rehearsed at least ten plausible and very detailed explanations for those questions. Once I was sitting right in front of her, not a single scripted response came to mind. But any good liar is an inventive liar, with a knack for improvisation. So I decided to take the most inventive approach I could think of on short notice.

"I see visions. I saw you here and I came as quickly as I could. I'm sorry I didn't get here sooner."

She went absolutely apeshit. *"You saw this in a vision?"*

"I said you wouldn't believe me."

She ranted a while longer. When she settled down enough for me to continue, I talked about my visions, when they started, how my mother had them too. I explained that they were the reason I got into the tarot in the first place. Since she already knew The Striker, I told her about the implants next and how I met Paul. I even told her about the website, though I neglected to mention my unauthorized bio. Maybe if she knew what a sick, twisted fuck her old pal was, she'd cut me some slack.

"That's bullshit! The Striker is a friend of mine. I've known him for years. He's weird…but he's no serial killer."

"Oh, really?" I asked, folding my arms across my chest. "You're so sure about that?"

Rose took a deep breath, ready to give me both barrels. Suddenly, she gazed blankly out the window. I *saw* a memory cascade through her mind with such clarity it felt like I was inside her head.

"My, what a charming necklace," The Striker cooed in that unearthly deep baritone. "Where on earth did you ever find it? An estate sale?"

"My dad gave it to me," Rose said quietly. She wasn't up to talking about her mom.

"It's simply wonderful. Look at how detailed these engravings are," he intoned, bending lower to stare at it closer, oddly not lifting a finger to touch it. "How very impressive. It looks positively ancient. What treasure does this precious key guard?"

"It doesn't open anything," Rose told him, a frown crossing her face. "It's just a good luck charm."

"Lucky, indeed," The Striker said, straightening his back again, not smiling like before. "But you're mistaken if you think it doesn't fit any lock."

"What do you mean?" Rose asked, strangely anxious from his change in demeanor.

"Why, isn't it obvious?" he asked, his smile returning, touching her chin with a long, spindly finger. "Any father who would give his little girl such a splendid present could only have one thing in mind…and that charm around your neck, dear Rose, is the key to your daddy's heart."

Rose opened her eyes with such a jolt I had to steady her shoulders to keep her from springing the trap. "The Striker…" she whispered, only now realizing that Martin wasn't the first or only man to exhibit a keen interest in her jewelry.

"I guess you don't think I'm so full of shit anymore," I said, easing my grip on her robe as she calmed down again. "Do you want me to tell you the rest of it or not?"

Rose nodded, her face pale and clammy, beads of anxious sweat pebbling her brow.

"Oh, God! The key!" she gasped, staring down at her bruised, bandaged, but otherwise naked chest. "I left it on the doorknob downstairs. In the bathroom. Maybe he didn't find it. Maybe there's still time to…"

"It's gone," I said curtly. I could still picture the doorknob perfectly. Unadorned. A small drop of blood drying on the shiny brass finish.

"How do you know?" she gasped, trying not to fidget.

"If Paul wanted it, he has it," I answered with a shrug. "It's gone."

"Gone…" she echoed, hanging her head with grief. I gave her a soft, comforting stroke on the top of her sobbing head. She rudely shook it off.

Hhmmph! I wanted to snort. Instead, I kept my mouth shut and folded my arms across my chest, slyly stroking the warm lump of metal hidden beneath my clean, starched shirt.

Well, not gone, forever, I mused, swallowing the words I so much wanted to voice before resuming my story again. *Let's just say you lost it.*

THE VOICE

Martin fumbled with the last lock on his door, hesitating in the hallway before opening it. What was he doing here? He should be marching into Paul's hellhole right now! How could he even think of stopping here first and wasting even more time?

The voice in his head that whispered to him on the way home warned him not to come here first. But no, he had to try the white room. Besides, he needed more equipment: his homemade ammo, his special ice pick for that fuckhead Michael and a Kevlar vest for when the bullets started flying. It would only offer a slim chance of survival if Paul wanted to go toe-to-toe with him, but he sure as hell wasn't going into that building without it.

He thought about the remote as he opened the final lock. Did it even exist? If he found it, would it actually work? Either way, he needed some extra insurance. Only the Book could ensure their survival. He needed the white room to find it. He needed his gear.

"No!" the voice nagged at him again as soon as he opened the door. "Go there now!"

"It won't take long," Martin tried to explain, rationalizing his dubious decision to both himself and the voice of his old and probably only friend: Johnny Bones.

He didn't recognize Johnny's voice the first time, yelling for him to run back to The Plaza after he stupidly went to the Carnegie Deli. He didn't recognize it the second time either, as he was leaving Paul's suite. When the voice spoke to him a third time in the taxi on his way home, he didn't even hear it. He was lost in his thoughts, debating battle tactics. Always blessed with the barest trace of an internal dialogue, Martin had been chattering in his own head so ceaselessly in the last half hour that he was starting to get a migraine.

"Can you step on it?" he shouted to the driver. "I'm in a hurry!"

The driver muttered, but stepped on it so hard Martin's neck jerked backwards. The traffic was lighter than usual. Was it a holiday? He wasn't even sure what day it was, though he thought it might be Friday. Clouds were gathering quickly, as if on cue. The dream of a peaceful day with Rose had long vanished and now the sun was going with it.

"That girl is not for you!" Paul screamed last night. When he found out about Johnny and Rose, he knew why. But when he replayed Paul's shouting voice on the ride home, this time he heard it differently. There was something in the way he said it. With the accent on the last word. If she wasn't supposed to be with him, then who?

That kid! Who was he? Where did he come from? What did Paul want with him?

To take my place. No, not just my place in the crazy clan vendetta. My gold. My girl. Paul wants Rose for him! But why? Just to hurt me? He couldn't imagine Paul caring about Bean's romantic longings. It didn't make any sense.

"You're wasting time," said an urgent voice in Martin's mind. This time he knew it wasn't his own. He shook his head, trying to clear it. His brain was already aching. Now he was hearing things. He rubbed his temples and took a long, deep breath.

I need to find that book, he thought, glad to hear his own familiar voice in his head.

"Go there now!" the other voice shouted.

"Johnny?" Martin asked, loudly enough for the driver to look back over his shoulder.

"Yes," Johnny grunted, like every word was a strain equivalent to lifting a boulder off his chest. "Go there. Kill Bean. Take the Book."

"Bean has the book? What about Paul?" Martin whispered into his hand, but the driver was still eyeing him in the rearview mirror.

The voice was silent. In the absence of any other competing internal dialog, Martin pictured himself wrapping his fingers around Bean's smelly, stubbly throat. Then an image flashed in his brain with all the clarity of a Polaroid. In fact, the image was a Polaroid...of Bean. Where had he seen it?

"Pinned on the wall behind the candles," came a new whispering. "In the chapel."

This time it didn't sound like Johnny. It sounded suspiciously like… Paul? No. It wasn't that much different from his own voice. Except it sounded…it felt…more grown up.

Martin clutched his knees. There was a strange new voice in his head that was *him?* But instead of the angry, sullen texture of his familiar thoughts, this voice was completely relaxed. Maybe even articulate. Adult.

"Where's the chapel?" Martin asked, willing the wonderful new "him" to return.

He sat. Waited. Nothing. Not even Johnny. His eyes snapped open and he pounded the armrest. He needed to find the chapel! He needed the white room!

"Step on the fucking gas!" he yelled, not sounding adult at all.

When the taxi screeched to a halt in front of his stoop, Martin threw some cash at him and barreled up the stairs, unfastening his myriad locks. I closed my eyes and watched him rummage around, gathering his supplies. Then I turned my attention back to Rose. Dear Rose.

Too bad Johnny didn't have the strength left to set Martin straight about his more misguided assumptions. Like what Paul meant when he said, "That girl is not for you!"

Martin was correct in thinking that Paul wanted her for someone else. But it wasn't Michael. It was me.

CORRECTION

I said earlier that I told Rose everything. That wasn't exactly true. After all, I was just starting to gain her trust. When I told her about Mother's deathbed plea for me to save Martin, her eyes lit up like a Christmas tree. And later, once her grief from the loss of her treasured family heirloom subsided a tad, she went right back to that salient point and barraged me with a slew of new questions. All about Martin, of course.

I obliged her curiosity, spinning the web of our strange, sad tale...even though I had to make some more judicious edits. Like the one I made earlier, when I told her about Paul and The Striker and the serial killer website. I left out the part about her being my intended victim. I figured she was scared enough already. She was still in that chair! Besides, if I told her she was the one dear ole Dad wanted me to kill, she'd start asking even more questions.

Like how and where and when.

And then, if I insisted on being completely honest, I would have had to tell her something even more terrifying: that according to my profile on the site, written five months earlier, I was supposed to have murdered her with an impaling device, after torturing her with knitting needles and pliers, in the Ambassador Suite of The Plaza Hotel on Good Friday at 3:15 in the afternoon.

Journal Entry: The Books of Revelation

I've got some big, fat acorns to squirrel away so I'd better start scribbling. When Paul told me to come up with some answers before I dirtied his doorstep, I took it as both a challenge and a reprieve. The good news was: I didn't have to see his detestable face for a while. The bad news was: pretty much the same thing. I really don't understand how I can hate someone more than I've ever hated anyone in my life and at the same time, miss his company when he's not around. One minute I'm plotting to murder him, the next I'm panting like a puppy, waiting for him to walk in the door. Fortunately, my obsession with Clan Kelly and the Hermetic lineage helped me stuff those fucked-up feelings and channel my energy into digging for gold. Even though I can't confirm everything conclusively and I've come up with a lot more questions than definitive answers, I've got some big nuggets to deposit.

I've been awake for almost two full days now, fueled by endless pots of coffee and surrounded by a mountain of books, my eyes glazed from reading countless pages of paper and Internet ink. Paul gave me some decent breadcrumbs to follow: the Clan Kelly feudal dynasty (which I'm now certain is linked to both the Hermetic lineage and the Celtic druids); the shift in succession from disciples to progeny (still not sure exactly when it happened, but I've got a new theory on why it's more advantageous); his lofty pronouncements about death and immortality (more to come); and his rage at the Church.

He has a serious ax to grind with Christianity, but why? Then again, why not? Anyone who's spent any time reviewing the history of Christianity can find plenty of ammunition to piss them off. For Paul, the wholesale destruction of ancient temples and writings associated with so-called pagan religions was a good starting point. Then you have the Crusades (the Children's Crusade, that's a sweet one), various witch hunts, and of course, the mother—excuse me, the father—of all heretical purges: the Spanish Inquisition.

Obviously, Paul can really milk a grudge, so his beef probably stretches all the way back to Peter and his own namesake. And since we're talking about King Kelly here, the Good Olde Land O'Green has to be a huge part of the story, most likely starting with Saint Patrick's war on paganism. But the more I pondered Paul's ravings, the less I thought they had to do with his loathing of Catholicism or his rival clans.

No, Paul's primary, defining characteristic, as far as I can tell, is his unbounded ambition disguised as disinterested contempt. His whole stinky-bum shtick is a perfect example. Here is a guy who is extremely intelligent, the High King of his very own secret feudal society, and with all the treasure and artifacts Clan Kelly looted, he's probably richer than Midas. Yet he dresses like a derelict, smells like a sewer and lives in a bombed-out tenement without modern plumbing. He's like one of those billionaires who still rides in, no, rides *and* sleeps in his '65 Ford LTD faux-wood-paneled station wagon, so he can thumb his nose at conventional society and act like all he gives a shit about are the simple down-home aw-shucks pleasures of life—fly-fishing, bird watching, eviscerating rivals. Yet there's a hunger burning inside him. He wants something and he wants it really, really badly. The zillion-dollar question, of course, is: what?

Immortality is the obvious, if preposterous answer. Paul is no spring chicken. Maybe he needs a recharge. Maybe he's a fucking vampire. He sure loves being alive. Never met anyone who loves it more.

Soul transmigration is a core belief of the Hermetic and Pythagorean traditions. Has he figured out the key to an eternity of Paulness? One of his more enthusiastic proclamations still rings in my ears: "Pythagorus, Apollonius—they shared something else in common—they housed the very soul of Hermes Trismegistus!"

What if soul transmigration is actually possible? Was he including himself in the list? His gigantic ego wouldn't have any problem sharing the stage with such luminaries, or kicking everyone else off the podium. What if he's already been around the block a few times and wants to take another lap?

The body-switcheroo he practiced on me was as real as real gets. Has he figured out a way to do it, not for a few seconds, or a few hours, but forever? If so, he'd need a host. A younger body, with a decent brain, like mine, or a lean, mean fighting machine with sawdust between the ears like his beloved prodigal son Martin. Is his fixation on the line of succession about more than passing down knowledge? Did the Master use one of his disciples as a host? When the line of succession became hereditary, was the shift less about discouraging rogue offshoots and more about improving ease and efficiency? If you're in the soul-transferring business, it might help to have a genetic link to your unlucky successor. And if genetic memory exists, it could provide a handy socket to plug into. Voila! How to become an immortal parasitic messiah in one easy lesson!

I can't believe I'm even thinking these things, let alone writing them down, but some of this stuff…it might be possible. Unlikely. Crazy. Absurd. But to my mixed-up, probably hypnotized brain…it could be possible. And if it's more than possible, if it's true, does that mean he's aching to slip into a new skin suit for another sixty years or so? Even if it isn't true, but he believes it is—a much more plausible scenario—what then? Will he try to psychically invade Martin? Me? Shack up together until the next generation comes of age? Go on and on like that for all eternity? Or to the end? But what end? If someone as ruthlessly ambitious as Paul did have an infinite amount of time on his hands, he'd need a really big project to keep him motivated, no matter how much he loved being alive or how long he lived. So what does he really want? What's the ultimate goal of his real-life sword-and-sorcery Clan Kelly RPG? World domination? Armageddon? Transcendence? Fun and prizes?

I went back to the beginning to search for the end: Hermes Trismigestus, or more precisely, Thoth. According to various legends, Hermes Trismigestus could have arrived on the scene as early as 2,000 or even 4,000 BCE. The Pyramid Texts are all about the Pharaoh's resurrection and ascension into the heavens—essentially a recipe for immortality. The earliest copy dates from 2,400 BCE and is probably the world's oldest religious text. That would imply a *very* long line of Masters and seems highly doubtful. The more likely lineage would begin in 500 BCE with Pythagoras. His Greek followers (especially Plato in his unburned writings) carried the torch for centuries, all the way down to one of the most interesting figures in the lineage—Apollonius of Tyana—who happened to be a contemporary of Jesus Christ and shared an interesting list of godlike similarities. There's a mysterious (virgin?) birth, plenty of miracles (casting out demons, raising the dead, curing the blind) and best of all: a heavenly assumption! Was he the real Christ? His best buddy? Co-Godman? Did they sit on the porch, having a glass of water-turned-to-wine? Talk about the good old days in the Garden of Eden?

Christ has never been a big interest of mine. One thing I absolutely have in common with Paul is my distaste for organized religion, particularly Christianity and even more specifically, the Catholic Church. As much as I'd like to think of myself as well versed in spiritual traditions, before today I had never spent much time poring over the gospels or other early Christian writings or beliefs, including Gnosticism (much like ninety percent of born-again Christians, I imagine). When I started dipping my toes into the murky waters of mysticism and the occult, I tried to avoid the Bible as much as I could—which is hard, because all the grimoires I've collected use incantations and magical symbols derived from the Torah or the Kabala—like the Tetragrammaton, the unpronounceable four-letter name of God, or the ten Sephiroth that make up the Tree of Life in the tarot. But as far as the Oh, So Holy Bible is concerned, I'd rather leave it than take it.

Then just as dawn was breaking today, while I was rooting through everything I could find on Hermeticism, Neo-Pythagoreanism and Neo-Platonism—what to my wondering eyes should appear but my barely glanced at copy of *The Gospel of Mary* (Magdelene). It was discovered at the turn of the nineteenth century in Upper Egypt but was never published until 1955, ten years after the discovery (also in Egypt) of the Nag Hammadi Library, a treasure trove of thirteen ancient codices, mostly Gnostic writings, which I've also largely ignored until today, with the exception of three chapters from the *Corpus Hermeticum*. After I gave Mary's Gospel a more careful read, I plunged into all the other codex translations. Lo and behold—the Gnostic material has so many Hermetic parallels that the two are sometimes indistinguishable. I've been speed-reading the Nag Hammadi Library, and so far I've tackled *The Gospel of Philip*, *The Gospel of Thomas*, *The Apocalypse of Paul*, *The Sophia of Jesus Christ*, *The Gospel of Truth* and a creation myth, *On the Origin of the World*.

I made the initial Gnostic/Hermetic connection in *The Gospel of Mary*. The first six pages are conveniently missing. Then it picks up where the resurrected Jesus is answering questions about the "nature of matter"—a totally Hermetic-alchemical concept. And next, you have this:

"And she began to speak to them these words: I, she said, I saw the Lord in a vision and I said to Him, Lord I saw You today in a vision. He answered and said to me: Blessed are you that you did not waver at the sight of Me. For where the Nous is, there is the treasure.

"I said to Him, Lord, how does he who sees the vision see it, through the soul or through the spirit? The Savior answered and said, He does not see through the soul nor through the spirit, but the Nous that is between the two, that is what sees the vision and it is…"

Pow! As soon as she mentions the *Nous*, a big Pythagorean tent pole, the next four pages are missing. In the next section, they're still talking about her vision, which is all about "seven divine worlds"—much like Hermes Trismigestus's *Poimandres*.

I found another Gnostic manuscript called *The Pistis Sophia* that is mindbogglingly weird. All the writings about Sophia are incredibly strange. In *The Sophia of Jesus Christ*, the resurrected Christ says to his disciples, including Mary Magdalene:

"I want you to know that First Man is called 'Begetter, Self-perfected Mind.' He reflected with Great Sophia, his consort, and revealed his first-begotten, androgynous son. His male name is designated 'First Begetter, Son of God,' his female name, 'First Begettress Sophia, Mother of the Universe'. Some call her 'Love.'"

The Begetter? The Begetress? The First-begotten androgynous son? This shit is so totally nuts. In *On the Origin of the World*, one of the more entertaining (and confusing) telling-it-like-it-really-was creation myths, *Sophia* is the creator of the world. *After* that feat, she creates a Yahweh-type God, who thinks He is the one and only God, and soon gets a lesson in humility from Sophia. She also creates Eve (first!) who is called Sophia Zoe. It's Eve who breathes life into Adam. Then seven archangels show up, look at Eve and wonder, "What sort of thing is this luminous woman?" The not-so-angelic angels then proceed to *rape* Eve, put Adam into a deep sleep, and while he's snoozing tell him Eve came from his rib and she really needs to obey him because he is "lord over her."

It goes on and on and on, contradicting itself over and over, making zero sense most of the time. In most cases, Sophia is the Prime Mover, The Great Mother consort of the First Infinite Light. She created the material realm and everything in it. In *The Pistis Sophia,* she's bushwhacked by the Rulers of the Twelve Aeons who are pissed at Pistis for striving toward the Light of Lights, so they create a "great lion-faced power" called Yaldabaōth who devours Sophia's light power. She then makes *thirteen* repentances, spending the next *hundred* pages trapped in the dark realm, before Jesus comes to the rescue and restores her Light.

Crazy, crazy crazy. But there's something going on with these Sophia stories that makes me think about Paul and his all-male-all-the-time lifestyle. Sophia means *wisdom* in Greek. To Gnostics, Sophia is usually the *syzygy,* or female counterpart to Christ. In all the Gnostic creation myths you have androgynous beings who pop up, then become yin/yang counterparts. But the males don't always have the upper hand. In fact, some of the writers are so gaga over Sophia that the misogynistic finger-pointing that inevitably follows seems like it was tacked on later to make sure disciples don't get the wrong idea and think She's at the head of the table. I'm dying to ask Paul more about Sophia when I dirty his door again, but he hates women, absolutely hates them. I'm guessing his response will be to nail me to the cross with the angel.

Speaking of which, these Gnostic writings have angels coming out the wazoo. They're everywhere. Angels, Archangels, good angels, bad angels, most of which are *androgynous* angels. What's the connection between them and Paul's crucified angel? Once again, I don't have a clue. What I do know is that at some point during or after the lives/deaths/resurrections of Christ and Apollonius, Gnosticism and Hermeticism were joined at the hip, Mary Magdalene sat in the front of the bus, and the patriarchal/monarchal model for Christianity and its dogma was just a gleam in Peter's eye. Fast-forward a few hundred years and you have a Christian Roman Empire, the Council of Nicea, Popes with fancy hats sitting on thrones, and a very successful campaign that wipes out just about every scrap of Gnostic and Hermetic literature. Gone, all gone, except for these few crumbling codices.

Another hundred years pass and St. Patrick rids the Emerald Isle of snakes and druids. The Celtic druids in Gaul were known to have frequent contact with the ancient Greeks, so it's logical to assume there was some Hermetic transmission between them. According to the writings of Julius Caesar, the Celtic druids were big believers of soul transmigration, and had a long, strenuous apprentice training program, passing down their magic bon mots orally, forbidding any written record of the great mystery. But... Paul hinted to me that somebody wrote it all down anyway. Is that what's in his big, fat, locked codex? Or in another book he's stashed away or hasn't found/stolen yet? And even if his book isn't the druid mother lode, it could be a collection of the complete Hermetic/Gnostic writings destroyed in the good old days. Whatever is in there, it has to be incredible. Otherwise, why would he wear that key around his neck?

I'm sure his book has the answers to everything I'm trying to make sense of, especially what Clan Kelly and the High King are really up to. God, what I'd give to see it. In one day, I've covered centuries of Hermetic and Gnostic teachings and I've barely scratched the surface. If it weren't for the whole "you need to kill the girl" thing, I'd be happy as a clam exploring this stuff day and night.

One thing I'm certain of—Paul's crucified angel is the missing link.

Every time I pictured that monstrosity I kept seeing The Hanged Man. So I pulled all the trump cards out of my tarot deck and just stared at them, totally intrigued by the parallels between them and the Hermetic/Gnostic creation myths. The tarot begins with The Fool, an androgynous archetype who is followed by The Magician, also somewhat androgynous, then The Priestess. I arranged the trumps in two lines of eleven cards, the first eleven going forward, the rest placed underneath them in the opposite direction, connecting The Universe with The Fool.

I started thinking about The Wheel of Fortune, how it kept coming up all the time for me. After reading these creation myths, I could clearly see that The Wheel (Jupiter) and The Universe (Saturn) were reflections of each other. So I shifted my arrangement and put The Universe on the table all the way to the left and The Wheel all the way to the right. I connected them with the other trumps and I couldn't believe what I figured out. All the trumps are paired! The Fool (Air) above Judgment (Fire) below, The Magician (Mercury) above The Sun, The Priestess above The Moon, The Empress above The Star. But that's not all. There's a triangle formed by The Priestess, The Empress and The Star—the three manifestations of Sophia: Virgin, Consort, Great Mother. And another triad, The Emperor, The Hierophant, and The Devil—the three manifestations of Hermes Trismigestus. That's where his catchy nickname comes from: Hermes Thrice Great. King, Sage, Sorcerer.

Does Paul know about all this stuff? Jesus, what's the matter with me? Why do I give a shit what Paul knows? Why am I spending all my time trying to figure out what he wants, what he knows—when the only thing he really, really wants is for me to murder Rose?

Talk about timing. I was launching into a rant about him and there he was, knocking on my door. I hid the journal and let him in. He came to congratulate me. Said he'd been drifting in and out of my head all day, following my progress and *guiding* me along. Was he wearing me like a puppet, picking out which books to read, which pages to turn, clicking the mouse on all the right links, giving me imperceptible subconscious suggestions, leading me like a mongrel pooch down the dark, dirty alleys of his twisted scheming?

He didn't specify. I didn't press. I was too immersed in what he had to say about my research efforts. "I see you've discovered the First Arrangement," he said, leaning over the table.

"It's the whole creation myth!" I said excitedly, pointing at The Fool.

"The Alpha…and the Omega," he said, looking at me like I was The Fool. Still, I could see a gleam of pride in his eyes as he said, "The key to the creation sequence lies in the starting point. Which is the first card? What's the chicken? What's the egg?"

"Well, if it's not The Fool, I guess it must be The Universe."

"It's a creation myth; the Universe doesn't exist yet," he said with a pained sigh.

I was stumped. I tried a few guesses and he got bored, or impatient. He laid his big paws on the table and parted the vertical rows I'd made right in the middle, like Moses parting the Red Sea. Now there was a gap between The Emperor and The Hierophant, The Tower and The Devil. "It begins here," he said, pointing to The Tower.

He laughed at my perplexed expression and laid it all out for me. "In the beginning there was only Chaos and the *Will* to Become, the *Intent* to act. Close your eyes and imagine that you're in a sensory deprivation tank. No light, no sound. You're floating in saltwater, so even the sensation of gravity dissipates. Now imagine being suspended in that senseless state without any thoughts, without words, because they don't exist yet. What are you left with?"

"Nothing. Without any sensation or internal dialog you wouldn't know you exist."

"Close, but no cigar. You have awareness. And with awareness, the *ability* to perceive—the *capacity* for intelligence. Unfortunately, you have nothing to perceive because there is no other. All is one. You're an entity with unlimited creative power, but no idea how to express that energy, how to come forth…to *become.* Imagine the agony of such a condition. And to make matters worse, the agony is eternal because time and space also don't exist. The Tower is what you might call the Big Bang. The first Singularity. From that eruption of Chaos came the great engine of creation and annihilation, the *Apeiron*, or Maelstrom. With the *Apeiron* came the *Nous*, the *Intelligence* first manifested in Sophia," he said pointing to The Star. "The Perceiver and the Perceived. Duality. Chaos into order and form."

"You know about Sophia?" I interrupted.

He rolled his eyes like I had just asked the dumbest question in the world and continued, pointing to each card as he spoke. "From Sophia came the Watery Darkness (pointing to The Moon) and the material universe. From the Darkness came the Second Light of the Divine Realm (The Sun). From the Divine Realm of pure creativity, came the first being and begetter (The Aeon). And so the Ethereal and Material planes unite at the Axis and the first cycle of creation is complete (The Universe)."

He went on like that, card by card. He had different names for most of them, their true names, of course, since he decided they were: The Hero/Fool, The Herald/Magician, The Oracle/Princess, The Matriarch/Empress, The Good King/Emperor, The Master/Hierophant.

He called those cards the "apocalyptic sequence" because they tell the story of revelation, where male and female Chosen Ones are enlightened by Hermes-Thoth and Sophia.

"Now things take an interesting twist. What story is told by the remaining trumps?"

Before today I had never looked at the cards in any context other than their individual interpretations. But after I made my big discovery that Paul called the First Arrangement and especially after watching Paul outline the story of the first twelve trumps, I was actually able to see a narrative in the next sequence. "It's a quest. For the Grail?"

"Billy! You just might be a genius after all. And the Grail is only one of the treasures. But if we're going to see the hidden map of this great adventure, we'll need another spyglass."

He rearranged the trumps, preserving the same sequence, but with all the odd-numbered top and bottom pairs almost touching each other and all the even-numbered trumps a few inches apart. The resulting pattern made me think of the double helix in DNA.

"The *Nous* transmits the sacred knowledge through Thoth and Sophia to the Herald and the Oracle respectively. The virgin Oracle begets The Matriarch, who enlightens The Good King and thus begins the Dynastic succession, or the royal bloodline. The Master Trismegistus passes down the secret teachings to worthy initiates, one of whom is chosen to receive the ultimate blessing. This is the Apostolic line of succession."

"Hold on a second, you told me that the Apostolic succession didn't work, and the Hermetic line adopted a royal succession with Clan Kelly. Are you saying you switched over to *Sophia's* way of doing things?"

"Ours is clearly a patriarchal succession," he said with a withering stare, "if anything should be obvious to you it would be that salient point."

"Yes, but it's still a bloodline legacy. What happened? When did it change?"

"The change came after Ceallach, our namesake, but that is not the story I'm telling. Both traditions, though differing in their methods of passing the torch, are almost identical in all other respects from this point onward." He thumped his bald fingertip on The Lovers (The Vows, in his interpretation) and declared, "These two cards are the key to everything," he said pointing to the upper/lower pair formed by The Vows and The Alchemist (Temperance). "Once you truly understand this pairing, everything else falls into place."

"The Great Work," I said, the light finally shining in my eyes.

"Yes, The Great Work," he repeated, like he was humoring me. "The Chosen One, whether heir or disciple, is shown the Prophecy (wouldn't tell me, I asked), vows to protect and guide the *Nous* (why does the *Nous* need protection? No answer) and swears eternal loyalty to his Clan. Once initiated, his training begins. He proves his worthiness and tempers his spirit in The Quest for the Elementals and The Trials of the Hero, ascending from apprentice to journeyman to knight and finally Sage. Having attained the

Grail, Staff, Sword and Stone, he and the Master penetrate the Threshold of the Divine. The Hero endures more challenges and finally surrenders his own ego and will to the Master completing The Great Work. He returns to the material realm in triumph, as the Lord of Two Realms…and it all comes full circle in—"

"Armageddon?" I asked, staring at The Tower. "All of this only leads to destruction? We're back at square one again?"

"Or onto bigger and better things," he said with a wide grin.

There were a million questions I wanted to ask, about the tarot, the Gnostic writings, Sophia, Hermes Trismigestus, Christ, Mary Magdalene…I had to know everything!

He cut me off immediately.

"Listen, son, you've done exceptionally well here, even though I gave your brain a nudge from time to time to keep your train on the rails. You've uncovered some very important information about our heritage, but you're never gonna get to the bottom of this no matter how many of those old books you poke your nose into."

"And that's because…"

"For starters, those writings were deliberately intended to disguise the truth in countless metaphors and scrambled codes to keep the idiots at bay. They've been translated, and re-translated back into the original demotic, Coptic or Greek countless times, every scribe adding his own pontifical touch in his glorious interpretation. Of the more accurate writings, there's more missing from the tracts than what remains, as you've seen in the Drivel of Mary. You've about as much luck hitting pay dirt in those dustbins as those literalist born-agains have of seeing the Rapture. However, I have a gift for you that should prove far more enlightening, if you apply yourself with half the dedication of these research efforts."

He reached deeply into his pocket and told me to close my eyes. "Don't go using yer second sight and spoil the surprise." I nodded and felt him place a large rectangular object in my left hand. "Okay, open 'em."

It was a tarot deck. Older than any I'd seen. The paintings were incredibly detailed and absolutely exquisite. I turned them over one by one, The Hero, The Herald, The Oracle—all the trumps labeled with Paul's titles. "These are amazing," I said, awed and yes, flattered by his incredible gift. I had a hard time spitting it out, but I managed to say, "Thank you."

"You've earned it," he grunted, taking the cards back before I had a chance to look at the rest of them. "If I'm not mistaken, you'll see more in them than any of those dusty books," he said, setting the cards down gently on the table. "But don't stay up too late gazing at them…this deck can be quite…entrancing."

"Is there something else I should know about them?" I asked apprehensively.

"Indeed, there is. Get a good night's sleep and meet me in the chapel tomorrow. I'm bumping you up to the advanced class, so make sure your eyes are bright and your head is clear. You've earned a little taste of the Gospel according to Paul."

Getting Nailed

The first three nails hurt so much that Michael's screams almost pierced his own eardrums. The fourth one hurt even more.

"Oops! Sounds like I grazed a bone with that one." The Striker chuckled. "I hope your protector won't be too distressed by my carelessness."

"Why are you doing this?" Bean howled, his blood leaking onto the black gummy wood beneath him, his bare hands and feet nailed to the altar in a perfect X shape. Martin would have liked the symmetry.

"You may have noticed that the nails I'm using have an unusual shape," The Striker said, ignoring Michael's question. "Although they're much wider on the top, they have no lip around the head to prevent you, should you summon the valor, from extricating your hands and feet from their painful grip. All you have to do is pull…and pull…and pull…starting with your left hand, I expect. You're a southpaw, correct? Shhhhhh. Don't bother answering, I'm rarely misinformed and time is fluttering away. As I was saying, after you free the first hand, assuming that's even a remote possibility for a sniveling brat like you, the Master has deigned, in his infinite generosity, to present you with two very compelling options—alternate battle plans as it were—you, of course, being far too inexperienced and frankly too doltish to come up with a feasible option unassisted."

"Fuck you, you fucking fuck!" Michael yelled, only to have The Striker *whack!* the nail through the palm of that aforementioned left hand with such joyous vigor that Bean's cursing invectives were immediately replaced by another round of bloodcurdling screams.

"Order in the court! Order in the court!" The Striker yelled above the din of Michael's tortured cries, pounding the nail again and again, punctuating each gleeful shout.

"Whoa! Whoa! What's all this racket in here?" Paul called out, slamming through the wall-portal. "You two could wake the dead!"

"Help me!" Michael cried, "This fucker is—"

"This fucker is trying to help you, if only you'd shut up and listen!"

"Help me?" Michael shrieked.

"If you don't put a sock in it, I will," Paul growled, his face looming over Bean like a blood-red moon. Michael instantly closed his mouth.

"That's better," Paul sighed, straightening up as The Striker retreated into the shadows beyond Michael's limited sight range. When he was convinced Bean was properly attentive, Paul continued: "Listen well, for I won't be repeating meself. I'm expecting a guest to come calling on you in a very short while, a recent acquaintance of yours. I imagine he'll be barging in here with a mighty big chip on his shoulder. I don't know where he got the idea, but Martin is under the impression you had something to do with the abduction of his poor, defenseless girlfriend. I'm sure you can imagine the distress that would cause. And while both of us know you've done nothing whatsoever to assist me in that nefarious plot, I don't believe he'll give you the benefit of the doubt, especially when he sees this peeking out of your pocket."

Paul daintily held the remote between his fat thumb and forefinger, wiggling it in front of Michael's face before sliding it halfway into the right pocket of his faded corduroys.

"This is a special remote control unit," Paul said, rubbing his hands together. "What makes it so special is the gadget it controls—a rather ingenious impaling device I've attached under the chair his pretty girlfriend is presently handcuffed to. Martin is going to come crashing through this wall in about twenty-two minutes, guns blazing, in the hopes of rescuing her with that item I stuffed in your pocket. Of course, he'll want to kill you before or after he takes it, so all you have to do is kill him first, this being a contest, essentially, and like any worthwhile duel, a fight to the death. If by some miracle you manage to pull it off, you'll seize a fortune that would spin your head around like Linda Blair if only I had the time to list its precious inventory. You get all that?"

"What happened to all that shit you said about protecting me?" Michael yelled.

"I have been protecting you lad, for all your life," Paul said with a solemnity that caught Michael so off guard he forgot about how much the nails hurt…for a second. "It seems we're long overdue for a father-and-son chat…with me doing most of the talking."

"Did you just say you're my *dad*?"

"That's the sordid truth, though we haven't the time to get weepy about it. Yes, you're the fruit of my very own loins and as such you're entitled to a fair crack at your inheritance. However, Martin claims the same birthright, which puts you pretty far back in the queue."

"That fuckhead is my *brother*?"

"Correct again. Even though Martin cares not a fig for his legacy, he's nonetheless entitled to all he's due, which is a hefty package. And you, sharing the same noble ancestry, have a miniscule window of opportunity to claim your bequest, though your chances of survival are slim and none, according to my reckoning. You had a crack at him last night but tripped me up instead. Fate is clearly on his side and I have no reason to assume the tide has turned in your favor. Yet regardless of the odds against you, I'd be remiss in my parental duties if I didn't offer some helpful tips in this, your hour of mortal peril. So if you can keep your mouth shut for a few more minutes, you might actually learn something that could save your hide…and claim the ultimate treasure."

"I don't want any gold! Just get me the fuck out of here!"

"Sorry, lad," Paul replied, sadly shaking his head. "You play a significant role in the grand design and though I seriously doubt you'll ever be taking a stroll down the red carpet, it's an important part nonetheless. If Martin fails to fulfill his obligations, I'll need another young buck to rely on. You're Plan B, son…assuming you survive this arduous challenge."

"You promised you'd help me," Michael cried, testing the grip of the nails, wincing with pain as he pulled his left palm up a fraction of an inch.

"Why, you ungrateful wretch!" Paul spat at him. "I've held back on your training until the last possible moment. All your other siblings save one have endured the most grueling labors imaginable to prove their worthiness…most of them dying in the process! I've spared you countless duels, wrapped you in a big, warm, fuzzy blanket. Even now, when my associate here would like nothing more than to practice his finely honed craft with you until the second before Martin arrives, I remain by your side, shielding you from the pain your brothers gladly welcomed. And you have the nerve to *complain*?"

"Please!" Michael yelped. "Just get me the fuck off this table!"

"Get yourself off," Paul snarled. "The Striker told you how. If you had an ounce of testosterone between your shivering legs, you'd have made some decent progress already. But before you make a wholehearted effort, let's quickly review your options, or you'll have no time left to choose between them. Option one: You can remain in your current position and extract only one hand, pretending you're still fully subdued and helpless when Martin busts in here, your body blocking his view of this pistol," he said, concealing the loaded Beretta on the altar between Bean's left hand and waist. "If he looks away, thinking you can't move a muscle, you just grab the pistol and shoot him in the back.

"The other, more courageous—or cowardly option—depending on your viewpoint, would be to yank all four limbs off and hide in the darkness of the hallway, firing as many rounds as you can when you hear footsteps coming, praying one of them finds its mark."

"How about this option? How about you pull these fucking nails out?"

"Think about what you're saying," Paul replied calmly. "What makes you think it'll hurt any less when I pull 'em out than if you tug your limbs free? Remember lesson one: It hurts a little less when you do it yourself. However, if you choose that alternative, you'll pass up your only real chance at ambushing a seasoned veteran that you have virtually no other possibility of defeating. I've thought long and hard about this, it's a brilliant plan! If you don't wet your panties and have anything resembling a decent aim, you could actually pull it off. You could win!"

"I don't want to win," Bean whined, almost in tears. "I want to get out of here!"

"Is that what the Book told you?" Paul challenged him. "Is that what it said as it led you to this holy place? You have the power inside you, boy. If you didn't, you never would have heeded the Book's magic call. Remember how good it felt to hold it in your arms? To follow its tug? It was leading you, son, like it's led so many others. If you listen again, it might even lead you to freedom and glory."

Michael stopped moaning. Stopped caring. He was doomed. Doomed. But as he experienced that ultimate surrender, another part of him shrugged it off like a mother lifting a car to rescue her trapped baby. Michael stopped…and stared at the Book.

Paul smiled at the change in him, at his own little *Turning*. "Good luck, lad…I wish you all the best," he said, backing out of the portal. The Striker followed wordlessly like a pale shadow. "You've always meant a great deal to me, son. Just not as much as Martin."

Armed and Dangerous

Martin picked up the top footlocker and slammed it on the floor. It weighed a ton. He opened the footlocker below and pulled out six ammo clips for the pistols (three painted red, three blue), four slim throwing knives and a CO_2 cartridge ice-pick injection device of his own invention. That was for Bean. Martin found it very useful for interrogations where time was a critical factor. Once he explained what the CO_2 would do upon being injected directly into the bloodstream, the subjects were remarkably compliant and confessed with a 96.5% accuracy rate. He'd bet every coin in his treasure chest that the kid would tell him where the remote was hidden in less than thirty seconds. Even if he didn't, Martin would still get the satisfaction of watching his frantic expression as his brain exploded.

Martin put on his custom-made, fatigue-green, pleated nylon vest and slipped all his accessories into their sewn-in sheaths, feeling a sharp twinge of anxiety that he didn't have two injector units to balance the symmetry. He groaned and took out one of the throwing knives on the left side, substituting the prick-pricker in its place, then rushed to the bathroom mirror to see how it looked. *Fuck.* It would have to do.

He quickly threw on his jacket again, pulled out the pistols and loaded the new clips of ammo into the chambers, red for one pistol (right pocket), blue for the other (left pocket). He holstered them in their interior straps, in case he had to pull a Wyatt Earp, did a few quick-draw warm-ups just to make sure they were perfectly positioned, and once he was satisfied that he had completed his preparations with the utmost attention to detail, he bolted into his blindingly bright room, sat in his white-on–white chair and closed his eyes.

NOTHING

Martin breathed slowly and deeply, ridding his mind of his previously frantic internal dialog. When he opened his eyes again, this is what he saw:

It may not look like much to you, but in that calm blankness Martin witnessed something so astonishing all he could do was gape. And blink. And gape even wider than before. The place he always called the dream world appeared, but now he could see where it was and what it was and what it had to do with him. He saw beyond the curtain of dreams into the other place. The wondrous place. Then the voice in his head started up again, but this time it wasn't Paul, or Johnny, or the "new" him shouting with another walkie-talkie message.

It was the voice of the angel.

ONCE UPON A TIME...

"Come," the angel said. Everything was golden. The sky. The clouds. The angel's face. Suddenly, more clouds gathered and the sky grew dark…darker…black. When the light returned, it was flickering. Candles. Groans. Crying.

He was in the castle of Lord Firth. Firth and his son were lying in a bloody heap. His daughter was crying, pleading for her life. Paul was too strong to be stopped, so Martin begged him to spare her. To his complete surprise, after much shouting and ridicule, Paul agreed, but only if he would swear a blood oath of unending loyalty.

Martin made his vow to save the girl. In blood. In the Book. Paul embraced him and said he was going to take him to the special place, as he had promised so long ago. The girl was bound and gagged, for her own safety, Paul assured him, and they entered a chapel where Paul tied her to the foot of a cross burdened with the nailed figure of an angel. Together, they climbed on the altar. Paul taught him the chant and they traveled beyond the curtain of dreams to that wondrous place he called the Maelstrom. When he and Paul returned, Paul kissed both his cheeks in congratulations.

The girl looked up at them, still bound and whimpering, her eyes soaked with fear. Paul opened his sickle. Martin thought he was going to cut her bonds. He slit her throat.

"You promised!" Martin cried, falling to his knees.

"I promised to let her live. I didn't say for how long. You'll have to toughen up if we're to finish this quest. You won't fare too well against Johnny's seed if you're getting all weepy for this mongrel."

Martin wanted to hit him, to kill him, but he was too distraught to do anything but cry. Paul let him sob for a moment. Then Martin flipped the switch, stood up and walked from the chapel without another glance back at the girl. He never even knew her name.

"Come," the angel said again. The castle of Lord Firth disappeared and he was in an underground temple, carved from the living rock of the cavern. The Master had been chained to the altar by a group of armed, angry men. Suddenly a girl appeared from out of nowhere, weeping with fear. Next a boy appeared, but he didn't look fully human. What they did to him was so awful Martin looked away, silently asking the angel to spare him the rest.

Then, in a blinding flash, he was in a small candlelit chapel, staring at a huge cross burdened with a crucified angel.

"Are you ready?" a voice said. It sounded like Paul's. It came from the cross. The same angel who brought him here was looking down at him, his face contorted in agony, his body pierced everywhere with long, rusty spikes, his skin painted red with blood.

"Do you understand?" the tortured angel asked, his face kind and loving despite his suffering. Martin nodded. The angel smiled and his face changed into his own.

Jolted by the shock, Martin found himself sitting in his chair again, staring into the whiteness. He ran from the room and down the stairs, his feet pumping furiously, streaking to Paul's apartment faster than he had ever run before.

"Do you understand?" the angel's voice echoed as he ran.

Yes, Martin answered silently as his feet flew faster and faster.

I understand.

He knew what he'd hidden from himself for so long. What his vow really meant, what Paul wanted him to do. Even if he died trying, he would never let that happen. Death would be a far better fate. But if today was his day to die, he had one more duty to perform, a responsibility more sacred than any quest he could attempt, any treasure he could acquire. He loved her more than he could ever love anyone. He had loved her for an eternity. Should he survive the battle with Paul, it would mean nothing without her.

He had to save Rose.

MISFIRE

Have you ever had a crush on someone who has a crush on someone else? And then you try to get them to like you more by putting down the person they're crazy about? Doesn't work too well, does it? I took my chances anyway and sure enough, it made matters worse. Even though I pointed out how loyal I was to stay by her side while Martin abandoned her in a foolhardy attempt to find a remote control that might not even exist and would probably get himself killed in the process like a big, fucking idiot... Rose glared at me with even more contempt. "I can't wait for him to come back here and kick your sissy ass," she said defiantly.

She knew what a risk she was taking speaking to me like that, knowing I could end the conversation with a slight tip of her chair. Still, she continued taunting me, making fun of my talents, challenging me to put on a show for her like I was some kind of trained seal.

"Okay, if you can see Paul whenever you want, what's he doing right now, Kreskin?"

I closed my eyes. "I can't see him," I lied, opening them again. "He's blocking me."

"Oh, he's *blocking* you. How convenient. And when your mother begged you with her dying breath to use your amazing powers and search for Martin, which was...let's see, eight years ago...somehow you couldn't pick up on his cosmic vibrations until last month, when you found a nice scrapbook about him, which was written by Paul in Martin's handwriting, in a secret chapel in a squatter slum with a gigantic crucified angel!"

"When you put it that way, it does sound a little..."

"Crazy?" she said, cutting me off again. "Crazy? Crazy? Crazy?"

I wanted to say something equally offensive, but I stupidly kept defending myself. "You think I'm so full of it, but if it weren't for these visions, I wouldn't have seen you get snatched by Paul, I wouldn't have come here and..."

Uh-oh.

"You watched him take me!" she yelled, her face red with hate. "I knew you were in this with him, you fucking liar! How could you let that fucking maniac do this to me? Because you showed me your fucking suitcase? Because I know how fucking sick you are?"

"If I wanted to hurt you, I would have done it already," I pointed out, after she hurled every conceivable invective at me. "Paul has it in for you because you're Johnny's daughter. I told you the truth. I saw a flash of Paul grabbing you, then nothing until I saw what he did and where you were. I came here as soon as I could and found Martin cleaning your wounds. He told me to wait with you while he looked for that fucking remote control. That's it. End of story. I hate Paul as much as he does. As much as you do!"

"That's not possible," she seethed, glaring at me like she wanted to pick up those knitting needles and give me a more thorough understanding of what she'd endured.

But she was still in that chair, wasn't she?

We both remained silent for a moment. She wasn't sure what to believe anymore, which, frankly, seemed like a pretty good deal to me… until she spoke again. "Here's what I think. I think you're crazy. I don't know if Paul is Martin's father or yours, but I do think you're his partner. I think you're a sick, twisted fuck. And a world-class liar."

I got huffy with her, as liars do, hoping that would intimidate her enough to shut her fucking yap. "Look, I don't care what you think. I'm not crazy and I'm not a liar. If you want to be pissed at someone, save it for Martin. He's the one that left you here. Not me."

I know that wasn't very nice, but it shut her up. If only for a few seconds.

"Okay, we'll play it your way," she said, digging back in. "Let's assume you do have your weird little visions…and you don't know where Paul is right now because…how did you put it? He's *blocking* you? But now that he's out of range, why don't you tell me what Martin is up to, since he obviously has more important things to do than protecting me from you."

I closed my eyes, seeing Martin clear as a bell. He was climbing Paul's stairwell as silently as a ghost.

"Well?" Rose demanded.

I stared at her blankly. I was getting so tired of this. I looked down at my hands, filtering out more angry insults. If I answered her question, there would only be more. The same thing had happened to me. Questions. Always more questions.

Suddenly, I had a flash of inspiration.

"Once upon a time…" I began, opening my eyes. Then I began reciting, word for word, the story Paul told me. I didn't say more than six sentences when her eyes lit up and her expression changed from "Who is this fucking madman?" to "He knows it too!"

"My mother told me a story like that!"

"Exactly like that…or kind of like that?"

"Not exactly," she said, closing her eyes, picturing her mother perfectly. "Her story started out differently. It isn't about a boy, it's about…"

"A girl?" I asked eagerly.

"Not just girl…a Goddess."

Gumption

Michael didn't think he had it in him. Neither did I. When the fourth nail came out, it took more flesh with it than the others. He didn't scream that time. He was in a different state of mind, a more purified consciousness. The only thing he felt was hatred and its ever-dependable sidekick, the lust for revenge. Oddly though, his thirst for vengeance wasn't directed at the instigator of his current torment, but at the man Paul said would be coming in only a few more minutes…to kill him. Martin. His fucking asshole brother.

"We'll see about that," he hissed, tossing the loose clump of flesh to the filthy floor.

He limped over to the lectern, which isn't too easy when you're limping on both feet, and placed his bloody hands on the Book. As soon as his red, dripping palms made contact, he felt something very peculiar, first in his perforated feet, then his hands.

He didn't bother looking at his feet. Why should he? The evidence in front of his face was convincing enough. There wasn't a drop of blood on the ancient leather hide of the book. There wasn't a drop of blood on his hands either. Nor were there holes. Or scars. It was like nothing had ever happened to him. A new strength came surging into his legs. His feet felt like a pair of anvils. His arms swung like wrecking balls.

The door was open now. The hallway beyond was as black as a crypt at midnight. But that didn't bother Michael. He picked up the sleek, cold Beretta, smiled at the angel and walked into the darkness like he was strolling along the Left Bank at sunset. When the darkness swallowed him up completely, that didn't bother him either. His eyes were shining from the inside now. And Michael Bean could *see*.

MARTIN GOES INSIDE

Martin climbed the stairwell with both guns drawn. They looked the same, but the ammo was different. Which one he'd use depended on what he saw.

When he reached Paul's apartment, he got his first big surprise. The door was open. That was not good. He stopped and listened. He heard footsteps inside. He waited until they stopped before proceeding. He was ready. No, he was more than ready. He was itching for it. The sooner he smelled gunpowder, the better.

He crept inside, his footsteps silent as a ninja's. It was quiet now. Very quiet. He moved from room to room. Ready. Tense. Then he heard them. More footsteps. He stood still, listening. He couldn't tell which hallway they were coming from—the corridor he navigated last night or the one just ahead of him, past the room with the tattered couch.

Was that the hallway that led to…the chapel?

He didn't move for the longest time. Keening his ears like a dog.

Then he heard them. More footsteps. Soft. Cunning. Light.

They didn't sound like Paul's clomping boots, but they sounded much too sly and stealthy for that stupid little creep, which could only mean two things. Either he'd grossly underestimated Bean's abilities—or somebody else was in there.

THE WITNESS

He moved between the walls. He didn't care if he was seen. Or heard.

He trusted in his power. Bullets could come. They would miss him. Nothing could harm him now.

He was here. But elsewhere. He had waited too long for this moment to take any further chances. He peered into the darkness, sensing everything. He felt Johnny watching him too, powerless to reveal his secret intent. His blood vow would always prevent it.

Even Paul, the Great Master, had been deceived. Remained deceived. And now he would have another chance. A slim one, admittedly, but a chance, nonetheless.

Paul would never have allowed it willingly. He had seen through that lie for untold years. But time was worth nothing, if not for planning…and Loren DeVilbiss, The Striker, The Lord of the Twelfth House…was ready to claim his due.

VISIONARY

Strange. So strange. When Bean entered the hallway and the last feeble flickers of candlelight faded behind him, he didn't think about how he was moving. He just did, one foot in front of the other. It wasn't like he could see with his eyes, exactly. He simply *knew* where he was. Something in his gut, right below his navel, was pulling him like a leash, like it had when he was holding the Book. He walked and walked, never bumping into a wall or even brushing against one. Walking, turning, until he felt the sudden urge to stop and sit, which he accomplished with just as much mindless efficiency.

Black. So black. He'd never felt so safe before. So calm. So cruel. He held the Beretta serenely in his hand, his finger on the trigger, his back against the wall, his feet pressed against the opposite side of the narrow corridor. The gun felt good in his grip. His thoughts were nearly absent. He stared directly ahead, wondering if his eyelids were open or closed. He couldn't be sure. He couldn't feel them. Yet somehow he was *seeing*. Not the grimy floor or the cruddy wallpaper—they were as numbly nonexistent as his outstretched feet. He began to wonder if he were really here at all. Was he a ghost? A puff of smoke? Black on black? He didn't know, but whatever he felt, whatever he *was*…he liked it. He liked it just as much as this new form of perception. If he could have put it into words, he might have described his altered vision as a cross between a daydream and a particularly vivid night dream. It resembled those vague mental images you get when you stare out the window, yet was combined with the crisper clarity and total immersion of an ordinary dream.

It was nice. The best of both worlds…his vision shifting from sleepy, cloudy pictures of people and places, always moving…busy, busy, busy… punctuated by sudden bursts of hyper-real (and unreal) panoramas he was witnessing from the inside, as if he were there. The pictures came and went, nothing so recognizable or compelling to distract him from the novelty of the experience. But when he thought about Martin, everything changed and he got the shock of his life. It wasn't what he saw that jolted him so entirely. It was what he heard:

"Never alive…and never dead…" the voice whispered. The voice was Paul's. The ear he whispered into…Martin's. Michael saw them together, like they were standing in front of him, not in this hallway darkness. In the chapel. He knew they weren't there now. But he didn't know how he knew that. He was seeing Martin's memories.

"Never alive…and never dead…" Paul repeated, his arms wrapped around Martin in an unbreakable bear hug, their hearts pressed so tightly against each other that they could feel every muffled thump.

"Never alive…and never dead…" Paul whispered again, his voice soothing as a hypnotist. "The angel knows everything…feel his tortured wings…see the hole in his heart…guide yourself there…to the absence… to the crack.…"

Martin was hugging Paul just as fiercely, his face pressed against those blister-red cheeks, staring unblinking at the angel only ten feet before him. They were standing together on top of the altar, their feet placed like sunken anchors, carefully positioned on top of the crude carvings that were almost obscured by the many layers of dried, caked-on blood.

"Never alive…and never dead…" Paul whispered more softly. "Feel our hearts beat together…slower…yes…slower and slower…"

Martin nodded, his eyes glazing over, his lids drooping, the angel smiling at him like an angry threat…his heart thumping softer, less frequently…right in time with Paul's.

"Never alive…and never dead…" Paul seemed to say. But no air escaped his lungs. "There! The crack is opening! Can you see it? Hold me even tighter…like I showed you! *Now…jump, boy…jump!*"

Michael's eyes snapped open. Or did they? He couldn't tell. But he wasn't in the chapel anymore, witnessing the inconceivable tableau of two men standing on an ancient altar, squeezing the last breath from each other.

His eyes were traveling to the other end of the hallway. There was only one man standing there and it wasn't Paul. Michael could see him just as clearly as he had before. Even clearer. It was Martin, and he was indeed jumping, into the darkness of the hallway. Running, no, loping directly toward him.

Like a werewolf chasing a rabbit.

ALL GONE

Black. Everything was black again. Not that calm, soft, velvety darkness where all was well and fear was just a memory. No, this was the same blackness that had swallowed him up like Jonah's whale only an hour earlier. He was scared shitless. The change came over him as soon as he *saw* Martin charge into the hallway, all his newfound bravado erased in the wake of his silent footsteps. Martin was coming for him! He was coming to kill him!

His ears pricked up for any sound. Nothing. Was he really coming? Was this all just another insane hallucination...like the burned-up closet? Was he going nuts? He couldn't see a fucking thing! But that's why he came in here, wasn't it? So no one could see him either. Yeah, that's right. That fuckhead would probably trip over his legs. Then he could shoot him! Wait, what was that? Muffled movement. Where was it coming from? He couldn't tell! Was Martin in front of him? Behind him? In the other hallway? He wondered how many bullets were in his gun. He hoped he had enough. Because if he heard even one more sound anywhere near him he was going to start firing.

Then he heard it. *Whoooosh.* It seemed like it was almost on top of him.

He clenched his jaw and squeezed the trigger. The trigger wouldn't squeeze. *Fuckity fuck!* The safety was on! But Michael Bean, who knew as much about firearms as he did about cold-blooded murder, didn't have a clue where to look for it. And even if he did, it wouldn't have mattered.

Because it was too fucking dark!

BLIND MAN'S BLUFF

"You're it!" Martin wanted to yell as he smacked Michael's head on his whooshing way past. He leapt over him like a sleek panther, his eyes dilated to their maximum aperture, enough to see Michael's comically horrified face while he fumbled to find the safety.

What an idiot, he thought, galloping silently away. When Martin leapt over him, slapping his head on the way, Michael gasped with relief. Then he heard more footsteps shuffling from the other end of the hall. Fuck! Who was it this time? As soon as he asked himself the question, his visionary ability momentarily returned and he *saw* the answer. It was The Striker. He was coming for him too!

WhatamIgunnado? screamed his fear-clogged brain. If he ran toward Martin, he was sure to deliver more than a playful punch next time. But he couldn't wait here either. The Striker's nearly silent feet were creeping closer. Could he shoot him? Could he…kill him? "Yes," said a creepy whisper in the back of his mind. "You can and you will."

Michael fumbled for the safety again and felt a tab of metal above his thumb. He flipped the tab, pointed the pistol, closed his eyes…and squeezed. *Bang! Bang! Bang!*

Yes! It worked! He wanted to scream with joy. But it wasn't time to celebrate yet. The shots were so loud he couldn't tell if the footsteps were still approaching. He listened. Nothing. *Maybe I got him.*

No such luck. Martin was standing in front of the chapel when he heard Bean's shots. He didn't hear the sound of any impact. Better yet, he didn't feel any. "Wow," he whispered, peering into the candlelit room. Everything he remembered was true. It was exactly like he pictured it… the altar…the angel. The only thing missing was the two of them standing on top of that blood-soaked wood, caught in that suffocating embrace… squeezing and squeezing until…No. He couldn't think about that now. He looked down the nightmare-black hallway and raised his pistol. He didn't want to kill the kid. Just clip him. The rest could wait until Paul followed him in here. Until Paul could watch him die.

Blam! Blam! Blam!

"*Ow!*" Michael yelled as a bullet tore through his shirt and bit off a slice of his armpit. "*SHEEEEIT!*" he screamed as the pain increased with every step, the idea never occurring to him that making more noise might not be in his best interests.

Bang! Bang! Bang! Thud. Thud. Thud.

Was he hit again? No. The next three slugs from Martin's pistol slammed into the plasterboard behind him. He stopped running and started listening. Everything was quiet.

What should he do? The Striker was behind him. Was he shot? Silently waiting? And in the other direction, toward the chapel, Martin was waiting too.

He felt another wave of panic. Then he was *seeing* again. As soon as he pictured Martin waiting for him in front of the chapel, he *saw* him there. Awesome! Every muscle in Michael's body relaxed. Even the bullet wound didn't hurt so much.

His feet started moving. He saw flickers of candlelight painting the hallway up ahead. And with the cool-headed courage only the doomed can feel, he recognized that if his time had truly come, then he was going to do his very best to take Martin with him.

It's time to go back there, he decided.

Back to the room with the angel.

Journal Entry: The Angel

When Paul was on his way out the door last night, I asked him one last question: "What's the story with the crucified angel?"

"Now you're on the right track!" he yelled, clapping loudly. Then he left.

What a prick. I was so exhausted at that point that I flopped down on the couch. I closed my eyes for a second, trying to peer inside the chapel, hoping if I gazed upon the angel one more time, I would *see* all his secrets. I didn't *see* shit. I thought about getting up to look at the tarot cards, something I felt more excited about than a kid waiting for Christmas before I hit the sofa, but I couldn't get up.

Ten hours later, I opened my eyes again, waking from the strangest dreams I've ever had. They were all about Paul's tarot and the story it told, which I completely understood while I was dreaming. I immediately wrote down as much as I could remember in my dream journal. But even though I scribbled as fast as I could, my insights faded with each second, until I got so frustrated that I quit and went over to the table to look at the cards, hoping I'd be able to recapture my lost treasures.

Last night, Paul had left the deck in a nice, neat stack on top of my cards. They weren't in a stack anymore. They were laid out on the table in the same pattern Paul had arranged my own cards—which were gone. My first reaction was rage. I hadn't touched the new cards, even looked at them! Yet there they were, in all their glory. I was certain Paul had snuck back into my apartment after I fell asleep so he could scare the shit out of me with the tarot switch. I was equally sure he had invaded my mind so he could fuck with my dreams. But as I bent over the table and gazed at those amazing cards, I knew it Paul hadn't done it.

How was this possible? How did I get from the point of seriously doubting Paul's sanity to even more seriously questioning my own? A sleepwalking tarot card reader? What's next—multiple personalities?

I sat at the table, trying to calm down, fully intending to gather up the cards and confront Paul with my latest out of mind/body experience. The cards had other plans.

He was right—they were mesmerizing. Every picture was like an open doorway, inviting me inside. A couple of times I could have sworn I saw the images moving in my peripheral vision, like they were peeking at me and as soon as they saw I wasn't looking directly at them, they began whispering about me.

When my eyes landed on the card called The Saint (formerly The Hanged Man), I saw a flash from my dream vision about the crucified angel. Every tarot deck I've seen depicts The Hanged Man upside down, hung by his foot. Paul's Saint is crucified. Lots of nails. Everywhere. A halo too, but no wings. So The Saint (any relation to Johnny?) isn't an angel. But what did the crucifixion signify? A sacrifice? Or persecution?

I thought the surrounding cards might offer an explanation, but they only deepened the mystery—and wonder. An androgynous Judge (Justice) precedes The Saint. She/He is sitting on a throne, holding scales in one hand—and the Emerald Tablet in the other. That blew me away. The others are just as strange and wonderful. Death is called the *Turning*. I know I've heard that before. Paul? The Striker? Anyway, it shows an angel ascending into the heavens, carrying the bloody Saint. Then comes The Alchemist (Temperance) with the angel and the Saint superimposed in Leonardo da Vinci's *Vitruvian Man* pose, standing on an altar with the four elementals. The next card is called Triumph, with a very godlike male figure seated on a throne. Two angels kneel on one side, a man and woman kneel on the other.

This card frightens and confuses me more than any other. First of all, it has a subtitle, The Lord of Two Realms, which appears to be painted over. Secondly, it looks a fuck of a lot like Paul. Since this card is called The Devil in other decks, what is this supposed to mean? The Devil triumphs as Lord of Heaven and Earth? Are we talking Anti-Christ here? When Paul shouted, "The Devil is jealous of me!" did he mean it…literally?

I got up and splashed some water on my face. I felt slightly less crazy and panicked, but I didn't want to look at those cards anymore. They called me back anyway. Maybe it was The Angel beckoning—that's the new name of the Judgment card. The four cards preceding it are some of the few cards in the deck that aren't renamed—The Tower, The Star, The Moon and The Sun. Then…The Angel.

It is absolutely stunning, by far the most masterfully painted card. The Angel is semi-androgynous, but masculine, like The Hero and The Herald. He is posed with his arms stretched out and feet together, like The Saint on his cross. Unlike that bloody mess, The Angel glows with golden light, free and floating in the clouds, smiling beatifically. His giant white wings reach upward, the tips almost touching above his golden hair. It is so incredibly beautiful. It should be in a museum, not on my crappy table in my crappy apartment.

Speaking of which, I need to get out of here and over to the chapel to see what Paul has waiting for me. As much as I'm semi-looking forward to another of Paul's theological discourses, I just want to know more about the angel. More later.

Well, I'm back—more or less in one piece. I keep trying to convince myself that what I saw and heard and felt in the chapel could not have happened. I've tried every explanation I can think of—that I was hypnotized the whole time, that Paul is simply a master illusionist. Unfortunately, even if his conjuring abilities exceed David Copperfield's, and my sensations of sight and touch can be manipulated to such an extreme extent, there is no way to account for the sheer *pain* I felt. Like everything else, it had to be real. I am the sorcerer's apprentice. But my Master isn't Merlin in a purple robe… it's who the fuck knows who, in a filthy, long, black overcoat.

I better start at the beginning.

On my way over to the chapel, I stopped to see The Striker. I wanted to know what, if anything, he was willing to tell me about the angel. Like Paul, all his replies were cryptic or insulting, until I changed direction and asked, "Who is Johnny the Saint?"

The Striker's eyes lit up like someone struck a match inside them.

"Johnny the Saint is the most dangerous man in the world," he said, sounding both respectful and contemptuous.

"To who?" I asked, completely taken aback by his response.

"To all of us. Especially to you and your line. To the Kellys."

"What about you? Aren't you part a part of the clan?"

"Not by blood. Viking stock. Druid High Priest," he replied, as if compelled to answer, but with no more information than necessary—name, rank, serial number.

Druid High Priest. Here we go again. Still, it opened an opportunity I wasn't going to waste. "So, do you know…"

"More than you ever will, at the rate you're progressing," he said, cutting me off from asking whether he knew the secret druid lore, if it was really written in Paul's Book, and what I was most curious about—whether he had mastered the druids' alleged prowess in sorcery.

"Tell me more about Johnny," I said, bobbing and weaving. He said nothing, so I pressed ahead, "Does he have something to do with the angel?"

"Oh, my! It thinks!" The Striker gasped, covering his mouth with bony fingers. I'd had enough of his crap. I didn't even bother with a follow-up, just put on my coat and headed for the door. As my fingers touched the doorknob, he gave me a parting shot.

"If you want answers, consider the source."

"I intend to. I'm going over there now."

"Not Paul. If you have questions about the angel…ask him."

"Ask the *angel*?" I replied, not sure I heard him correctly.

The Striker laughed in that deep voice. "Isn't that what all your grimoires are for?"

I walked out, shaking my head. Was he seriously suggesting that I *invoke* an angel? Without even knowing "who" the angel was? Apparently. But that was impossible. I had never even attempted to conjure a spirit. I sure wasn't going to break my cherry in that creepy chapel, calling forth whoever or whatever happened to be floating between those piss-soaked walls. Most of the grimoires I've read use the same basic recipe for invocation: create a protective magic circle (carved into the floor using a consecrated ritual sword, which I didn't have); wear a protective amulet (which I didn't have); carve a lot of magical symbols in the circle and then recite all the invocation phrases from memory (which I could do, but without the other stuff it didn't make a difference).

Suddenly, I had a one-word flash of inspiration. *Prayer.* I could pray to the angel and see what happened. It was a chapel, right? What do you do in chapels? Pray. Mother was never a churchgoer, so I didn't have any templates to work with, but I figured whatever success I might have would come from a combination of desire, heartfelt sincerity and of course, my big, fat *gift*. Maybe it was finally going to provide me with something other than an effective eavesdropping device.

I rehearsed various prayers all the way to Paul's place. Most variations began with "Dear Angel." That was way too corny to say with any degree of passion, but I felt confident the right words would come to me when I was kneeling, yes, kneeling in front of the angel.

Paul was waiting for me in the chapel. I was about to ask him if I could have some "private time" when he gave me a hard, blank-faced stare and left me alone without saying a word. What happened to the big speech? The Gospel according to Paul? Did he know what I'd been thinking about all day? Was he inside my head without my even knowing it? Honestly, I was just happy to be left alone, so I didn't give it another thought.

I kneeled on the pew-like stand behind the lectern, staring at the golden rays emanating from the angel's heart, his gently smiling face, the hundred or so spikes driven into his wings and torso. I hadn't even started to pray when I felt a warm glow come over me, like the angel was calling out, beckoning. Like it wanted to share a secret.

I closed my eyes and started praying. My prayer was simpler than I thought it would be. Only three words. A question I asked over and over. *Who are you? Who are you? Who are you?*

Soon a vision flooded my eyes with such clarity I felt blinded. I think

I fell and hit myself. There was blood on my forehead when I got up. But my head didn't hurt and my fears had melted away. When Paul came in, he gave me the biggest smile I'd ever seen.

"You saw it, didn't you?"

"The angel? Yes, but I still don't understand about the cross and…"

"Never mind that," he said dismissively. "What did else you see?"

"I saw this place. I don't know how to describe it. It was so amazing. Everything was swirling. It felt like I was being crushed…dying. Then we must have passed through something. There was a temple."

"Yes, yes," he said, nodding eagerly.

"I saw two people in robes, turning a wheel…" I continued, my eyes focused far beyond the wooden creature nailed to the crucifix above me. Then I asked the only question that seemed to have any true importance: "Is it real?"

Paul lowered his head, resting his ruddy chin on the tripod of his knuckles. "Real…" he said softly. He paused for more long seconds, then spoke haltingly, as if the precision of every word was critical to even the remote possibility of comprehension.

"The Wheel is…a construction…of *intent*," he said finally. "The power is in the *intent*…the *will*…of the Master. In the creation of the most powerful ritual objects, the Master molds his *intent*, with the guidance and participation of the angels and the *Intelligence*. True creativity is within the purview of the Master, occasionally even the gifted initiate. Such abilities are the luminous heritage we share with the angels of the divine realm. Those beings of the twin universe use that power effortlessly, as humans do in the realm of dreams. But to do so fully in the material realm takes extraordinary energy."

He paused, longer this time. I assumed he was searching for the right words again, but he did not speak. He cupped his hands in front of him like he was holding a delicate invisible vase. He closed his eyes, lowered his head and became completely still. A true flesh-and-blood statue. I stared at his face. It was smooth and waxy. The mask revealed nothing. What was he doing? I thought he was in some kind of meditative trance. Instead, he did the most extraordinary thing I have ever witnessed. I looked in his hands and a golden light began hovering above his calloused palms. I stared in wonder as the glow took shape: round, then elliptical, then ovoid, becoming more solid with each passing moment. As it gained mass it settled downward, finally resting in his palms, fully formed. A golden egg.

Slowly he opened his eyes and looked into mine. His face remained blank, but I could sense he wanted to smile or make some expression to share the moment with me. He did it in a way I never could have imagined and still can't comprehend. He held the golden egg between his thumb and forefinger, placed it in my hand, then closed my fingers slowly around it. I felt the heavy weight of it in my grip. It was so smooth, so warm. Living?

"It's real," I gasped, wanting to applaud, cry, hug him. It felt that intimate. He nodded, the hint of a smile finally forming on his lips. With that simple movement the egg began to disintegrate in my hand. I opened my palm and it turned into a bright, golden glow again, hovering, as if releasing its spirit to heaven. An ascension of sorts. Then, like a single birthday candle blown out by a child, it was gone.

"It takes too much energy to hold the form in our world," he said, breathing deeply, sounding almost apologetic.

"So the Temple, the Wheel, it's all…"

"The elementals were created eons ago, after the completion of the Sanctum Santorum of the Temple. They were forged jointly with the *intent* of the Masters, the *Nous* and the angels. Together they form the Wheel. It is a *replica*, a balancing counterpoint, a *mirror*…of The Great Wheel in the Maelstrom…the Axis."

"All this still exists?" I asked, my heart pounding.

"It exists now only in the divine realm, as you saw. A mirror of the mirror we made. It can still be used, very sparingly, but only by those with the greatest mastery and the strongest intent. The Temple was destroyed in our dimension but not the elementals. Soon it will be rebuilt. Then the words of the Book will make it come alive in both universes. The Wheel will turn. The gateway will open. The glory will be fulfilled."

He opened his shirt and showed me the key hanging from his neck and the scars on his chest. They were the same shapes as my implants, but much more horrible. He reached beneath the altar and placed the Book on top of the blood-caked wood, turned the key, opened the binding. He stood with me facing him, the angel looming over his head, and began reading. It was a very long and very sad tale. I listened raptly to every word, memorizing every intonation and gesture, putting my photographic memory to good use, for a change.

I'm going to keep it simple, but it's like whittling a five-act Shakespeare play into sound bites:

In the fifth century CE, after much persecution by the Christian Roman Empire, the Master (his name is never spoken) gathers his disciples and all the manuscripts he's managed to salvage from the book burning bonfires. They sail to Erin (his homeland, which was unexpected) and take over a ruined abbey built on top of a hallowed Druid site by early Christian missionaries. The Master poses as an abbot, his disciples as monks. They make copies of the codices and scrolls they've hidden in caves below the chapel and begin construction of an underground temple, because the time of the prophecy is finally at hand.

Under the light of the full moon, the Master spies Morgana, the Queen Matriarch/druid high priestess of Clan Something-or-other (Paul's Gaelic was incomprehensible), performing a magic ritual atop the abbey tower. She's naked, beautiful and happens to be Sophia incarnate, his *syzygy*. Naturally, they fall in love. He breaks his vow of celibacy. She cuckolds her husband King Bradan and immediately becomes pregnant. This is a big problem because a) she hasn't had sex with Torcan in over a year; b) she can sense it isn't a girl, and as a Matriarchal monarch with no successor, she's getting antsy; c) if he's found out, The Master will lose face with his disciples and incur the wrath of her entire clan.

When her belly starts to swell, Morgana takes a sabbatical at the monastery, where she maintains silence and solitude until she's ready to deliver. A son is born with the mark of *An Té atá Tofa*. He is named Ceallach. Pronounced *KELL*-ahk. As in *KELL*-y.

Paul stopped reading so he could explain the true meaning of the name. He said Ceallach means "Temple." In Gaelic *ceall* means church or monastery, though Paul said the more proper translation was temple, not merely a place of worship—the literal House of God. "Ceallach was the *vessel* and the tabernacle of all that came before, the perfected union of Hermes and Sophia," he explained. "'Bright-headed' is a frequent and related interpretation, referring to both his golden hair and the light of the *Intelligence* residing within him. Later, his name became synonymous with war and strife, for reasons that will soon be clear."

Paul returned to the book, explaining how they hid the secret of the baby's parentage with a classic baby-left-in-a-basket-at-the-monastery cover-up story. The Master loved the child more than life itself. Morgana took more sabbaticals at the abbey to be with him. They both made the best of a difficult situation, declining to reveal Ceallach's parentage until he came of age at the time of the *Becoming*.

Then they get a disturbing message from the great beyond. The angel appears to warn them that the *Becoming* may fail (due to unspecified reasons), so they better make use of the time they have left by coming up with a good Plan B to ensure the continuation of their lineages, because the next crack in the *Becoming* window wouldn't open for a long, long time. The Master, a sworn pacifist who has been on the lam from Christian zealots, knows they will never stop hounding him, so he begins work on a very special codex to preserve all the teachings, should everything go to shit.

Paul paused to breathe in deeply, laid his hands upon the parchment leaves and simply said, "The Book."

Wow. What a chill I got when he said that. Collectors are always looking for treasure—and *this*, this one-of-a-kind, immaculately preserved fifth century codex containing the compiled knowledge of all Hermetic and Gnostic teachings, perhaps all sacred teachings from the time of ancient Egypt or even earlier—this was more priceless than any object I could even imagine. The almost physical lust I felt for the Book made it difficult to concentrate as he continued with a very detailed description of how the Book was made and consecrated (the one part of his story I was forever forbidden to tell or record by any means).

Paul spoke more vaguely about Morgana preserving her heritage. He didn't say a second codex of druid lore was created, and when I asked him, he gave me such a baleful glare that I kept my mouth closed for the remainder of his narrative.

Whatever she's doing evokes a very bad dream about the Master and Morgana's daughter—even though she doesn't have one. Hearing her terrified screams, Bradan comes into her bedroom to comfort her and bingo, she's pregnant again. This time, she knows it's a girl. She doesn't tell the Master, but it's a small island and news travels quickly. The Master is not pleased. He's even less pleased to hear that her baby also bears the mark of the chosen one. She names her Róisín Dubh (Little Black Rose). Uh-oh.

Years pass. The temple and the Book are near completion. The Master gains popularity teaching some of the locals, mostly royals and druids, since they're the only ones who can read. Ceallach is growing into a fine young man, Róisín, a lovely lass. Then Bradan, in a rare display of kingly assertiveness, declares that Little Rose must begin studies at the monastery. Morgana, who's been trying to keep her far away from the Master, has no choice but to agree, or else risk a chance of Bradan getting wind of their affair because she doth protest too much.

This is where things get really interesting, not so much in the story as in Paul's telling of it. He started out talking in the measured phrases of someone who has recited from the Book verbatim for a gazillion years—then he suddenly goes off-script, fumbling, looking at me intently to see if I noticed any glitch, while I keep my best poker face on and act like I'm oblivious. The context of his edited version is this: Morgana tells the Master about her dream —where he kills Róisín—and she demands a blood oath of protection. Paul said that a very powerful ritual was conducted (details omitted), then he immediately went back to the rote incantation, picking up where Róisín begins her studies—and Morgana seems a lot less nervous about it.

Her peace of mind doesn't last because Róisín gets a huge crush on Ceallach and vice versa, neither of them the least bit aware they're skipping through the incest minefield.

More time passes and Ceallach and Róisín prove very adept at their studies, including Advanced Magick and Alchemy, and are initiated into the Gnostic/Hermetic/Druid club, vowing their commitment to the Way and the Great Work. During the ceremony, the angel is invoked and dramatically appears on the temple altar. Even more dramatic is the angel's declaration that Ceallach and Róisín will join with him in the *Becoming*, instead of M&M. Morgana accepts it gracefully, since her line has always passed on the torch to the next generation. The Master...not so much.

Knowing their remaining time together is short, the Master and Morgana reveal themselves to Ceallach as his good ole Mum and Da. Predictably, his reaction is a mixed bag. Nice to know, wish you told me sooner. Tears are shed and hugs shared. Róisín is not to be told so she doesn't get all cranky with the adulterous Queen in front of Bradan who will certainly bar her from ever returning to the monastery. Ceallach, who is now head over heels in love with Róisín, is also warned not to consummate their passion, because well—she's his half-sister. For good measure they guilt-trip him, saying the angel will "glorify your purity." Very Catholic. Regardless of their admonitions, Ceallach wants some private time with Róisín, so they can express their heartfelt emotions before the big event. Does he heed his parents' warning? Unspoken—at least in the section Paul read—but there are a lot of sacred oak groves around.

Then, because you can't tell any Irish story without a war popping up, Eoghan, a clan chief from Hy-Many, decides to make a land grab in the peaceful kingdom of Morgana because...why not? They're pussies!

He's got a sizeable army, thirsty for blood and backed up by none other than Bishop Patrick, who is travelling with them because he's heard rumors of an abbot in the neighborhood that sounds suspiciously like public enemy number one on the Church's hit list. Eoghan sends an emissary to Bradan, saying he can either cede the territory, or fight and die. Instead, he chooses door number three, offering Princess Róisín's hand in marriage to Tormac, Eoghan's mean-as-a junkyard-dog son. Bradan kicks in a nice-sized parcel of land and many goats and cows as a dowry if he'll take the deal. He takes it, because less bloodshed and more land mean bigger and better wars to come.

A messenger is sent to the abbey to pick up Róisín and drag her back to the castle. Morgana learns that not only has Bradan sold out her Queendom, he's pimped off their daughter too. She sends the messenger away empty-handed and keeps Róisín under wraps, preparing her for the ceremony that afternoon which will hopefully silence the war drums in the Glory of the *Becoming*. All of this is occurring on Good Friday, by the way, in honor of Yeshua's "needless" sacrifice (Paul editorializing again).

Meanwhile, back at the castle, Eoghan and Tormac are tapping their toes wondering when the bride-to-be will make her appearance. Patrick is anxious to prepare his own Good Friday celebration, stirring up trouble at another druid megalith site, with Eoghan's soldiers in attendance to quell any protests. But Tormac's messenger returns and announces that Róisín and Morgana are refusing to leave the abbey.

"Abbey?" Patrick's ears perk up, and they march off after our heroes, while everyone in the abbey marches into the Temple cave. The Master and Morgana invoke the angel while two disciples turn the Wheel. Everyone flies through the Maelstrom to the Axis, where the angel is waiting. The Master, acting very humble about being left out of the ascension party, bids his son a teary farewell as Ceallach, Rosie and the angel unite.

Then everything goes to shit. The Master returns to terra firma. The kids get cold feet and follow him. Unfortunately, Ceallach has already begun morphing into a human/angel hybrid. He comes back monstrously crippled to find Eoghan and his clan waiting. Patrick fires up the lynch mob and Tormac takes great pleasure in crucifying "the demon" Ceallach, while the Master is helplessly chained and Morgana is nowhere to be found.

So concludes the story of the crucified angel.

"And the beginning of the New Way," Paul declared, closing the book.

I asked him to tell me what happened after Ceallach's death, but he shook his head and said, "Come, receive your legacy."

I walked up to him as if I were in a dream. He opened the Book to the middle. There were two blank pages. He told me to lay my hands upon them. Then he opened his sickle and slit my throat.

I gurgled in horror, clutching my neck to stanch the flow. I felt the size of the gaping wound. My throat was sliced all the way to the trachea. Paul whispered that he could save me, but only if I could write my name on the pages before the life drained out of me.

I remember looking into his eyes as if asking for a pen. He laughed as the blood spurted from my neck in six-foot arcs, covering both of us, the book, the altar. Everything. I'd never seen so much blood. It was so *red*. By the time I lowered my finger to the pages, my hand was trembling, my legs twitching, about to collapse. I wrote my name from that river of red cascading from my open-hinged throat. It looked like a finger painting. But as soon as I finished, the pages soaked up all my blood. Blank pages again. Blanker than blank.

Paul told me to press my palms on the parchment, and I felt a warm glow suffuse my whole body. The bleeding stopped. I felt my neck. I didn't need a mirror to know the ragged wound was gone. Gone like my ink. With my hands on the Book I was told to make a vow to honor the angel and guard the secrets of the Book "for a thousand Aeons." If I did not, then the Book would take back my blood. If I did, and betrayed my vow…

"I won't," I promised.

Paul smiled and locked the book, placed it on the lectern, then jumped on top of the altar, holding out his hand. I knew what he wanted. I wanted it just as much. When he took me to that terrible, wondrous place, then farther still, to the realm of the Golden Temple and back, I knew who I was, what I was, what I'd always been.

I was a Kelly.

COLLATERAL

When Martin peered inside the chapel, the flood of memories was overwhelming. He could almost see the angel from his vision nailed to the cross before him, still breathing, though barely, leaking so much blood that the floor ran red. But this angel was only made of wood and the cloak of blood covering the angel's perforated body was caked and crusty.

Martin looked from the angel to the altar. Four nails were pounded into the wood, each rising like an abandoned tower, surrounded by little moats of fresh blood. Who was the victim? Where was he now? What happened here? His eyes travelled to the cabinets below, but there was no sign of the remote control. Did it really exist? There was no way to know, but after a cautious and thorough exploration of the entire room, he was certain it wasn't here. He was surprised Paul hadn't shown up yet. That was not a good sign. He liked to make a dramatic entrance, and the longer it was postponed, the more dramatic it would be. Martin was also surprised to discover the books in the cabinet beneath the altar were gone.

Only one volume remained. Martin snatched it off the lectern as soon as he entered the room. The Book was lying next to him now, beneath the angel. Waiting, like he was, for the moment to unleash its power.

SHOWDOWN

Bean stood outside, two feet from the open door. He knew where Martin was hiding. He could still *see* him. And now he could *see* something else. The Book. Yes, the Book. He thought about how weird his new vision was, until a deeper part of him silenced his internal dialog like a slap in the face and said, "Look! Listen!"

He looked through his closed eyelids and saw Martin again, holding two big silver guns in each hand. Then he *heard* Martin listening to him. Whoa! This was even stranger than the *seeing*—like he was listening through Martin's ears, hearing his own breathing, his own heartbeats.

Michael knew he had a chance. The chance Paul promised. His vision was so clear that when Martin rose to attack, he would be completely vulnerable. All he had to do was sit tight, keep his finger on the trigger and wait for the perfect moment.

When the perfect moment came, it was Martin who seized it. He stood up and fired one lone slug through the wall right where Michael was waiting. Martin had his gifts as well, and he'd been practicing them far longer. The gifts of sight and touch. Taste and smell. Hearing and speed. In the end, the only benefit of Michael's newly acquired talents was his uncanny ability to watch a slow–motion bullet as it tore through the extra-thick plasterboard and into his fairly thick skull.

Quantum Leap

When you flip a coin, what are the odds of getting heads or tails? Fifty-fifty, right? And when you pick six numbers out of sixty in a lottery, the odds are one in 50,063,860, right?

Wrong. The odds are still fifty-fifty. Ridiculous? No. Because either something is going to happen, or it isn't. Even if there are a zillion possibilities, only one of them will occur. And the variable that may have the greatest effect on whether something happens or not...is the person observing it. Especially if Loren is involved.

Loren has a talent you would scoff at, that you'd call impossible, or fantastic, or any other gawking superlatives that come to mind. When the bullet left Martin's gun, Loren traveled with it. Through the wall, where it lost much of its velocity, through the bony helmet of Michael's skull, where it slowed down even more. He rode the spinning hunk of metal like a surfer, bending the quantum waves.

It was a short ride, but extremely exhilarating. This was his supreme talent, twisting the web of probability, until a million possible outcomes narrowed further and further, to a thousand...then a hundred...and finally... only one. The right one.

When he was finished, he turned his attention elsewhere, drained but encouraged by his efforts. It was too early to gauge the extent of his success, but he wouldn't have long to wait. So in the meantime, in between time, he retreated to the place where he'd been hiding, the place where he felt most at home, regardless of the toll it took on his body to remain there. It wasn't another secret room, like the one Paul occupied, his eyes rolled backwards, grinning, watching, waiting.

He went back to the place where every beginning ends and every end begins. He went back...to the Maelstrom.

THE NOT-SO-OK CORRAL

After he fired through the plasterboard and heard Michael's body thump against the wall, Martin ducked down and peeked through a six-inch gap under the bottom of the altar, watching the doorway, guessing it wouldn't take long for the next set of footsteps to arrive. Paul's big clunky boots.

Martin's plan was going perfectly. Well, almost perfectly. He wasn't totally certain Paul witnessed Michael's demise as he intended, or even whether he was lurking close by. If not, the gunshots would lure him and then...

Just a little more time and I'll be back with Rose. He kept perfectly still. Looking. Listening. Waiting. Usually, those were his three favorite pastimes. What was taking so long? He cursed soundlessly, staring up at the face of the angel. Was it smiling at him?

BLAM! The bullet grazed his hip. Without looking, Martin pumped six shots under the altar back to the doorway. The shooter had to be Paul. Why didn't he hear him coming? Martin did a body roll to the wall away from the candles. He looked at his hip, crouching motionless in the darkest shadows. It was only a scratch. He thrust his guns out...staring at the open portal...waiting...listening.

The shooter was listening too. Then, quite fearlessly, he stepped inside the room. It was Bean. He was looking down at him with a big, crazy grin on his face. A thin, red trickle ran from a hole in his forehead, skirting around his eyeballs like two boulders in a stream, cascading down each cheek into his frozen, smiling mouth.

The kid. The kid had shot him. And he did it with a bullet in the middle of his brain.

Martin was so shocked that he hesitated, just for a moment. It was all the time Bean needed. *Blam! Blam! Blam!* Two of the shots missed Martin completely. The third hit him in the middle of his chest. Martin felt his body stiffen. He stared aghast at the bright red gravy on his drab green vest

Why hadn't it stopped the bullet?

Bean took a jerky step into the room, wincing at the tightness in his face. Was he smiling? It sure felt like it. But when he tried to relax his cheek muscles, nothing happened.

Even though Martin was still cloaked in the shadows, Bean could see him perfectly, slumped against the wall, raising his gun-clenched hand with extreme difficulty, like someone had dumped concrete all over his shirt and it was quickly stiffening. Bean tried to shoot him again, but now his own arm could barely move. His legs were still working and they dragged him farther inside, hoping he could touch the Book before Martin fired again.

Blam! Blam! Martin pointed at his slowly moving target and missed. Twice.

Blam! Blam! Blam! Michael found some feeling in his arm again and fired back where Martin was crouching. He missed by a mile. *Blam! Blam!* Martin tried again, but his arm was so stiff and heavy he barely missed his own feet. He was about to squeeze the trigger again anyway when Michael fell to his knees and then on his face. He couldn't move at all.

To those of us observing from our far-flung locations it was the lamest gunfight in history. Sergio Leone would have laughed his ass off, but none of us were. Not Paul, not Johnny, not me, not even Loren.

"Hey, open your eyes," Rose said, halting her druid tale, thinking I was bored, I suppose. When I remained silent with my eyes closed, she soon realized my attention was focused elsewhere. "Why are you grinning like that? Can you see him? Is Martin okay?"

I could have told her, but I didn't. What would I say? From her perspective he was in terrible shape…but he looked okay to me.

CREEP SHOW

Bean heard them coming. He could feel the pistol in his hand, but couldn't lift his arm. His eyes felt like two portholes, with an equally limited view. The scene was horrifying. When Paul walked into the room, his eyes still rolled backwards, Michael thought he was in a monster movie. When The Striker followed, he was sure of it. He carried a hammer in one hand, the business end covered in blood. His other hand was dragging a body stuffed in a burlap bag. Most of it anyway. The bag was split like a baked potato. So was the body inside. A winding cord of entrails followed in his wake.

Loren dropped the bag and its messy contents only a few feet from Michael's face. Then he turned solemnly toward Martin, bent down and felt for a pulse.

"How is he?" asked Paul.

"Gone," answered The Striker.

"Oh, my," Paul sighed. Turning to Michael, he winced exaggeratedly at the bullet hole in his forehead, then turned to Loren. "I guess it's two-for-one day, eh, old friend?"

The Striker let out a rumbling laugh and took the Beretta from Michael's hand like he was plucking the last petal from a daisy. He gave it to Paul, who dropped it into his pocket.

"Pleasssshh," Bean managed to hiss. "Hellllfff meeee"

"Shhhhhh…don't tax yourself." Paul grinned "And don't you worry about any funeral expenses. The fire will take care of that."

"What fire?" Bean tried to say, but his tongue was paralyzed.

"This one," Paul replied, with his arms stretched wide.

Nothing happened. Or nothing seemed to happen. Then he smelled the smoke.

JUDAS

"And then there were two…" said Paul, peering through the gathering smoke at the bodies on the floor. "I guess it's down to you and Billy now."

"He's not worthy," said The Striker without a trace of humor, for once.

"I admit he's a tad slow on the uptake this time around…" Paul said, bending over Martin's body. He held the blade of his sickle to Martin's nostrils, searching for a whiff of breath reflected in the chrome. He straightened up, pocketed the sickle and pulled out Martin's gun, adding, "Even so, he's far more worthy than you."

"I don't understand. What have I done?"

"Oh, we both know what you've done, so let's stop playing patty cakes. You were plying your craft on Bean, stacking the deck against Martin. I know you're gloating inside, thinking your treacherous gambit has paid off—in spades, no less. I've always been one to applaud ambition and treachery, but you've truly crossed the line here. This isn't a contest, Loren. There's more here at stake than that."

"I know what's at stake," said The Striker without emotion.

"Aye, that you do. Which presents another problem. Billy still has much to learn, and I can't imagine you being too helpful, with your own prospects on the line. I've always said I'd give you a fair shot. But when it comes right down it, blood is blood and I have to protect the line. Surely you understand that."

"I'm part of the line."

"Yes, but not by blood," Paul said, watching the smoke gather on the ceiling, raising the pistol higher.

The Striker clenched his jaw so hard it loosened the nails in his temples. "If that's the way it has to be, then put down the gun. Let's settle this the way it should be settled."

"Sorry, Loren," he sighed, pointing the pistol at The Striker's high, domed forehead, "I don't have time for a whole gladiator thing right now."

BANG! It wasn't the pistol firing. It was the sound of the floor collapsing beneath The Striker's naked feet.

Paul leaned over the gaping hole in the floorboards, shaking his head. "Oh, my goodness!" he shouted as The Striker brushed the dust from his body two floors below. "I'd take a shot at you, Loren, but I'm sure the gun would jam. Or backfire. You really take luck to a whole new level!"

"Why don't you join me?" Loren shouted. "It's only a short hop down here for you."

"I'm afraid I must decline your gracious invitation...though I'm sure I'll be seeing you later," Paul shouted back. "Then we can have that little tussle you're craving."

"I look forward to it," The Striker said, pulling a three-inch splinter from his bicep.

"Oh, I surely do as well!" Paul dropped Martin's pistol to the floor with a loud clunk as he pointed to the purple-veined length of The Striker's bony, bloody arm. "It should be quite a battle...a real nail biter. Look at the reach you have on me!"

Loren looked up with a sneer. Paul gave him a salute and watched him disappear in the smoke, then turned around and knelt beside Martin.

"What a pity," he said, gazing into his wide-open eyes. "They're so beautiful. I might as well keep one."

PLAYING POSSUM

Tetrodoxin and curare. Separately, either one could kill you in high enough doses. In much milder concentrations, the combination does something quite remarkable: it simulates death.

Tetrodotoxin, also known as fugo poison, is an extract taken from the puffer fish. It induces a coma that is virtually indistinguishable from death. In Haiti, the substance is used in Voodoo rites of zombie creation. The witch doctor usually administers the drug in low doses over time. Gradually, the victim becomes more helpless and dependent, unable to even feed himself. Eventually, he's drugged into a deathlike state and buried in a ritual ceremony. Later, the doctor digs him up to put him back to work…as his personal slave. Martin made his own special variant of the potion, combining it with an extremely low dose of curare. Curare, he learned after many long nights in the public library, is used in blow darts by native jungle tribes to paralyze their prey. It creates complete paralysis almost instantly, though the victim is still alert, and able to feel pain.

One of his pistols was loaded with special ammunition…gel caps filled with a mixture of that wonderful potion and a generous dollop of fake blood, just for color. The gel cap cartridges were designed to penetrate at least one layer of clothing and enter the bloodstream, much like an aerosol hypo. He intended to use it on Paul, so he could have some extra fun with him before he killed him for real.

Unfortunately, Martin made a very careless mistake in his rush to suit up for the big shootout. He put on the wrong vest. It looked just like his other Kevlar vest, but it had some special modifications. It was designed to perform a triple function: stop bullets, release blood squibs (so the attacker believed the bullets hadn't stopped) and release a small amount of the Magic Potion into his bloodstream via a spring-loaded injector he had taken from an Imitrex migraine kit. Martin called it his "doomsday vest." It was about to live up to its name.

He got the idea for it when he was bounty hunting. He'd taken a slug in his regular Kevlar vest on three separate occasions, making a big show of toppling over and then popping back up like a jack-in-the-box, guns blazing. Wouldn't it be cool to add a little razzle-dazzle with some blood squibs, like in the movies? He did just that, and rigged a parachute rip-cord to trigger the squibs when a bullet came near him, resulting in some very entertaining arrests, while sparing himself the extreme discomfort of actually being shot in the chest.

Never one to rest on his laurels, Martin took his invention to the next logical level. Logical, that is, for someone like Martin. What if he *really* looked dead? That would make for an even more dramatic reprisal…right? He did some research, discovered the amazing properties of tetrodoxin and curare and went back to the drawing board, creating the doomsday vest. So, when Michael fired his completely unexpected and remarkably accurate bullet, instead of doing his standard dead-man-fake-out routine, Martin was totally paralyzed. And much, much worse…he could still feel *everything.*

Bean was pretty much in the same anchored boat. The bullet lodged in his brain could have killed him at any second, with the slightest jog of his body. It also could have restored all his motor functions, with the same little nudge. When Paul spoke to him and he tried to answer, the warped lump of metal in his brain shifted, three millimeters south. It wasn't much, but it was enough. The spreading paralysis that kept his hand clutched on his pistol and his mouth smiling like Dr. Sardonicus instantly became total paralysis. The effect wasn't much different from Martin's potion. And like Martin, he could feel *everything.*

Michael had a hard time making sense of it. When the bullet moved and his tongue froze and stiffened, he wondered what had happened. Was this what it felt like to be dead? He heard stories of people floating outside of their bodies, but never watching from the inside. He could hear and smell too, which was also strange. He watched Paul come over and look into his eyes with that big fucking smile on his face.

Then he walked over to Martin.

Martin watched with his paralyzed eyes as Paul came closer, his steps sounding like the wheel of fortune spinning at the San Gennaro festival. Where it stops, nobody knows. When he held the sickle up to his mouth, Martin was terrified. When he stood back up again, Martin felt a huge wave of relief. Hallelujah. Martin thought that maybe, just maybe, he was going to get out in one piece. Then the fire started. That was bad, but it only went downhill from there. After Loren crashed through the floor, Paul came back. As he leaned over him, Martin couldn't even blink. But he could feel Paul pry his eyelids apart. He tried to move his fingers. He tried again before the blade descended.

Martin's agony was surprisingly surpassed by his torment for fucking up his chance to kill Paul. But the drug had to wear off eventually, right? It was already past the five-minute mark. If he woke up right away, there was still a slight chance he could kill Paul, escape the fire, and save Rose. Then he heard the firemen arrive and fall silent, one by one. Paul put on a black and yellow fireman coat...and picked up his book. At least one of them was smart enough to have an escape plan. Paul looked at him one last time with his gas mask on. He winked before dangling his own eye in front of him. It looked so small now. Bye-bye.

Martin felt the wood get really hot beneath him. He thought about Paul, still alive, while the flames licked at his back. Then he thought about Rose and cursed himself again.

Stupid! Stupid! Stupid! screamed the trapped voice in his head. The smoke was starting to strangle him, and he still couldn't move.

OUT OF THE FRYING PAN...INTO THE FIRE

Bean watched as Paul took Martin's eye. Paul did it so...professionally, that there was hardly any blood. He used his thumb and forefinger to pop out the eyeball, then snipped the muscles and nerves with his long, curved knife. When he was finished, the eyelid sank into the empty socket like a loose tarpaulin. Michael guessed, correctly, that he'd done this before.

The smoke thickened, but Michael couldn't cough, no matter how much he wanted. *You can't be dead and want to cough, can you?*

He watched Paul depart and tried to shout, "Please don't leave me here! Don't leave me all alone!"

His lips didn't even quiver when he tried.

Twitch. Twitch. Martin's finger moved like Frankenstein's monster, tapping against the wooden floor that was only minutes away from total ignition point. The smoke was overwhelming, thick and greasy gray. A section of the floor near Bean's body was already beginning to flame. It was the second thing Martin noticed when he willed his legs to stand. The first thing was the gel cap pistol Paul had thrown on the floor. Martin pocketed both pistols and crawled on his belly to minimize the smoke inhalation. He was only a few feet into the hallway when he found the second fireman's body. The heat was incredible and growing worse by the second.

His one remaining eye stung as though an army of fire ants were biting it. The other ravaged socket hurt even more. He wrestled the oxygen tank from the fireman's body and stuffed the hose into his mouth. *Ahhhhh.* He took three deep breaths and stripped off the fireman's tank, mask, coat, pants and boots in less than half a minute. He put everything back on even quicker, shoving his pistols in the big coat pockets. He was about to make a mad dash down the hallway when he felt an irresistible urge pulling him back to the chapel...and Bean.

The walls and floorboards were burning, igniting Bean's army coat. There was a plastic rectangular box poking out of his front pocket. The remote. Holy fuck! How could Paul have left it behind? Had he forgotten it in his haste to escape the fire?

Bean was even more perplexed when Martin first stood up. *Am I the only one who's dead around here?* He watched helplessly as Martin left the room and came back wearing the fireman's gas mask and clothes. Bean stared in horror as his own jacket began to flame. When his dreads caught fire like candlewicks, he tried to shout at Martin.

Don't just look at me! Do something! Martin did. He snatched the remote right before Michael's pants caught fire, giving it a flip in the air before holstering it in his pocket. He did everything but blow imaginary smoke from his cocked fingertip. There was enough smoke around anyway.

"Thanks," said Martin in a muffled voice behind the gas mask, tipping the brim of his fireman's hat. Then he walked away.

No! Don't go! PLEASE SAVE MEEEEE!

Martin turned around quickly, staring at the kid's open eyes, studying the grin still frozen on his face. Hmmm. That was weird. He could have sworn he heard somebody screaming. Then he shrugged and walked down the hallway.

NOOOOOO! COME BACK! DON'T LEAVE ME! Michael tried to yell. But still no sound left his lips. And Martin didn't come back.

He could smell his scalp frying like bacon. The smoke grew black. The altar was burning. Now the angel too. The flames from Michael's clothes and flesh joined the glow. When his skin began melting like candle wax, he realized the biggest truth about his sadly mistimed encounter with Paul.

There really was a Hell, after all.

PAUL'S GIFT

After he shed the fireman's gear in the burnt out basement of the apartment across the street and whumped his way past the gathering crowd, Paul settled comfortably into the back of the black Lincoln Town Car waiting for him on Ninth Street.

As the Lincoln sped away, he pulled out his present, wishing he'd had time to wrap it. But it looked so perfect in its natural state that it would be a travesty to conceal its beauty, even for a few moments, regardless of the dramatic effect a slow unveiling would have. He turned it over again and again in his hands, reveling in the cool, round smoothness, the few pebbled buds of texture caressing his blunt fingertips like the bumps on a milk-swollen nipple.

He put the orb in his top shirt pocket and patted it gently.

It's going to make quite an impression. He imagined the look on her face when she saw it. He wondered if she would guess right away where it came from, or whether he'd have to spell it out. *She's pretty clever. I'm sure she'll know.*

The buildings were a blur as the Lincoln rocketed up First Avenue. When they passed Forty-Second Street, Paul pulled out his gift again, dangling Martin's eyeball from its severed muscles. *So beautiful. So blue.*

It sure would make a nice key chain.

HERO

Martin was barely out the chapel door when he heard more firemen shouting from the hallway. His instinctual reaction was to reach for his guns. Then he had a moment of inspiration. "Down here!" he yelled from behind the mask, his voice so muffled it could have been anyone's. He walked back into the chapel and rolled Bean's body on the floor until the flames went out. Then he carried him back into the hallway, almost bumping into the other fireman as they arrived. "He's alive!' Martin shouted as they moved to let him pass.

He made it out of the building so quickly he surprised himself. All the remaining firefighters outside were doing exactly that. Fighting. Every window was gushing flames. He dropped the stiff, charred body onto an ambulance stretcher. "He might be alive," he lied and trotted away. They looked at him like he was a hero. It felt kind of nice.

He looked in every direction as he passed the fire trucks and the cop cars. He knew Paul had already gone, but what about The Striker? There was no sign of him and no one else was even looking in his direction. *Nice disguise.* He took off the mask and tank as soon as no one was watching. He kept the coat, since his own was covered in blood. He doubted anyone in The Plaza would try and stop a fireman from entering.

As he passed the fire chief's van, he saw a flash of light in the corner of his remaining eye. Keys. Excellent. "This should cut my travel time," he said, hopping inside. He grabbed a pair of aviator sunglasses from the dashboard and put them on. Not as dark as his empty eye socket, but they'd do. He felt the guns and the remote in his pockets, stepping on the gas like a drag racer. By the time he hit Avenue B, he was flying.

I can still make it. All that matters now is Rose.

MR. HYDE

Paul was getting close. I'd been blocking him out all day. Didn't want him taking the helm, or eavesdropping on our mutual yarn-spinning. Now I wanted him to look at her through my eyes. To see she was still alive. And waiting. "Come," I beckoned, inviting him in to savor the view.

Then something happened.

"Why are you staring at me like that?" Rose asked, more alarmed than angry. I couldn't respond, even if I wanted to. I was in the car with Paul, inside his head, pulling in front of The Plaza's lobby. And I was stuck.

"Answer me!" she demanded.

I still couldn't speak. Now I was in the lobby pressing the elevator button. I looked in the mirror while I waited for the doors to open and saw Paul's reflection staring back at me.

"Say something!"

The eyes slowly opened. "He's coming," said the lips beneath them.

"Martin?" Rose asked desperately.

"No." The face smiled. "Not Martin. William."

"What are you talking about? You're William! Do you mean Paul is coming? Is that what you mean?"

The face watched Rose squirm in her spike-loaded chair before answering. "William…Paul…what's the difference?"

Journal Entry: Damned

The deeper you go, the deeper you get. Paul called me today. On the phone. Told me to meet him uptown…at The Plaza Hotel. He was in the Ambassador Suite. A middle-aged man with thick, red hair ushered me inside, to what I guess was a sitting room. I was floored by its size and opulence. The next shock was bigger.

Paul looked…incredible. Immaculately groomed and tailored like he just stepped out of a *GQ* fashion shoot. He was dressed in a dark gray, light, wool suit that had to cost a few thousand. His shirt was black and buttoned to the neck. His hair was shining white and pulled back in a neat ponytail. His mustache was meticulously trimmed, his skin glowing. He looked like a straight Karl Lagerfeld. A big, crazy, straight Karl Lagerfeld.

Paul introduced me to the lanky redhead—Ryan Murphy, his attorney. Murphy shook my hand with a big phony smile, like I was someone important. Said I needed to sign some documents. I asked Paul what was going on.

"Your change of identity," Paul said proudly. "Your *retroactive* change of identity. In a few short years, the internet will be the repository of your entire personal history, so before that occurs, we're making some preemptive adjustments. After we've finished, all information and documentation related to you—birth certificate, social security number, driver's license—will substantiate your identity as William P. Kelly."

"What's the 'P' stand for?" I asked needlessly.

"It sure as hell ain't Patrick," Paul laughed.

"How the hell can you even do something like this?"

"The common term is connections. The reality is much more complicated, particularly if you want the public record to withstand the scrutiny of any serious investigation."

"Why would I be…?"

"You may find yourself growing more ambitious as time goes by.

Wealth and power tend to inspire a passion for more of the same. Should the time arrive when a higher public profile suits your objectives, you'll have a pedigree suitable for framing…after you've fulfilled your obligations, of course. We've already contacted any students, neighbors, workmates or anyone else that's ever had more than a ten-minute conversation with you since kindergarten, and made the necessary…arrangements…to keep the story consistent. In short, you'll be a new man, William."

Ryan handed me a packet containing my new passport, driver's license, social security card, Tetron ID, medical records…all to be kept in escrow until I "fulfilled my obligations."

I could barely keep the pen steady in my shaking hand as I signed the stack of papers.

"What's 'Tetron'? I've never heard of it."

Paul was about to answer when Ryan took the floor. "It's a holding company. Armaments, aerospace, real estate, etc., but our deepest interest is in the technology sector—computing, robotics, artificial intelligence and bio-engineering."

"*Our?*" I asked, glancing at Paul, then back to Ryan. "Are you a shareholder?"

"I meant to say the company's holdings," he backpedaled, looking at Paul to check on the extent of damage control necessary. When Paul's face changed to the dead mask, Murphy was so rattled I thought he might start doing a Rodney Dangerfield with his tie.

"And the primary shareholder is…?" I prodded, enjoying his discomfort.

"Why your father, of course."

My father. Out of all the Clan Kelly kin, I was in all likelihood the very last person to become privy to that information.

"So, how extensive are Tetron's holdings?" I asked, none too subtly.

"I believe he's more interested in the current valuation than the portfolio listings," Paul said to Ryan, with a kingly wave of his hand, authorizing the disclosure.

"If the market is still up by the end of the day, and this is only a guess, mind you, the company's net worth should be in the neighborhood of 12.2 billion dollars U.S."

"U.S. dollars," I gulped. "They're my favorite kind."

Ryan smiled. "It's been a pleasure meeting you, sir," he said, packing his briefcase with the new me. "If you need anything, anything at all, don't hesitate to call." He handed me his card and left. The red-and-black Tetron logo looked like it was designed by Goebbels.

"Nice graphics. Very Bauhaus."

Paul smiled and put his big arm around my shoulder. I could feel the fabric of his suit. It was definitely cashmere. I asked him why we were meeting in a hotel suite.

"This is my home, William, or one of them. How do you like it?"

I liked it a lot. I was also thinking he looked even scarier in a suit than his usual outfit. Why would someone who usually dressed like a bum maintain a permanent residence in The Plaza Hotel? Paul seemed to hear my question and began talking again.

"The land beneath these foundations belonged to the first of our clansmen to settle in this brave new world. It was a bog back then, but your namesake William Kelly didn't mind. He could feel the power flowing beneath his feet like a lodestone. Much has changed since then, except the power. Can you feel it, Billy? Doesn't it feel like home?"

It did. I'd never felt so calm and comfortable, and yes, as strong as I did in that room.

"How did you get so...?"

"Stinking filthy rich? I've made some savvy investments over the years. You could say I have a preternatural gift for futures speculation: currencies, gold, commodities. Plus, we're sitting on a basketful of primary patents. All of it, everything I have, is yours to share, once you fulfill your duty."

My duty. He repeated the scope of my obligation, sounding more like his attorney: "You must, by your own hand, cause the death of Rose Turner on the afternoon of Good Friday. Otherwise, you forfeit your entire legacy. Including your life."

"Paul…I don't want to kill her."

"Billy…you have no choice. You're damned if you do, more damned if you don't."

"If you want her dead so much, why don't you do it yourself?"

As soon as I saw the grimace on his face, I knew. "You can't kill her, can you? The Master made a pact with Morgana and you're stuck with it."

He didn't say anything at first. His face turned to stone. "If I kill her, there will be extreme consequences. We are too close to the end to take such risks. The vow is only binding on the Master. You are not even a full initiate in the clan. You can, indeed, you *must* do what is required. It is essential to our success and your continued existence. This is your sole path to awakening, your initiation rite and your membership fee. You must assume your rightful position in the clan hierarchy. You can't be a ruling Lord without at least one significant kill to your credit and there's no target more significant or necessary than the girl. Plus, on a purely pragmatic level, I'll have to kill you if you don't. Or let you rot in prison. I know it sounds corny, but you simply know too much."

"I hardly know anything! Look where we are!" I protested, gesturing at our opulent surroundings. "Besides, you can trust me. I'll never tell anyone."

"Billy, you're missing the big picture here. You're still thinking about what you're going to lose, instead of what you'll gain."

When he saw my eyebrows lift in a spasm of greed, he slapped me on the back. "Come with me. There's much more to your birthright than wealth, power and influence."

He led me to a white door and unlocked it. The room was enormous, filled with sunlight from a row of large windows. Against the far wall was a sight even more unexpected than Paul's new wardrobe. It was another angel, even bigger and more beautiful than the first. Maybe even older. The paint was dull and worn and chipped away in places, but there were no nails or other disfiguring attachments. It was bound to a mammoth cross by sheets of white linen. I walked closer and stared at the chest. The golden rays shone like the midday sun. I looked at the face and saw the resemblance.

It was even more striking than before. I looked away, to the altar in front of the angel. It was covered with a white linen sheet. A cabinet was open beneath. Twelve volumes on one side. The big one on the other.

The Book of Paul.

"Pick it up. Put it on the altar."

The sensations I felt are nearly indescribable. Like I was on fire. Like I was the angel. After I picked it up, I didn't want to set it down. I wanted to hold it against my chest forever, embracing it like a lover I would never see again. Paul pointed to the altar. I nodded, setting it down, but I kept my hands on the cover, rubbing my fingers across the ancient leather.

Paul reached to his neck and drew out a thin chain and the tiny key.

"This is your inheritance too. All of it." He made a sweeping gesture from the Book to a wall behind us. I barely noticed it when we walked in. It was a floor-to-ceiling bookcase. The higher the shelves, the more ancient the bindings looked. On the top shelf were scrolls. This room wasn't merely a chapel, like its horrifying counterpart. It was a library.

"Where did you get all these?"

"Here and there, over the years. It would be more accurate to call me a conservator than a collector. We possess much more than you see here. We will never again risk the dangers of consolidation and wholesale destruction as in the Egyptian cataclysm."

"Are you talking about the Library of Alexandria?"

"Yes, and the Temple of Serapis, also known as the Serapeum. Many of the most important texts were housed there, including the works of Apollonius. After the emperor Theodosius outlawed paganism, Pope Theophilus began destroying all the pagan temples in Alexandria as well as the Great Library. We cleared out the Serapeum first, while the pagan revolt was being crushed. Then under cover of the fire we set, the Library was rescued."

"Are you actually claiming that our ancestors burned and looted the Library of Alexandria?"

"*Rescued,* not looted. You're a funny duck, Billy. You look at me like what I'm saying is the most preposterous statement you've ever heard, yet you're gawkin' at an entire wall of ancient scrolls and manuscripts. Where do you think they all came from? A Sotheby's auction?"

I just stood there, unable to speak. He shook his head and marched up to the bookcase, dragging me by my wrist. He pulled out a slim volume and told me to open it. It was the *Gospel of Mary*. The complete *Gospel of Mary*. "Hhmmph!" he snorted at my dazed expression. "That couldn't be an authentic codex, could it? No, that's impossible! There isn't a single complete copy of the *Gospel of Mary* to be found anywhere in the world! Oh, my, but what do we have right here next to it? Well, I guess you can keep that one, Billy, because I have *five* more copies…in this bookcase alone! Where could they all have come from?"

"I'm sorry…but this is so…incredible," I muttered.

"So are the contents. You read Coptic, correct?" he asked, pointing to the book.

"Right," I replied. The missing pages. Now I know why they cut them out. The story begins with Jesus being resurrected in the tomb. *Being* resurrected. Mother Mary and Mary Magdalene told the other apostles to seal them in the tomb with the body of Christ, "For they knew in Faith (*Pistis*) and Wisdom (*Sophia*) that he would soon return."

Suddenly a great light fills the cave, the stone rolls away, an angel appears, and bada-bing,bada-boom, Jesus is back! After many hugs and high-fives, they all go to visit his disciples, who are hiding out from the Romans in the home of…Apollonius. He apologizes for unmentioned "transgressions." Christ forgives him, kisses him, calls him his brother, then he begins his sermon, telling everyone of his journey to the divine realm and back.

"Apollonius? What's he apologizing for?"

"He made a mistake.…well, a few of them," Paul said, turning to face the angel. "First and worst, he fell in love. Love is always tragic, but in this case, as with your current malady, it was disastrous.

"She was…as he was…in the beginning. His mate in more than name.

She bore them twins, male and female. The angel appeared at their birth and revealed that the time of the prophecy was at hand. The babes had been chosen. *They* had been chosen—not the elders. Needless to say he was…devastated. Even so, he had sworn to fulfill the will of the *Nous*. She told him how they could transmit the *Intelligence* directly to their children without sacrificing their own lives—the path her line had always followed. She said it was the only way to ensure complete *knowing*. 'Our memory and all that has come before is in their blood. They only need to awaken.'

"He *saw* the truth in her words, but he had taken the old path for so long, *Turning* inside dedicated disciples, all more than willing to sacrifice their mortal flesh for the greater good. Now he was supposed to merely pass on his hard-won knowledge when the boy came of age—so *he* could be the Master?

"It was never his intention to consume the boy. He loved him dearly. He tried so hard, but his will to survive was so old, so hungry, it would not be denied. When they returned from the Maelstrom, his mate had passed the *Intelligence* to their daughter as intended. But he had taken the boy, as he had so many others. The women cursed him in his new young body. Abandoned him. And the *Nous*…the *Nous* sent Yeshua, to cleanse his sin and *set things right*. Wasn't the loss of his family, wasn't their scorn, their abandonment, punishment enough?

"Well, one of them had to go. You can't steer a ship that big with two captains at the helm. When Yeshua and his disciples arrived in Jerusalem, Apollonius suggested preaching in a more hospitable environment. The Romans didn't want any messiah. How could he know that the High Priest of the Sanhedrin was listening? He warned Yeshua they were coming. There was still enough time to escape. That would have been a win-win. But nooooo, Yeshua was convinced that *he* was the chosen one! Well, he was, but not the first. There's such a thing as seniority. Still, he wouldn't budge. 'The *Nous* guides my destiny.' Some destiny. Right up to the very last minute, he still couldn't believe the cavalry wasn't coming to pull him off that cross.

"Then Mary acted like I was to blame! 'You haven't won!' *Really?* Just look at him! Not that I said that to her. But she still kept digging away at me, 'The world will hear his message! She will tell it!'

"Mary Junior. *Well, fuck me!* Just one look at the two of them together and I knew. Big Mary didn't have one child...she had *two!* The new Matriarch! When Yeshua came back, he blessed *Sister Mary* to carry the word. Well, the boys didn't care for that, I can tell you. They toed the line for awhile, out of respect for Yeshua, but Peter...well let's just say the Rock wanted to roll...right over Mary. He vowed revenge on Apollonius too. Four centuries later he delivered, through Patrick. But he who laughs last, laughs best, and before long we'll be splitting our ribs. Which reminds me, I have another gift for you."

He walked back into the sitting room. Following, I said, "You started talking about Apollonius in the third person and ended in the first."

"And?" he replied, looking at me curiously.

"Are you saying what I think you are?"

"Billy, do you honestly need to ask that question?"

"I just want you to come out and say it."

"He who has ears, let him hear," Paul replied sternly. "I have been talking to you of nothing other than this subject since we first began our dialog. What more is there to say?"

"Well, you could say, 'Apollonius, Pythagoras, Hermes Trismegistus were all previous incarnations of *me!*' or, 'I've passed on my soul from body to body for thousands of years and I'm about to do it again.' And, 'I personally knew Jesus fucking Christ and was sort of responsible for getting him crucified, but he forgave me after his resurrection!'"

"Very well phrased, Billy. But Yeshua said it best, when Pilate popped the question. 'It is as you say.' Short and sweet. Now are you ready to look at your present?"

I'd been agonizing about this for weeks. Squirming with doubt, scared to death it might really be true. I thought I would feel something akin to dazed astonishment if he finally came out and said it. But now that he had, with the casual indifference of an Olympic athlete displaying his medals for the umpteenth time, I felt like I'd been robbed of my big moment.

"Yeah, sure, whatever," I grumbled, shaking my head in frustration.

He led me over to a huge armoire. "I think you'll find this infinitely more useful and satisfying than that moldy old text," he declared theatrically, opening the ornately engraved doors. I stood there speechless. It was filled with all this S&M gear: masks, ball gags, and very weird, very nasty torture tools. He grinned at my shocked expression and pointed to a bizarre metal contraption on the bottom shelf.

"What the hell is that?"

"An impaler," he said proudly, "for your big date!"

"An impaler?"

"It's a real beauty, isn't it? Think of it as a helping hand to see you through. The device is spring-loaded, triggered by off-balance movement. I'll do the heavy lifting, get her settled down nice and cozy. All you have to do is give her a little tip and the machine will do the rest. *Ca-ching!* But don't press the black button on the bottom. That's the fail-safe locking mechanism, in case something goes wrong and we have to keep her on ice."

"Oh, God...please, don't make me do this."

"*Make* you?" Paul snarled. "I should think you'd be chomping at the bit after all I've offered. Unlimited wealth and soon, unlimited power—what more could you possibly desire? I can't believe I'm still encouraging you with the promise of rewards. We should be far past that stage by now. You should be killing her for the sheer pleasure of it. Trust me, I know you better than you know yourself. You'll take to murder like a duck to water."

"You're wrong about me. I'm not who you think I am."

"No, you're wrong about you. You are part of us. We are the same."

"I'm not anything like you!"

"Perhaps you're right," Paul said calmly. "Maybe you're not a bit like me. Maybe I'm exactly like...*you!*"

He let out a thunderous laugh that scared me even more than his bizarre declaration. When he settled down, he gazed into my frantic eyes and spoke in a soft, sinister voice.

"You think your achievements and transgressions are restricted to the choices you make in this lifetime, but you are wrong. I am everything and everyone that has come before me, as are you. Your blood carries the knowledge and memories of every preceding generation. The sins of the father are truly the sins of the son, passed down endlessly, regardless of the veil of forgetfulness that hides the truth from your awareness."

"What the fuck are you talking about?"

"Exactly who do you think you are, William?"

I thought he meant I was out of line with my question. Then I realized he was literally questioning my sense of identity. I told him exactly who I thought I was. He laughed.

"You didn't even know your own name until I told you! In your veins flows the blood of the most illustrious and accomplished forebears that have ever walked the face of this truly god-forsaken planet, yet you know nothing of your heritage other than what has been revealed to you by me. Yet, regardless of the near totality of your ignorance, your blood knows the truth. And your blood aches to awaken to your forgotten glory."

I said nothing. He kept pushing.

"You did so well in the chapel. You saw the angel. You witnessed the power of the Book. It brought you back from the brink and took you to your true place of birth. Yet you still can't remember *yourself*. But in spite of what you can or cannot grasp, there's one thing you can sense right down to your very bones, of this much I am certain—that the only thing that matters in this or any universe is the Wheel and the power to control it. Not just enough for another *Turning* so we can buy enough time to dance this ballet all over again. The power to control it utterly, completely…and forever. This is our destiny and the only thing standing in the way is your foolish, futile resistance. We can do it this time! So play your part and kill that *bitch!*"

I opened my mouth to speak, but he pressed a blunt finger to my lips. "No. No more talking. You know what must be done, so do it."

"I love her," I pleaded.

"We always hurt the ones we love."

"I don't care if you send me to jail or do whatever you want. I…won't… kill her."

"Yes…you…will. And in the end it won't be because of threats from me. You will kill her out of your own hatred and jealousy and greed…your lust for power and vengeance. You will kill her because you *always* kill her. That is your role, your destiny—your true *self.*"

"What if I kill you instead?" I seethed, thinking about Mother again.

"You're welcome to try. You can make your bid as you have so many times, with and without the wizard's aid. Loren doesn't know the whole story, yet he plays his part, as do you. If he hasn't already, the serpent will ask you to betray me. Maybe you will and maybe you won't. The story changes with each telling, so there's no way to know that yet. But in your quest to slay me, unlike your murder of the dear, sweet princess, you have always failed. That has never changed, not a single time. So stop whining about your petty emotions and save your energy for the work that still awaits us after the *Turning*, when we rebuild the Temple and forge the Great Wheel."

"You're actually going to make them…in our world?"

"We're already well on our way." He raised a finger and walked back in the library. He returned with his arms full of scrolls. They weren't ancient. They were blueprints. He spread them across the table. "We have to clear the property first. There are some buildings cluttering up the landscape that need to be demolished. We're going to need plenty of room."

He wasn't kidding. It was amazing. Truly majestic. A massive temple complex with an enormous tower. Exactly what I always imagined an insanely huge pagan temple would look like, maybe in Atlantis.

"It's sure going to attract attention."

"I certainly hope so," he nodded proudly.

"Are you trying to start a Holy War or something?"

"Not something. Precisely that. We can't end this epic story without a big finish. Good versus evil, angel versus devil, Pagan versus Christian versus Muslim."

"What's going to happen? What does the Wheel actually do?"

"What doesn't it do? If I can make a golden egg out of pure aether sit in the palm of your hand in the world of dead gravity, what do you reckon could be accomplished at the heart of the Maelstrom if you possessed such an instrument?"

"You could do anything...make anything."

"Yes, but I only want to make one thing."

"What?" I asked, suddenly afraid to hear his answer.

"A God."

"A God," I repeated numbly.

"Even if I do nothing, even if I'd never been born or chosen or filled with the spirit—the *Becoming* will still occur," Paul continued, disregarding my stunned reaction. "It was ordained by the prophecy six thousand years ago. The Singularity will set the stage, and shortly, very shortly afterward, the *Intelligence* will become fully manifest in human flesh. There is nothing in this or any universe that can stop that from happening. It is the irresistible intent of the *Nous*—the point, the *sole* point of everything that has ever existed. To facilitate the proper outcome of this event is what we have dedicated our lives and our deaths to since the building of the first Tower in Babylon—and the Great Wheel beneath its foundations. Our enemies have tried to steer the *Nous* in their favor, convinced that their path is the only true course to victory. But regardless of what they do or believe, or what we do or believe, the *Becoming* is inevitable. The only questions that remain are *when* and *where* and *how* and most importantly to me...*who*."

"Who?"

He gave me a sly smile, striding back to the altar, resting his hands heavily on the ancient leather codex.

"If there's a God to be born...he'll surely be holding the Book."

CATCH

I came unstuck from Paul's mind just as the elevator opened.

"Honey! I'm home!" he shouted as he walked inside. Rose looked at me in absolute terror. I thought she might trigger the trap just from the way she was quivering.

"Well, if it isn't Billy the Kid!" he cried, savoring our expressions. "Hello, darlin," he said sweetly, walking over and giving her a kiss on the forehead while she tried to duck it. "I see you're all bright eyed again. Hmmm. Even had a little drinky!"

He gave me a dirty look and set the Beretta down on the tea table. Daring me. He even turned his back to take his overcoat off, draping it over an eighteenth century love seat. When I didn't move for the pistol, Rose glared at me with such anger and betrayal that I thought she would trigger the impaler again. All in due time, I wanted to tell her. All in due time.

"I don't know why Martin bothered with those band-aids," Paul said, turning around. "It's not like you're going to leave this place alive."

"Shoot him!" Rose screamed. "Pick up the fucking gun and shoot him!"

"Why in the world would he do a foolish thing like that? Even if he wanted to rescue you—and I can assure you he doesn't—he'd still need to get you out of that chair."

Paul waited for me to say something or do something. Rose motioned with her chin toward the pistol again. I looked at her and the Beretta and Paul's smiling face. Then I closed my eyes and tried to find Martin. He was in the elevator, pounding the button. I could see the bulges in his big coat pockets. I knew what was inside.

"What were you just looking at?" Paul growled as I opened my eyes. "Is there something you want to share with us?"

His glare felt like a crowbar, but I didn't think he knew. Even so, I had to buy more time. "What's that?" I asked, staring at the bulge in his shirt pocket.

"Oh, this little trinket?" he whispered, giving me a conspiratorial wink. He stood up and clapped his hands over his head like he was calling the tribal council to order. The stench from his armpits was almost enough to make me heave.

"Why, this is the most glorious jewel I've ever laid eyes on. The Star of India, the Hope Diamond…mere baubles by comparison. I was going to stop by Cartier on the way over and have it put in a proper setting, but first I wanted to show it to the lassie in all its unadorned perfection."

Paul dipped his fingers into his shirt pocket like a magician reaching for a rabbit. I had to hand it to him, he sure had a flair for showmanship. He pulled it out slowly and when it was fully exposed, he swung it back and forth like a hypnotist's pendulum.

Hypnotized we were. For about three seconds. Rose let out an ear-splitting shriek when she realized who it belonged to. Her scream went on and on. Then she stopped as suddenly as she'd started, staring at the fireman in the doorway.

"I think that belongs to me," Martin said.

"Here you go!" He threw the eye toward Martin in a low, lazy, underhand arc. Like a softball pitch. Martin watched it fly and felt the pistols in his hands taunting him. His reaction was instinctive. He dropped the gun in his right hand and caught it. It was all the time Paul needed. He made a lightning fast tuck and roll, snatching up the gel cap gun Martin dropped.

Shit! screamed the voice in Martin's head as he saw Paul's "gotcha!" grin and watched Rose's face dissolve in terror.

If there had been time, I would have told him not to be so hard on himself. How could he not catch it? After all, it was *his* eye.

CAPTIVE AUDIENCE

Martin didn't dwell on his fuck-up. He made another one instead.

"Are you okay?" he foolishly asked Rose, putting his eyeball and sunglasses in the big coat pocket while he kept his remaining gun on Paul. Rose let out a horrified cry when she saw the empty socket, which gave Paul a sufficient distraction to pop back up behind Rose's chair and grab the wood with his spare hand. *Sonofabitch!*

"Can't say that she is," Paul grinned triumphantly, covering Rose's mouth with his hand as she tried to answer. "But I'm glad to see you're back in the pink, Martin. Did you think your sleeping beauty act could throw this ole hound dog off your scent? I must say though, I admire the fancy weaponry. Tetrodoxin gel caps! My, my! What was the plan? Have your cruel way with me while I'm helplessly paralyzed? What do you think about that Billy?"

"What the…" Martin mouthed, finally noticing me in his significantly more limited peripheral vision. He wheeled around, his mind flipping through all the images he'd seen in the Chapel, still not finding a match. "Who the fuck are you?"

"I'm your…" I started, but Rose cut me off.

"I knew you were lying! I fucking knew it!" she yelled at me, then turning to Martin, "He told me he came here *with* you. But he's with Paul. They're partners!"

"Oh we're much more than that," Paul chuckled, gleefully entering the increasingly volatile discussion. "We're cut from the same cloth, me and Billy. Just like you, dear boy."

"What's he talking about?" Martin asked, aiming his gun at me.

I looked at Paul, hoping he would tell him. He gave me the nod instead. But now that I was finally free to spill the beans, I was extremely hesitant, especially with him pointing that gun at me. "Paul is my father. Our father," I said, bracing myself for his reaction.

Martin said nothing, did nothing, except look from me to Paul blankly.

"Go on. Tell him the rest. Tell him about your dear sweet mum," Paul goaded me.

I took a deep breath. "I'm Norine's son. Paul raped her the day he took you away, when she went in the house with him. She asked me to find you. To help you."

"Norine? Where is she?"

I cursed Paul and said, "She's dead," coughing to hide an unexpected swell of emotion. "She died of cancer in Port Richey, Florida on September 23, 19…"

"No need to get technical," Paul cut in. "A simple 'She's dead' will do. But you're leaving out the best part Billy, the very best part!"

"What's he talking about?" Martin asked, his pistol aimed at my heart.

"Tell him!" Paul yelled at me with a whoop. "*Tell him!*"

I just stared at him. I couldn't say it. I couldn't do that to Martin.

Paul could. "She was your mommy too, lad."

"That's not possible," Martin croaked, looking from Paul to me, and back again. Before he even saw my nod and Paul's sadistic smile, his own heart told him it was true.

Martin became completely still. He swallowed a fist-sized lump in his throat. A wave of old memories surged while he mouthed her name. Norine. He had left her alone with Paul. Yes, he was just a kid. But he didn't protect her. And he never saw her again. It was all his fault.

"*You fucking fuck!*" Martin screamed, pointing his gun at Paul's forehead.

"*Do it!*" Paul cried, leaning on the chair. "Do it and I'll take your other bitch with me!"

Martin looked at Paul's hand—just one push and…

He had to think. The remote! He reached his free hand into his pocket and pulled it out. "Back away from her," he said, pointing it at Paul like another loaded weapon.

"Oh goody!" Paul laughed, not moving a muscle. "Mission accomplished! I guess all you need to do now is figure out which numbers to press and disarm my little invention."

Martin looked at the face of the small rectangular device for the first time. There were ten buttons on it, numbered one through zero…and a big red button on the top. It was easy to guess what the red one was for, but even if the release code was only three digits long, the number of possible combinations was…fuck…a thousand!

"What's the matter, Martin? Cat got your calculator? Oh, I suppose I should warn you that punching in the wrong combination automatically springs the trap."

"What's the code?" Martin demanded. "You're not faster than a bullet."

"You're welcome to test that theory. But what if I were to keel over on this little tart in me grisly death throes? I reckon that would spill the apple cart too, eh?"

Martin looked helplessly at the remote and then at Rose.

"Well, now that you've decided not to place a wager on the fast-bullet-versus-big-man-falling-over contest, I'm quite sure I don't care for you pointing that gun at me any more. Drop the weapon, or I'll give her a push right now and see how well this thing works."

Martin stared at Paul down his pistol sight.

"Bullets have a tendency to miss me, as you well know. Last chance. Drop it now or brace yourself for the grand finale."

He dropped it. "Fuck," muttered Martin and Rose at the same time.

"Wise choice," Paul said, coming from behind her, picking up the pistol, placing it on the table beside the Beretta, relaxing in the chair next to it.

"I know I haven't been as honest with you as you might have liked Martin, but I'm not alone in my heartless betrayals. Your brother here is a charming storyteller, but I do believe he left out another unwelcome surprise. He's known your little slut here for quite some time. Did she ever tell you about their late, late nights together?"

Martin looked from Rose to me and saw the look of shock and shame on our faces. We were tripping over each other's words, trying to explain when Paul out-shouted us.

"And that's not all...he's in love with her, Martin! In love!"

I didn't know a single eye was capable of conveying that much hatred. Or sadness.

"He's lying," I lied. "I don't love her. We're not even friends anymore!"

"No, they're certainly not friends. Alas, she dumped the poor lad. Broke his little heart. Yet still he loves her. You can see it in his face—that tormented grimace worn only by those who have loved and lost. That's why he's here. He can't bear to see her in the arms of another man, especially his handsome, muscular brother with that big pile-driver between his legs. Jealousy seethes like a pestilence inside him. He wants her to die, so you can't have her!"

"He's lying! You know how he lies...all he ever does is lie!"

Martin did know. It was the only thing that kept him from shooting me.

"Oh sure, I've been known to tell a fib or two. But I can tell from this poor girl's expression that you've been spinning some fancy yarns of your own, eh Billy?"

Rose nodded to Martin. Then she gave me that look again. *Bitch!*

"Tell them the truth!" I shouted to Paul. "

"The truth? Well if you insist, I'll tell the whole sordid tale, but it may take a minute or two and I'm not fond of being interrupted once I have a full head of steam."

Bang! Paul shot me in the chest. The impact was thunderous. My shirt was soaked red. Was it blood? My body began to stiffen. *Fuck. This is it.* But I didn't die. I just became more stiff and numb until I was frozen like a slab of meat in a butcher's freezer.

"Ah, that's better..." Paul sighed, keeping his pistol trained on Martin as he kicked my shoulder, positioning my body so I had a perfect view of them out of my unblinking eyes.

"Billy's a bit of a Chatty Cathy," Paul said to Martin with a wink. "It's hard to get a word in edgewise. Isn't that right, lassie? I'll bet he's been chewing your ear off."

Rose was trembling with abject terror. Martin seemed completely unfazed, his single eye tracing Paul's every move like a sniper scope as Paul settled into the chair across from Rose.

"I know you're not much of a talker, Martin, so I'd appreciate it if you stay in character until I've had my say. I'm sure you're not anxious for another Rip Van Winkle session. And Rosy, you won't be needing this gag shoved down your throat again, will you?"

She shook her head, cringing at the sight of the dildo gag on the table.

"Good, good. Now Martin, I'll need your word of honor as a warrior and a gentleman that you won't snap Billy's neck while he's dozing. You might not enjoy my account of his nefarious deeds, but it wouldn't be a proper sibling duel with him handicapped like this, eh?"

"I won't kill him," Martin said tersely, thinking of Norine to keep his bile down.

"Well then," he began, giving my corpse-like face a little wave as he spoke to Martin. "Rosy and Billy met when she etched his morbid and quite disturbing tattoos. Billy got all hot for her, and read her tealeaves in his dingy abode. He had one glass of wine too many, and made the fatal mistake of showing her the body parts he likes to collect. I think these serial killer types call them trophies. Not that he's a serial killer. Too big a wuss. At any rate, she didn't call the police so I assume she came to the same conclusion, or else she's extremely derelict in her civic responsibilities.

Billy came to me after she left him in the lurch, seeking dear ole Da's burly shoulder to cry on. 'What's her name?' I ask, me dander rising. 'Rose Turner,' he says. Johnny's girl? Oh my. Well, that put another light on the matter entirely. When I told Billy how her clan betrayed us, he was livid. She had to die. In the worst way possible. Thinkin' I might have some experience in the area, he asked me what was the slowest, cruelest, most gruesome, horrible method of execution I could contemplate. Something really...*evil*."

"Please stop..." Rose blurted out.

"Tsk-tsk...it seems that no one in your family can keep their promises... or their mouths shut. Martin, would you be so kind as to gag her for me?"

400

"Not a chance," Martin said, his knuckles white.

Blam! Paul blasted him too. "Looks like I'll have to do all the work around here," he groaned. He picked up Martin's body and then mine, plopping us down in two chairs across from him and Rose, arranging our stiff limbs neatly like we were stuffed animals. We watched mutely as he shoved the penis gag back in Rose's sobbing mouth, set the gel cap gun on the table with the other two, and sat down again facing us.

"Now where was I? Oh yes, cruel, horrible deaths. Crucifixion is a good candidate. Slow…agonizing…plenty of time to think about your approaching doom while your body cries out in anguish. And for any loved ones unlucky enough to be watching nearby, the pain and suffering is absolutely excruciating. Not only do you experience the gut-wrenching loss when the sad end finally comes, but the *anticipation* of death is even more unbearable, especially if your hands are tied, and there's nothing in the world you can do to prevent it. Do you boys understand the essence of what I'm saying?"

Silent, frozen, unblinking stares. Waxy, flat expressions.

"Hhmmph! Well, I suppose you do. But wait! It gets even worse. After she draws her last ragged breath and you're left completely and utterly alone in your grief—suddenly you're assaulted with an even more painful torrent of guilt. Oh the *shame* of it all! She was right there in front of me, terrified and totally helpless and I did *nothing!* I just sat there like a gutless, nutless puppet and *watched her die!* How can I ever sleep again without seeing her terrified face begging for help in my nightmares? How can I get through day after day after day, replaying that terrible scene over and over and over in my head like an endless tape loop until I finally find sweet release in death? It must be intolerable…don't you think?"

He savored our mute attentiveness for a few moments before proceeding.

"Crucifixion. Billy liked the idea. It seemed fitting, ironic even, turning the tables on Sophia's spawn—those cursed O'Neils. Now we'll finally have our revenge for what they did to poor Ceallach when he came back from the Maelstrom at his sniveling slut's insistence. She came back whole, of course. Traitors never suffer at their own hands. But the merging had already begun...and Ceallach...he came back so crippled. Monstrous. An angel of flesh and blood is not a sight a father can bear with any grace.

The Master was already manacled when Ceallach returned. They had been waiting: her father Lonán; Eoghan of Hy-Many and his vile son, Tormac, the cruel, heartless lad her cuckold da sold her off to. And to make matters worse, there was an interloper—Bishop Patrick—determined to exact his own vengeance against the sons of Apollonius, served four centuries cold.

The Master struggled against his chains while his beloved son writhed in agony, the lad's grotesque, almost reptilian wings flopping limply on the altar. But he was helpless to protect the boy, his power drained dry by the strain of staying in the Maelstrom so long, watching what should have been Ceallach's ascension into glory.

"'What is this demon? This abomination?' Patrick cried, fueling their rage. His prodding was all it took to complete the travesty.

"Tormac hoisted up Ceallach's twisted body and nailed him to the bare cross in that cursed chapel, pounding in spike after spike. There were so many. The Master felt each one as if it pierced his own flesh. It took so long for Ceallach to die. Even with all that blood pouring out. The Master tried to rescue the boy's soul, to draw his luminous essence back into his own heart, but they were both too weak. When the final nail was pounded in, when his poor heart finally stopped beating, The Master swore his ever-lasting vengeance against those cursed cunts."

Paul stood in front of Rose, slowly lowered his face, and shouted so loudly I thought the windows would break:

"YOU KILLED MY BEAUTIFUL ANGEL!"

Then, as if he'd never raised his pulse, he smiled and began circling the room again.

"Alas and alack, such a sad, sad tale. But it put me back on track with Billy's request. Crucifixion? Not on her life! She doesn't deserve the honor of dying like noble Ceallach. *Impaling!* That's an excellent alternative. Efficient and dependable, with centuries of tradition behind it. When the Persian emperor Darius the Great conquered Babylon, he impaled *three thousand* citizens. The Romans enjoyed impaling almost as much as crucifixion. They'd often showcase their stylish merits side by side, one victim hung on a cross, another one writhing six feet off the ground with a wooden stake up his arse. Quite a sight, I can tell you. Kept the crime rate looowww. I'm sure you wouldn't think it such a slow death like crucifixion, but you'd be surprised. A properly orchestrated impalement can keep the condemned alive even longer! Executioners are a very inventive breed and take great pride in their work. They would gain enormous satisfaction in staging the most lengthy and agonizing methods of impalement, almost like it was a contest. For example, to reaaaaalllllly drag things out, they would use a blunted stake, so when it was rammed up your arse—or your cunt with whores like yourself, Rosy—the stake would push many of the vital organs out of the way as it was thrust inside. And then, once you were fully impaled, the stake would act like a plug, you see, to keep your blood from draining out too quickly. Voila! There you are, stuck on a pole for days. But as much as William and I would savor that spectacle more than front row seats at the Coliseum, we'll have to make due with watching you squirm in agony for a few hours instead of a few days. But that's still a good chunk of time for us to enjoy the spectacle, before you bleed out."

Rose had been making horrible gurgling noises throughout Paul's gruesome description, her eyes streaming tears, her nose running, her throat swallowing frantically. When Paul stopped talking and leaned down in front of her again, she closed her eyes and turned her head, as if an ostrich-like evasion could protect her from what was coming next.

"Oh, dear. I haven't upset you with all this talk, have I? Look at your face, sweetie, you're a feckin' mess!" Then he raised his hands to the ceiling and cried out, "Hey, Johnny! Are you nice and cozy in that padded cell? Got plenty of crackerjacks and goobers? What about you, Martin? And Billy?" he asked, moving in front of us. He rapped on the top of my skull with his knuckles. "Knock, knock! Anybody home?" Then bending down next to Martin's ear he yodeled, "Helllllooo! Can Martin come out to play?"

"My word, these lads are thick. Hey Rosy, have you ever felt like you might as well be talking to yourself with these two? I sure hope all is well in their noggins. They have such great seats for the show. It'd be a cryin' shame if they missed a single second, especially Billy, since he put so much care and planning into this. Let me tell you, Rose, I've never seen the boy so excited! When I described the whole impalement procedure, I could see those gears turning right away. 'We can make a deathtrap!' he shouts. 'Even put a timer on it so the exact moment of her death will coincide with the crucifixion! Both crucifixions!'

"See how revenge becomes a dreadful cycle you can never escape from? Christ gets himself killed, Patty nails Ceallach, and now we have Sophia's last living female descendent ready to bite the dust on Good Ole Good Friday! Ahhh, tradition! Oh, but my, look at the time. And me, running off at the mouth again. You'd think I was in the fourth quarter of the Super Bowl, ahead by a field goal, trying to eat up the clock 'til the two-minute warning. Here, let me get that cock out of your mouth, so you can give me both barrels before the boys wake up and start barkin'." Paul removed her gag. "Go ahead, sweetie, let me have it...take your best shot, one last blast of hate, some cream for my coffee."

She stared at him. Said nothing. Paul seemed incredulous. "Don't tell me you're gonna get all lovey-dovey like your mum before she died? You're not going to *forgive* me?"

She remained silent. Martin was still a block of ice. But sensation was beginning to return to my hands and feet when Rose finally said, "You are so pathetic."

Paul's face went completely blank. His skin flushed red as a furnace. I knew he was about to blow, but he began howling with laughter. It was terrifying, but it gave me the chance I was hoping for. Somehow, miraculously, I sprang out of my chair and grabbed a gun off the table. Paul wheeled around so quickly he was a blur.

"Oh, it's only you. First one down, first one up. I was actually worried there for a second. I thought it might be someone who knows how to use that thing."

I pointed the gun at his face, unsure of what type of ammunition it held. I didn't much care at that point. "Tell her you were lying about me," I said, surprised at how threatening my voice sounded. "Tell her all this shit was your idea and you were blackmailing me."

"Why should I tell her? You just did," he said, strolling behind Rose's chair again, gripping it. "I don't think either of us have a great deal of credibility with her right now."

Rose was about to speak when suddenly Martin sprang up and grabbed the twin pistol. The Beretta still sat there, all alone, far from Paul's reach, but he still held the best weapon.

"Let her go!" Martin demanded. Paul said nothing. Did nothing. Complete silence.

But then, from out of nowhere, came Rose's voice, "I am so sick of this shit!" she yelled, shocking everyone. "Would one of you fuckers just shoot him?"

All eyes turned to her. Martin moved in, thrusting his gun out at Paul.

Paul tilted Rose's chair forward a fraction of an inch. "Stalemate."

Not necessarily, I thought about saying, but I decided to let Paul get in the last word. Then I shot him right in his lying face.

3:15

I let out a gasp of relief as Paul let go of the chair and fell over...backwards. The huge thud from his fall didn't set off the trap either. I wanted to scream, to jump up and down, pop open some champagne, grab Martin and Rose by the hands and do a victory dance. I did it! Me! I shot Paul! In the face! Yes, it turned out to be just another gel cap, but still, I did it!

Then I saw the clock, the laughably ornate Louis XIV monstrosity on the table. The time was 3:13. Rose stared at Martin like Maria stared at Tony in *West Side Story* when she knew everything had gone terribly, unstoppably wrong. Martin stared back at her with the same panicked look, then pulled the remote from his pocket and stared at the keypad just as desperately. *Tick. Tick. Tick.*

Remember *The Amityville Horror?* The new homeowner would wake up every night and the time on his digital alarm clock would always be 3:15. After I finished reading it, I used to wake up at the same time, night after night. I didn't see any ghosts, but I thought there must be something strange about that number. But as I heard that big clock ticking and the faint echo of a parallel rhythm emanating from the impaler, as I watched Rose sob with fear and saw beads of sweat accumulate on Martin's brow for the first time in his life, I knew that number was more than just spooky. It was the number of death.

"The code is three-fifteen!" I shouted, as the final seconds ticked away. Martin looked at me suspiciously for one of those precious moments and by the time he typed in those three sinister digits, the clock started chiming. Chiming? Who has a clock that chimes at 3:15? Only one person I know. And even though the numbers Martin punched in were indeed the correct ones, he was one second late. One single doubting second. All our hearts stopped at once as a brand-new sound drowned out the clock.

The sound of that final...*ca-ching!*

DISAPPEARING ACTS

The steel pole shot up from beneath Rose's chair with the force of a Titan rocket. She let out a scream to end all screams. Martin ran over as fast as he could. When he saw her head fall limply to her chest, he turned on me.

"Hold it! Look at her!"

Martin looked back at Rose's hanging head. He was about to charge me again, when he saw it move. She had fainted. The two metal cocktail trays I rigged under her seat while she was still unconscious had served their hoped-for purpose. Whew.

"Rose!" he yelled, rushing over. She was coming around. When her vision cleared and she saw Martin's ravaged face again, she cried and cried. He leaned forward to kiss her, then looked under the chair and saw the metal trays. He turned to me with an astonished look that went far beyond simple gratitude or admiration.

"Here," I said, tossing him the handcuff keys I'd pulled from Paul's coat pocket. Martin unlocked the cuffs and was about to pick her up when she pushed out her hand to stop him.

"Wait…" she said, gasping. "Be *very* careful. Lift me straight up."

Martin looked at her in bafflement, so she repeated herself. "Slowly. *Very* slowly."

I came over to see if I could help, but Martin gave me a baleful stare that discouraged my further involvement. He put his hands under her armpits, his legs straddling both sides of the chair. He lifted her straight up, exactly like she wanted. Slowly. He was so strong it looked like he was helping her levitate. When he raised her about four inches, a look of relief came over her face that bordered on rapture. When we saw the seat of the chair below her, it was easy to see why. No wonder she fainted. The metal trays did their job, for the most part. They stopped the pole—but not before it shot up three inches through the seat. The pointed tip was poking up like a periscope. Yet there wasn't a drop of blood. Where had it gone?

Rose gave us a clue. "Put me down," she told Martin with a delirious smile. "Then make sure my asshole's okay."

Clean as a whistle. When Martin finished his proctology exam, he picked up the Beretta and shoved it in his pocket. Then he leaned over Paul's stiff body, staring into Paul's unblinking eyes, knowing he was looking right back at him, knowing he'd heard everything, even seen Rose escape from his limited vantage point on the floor. He gave him the finger, grabbed Rose by the waist and made a big deal out of kissing her right over his face.

Rose looked at me for the first time that day with something resembling gratitude. I didn't have time to savor her fleeting appreciation. Martin picked her up and carried her into the adjoining bedroom so she could collect her breath. She hugged him with extraordinary love as he gently placed her down on the satin bedspread.

She promptly hopped off again, running into the bathroom to pee. While Martin waited outside the bathroom he did a quick mental calculation of Paul's body weight, the proximity of the blast and the absorption rate through his unclothed skin. He calculated that he would remain in his coma for another three minutes and twenty-six seconds. Good. He couldn't wait to go back in there and take full advantage of his vulnerable condition, with every bit as much gusto as Paul had shown.

This was why he brought that ammo in the first place. This was going to be great. But he didn't want Rose to watch. She might get the wrong idea about him. So he waited, getting more impatient with each passing second. When she came out, he'd tell her she needed to stay in the bedroom a while, watching the TV or something, until he finished the job. He didn't want to rush things. Didn't want any distractions. And after Paul was dead, he'd usher her back to their own room for a quick change and...

Boy she sure was taking her time in there.

"You okay?" he shouted nervously.

"Yeah, I'll be out in a minute," she answered happily.

Martin counted it down outside the bathroom, and when she didn't emerge in exactly sixty seconds he felt too nervous about leaving someone as dangerous as Paul unguarded any longer, so he came back into the sitting room to give him another booster shot.

Martin walked through the door and his eyes, excuse me…his eye… bugged out. Paul was gone. And so was I.

Rose came out of the bathroom only a few seconds later. When she entered the sitting room, she looked at Martin and let out a horrified gasp, "Where the fuck are they?"

Ca-ching!!!

Three eyes turned, fearing the worst. But it wasn't Paul's sickle opening. The impaler's steel spear had shot up two more feet through the cocktail trays. Ouch. Those were some really strong springs in there.

Lucky me, she thought, sighing with relief. But when she turned around, she sucked it back up again. Now Martin was gone too.

The Library

I had to go in there alone. Well, not completely alone. I dragged Paul with me. I found the door key in the same pocket as the handcuff key. It was bigger and brighter and surprisingly heavy. It turned easily in the lock, but when I opened the door, I had a hard time concentrating on my most important task: dragging Paul in there. *Ooof.*

I dropped Paul's legs on the floor inside, locked the door behind me and wiped the red goop off his bullet-bruised face so he could have a good view of my imminent triumph. The Book was on the altar. I knew it would be. I walked over and pressed my hands on the stiff cover, my eyes drifting back to the thin chain around Paul's thick neck and the dangling key. I fished under my shirt and pulled out the other key, the key I had won (not stolen!) from Rose.

I felt quite proud of my coup, the way my mind pushed against hers, against her fingers, pressing the key into her chest until the blood flowed out. My mind was still pushing when she ran to the bathroom, guiding her hand as she hung the chain around the doorknob. Yes, it was quite a feat. Paul thought so too. You should have seen his face as we passed each other in the hallway. He winked at me right before he knocked on the door. *Bop-ba-ba-da-da!*

"The key can only be seized upon her death, or if she removes it voluntarily," he explained when we were making our plans. "If you get her to take it off, then you'll have earned that trinket same as Loren did, fair and square...though, I'm sure he would disagree. Of course, Johnny will want it back, and my guess is he'll find a way, same as he did with The Striker. He will try to stop you, maybe even kill you, but that's your risk. Yet I'm guessing he'll be watching me instead, trying to get his bitch to make a run for it."

Johnny the Saint's key. Loren's key. My key. I had beaten all of them. Paul too. My chest puffed out as I stared at him, helpless on the floor.

But I didn't feel a twinge of remorse. Look how he kept pushing for it. The way he lied about me to Martin and Rose!

I gazed into his open eyes, savoring my victory. I placed my hands on the Book. I felt its power surge through me as soon as I touched it. I grasped the key hanging from my neck.

It didn't work. There could only be one explanation. A second book. Was I in possession of the one and only key to the one and only book of the druids? Was it hiding in plain sight here in the library? Not even knowing for certain the book existed, I went crazy looking for it, knowing I had a very small window of opportunity before Martin broke the door down or Paul woke up and ripped my head off. I skittered like a crab in front of the shelves, scanning the spines of the hundreds of volumes stacked inside the fourteen-foot-tall bookcases. Almost all of them had no identifying markings, so I tried to *see* which one it might be. That didn't work either. As each second ticked away I became more frightened. My breaths were coming in gasps. I looked down at Paul. He was still gazing at the ceiling with lifeless eyes. Was he dead? Overdosed? I thought about going over to feel for a pulse, but I didn't know whether a pulse even registered with the tetrodoxin-curare cocktail. What was I thinking when I dragged him inside with me? Did I think I was going to kill him in a more private setting? Was I subconsciously protecting him from Martin? Or hoping the Book could protect me from his wrath at my betrayals once I had it in my grasp? Did I even have a fucking clue?

I stifled my rising terror and made one last attempt to find the other book. Then I heard him.

"It's not here."

I breathed a tentative sigh of relief when I saw it was The Striker and not Paul. He wasn't holding a gun, which provided even greater relief. "Hello, Loren."

"Put that gun down, you fool," he hissed at me. Literally. Even without any sibilant "ess" sounds he still managed to hiss at me. He was standing between the altar and the angel. How did he get in here? Why was he still wearing that loincloth? Did he hail a cab in that?

"We need to get him up on the altar. Now," he said, with a very convincing urgency.

He pulled the white sheet from the altar with a crisp *snap*. My eyes drifted across the surface. Dark, unblemished teak. A pattern of carvings covered the entire surface. They seemed to move when I looked directly at them. I couldn't look very long, though. The other objects on the altar were too compelling. Three massive spikes. To the left of the spikes a large, strange looking hammer. The mallet seemed to be made of iron. The handle was thick and wooden. Then, I saw the knife. A very long, very old, very sharp knife.

"Do you understand what must be done?"

"Yes."

"No, you don't," said The Striker, peering at me through those droopy lids, his eyes darting down to my dangling key. "You're still asleep."

"If I'm so woozy, how come I'm holding the gun...and your key?" I pointed out, pulling the pistol from my waistband.

"The key won't help you," said The Striker, pulling his ball-peen hammer out from the side of his tribal leatherwear. "The other book is not here and your gun is useless."

"Tell that to him," I said, pointing to the crumpled body on the floor, acting a lot more confident than I felt, hoping he couldn't tell.

"Put the gun down. You don't know what you're doing."

"I'm going to kill him and take the Book. I'm going to end this."

"You can't kill him. But I can. Leave Paul with me. Go kill the girl."

"I don't think so. I can kill Paul...and you too."

"No, you can't," he said, completely unperturbed.

"And why is that?" I asked, still tingling from the power of the Book.

"Something will happen. It always does. You don't have my kind of luck."

"Oh, really?" *Blam! Blam! Blam!* I fired three gel caps at The Striker's pale white chest. Excuse me, his bright *red* chest. *Plop.*

"Ha! It looks like I found my four-leaf clover," I laughed, shouting at his fallen body, squeezing the key in my clenched fist. "Score one for Clan Kelly, *you fuck!*"

I bent over, staring into Loren's open, droopy eyes. Then something happened to my head. I felt a wave of dizziness gripping my skull, pulling me to the ground. It felt like I was in the middle of a giant black hole, being sucked down by an unimaginable source of gravity. I closed my eyes, willing myself to stay upright, but as soon as my eyelids shut, I was greeted by a vision…Loren moving his fingers…Paul standing up again. And just when I thought things couldn't get any scarier…as my head hit the floor… as I opened my eyes…as I saw Paul hovering over me…

He winked.

Journal Entry: Clan Kelly

I've been pacing around my tiny, shitty apartment all day, banging my head into the plaster walls, wondering whether to write this all down, whether any of it could possibly matter, now that I've taken a good, long look into the crystal ball and can see the tide that's rising, inevitably, irresistibly, crushingly towards us. Us, not me. I won't be alone when the tsunami comes crashing down. No one will be spared from the onslaught. Even if some stragglers manage to hide in caves, it will all be waiting to greet them when they emerge. It is coming. It cannot be stopped. And afterward, nothing will be the same.

I'm not talking about the *Becoming*, though Paul insists its inevitability is bound to the same timeline of the thing I fear even more than the prospect of the God O'Paulo. Maybe he can still be defeated. Johnny and Rose and Martin could succeed, with or without my help or opposition. Paul, or at least his body, could be killed, unlikely as that seems, particularly if I have to be the triggerman.

Science is what I fear.

When I woke up today, it was the farthest thing from my mind. All I could think about was Paul, his wealth, and my new identity. I went back on the web, now that I had a filter to sift through all those Paul Kellys. Tetron. Paul's cutesy contraction of the Tetragrammaton. A perfect name if you're in the God-building business. My search paid off quickly: "Tetron CEO raises millions for Policemen's Benevolent Association at Metropolitan Museum gala."

There was a picture of him in a tuxedo. Paul Kelly. My father. The saint.

Digging up more on Tetron was difficult. As a private company, it had few disclosure obligations. I kept clicking around and found a few more links associated with fundraising events for the police and fire departments. Next, I tried searching for Tetron subsidiaries. *Bingo!* I found a company called Intragon, a pioneer in stem cell research.

Stem cells are strange. Normal cells—that is to say, specialized cells—divide about fifty times and then *pfffft*, they're done. So in a very real sense, your body is always dying, and always being born. But stem cells keep dividing endlessly. In science jargon this is called "pluripotency." Very plural, very potent. Immortal.

As I was reading about stem cells, I came across a very interesting piece of information. When a group of scientists isolated the protein that controls the self-renewal process of undifferentiated stem cells, they called it "Nanog," after the mythological Celtic island of everlasting life: Tir nan Og. Land of the Ever Young.

Intragon. Tir nan Og. Nice anagram. But why would Paul care about stem cells as a path to life-extension or rejuvenation? He's clearly perfected his own beat-the-reaper system. Was he trying to build organs from scratch? Spare parts? I knew it was theoretically possible, but that kind of technology was probably decades away. Then again, time was another asset Paul possessed in abundance. Maybe he's building a better mousetrap. Or an entirely new mousetrap. That gave me an idea and I searched for bio-engineering. *Bingo*, another hit…a company called Ogamete. I did a patent search and found several awarded to Ogamete for gene-sequencing and splicing. Then I hit the jackpot with another Tetron holding called Quadcom. It has four divisions (natch): computer technology, nanotechnology, robotics and artificial intelligence. The computer sector is pursuing highly experimental research into biological and quantum computing. Bio-computing utilizes molecules like DNA and proteins to store, retrieve and process data. Quantum computing makes the miniscule molecular scale look colossal in comparison, using atoms to make all those little 1s and 0s. I'm quite sure the nano-technology sector contributes significantly to both less-is-more approaches.

Moving on to the robotics and AI divisions, I ran across an article by the *former* Quadcom head of AI R&D. Former? He quit working for Paul and he's still alive? That in itself was amazing, but the article had my brain doing flip-flops. It was all about the Singularity. I heard Paul throw the term out along with a handful of other hokey sounding initial-cap spectacularisms, like the *Becoming* and the *Turning*, so I didn't pay much attention, but after reading this and everything else preceding it, I was scared shitless. The article talked about an explosion in super-intelligence that would occur after computers became smarter than humans. He called this tipping point the Singularity—after which computers would design more and more intelligent iterations of themselves at an exponentially rapid pace, resulting in…

Nobody knows.

Not *nobody knows* in the sense you can never tell what the future will bring. Nobody knows because after the Singularity it will be impossible to predict *any* foreseeable future. In a post-Singularity world, humans will be unable to even *imagine* the intentions or capabilities of the emerging super-intelligence. Terminators? Maybe. Extinction of the human race? Very possible. Entirely new cyber-bio life forms? Why not?

Sounded a lot like the *Becoming* to me. And Paul being Paul, I was quite certain that his scientist minions were working around the clock to ensure that when the Singularity occurred, Paul wound up in the driver's seat. How? The super-*intelligence* would have to be integrated in some way with the *Paulence*. That outcome, and that alone, must be the true mission statement of Tetron.

I couldn't wait to see Paul and hear it all from the horse's mouth. But he wasn't downtown or at The Plaza. I couldn't *see* him anywhere. Then suddenly, I realized I didn't need any hocus-pocus to track him down. Today was St. Patrick's Day.

The parade had barely started when I saw him ride by on a float with the police commissioner. He was standing next to him, waving to the crowd, his hair pulled back in a ponytail again, wearing a black-and-red tartan. I watched him wave and smile as I walked along the sidewalk crowded with blind-drunk shamrock wearers, moving at the same pace as the float. It was easy. I just had to avoid stepping in the puke.

He didn't seem to see me. But I noticed something curious. Some of the people were waving back at Paul more enthusiastically than the rest. Trying to get his attention. When they got it, they seemed grateful, like they had touched the Pope's robe. Then I noticed something even stranger. All these sycophants, many of them cops, were wearing a ring. The same ring. A golden serpent band with the wings and head of an angel. As I passed, I asked one of the cops where he got his ring. He looked at me like he was going to slap on the cuffs and haul me away. I shut my mouth and kept on walking alongside the float. But the cop began following me. That's when Paul saw me. And winked. He caught the cop's eye and waved him off. The cop nodded, tipped his hat and backed away.

Paul gave the Commissioner an elbow in the ribs and pointed to me. I could read his lips. "That's him. That's my boy!" The commish gave me a big wave and a smile to match. Then he took off his hat. To me. I flushed with embarrassment as Paul waved for me to join them on the float. I felt too shy, so I walked alongside the entire parade route and watched all the other ringed attendants (disciples? soldiers?) waving. There were so many.

When it was over, Paul took me out for a drink…at a dingy Blarney Stone. He sure likes slumming it. Green beer and Bushmills flowed like twin waterfalls. The place was plastered with shamrocks and crowded with plastered Irish and Irish-American drunks. About two-thirds of them wore spiffy angel rings. When an Irish-wannabe couple wobbled in drunk from the street, they wobbled back out before they had a chance to order a drink. There should have been a sign posted on the door: CLANSMEN ONLY

Paul and I settled into a booth in the back. He was getting stinky again, so I leaned as far back as I could. The burlier ring-wearers sat at the tables and booths surrounding ours. Paul's royal retinue? They made a big show of not looking in our direction, not even listening in our direction. Paul didn't seem to notice them at all. I didn't care. Instead, I dug right in, asking if my theories about Tetron, the Singularity and the *Becoming* were true.

His reply was terse and terrifying: "More or less. But you have the general picture."

"When is all this supposed to happen?"

"According to the prophecy…2031. But at our current rate of development, we'll shave off a few years. Let's say 2029."

"Then what?"

"The future is a probability curve that can't be analyzed with any certainty. Combine that with what you've already learned about the unfathomable nature of the post-Singularity *Intelligence* and your guess is as good—well, not nearly as good as mine. But don't waste a minute fretting over the infinite destructive possibilities. Think of all the fun we're going to have along the way! It will all be one glorious adventure, start to finish!"

As much as I wanted to keep pumping him for more info on the pending Armageddon, Paul unexpectedly steered the conversation in another direction. "What's the biggest problem with immortality, from the Hindu perspective?"

I wanted to get cute and say, "The saris," but I could tell he was about to throw me a big bone, so I answered, "You can't remember anything when you reincarnate, so it doesn't make any difference that you live forever. You have to do the same shit over and over, making the same dumb mistakes a few hundred times—or become enlightened and get kicked upstairs to the divine realm."

"The dreaded karma. Memory is the key to everything. Not just identity. Everything. It's all there, in the DNA. The whole story, every word of it. From the first trace of slime to all the slime in this bar, everything came from the same source code. We know proteins talk to each other, but how do they know what to say? Cellular memory. Without words, they know. Soon we'll have the whole script. Science will lead the way."

"The way to what?" I asked, seriously intrigued.

"To the end." He paused a moment, then said, "I'm going to tell you a secret more arcane and profound than the legend of Solomon's ring and his captured genies, a true story by the way, though trashed up in more of that *Arabian Nights* crap than I care to endure."

"Okay," I said, wanting to hear more about that but asking, "what's the big secret?"

He looked around the room theatrically, then cupped his hand to my ear and whispered, "Science is magic."

"Science is magic?" I asked, not sure why I was whispering too.

"No. Science *is* magic. See the difference? They are one and the same. Ask the best minds in every field—mathematics, chemistry, biology, physics—they'll all tell you."

"Tell you what?"

"That everything we see and know and believe to be so solid and dependable is at its core more unfathomably complex and ineffably mysterious than all the Gods or daimons that have ever been invoked since the dawn of time. But in the end, we will know...or at least, I will. And between what we've already discovered and what will soon be revealed, it won't be long before we won't need these time-consuming rituals, or women to make the vessel."

"The 'vessel'? What's the vessel?"

"*Who*, not what. If you want to live forever with your memories and identity intact, you have three options. The first two we've discussed and they comprise the Apostolic mode of succession: first, train willing and dedicated disciples and take possession of their physical bodies in much the same way as I have already demonstrated to you; and second, reincarnate and have your loyal followers search for your new body, as they do with the Dalai Lama, then through the use of some very non-Buddhist ritual magic, awaken the memories of your past lifetimes. The third, and by far the most effective and powerful approach, is to train your own biological descendant and awaken the cellular memories already encoded in their DNA during the act of soul transfer—the Dynastic mode of succession."

"The *Turning*," I said with not a little awe.

"That colloquialism has been applied to all these approaches. But it became clear to us that biological successors held so many advantages over the other methods that those options were abandoned entirely, except in cases of dire emergency, which occur with much greater frequency than I care to admit, but are not unexpected."

"What kind of emergency?"

"When you're in a nearly continuous state of war, as is the case with us Kellys, you can't always be so picky about your host body, especially not with a double-headed ax buried in your ribcage. So you simply hitch a ride in the nearest available open-eyed human, usually not so hard, because hot-blooded murderers always love to gloat. You stick around long enough to torment them to the point of suicide—the reason for most exorcisms, by the way—then perform the ritual properly with the vessel. Of course, from time to time you'll get a bullet in the head from a high-powered rifle and you're back in the Maelstrom again, ready to be recycled. Which, I might point out, is the true genius of our clan's approach to the whole messy business. Not only do we utilize all the advantages of *Turning* with a vessel that houses the genetic memories passed on to him—we also have an army of loyal soldiers and druids who will stop at nothing to discover the Master's reincarnated body should the *Turning* fail."

"So there's no way you can really die," I was so astounded by the implications of his virtually fail-safe method of ensuring everlasting life that I felt giddy. "How old *are* you?"

"This being has existed for..." He paused and took a deep breath. "What you don't realize, what nearly no one realizes, is that we are all eternal. That's the message Yeshua tried to bring, before Peter and Paul made him the one and only Son O'God. That's the message of Hermes, Pythagoras, Apollonius, the druids...of all our kind. We are immortal. Physics 101. Energy cannot be destroyed. You could go so far as to say that all of us are billions of years old. But the gift of us luminous beings, the one thing that makes us feel mortal or immortal, is our sense of self, our identity, which immediately ceases to exist without our memories. Memory as I said, is everything."

"Is that what the Book is for? Does it restore your memories after you've Turned, or reincarnated?"

He got real pissy. "The Book does far more than that, but you are in no way worthy of that lesson. Today we are speaking of the vessel. Martin is the vessel and the Guardian."

"Guardian of what?"

"Of this vessel," he said pointing to his chest. "Until the *Turning* is complete. Then if you do your job, you will assume the role of Guardian until the *Becoming*. This is the last *Turning*. The last time we have to ride on this ridiculous merry-go-round."

"Isn't there another way to do this…that's not so…parasitic?"

"There is also a fourth option, but it is even more cruel. I would encourage you to avoid it like the plague. It is Loren's path. He is very old indeed."

"What does he do?" I asked, a shiver running down my spine.

He paused a long time as if debating whether to tell me. When he spoke again I could see why. It was a dire warning. "He feeds on souls… both here and inside the Maelstrom. But again, that is not a topic you should approach with any fascination. It is a curse for both the victim and the feeder. The consciousness of the consumed is never fully assimilated, and you acquire, in a very real sense, eternal roommates."

I could easily picture The Striker gleefully devouring the very essence of his victims. Even "living" with them. My mind wandered down that dark corridor, then I suddenly remembered a question I'd been dying to ask. "What happened after Ceallach died? How did the wise, kind Master turn into mean old Paul Kelly?"

"Hah! I like that, Billy. And since it's Saint Patty's Day, I can't think of a better time to tell you about the birth of our Clan and the story of the empty vessel."

"The *'empty vessel'*?" What hellish new wrinkle was unfolding?

"The term had also been used in the Apostolic succession. The Chosen One would willfully surrender his ego by degrees through mediation and other techniques until his mind was reasonably uncluttered in preparation for the Master's tenancy. But after Ceallach, it took on a whole new meaning. We drew a line in the sand. Traitorous bitch or not, it was clear Sophia's clan was right about one thing—a biological heir was the only proper vessel for a completely effective transmigration. Only this time, it wasn't going to be another handoff. A solid, experienced leader was needed if we were to survive the centuries of hardship sure to follow in the wake of the Holy Empire's triumph. The Master alone must endure. And the Chosen One must sacrifice himself just as the disciples had done.

"Utter ruthlessness was required. The natural inclination to love and care for one's progeny, to have any degree of attachment, was not a viable option. Fortunately, the entity that emerged after Ceallach's death was up to the task. After Tormac drove in the last nail, he thrust his sweaty face only a nose-length away from The Master to crow his triumph. The Master leapt into Tormac's body and Tormac's gloating conquest quickly turned to screaming horror, followed by a two-day coma. The Master's disciples knew what had occurred and took the Book to his chamber.

"When he awoke, the Master had changed irreversibly, his essence contaminated by Tormac and his own unquenchable fury at the killers of his martyred son. After reading the Book he was an entirely different breed, a true Warrior Sage—the right man for the job that had to be done. The new, improved Tormac was cruel and wise beyond measure. He married the Black Rose as ordained, and a boy was born nine months later. He was named O'Ceilleigh after his true father Ceallach. But the Master wasn't about to make the same mistake again and let compassion interfere with the primary mission—the absolute necessity of his continued existence. He stole the baby from Rose while she was bathing, and took him to a horrible crone, who was paid to make him suffer. Then, at the right time, he rescued the lad, the boy so traumatized he was only a shell of a person, not enough there to care for himself or care about. The perfect empty vessel.

"He knocked up poor Rosie another eleven times, until she died in childbirth with her twelfth son. Morgana was never seen again in her lifetime, though she was certainly present. Tormac murdered Eoghan and Bradan, assuming High Kingship as Master of the unified clans. Soon afterward, O'Ceilleigh had his initiation ceremony and exceeded all expectations in his apprenticeship. The *Turning* occurred twenty-two years after

Ceallach died. That glorious Good Friday when Tormac took O'Ceilleigh and assumed his identity is the day we mark as the birth of our true lineage— the founding of Clan O'Ceallaigh.

"Since that day we have prospered in every way. We have eschewed the outward trappings of royalty, since our ambition has nothing to do with the respect and admiration of the masses or our peers. When another Ceallach, son of Tuathal, founded his O'Ceallaigh lineage, we were more than happy at the camouflage it afforded our own thriving clan.

"Our new succession mode was followed in every subsequent generation for fifteen centuries. I did it to Martin as my father did to me as his father to him—taking the child from his true mother at birth, leaving him in the custody of some cruel, heartless bitch we call the surrogate. However, it was important for the vessel to believe she was his real mother, so the trauma would be as effective as possible in accelerating the process. Even the trauma had its own prescriptive guidelines, the preferred method being the death of the surrogate at the hands of the subject."

The surrogate. The subject. The trauma. I couldn't believe what I was hearing. Paul ignored my horrified expression and plowed ahead.

"The next task was to train the subject in the art of *unthinking*. Unthinking has two goals: to free you from the slavery of your thoughts, and to open you to the realm of true knowing, beyond the shackles of limited possibilities we call our mind. Simultaneously, the subject is taught to withstand astounding levels of physical pain, utilizing a combination of unthinking and other biofeedback techniques during daily torture sessions.

"After a reasonable degree of progress is made in these areas, the vessel is gradually initiated in our mythology, which elicits an aura of mystery along with an overwhelming desire for participation. It is then that he is formally initiated into the clan and continues to hone his skills through a set of increasingly difficult challenges. These challenges are interwoven with the system's mythology and are highly ritualized, as well as substantially rewarding for the subject, according to a predetermined set of key motivators selected by the Master to induce the highest level of commitment and positive reinforcement. For me, the worm on the hook was knowledge. For Martin, it was treasure.

"For the remainder of his training, the apprentice learns all the essential tenets of our society, and his ambition is constantly stoked with ever more difficult challenges and fulfilling rewards. The challenges usually take the form of quests for ritual objects or duels…first with the outside clans, then between his own clansmen. The High King—that's me, of course—rules the reigning clan. Clan Kelly and the other royal clans are divided into twelve houses. The Lords—one of whom you've already had the dubious privilege of meeting—preside over the houses."

"The Striker…" I interrupted. Paul shot me a dirty look and kept talking.

"The houses follow bloodlines, though outside talent is permitted after swearing blood oaths. You've seen many of these disturbing gentlemen on our website. Each of these initiates and the other clan descendents go though their own training. They're given a number of tasks, including quests and duels, plus sundry extortions and executions required to maintain our continued privacy. If successful, the apprentice is granted the title of Knight. From time to time, the most daring of these will make his own play for the throne.

"The vessel, because of his more rigorous training and direct connection to the king's bloodline, has now attained a level of unshakable confidence, believing there is nothing in the world beyond his ability. And with that assurance comes an equal conviction in his own entitlement. Not only can he do anything, he deserves everything he craves. This is the exact point where ambition, mastery, courage and ruthlessness attain their proper balance. The vessel swears a blood oath to the Master and is anointed the Guardian, for his role is to both house and protect the essence of all his forebears, all their accumulated knowledge and power. He is shown the Book, the map to the Maelstrom. There he is taken to witness the full glory of its majestic power, and upon his return, the Guardian is prepared for the final act, when he will travel again with the Master to the Axis so he may be reborn.

"We've made some mistakes along the way. Yeshua. Ceallach. And now we have the tragedy of Martin. I always considered him to be my most well-wrought creation, the most perfect vessel of all. He was the youngest to achieve full-fledged Knighthood. Yet, he's lost almost everything I filled him with: his lust, his ambition and worst, his hate. Now we're both paying the price for my mistake. I should not have been so ruthless with him. Martin was always such a sensitive lad, with the most tender heart you could ever hope to find. So much the better, I thought. An open heart means an open mind, exactly what was needed. And after a trauma that couldn't have been more thoughtfully orchestrated, Martin's brain was like a heap of soft pink slush. How perfect, I thought. How empty. And better still, he could unthink before I even taught him how. Well, well, well. I was glowing with pride! The boy was a natural! A prodigy! When I taught him the technique, you should have seen how he excelled. He could hold back his thoughts for minutes. Then hours. Unheard of!"

Suddenly, a deep sadness crept into his voice. "Martin liked unthinking so much he did it all the time. He used it like a machine to erase all those painful memories and shield his tender heart. Now the machine is running by itself, wiping away everything of value, the baby with the bathwater. And with hardly any time left, he must recapture all he has learned in order to fulfill his destiny and ours. He must remember."

"What about you? After all this time, do you remember…everything?"

"I have the capacity and the access. More often than not, I lack the inclination. In this way I share Martin's predilection to…compartmentalize… especially with the she-cunts."

"Why do you hate women so much?" I asked, cringing at his unfettered misogyny.

"Clan Kelly is a warring clan. Always has been…always will be. Women humanize us. That's what we need to rise above. Mercy. Compassion. Love. As soon as a baby breathes air, his mother sucks the life she gave back out of him while he's sucking on her tit. Training the poor lad to need her, to love her. That's the source of all pain in life. And that's what must be squashed like a bug on your boot heel—that fatal dependence. I squashed it. And by God almighty, you will too! It's the one thing us Kelly boys will never have need of…that sick, sapping motherly love."

"You still can't have babies without women, even with insemination," I pointed out. "No women, no lineage."

"You can't have babies without them…yet. But that's changing. We are the last generation born into a world shackled to a cunt to spread our seed.

"Three cheers to science!" he roared.

"Hip hip hooray!" a hundred voices blared.

After the noise abated I said, "You know, your manly man club isn't a whole lot different from the Church."

"We bear no resemblance to that worm-ridden institution whatsoever! We breed, we pass along the *truth* to our followers. And we've never been kid-fuckers."

"Yeah, but for you, breeding is spelled R-A-P-E. Sex for procreation purposes only. Very Catholic. Even back in the good old days, you were into celibacy and self-denial. I'll bet Sophia's clan has a lot more fun with their goodies. That seems more like true paganism to me. This setup you have now, it's a little bit…*gay*…don't you think?"

Paul said nothing. I thought steam was going to come out of his ears.

"And about that whole 'passing along the *truth*' thing," I pressed on, testing just how far I could push until I reached ignition point. "If your loyal subjects here knew about those little 'mistakes' you mentioned earlier… like what you did to Christ, like you might not actually be the true Chosen One anymore…I'm not sure they'd be hootin' and hollerin' every time you make a beer belch. I'll bet there'd be a lot of angel head rings turning up in pawn shops."

"Oh, really?" Paul roared, standing to his feet. "Let's test that theory."

"Hey, lads! Listen up!" Total silence. Crickets. That in itself was a major miracle for any Blarney Stone in the world on St. Patty's Day.

"I'm very sorry to inform you all that I haven't been completely honest in regards to our sacred objectives. In fact, our ancient ancestors had a hand in Christ's demise and now those O'Neil cunts are looked upon more favorably by the big man upstairs than my humble self. All that being said, I need to know…*are you still with me?*"

"*LONG LIVE THE KING! LONG LIVE CLAN KELLY!*" they shouted deafeningly.

"Thanks so much for your support, lads! The next six rounds are on me!"

He sat down, smoothed his hair back and smiled. I opened my mouth to ask another question, but he held a blunt finger to my lips.

"Yes, I know. I've answered so many of your questions, only to raise a thousand more. But there's one thing I need to know too." He paused, taking a deep gulp of whiskey.

"Do you want it bad enough, Billy? Are you ready to claim your legacy?"

"What exactly does that mean…my legacy?"

"You will rule by my side as you always have. After you kill that stupid cow in front of the Guardian, of course."

"I have to kill her in front of Martin? He'll rip my fucking head off!"

"You underestimate your own power. When the time comes, you'll hold your own. You must kill that rotten shank while he watches so Martin will fully surrender to his fate, to his clan, to his king and to his vow. All love and the hope of love must be annihilated in him completely, as I have done at every fork in the road. Now it's your turn. You must cut his last tether to this world. He must turn fully to our side, and against Sophia and her foul spawn."

"Why don't you take me instead of Martin? I'll trade my body for Rose. It's not like I'm doing much with it anyway. We both like the same stuff… well not all the same stuff, but you know what I mean."

"You're a little soft for my tastes. Martin is a thoroughbred. Blood, bones and muscle. He's got what I need to reach the finish line. All that clean living, don't you know? I appreciate your generosity, though, if not your motivation. Still, I'm afraid I'll have to pass."

"Don't you want a pound of brains to go with the brawn? Talk about horsepower. Martin is not exactly…"

"You don't have the right to carry that boy's dirty laundry, let alone besmirch his abilities!" Paul shouted, instantly livid. "You know nothing of him whatsoever! If you did, you'd know he has just as fine a gearbox as you. Besides, I'll be doing all the thinking for both of us soon…and you'll have your hands full with Tetron."

He was trying to tempt me again. It was starting to work. But some stronger part of me came rushing out, surprising Paul and even myself. "I won't do it. Not for you, not for me, not for all the money and power in the universe."

"If you won't do it for me…" he began softly, growing louder with every word. "And you won't do it for yourself…then do it for something that really matters…"

Then he raised his glass and shouted to the rafters. When he shouted a second time, the whole crowd joined him, raising their drinks and angel-head rings to the ceiling:

"DO IT FOR THE GLORY OF CLAN KELLY!!!"

THE LOCKED DOOR

When she saw that Martin had disappeared, Rose shrieked like Jamie Lee Curtis in the first *Halloween* movie. *"Marrrtiiinnnn!"* Then she ran around the corner.

"Oh, God! There you are! You scared the shit out of me!"

Martin was crouching outside the white door, staring at her like a pistol-packing Cyclops, a finger on his lips. When she crept over to him, Martin handed her the Beretta, told her to go back into the bedroom, lock the door and stay there.

"No fucking way," she whispered, shaking her head violently. "You are *not* leaving me alone again."

Martin grimaced like her response was causing him physical pain, then turned his attention to the door, twisting the brass handle. It was locked. He fired a bullet directly into the keyhole. It still wouldn't open. Rose cowered beside him, praying the door would stay locked and Martin would flee with her to the elevator. But that wasn't going to happen. Not if he thought Paul was in there.

Martin fired again, the *bang* so loud she covered her ears with both hands. Still the door refused to budge. He was about to empty the rest of the clip into the lock, when he heard something on the other side of the door that was even louder than his pistol.

Boom!!! Then again. *BOOM!!!*

"Holy Shit. What the hell was that?" Rose asked, trembling.

Martin shook he head. He didn't have a clue.

But it sounded like a wrecking ball.

CLASH OF THE TITANS

The Striker rolled toward the altar just as Paul leapt into the air and crashed his boot heels where his head had been resting. Loren snatched up the big iron mallet, his other hand still gripping his own trusty ball-peen hammer.

Ca-ching! "I'm so glad you arrived on time, old friend," Paul purred, wiping his face with the dull side of his sickle. "To every beginning an end, to every end a beginning."

"You will fail without me," The Striker replied, circling around Paul in a wide orbit. "William cannot protect you as the Guardian," he said, pointing at my inert body. "But I can. Together we'll be more powerful than all the Clans combined. Honor me with your glory."

"You tryin' to sweet-talk me now?" Paul chuckled, pacing around him in front of the altar, tightening his circles with every lap. "Do you really think I need a traitorous Dutch boy to turn the Great Wheel?"

"So be it," The Striker said.

Paul stopped moving. "You know something, Loren? I've always admired you."

"And I you," The Striker replied honestly, still circling around him.

"So, I'll tell you what I'm going to do," Paul said, his body now perfectly aligned with the lectern, the Book, the altar and the angel. "I'm going to let you keep your head."

Whooooosh! The Striker swung the iron mallet in a blinding four-foot arc. Paul tilted his body to the side at what would have been the precise moment of impact, wheeling around with his blade while the force of Loren's swing and the weight of the hammer pulled him off balance.

Clang! Paul sliced the handle of the ball-peen hammer neatly in two, the head falling to the floor, the haft a useless stump in Loren's grip. Loren regained his balance just in time for Paul slam his fist into his face, smashing his long, aquiline nose. Not easily deterred, Loren quickly countered, connecting a solid blow to Paul's shoulder with the iron hammer. *Crunch!*

I propped myself up on my elbows, finally able to move again. But I didn't know where to go or what to do. Should I start shooting? The gun was still in my grip. And if the answer was yes, who should I aim at first? The two of them were going at it like rock-em-sock-em robots, only six feet away from me. The way their fists, hammers and sickles were flying, I could get killed just trying to stand up. So I crawled behind the altar, peeking around the corner. So much for Mr. Triumphant.

Clannnnng! The sickle lodged itself in the handle of the giant iron hammer. The Striker punched him in the throat. *"Aaack!"* Paul gacked, hitting the floor with a thunderous *boom!* Loren dove on him, both fists scrunched together, targeting Paul's solar plexus. Paul lifted both knees to his chest and kicked his leaping adversary in the gut with so much force that he landed on the altar with another resounding *boom!* Then Paul charged to the altar like a juggernaut, grabbed Loren by the throat and crotch, lifted him over his head and slammed him down on the altar again in a bone-crunching thud. *Boom! BOOOOOM!*

Paul pummeled him against the sacrificial slab again and again, lifting his limp, bruised body over his head one final time and flinging it to the base of the angel's cross where his head slapped against the wood with a sharp, wet *crack.*

The Striker lay motionless at the foot of the cross, the back of his skull bleeding, propped against the wood like a hard pillow. His long, skeletal frame sprawled across the floor, his feet pointing toward the altar, his blue-veined arms spread akimbo in a crude parody of the glorious white wings poised directly above him.

Paul laughed like a madman and grabbed the handle of his fallen sickle, yanking it from the mallet with a wine cork *pop.* He drew his arm back like a baseball pitcher warming up, then threw his sickle straight for Loren's neck like a ninety-mile-an-hour fastball.

Chiiiiiingg! The blade lodged on either side of his throat, the long, curved arch forming a razor-sharp collar around The Striker's gasping trachea. A thin red stream trickled from the lump of his Adam's apple, until it gathered at the blade's anchor points, anointing the cross with its first taste of blood. The wood sucked it up like a straw.

Paul looked at the knife and the spikes on the altar, then shook his head and reached under Loren's loincloth. What the fuck was he doing? Looking for nails. There was pouch full of them—a nice assortment of lengths and gauges. Paul used them quickly and judiciously: long, thick nails for his hands and feet, pounding the steel mercilessly through the yielding bone and muscles into the floor; small, thin nails for his eyelids. He nailed them to his brow.

"There, that should hold you awhile," Paul said, rubbing his hands together. "This momentous occasion requires a proper witness, and I can think of no one more qualified for that vital role than you, dear Loren… my faithful wizard!"

The Striker said nothing. Saw nothing. Paul was so happy he didn't care. He was staring at me as I stood by the door, turning the handle. "Whoa there, Nellie!" he shouted, raising the hammer, letting me know how accurately he was prepared to throw it at my quivering face. "Judging from the way you took me down before, and your treasonous negotiations with that slithering snake, I can only come to the conclusion that you mean me bodily harm. And while we're on the subject of unvarnished betrayals, how could you let that stinking harlot live? Cocktail trays? Are you still numb to the threat she represents? Or are you so sick with your tainted affections that you're willing to trade punches with me rather than send her off to Hades? Is that the God's honest truth? Do you really want a piece of…me?"

I shook my head vigorously. *No! No! NO!*

"I'll take that as a yes," Paul grinned, clenching his bloody fists, one finger curled and beckoning. "Let's see what you got, then. Come to poppa, Billy boy!"

Up and Down

Wham! Martin punched a hole through the wooden door like Bruce Lee, reached inside and turned the door handle. He shouldn't have bothered. I had just unlocked it. He threw open the door, ready to fire. When he saw us, he watched instead.

"Holy Fuck!" Rose blurted out, peeking around the doorframe.

Paul and I were too preoccupied to pay much attention to either of them. He was coming at me like a giant Kodiak bear, his nailless hands raised like claws. I tried to think, but a voice inside my head issued a different command, "Shoot first, think later."

Blam! He went down like a rock. Then he rose from the floor like a winch pulled him up by the shoulders, with no visible use of muscles.

Doesn't anyone stay down around here? I wanted to scream, so scared my whole body was shaking. He was only six feet away. *Blam!* Another gel cap exploded across his shirt as he closed the gap between us. He still wasn't falling down! I fired again. *Blam!* Another direct hit and still no reaction. I pulled the trigger one last time as he was almost on top of me. *Click.* Oh shit. He grabbed my collar and the belt of my pants, lifting me over his head like a stuffed doll. He slammed me on the altar with a thud that nearly knocked me out, dropping the empty pistol to the floor with a loud clatter.

Paul ripped open my shirt, exposing the glowing implants to his hungry eyes. He picked up the sacrificial blade, raised his hand up high, while I raised my arms to stop him.

"This is how you do it, boy. You always liked to talk too much!"

"The same could be said for you," I replied, my fearlessness suddenly returning. Paul was stiffening in his knife-held pose like a block of carved glacier ice. Then he fell back to the floor the same way he had risen.

Without any effort at all.

Togetherness

I sat up on the altar, buttoning my shirt again. There were only two left at the bottom. "Thanks so much for all your help, by the way," I grumbled to Martin and Rose.

Martin didn't seem to notice. He was staring at the angel.

"No thanks necessary," Rose replied. "I was hoping he'd kill you."

I ignored her remark. She wasn't even looking at me. She was staring at the cross too, at the way Loren was attached to the base of it, his eyelids nailed-open, his unmoving eyeballs devoid of animation—as far as she could tell.

"We'll be getting some visitors after all that gunfire," I said as she huddled under Martin's arm in their cowardly outpost by the doorway. "You'd better get out of here."

I knew any police intrusion was unlikely, given Paul's control over the house staff. Judging from Martin's non-reaction, I guess he knew it too. Still, I was anxious to be rid of them and have some quality time alone with Pop…and Loren…and my newly claimed legacy.

"He's not dead," Martin said, leaning over Paul's body.

"I'll take care of it," I assured them, prying the knife from Paul's stiff hand, tossing it across the room. As I bent over, I noticed Rose's key dangling freely from my ripped shirt. I straightened up quickly, turning away from them, hoping they hadn't seen it.

"As if!" Rose yelled, clenching the Beretta. "Why should we trust you? Just when I thought that maybe you weren't a total lying piece of shit you disappear with him in here and lock the door!"

"I saved your life!" I shouted, hoping she'd back off so I could pull my shirt together and hide the key. "And in case you didn't notice, Paul was trying to kill me too!"

"Too bad he didn't," she shot back, undaunted. "You never told me about the cocktail trays. You're a sadist. A killer. Just like him."

"I didn't tell you about the trays because I wasn't sure they'd work. I knew Martin was coming, that he had the remote. I was protecting you until he got here!" I shouted, pointing at her—and inadvertently exposing the necklace on my chest. Rose was staring at the key. I should have known better. It's not polite to point.

"You fucker! You stole my key!"

I didn't defend myself. What was the point? There wasn't time anyway. Martin was coming at me like a steamroller. Rose grabbed his sleeve to stop him, not because she didn't want him to hurt me, but because of what she saw behind Martin's back.

Paul was rising from behind the altar.

"I'd rather discipline Billy meself, if you don't mind. And I have to say, that potion of yours sure packs a whollop! Too bad you don't have a few more shots left. I'm beginning to like it better than Bushmills!"

Martin wheeled around in a blur. *Blam! Blam! Blam!* Paul ducked below the altar with unearthly speed the instant Martin fired, like a reverse jack-in-the-box. Then he popped up again just as quickly. *Blam! Blam!* And down. *Blam!* And up and down and up and down until the final sound from Martin's gun was a ghastly, echoing *click.*

"That wasn't very nice of you," Paul said, waving his finger, not the least bit fatigued from his lightning-fast gymnastics. "I'll be expecting a bit more respect from you, now that you know I'm your ever-lovin' da."

PFFFFT! PFFFFT! PFFFFT! Martin hurled his throwing knives in quick succession. Paul caught one in each hand. The third one hit its mark, burying itself to the hilt directly below his clavicle, barely an inch above his left lung. Paul stared at the haft and at Martin. Then he flung back the knives in his bloody hands, followed by the one in his chest, even faster than he caught them. Martin somersaulted toward the altar and the knives whooshed past him, sticking in the wall behind him one after the next, vibrating like tuning forks. He huddled behind the altar next to the books, loading a fresh clip as fast as he could, then leapt on top of the altar, ready to make his final stand.

Funny thing what happened next. Paul was making the very same leap at the very same time. He grabbed Martin in a choking bear hug so brutal that his pistol fell from his grip, dropping harmlessly behind the altar.

Martin wheezed as all the breath was squeezed out of him. Rose fumbled for the Beretta, but even she had to pause in her loyal defense as Paul rolled his eyes backward and began chanting in the deepest, eeriest voice she had ever heard:

"Never alive…and never dead. Never alive…and never *dead!*"

HORROR

It had been a bad day. A bad two days. Now it was getting worse. Rose pointed the Beretta squarely at Paul's broad back. But she couldn't pull the trigger. Something was stopping her. She tried to speak, to call out to Martin, to scream with all her might, but as the word left her mouth it seemed to crystallize in the air. *"Maaaaaaarrrr…"*

Why was everything moving so slowly? Her feet were glued to the floor. Her finger couldn't squeeze the trigger. And now her eyes were slowing too, locked on the blackness of Paul's shirt, unable to move, to turn even a fraction of an inch toward Martin's face, his chin nestled in the crook between Paul's neck and shoulder. What was happening? She thought I shot her with the tetrodoxin, but it wasn't anything like that. I was in the same boat as her, staring at the altar in wonder, not blinking, not moving, not able. Wisps of smoke from Martin's gunshots hung motionless in the air, like gray cotton candy clouds suspended by wires from the ceiling.

"Never alive…and never dead…" Paul chanted again, still moving, though barely. Martin was moving too, immune like Paul to this new source of gravity. He hugged Paul back just as hard, his breath and heartbeat slowing with each crunching squeeeeeeze.

If Rose were able to move, her expression would have changed from bafflement to horror as the sound came out of Martin's throat from a place as deep and hollow and ghastly as Paul's: *"Never alive…and never dead…"*

Rose wondered how her mind could still be working but not her body. She felt like she was in one of those nightmares that keep getting worse, the ones you can't wake up from even though your heart is racing so fast it feels like its going to explode with your very next breath. And what made her horror even more extreme, what made it absolute, was the sound coming from somewhere behind the altar. From the angel? No. From the man she thought was her friend, but was in truth, her mortal enemy.

"Never alive…and never dead…" The Striker droned, over and over.

DUET

Johnny the Saint sat in his cramped cell and watched the ceiling and walls disappear. He spoke the ancient phrase and flung his body to the floor, in the same pose as Loren, but in the opposite direction. He lifted his hands to the blue sky, not the gray stone ceiling above him and joined the choir. *"Never alive...and never dead..."*

Loren tried to resist. Johnny shouted his command again. This time Loren obeyed.

"Never alive...and never dead..." they chanted as one.

Only a handful of souls had been able to accomplish this task unassisted. Johnny was one of them. Loren was another. But now they toiled together, bound forever by their vow. No, not forever. For life. When the crack opened and they jumped inside, no one was there to greet them. Good. Just in time.

Johnny groaned in agony as the Great Wheel turned, grinding his head and bones and body into dust. Loren groaned in pleasure. Together they moved through the swirling mass with all the silent souls...all the angels...always dying, always being born. Together they moved...one person, one being, one mind...to the Axis.

MARTIN REMEMBERS

Martin remembered everything. He knew where they were going and what he could do there and how much it mattered. He remembered the rest of the stories. Not only Paul's…but Kathy's too. He remembered that he was the only one who knew both sides of the tale. He remembered what he could gain with that knowledge.

His eyes opened wider. Not his remaining eye. He was whole again, seeing first with both eyes, then with none…seeing with his entirety, his luminous self.

He saw it coming. The light. The darkness. It was so beautiful. They were past the portal, moving inside…to the place where they had always been…always here, always near, always just beyond reach, beyond sight and sound and breath. Beyond death. Beyond life.

He remembered what would happen next. He welcomed the transformation. His heart wept with joy, and he smiled. It was a real smile this time, unencumbered by all the memories that seemed so trivial in the glory surrounding him. None of that mattered anymore, not the pain, or the sadness, or the fear, or the lost hopes and dreams.

Nothing mattered. Nothing ever mattered. Except this.

When Paul yelled, *"Jump!"* he jumped gladly…off the widest, deepest cliff from which any human could leap. He never landed. There was no other side. And when he exploded into his once and future essence, he smiled again with a shudder of gratitude.

He was home. Home at last. In the grinding, churning heart of the Maelstrom.

DEAL WITH THE DEVIL

Rose was starting to move. Like a freeze frame in a movie theater flickering back to life, cranked slowly forward by the projectionist's rotating grip, she was moving again…her lips closing, ending the scream she seemed to have released hours ago.

"*Maaaaaarrr…*" became "*Martin!*" She was also squeezing the trigger again, aimed at Paul's back. Paul and Martin were motionless, as she had been only seconds earlier. Their crushing embrace looked almost tender in its stillness, like a sculpture of a father-and-son reunion, meeting in the airport after a four-year tour of duty in some faraway war zone. The image flashed in her mind for only a fraction of a second. She knew she would never have an opportunity like this again, with Paul so utterly defenseless.

"If you shoot him now, Martin will die," The Striker rasped loudly.

She turned around, gasping for breath. Good. He was still nailed to the floor.

"Lower the pistol," he whispered, minimizing the movement of his windpipe. Each utterance was slicing him deeper with the sickle blade.

"Fuck you!" Rose shouted, out of her mind with fear. She didn't know where to look, where to point her gun, where to fire. I was still frozen. So were Paul and Martin. Rose stared at them. Oh, God! Martin's gouged out eye was back again, like nothing ever happened! What was going on here? This was so insane! She shook her head to clear it, pointing the pistol at Paul again. At his head.

"If you shoot him, Martin will die," The Striker repeated, clearly exasperated at the effort she was forcing him to make.

"Why should I listen to you? Why should I trust anything you say?"

"Because your father is making me tell you this," he said, the blade carving his neck wider with each syllable. "For some reason he cares about you…and Martin."

"My father is *making* you?" she asked hysterically, the gun shaking in her grip.

"Yes. This is his will, and I must obey," The Striker said with a barely perceptible nod. "While he holds the Wheel, I am required to assist you, but he must hear me as well. That's the price he has to pay for the use of this mouthpiece, for there's something I want to share with you too. I think it will help us pass the time more enjoyably, while we're waiting for those two…to finish."

"Finish *what?*" Rose shouted, her face darting up to the figures on the altar, locked in their terrible embrace. "What are they doing up there?"

"That is not what I wish to discuss. I want to talk about Kathy."

"Kathy? My mother?" Rose shouted, completely baffled.

"Yessssss," he whispered, his voice gurgling now.

Rose couldn't speak. She was barely able to stand.

"Sit down," The Striker said soothingly. "I wouldn't want you to injure anyone with that pistol. Especially me."

Rose slumped at his feet, the conjoined shadow of Paul and Martin casting a pall over her face.

"There, that's better," The Striker sighed, indifferent to any pain the sickle was causing him. "You've been under the impression that your father killed her, yes?" When Rose shook her head, he seemed saddened by the news, then brightened up again. "Well, goody for you. That will save me a few nicks from this razor. Did he, by any chance, reveal the actual perpetrator of that horrendous crime?"

Rose shook her head again.

"Care to venture a guess?" The Striker asked, a sneer curving his lips.

Rose suddenly became more animated. So was her pistol. She pressed it above the bolt in his temple, shouting, "If he knew you killed her, why didn't he tell me?"

"He knew you'd attempt to exact your revenge, just as you're contemplating now. And then, sweet darling, all your father's carefully laid plans would lie in ruins."

"Plans?" she cried, unaware she was already squeezing the trigger. "*What plans?*"

"Lower the gun," he warned her, "or you'll destroy everything you've ever loved in this world." Her arm collapsed into her lap like a strand of linguini.

"Good," The Striker croaked. "We don't have enough time to fill in all those horrid blanks from your childhood…poor Johnny would be drowned in the tide he's holding back. And as much as that would delight me, my vow prevents me from abetting that outcome."

"Your vow?" Rose asked, unsure what to do with her shaking hands.

"Your father and I have an arrangement. He doesn't prevent me from fulfilling certain goals I have, and I assist when his only child is in mortal danger. A much more difficult task, I admit, since you were foolish enough to surrender the key. My key."

Rose clutched her naked neck. "You're lying! Why would he make a deal with you after you killed my mom?"

"Because she isn't dead," The Striker said, gasping with delight. "Not all the way."

"*What are you saying?*" Rose cried, completely frantic.

"She's in heeeeeeere…" The Striker hissed. "Inside meeeeeeee."

Rose almost puked. The Striker giggled as her breaths came in short, lurching gasps, the bile rising into her throat, her stomach lurching with horror. "Yessssss…that's good," he wheezed. "Feel my hate! Choke on it! Like I choked on Kathy's soul when I ate it!"

"*You crazy fucking shithead!*" Rose spat, pointing the pistol at his face.

"Oh my, such an ill-mannered young lady! I must say that your mother is appalled, simply *appalled* at your use of such foul language in her presence."

"Her presence…" Rose echoed, her skin crawling with goose bumps.

"Yessssssss…she's watching right now, listening to every word we share, but alas, not from some lofty perch in heaven, nestled on a soft pink cloud. She's watching through these stapled eyes, listening with these ears. Come a little closer, dear. Maybe you can hear her too. I'd be surprised if you couldn't…considering how loudly she's screaming."

Rose crept closer and pushed the sickle farther into his throat.

"No? Don't even want to try?" The Striker spat, delirious with pleasure in spite of the blade chewing at his neck. "Tsk. What a pity. It would be like a family reunion! Johnny could tell you himself why he never avenged poor mummy. Because he's still trying to save her! He protects me for the same reason you shall, in the desperate hope of rescuing her on some distant day, bringing her home to his own aching heart, or in failing, share a bed with her inside me. And here's another amusing twist: There are only two people that can help him achieve his fervent prayer, and they're both here in this room. But neither can aid you while the Master lives. So if you care about saving poor Kathy, get your hand off this blade and point your gun at Paul's head, but don't pull the trigger until I say. I want him dead even more than you or Johnny, so you can trust me just this once."

Rose let go of the blade and raised the gun to Paul's head, her hand quivering with fear and hatred.

"Yessssss…that's good. I think we understand one another. Now take a deep, slow breath, steady your hand and make sure your aim is true. When I give you the word, squeeze the trigger and get ready for the ride of your life…or death. Johnny is releasing the Wheel now and the Guardian will awaken."

REUNION

"Come Ceallach," the angel said. The Princess and the Great Mother were the first to go. Then he and the Master passed through the Curtain of Dreams.

"It's beautiful," he said to the Master as they gazed upon the golden light of the Axis. He felt so much younger than his seventeen years, almost like the boy who sat on his father's lap the first time he told him the story. Róisín and Morgana were waiting for them at the Axis, Róisín holding the angel's hand as they hovered above the Great Wheel.

"Yes, it is beautiful," said his father, having witnessed the glory many times before.

"Come," the angel said again.

"Come Da," Ceallach said eagerly, pulling his father's hand, smiling as the princess beckoned him.

The Master let go of his hand. "I cannot."

"But you said I would take this voyage with you, you said we would…"

"What was whole must be joined again," he said, looking beyond him to the Great Mother. "It is your time now. The time of the *Becoming*."

"What's going to happen to me?" he asked, looking not to the angel or his beloved princess, but to his father and Master who had spoke to him of this wondrous place so often.

"I do not know," his father said, his eyes full of longing.

"Where will the angel take us?"

"I do not know. This—your journey—has never been made."

"Will I still be…me?"

"You will be changed."

"What will happen to you? Where will you go?"

"I will return."

"But all our enemies were in pursuit! They will surely be waiting!"

"My fate rests with the *Nous*. It is the will of the *Nous* that I remain behind…and that you become one with her and the angel."

"Come," said the angel more urgently. "It is time."

"Will I see you again?" he asked, resisting the pull of the angel.

"Not in this way. Not with these memories."

"Da! Don't leave me!" he cried out, his heart breaking.

"I will never leave you, son. I will always live inside you."

"But you said we couldn't die! You said we'd never die!"

"We cannot truly die. We…change."

"If I see you again, will I remember who you are?"

"You won't care. You will be love…all love. Go with her…you'll be so wonderful. *You are…so wonderful!*"

"I don't want to lose you!"

"Trust the angel. Don't resist," his father said, his voice choked with emotion. Then the Wheel suddenly began turning again, the screaming winds of the Maelstrom almost deafening.

"Da! Don't leave me! I'm scared!" Ceallach cried out, struggling to reach his father's side, but the pull of the Axis grew in direct proportion to the grinding force of the Maelstrom and soon he found himself clutching the angel as his father waved farewell, still resisting the terrible vortex.

"I will always love you," his father said as his body began to disintegrate.

"Daaaaaa!" Ceallach screamed.

But the Maelstrom had blown him into dust.

Ceallach cried out in anguish. The angel held him as he wept. Róisín wrapped her arms around him and kissed the top of his head. They clung to each other and their hearts began to glow like the angel's chest as he cradled them in his giant arms.

"We must go now," said the angel without speaking, and they began to descend into the Axis. Their hearts ached with longing as they looked into each other's eyes. Then the same terrifying thought entered both their minds. They didn't have to speak it. They were already joining with the angel and knew each other's mind the same as their own.

"We will be lost as well! We will cease to exist to each other! Only one being will be born in the angel! This new thing will leave us both behind, as it abandoned the Master!"

"No! I love you! I won't let you go!" Róisín cried, her strong, willful soul parting from Ceallach and the angel. He echoed her cry, their hearts blazing with love.

Suddenly, Ceallach was assaulted by the image of his father being chained to the altar by Tormac. Ceallach shouted to the angel, "We have to help him! They'll kill him!"

"It is too late. Our merging has already begun. You cannot go back. You cannot live in that world again until we become whole."

"No!" Ceallach shouted, tearing himself free of the angel. Then clutching the princess close to his heart, they flew headlong into the merciless jaws of the Maelstrom.

"COME BACK!"

He turned to look. It wasn't the angel calling after him. The angel had disappeared along with Róisín and everything else he had seen beyond the curtain of dreams. What was this place? Who had called him?

"I thought I lost you!" the voice shouted from far away. It was Da, his arms extended.

"Da!" he cried, rushing to his father's side, gripping him in a crushing embrace. When he pulled back to look upon his beloved father, he was filled with terror.

"You're not Da!"

"Yes, it's me!" Paul cried. "I've missed you so much!"

"No, you killed me. You want to kill me again."

"No, *they* killed you! I tried to save you! Don't you remember?"

"You took everything from me!"

"No, Ceallach. I let you go. To the angel. To the girl! She betrayed you!"

"I'm not Ceallach."

Paul looked at his son's crying face and saw Martin looking back. Then he began changing...to another, younger boy, then another and another until...

The boy was so beautiful. So innocent. So desecrated.

His name was Paul.

"Da, don't take me…please!" his young self pleaded, as he had long ago.

"I must," the old man replied, his chest heaving in pain. "Don't you see? We are so close to the end!"

"Da…I'm scared, please let me go!" he cried out, begging on his knees now, his face soaked with tears.

"Don't be afraid," Paul said, kneeling down, holding his own small wet face in his big hands, weeping with him. "You'll still be here, inside me."

"No, I won't! I'll be gone!" the boy cried, his face morphing into the son of Ceallach, then his son after that, and on and on until it finally came to rest in the anguished face of Martin, in the wheat field again.

"You killed all of them!" little Martin screamed. "They wanted to live, just like you!"

"No! It's that girl! She's got you all mixed up!" Paul shouted at the boy.

But the boy was now a grown man. "It doesn't have to be like this," Martin said calmly, standing up in his perfect adult body, holding Paul's hand, helping him rise.

"Come Da," Martin said, pulling Paul's hand toward the swirling glow of the Axis.

"No! We will Turn in the Maelstrom!" Paul commanded, pulling Martin's hand with all his strength, his tear-streaked face hot with rage.

Martin shook his head and pointed to the Axis, effortlessly freeing his hand from Paul's viselike grip. Together they stared into the vortex as The Great Wheel turned. Something was rising from the molten, twisting core, taking shape in front of them, gaining form and substance, its great wings even more majestic than the Axis.

The light streaming from the angel's chest was blinding in its brightness, but Martin could see. He reached up and touched the angel's hand. Then they were floating together above the Great Wheel.

"The story has a purpose," the angel said as the winds of the Maelstrom accelerated, roaring faster and faster…swirling, grinding. "We're doing something together…something that will change…"

"Everything?" Martin asked hopefully, a boy again.

"No…" the angel said. "One thing." The voice was different now. Lighter. Softer.

Martin looked into the eyes of that beautiful creature and its face began changing, first to Norine, who rubbed his hand on her soft, soft cheek, then to Johnny, smiling that ten-thousand-megawatt smile, and finally to Rose. It was Rose who finished the angel's thought, Rose who whispered in his ear as the winds began tearing him apart again, the swirl of his atoms blending with the fiery essence of the angel. When he finally heard the other words he had no ears to hear them with, and the words, like all words, barely mattered. Yet he knew what they meant, what the angel meant, what he had always wanted for him and Rose.

Suddenly a black cloud swarmed around them like a billion starving locusts, and Paul's voice melded with the angel, repeating the words as he began to take shape, wrapping his beefy arms around Martin's chest, squeezing him harder and harder, bringing him back, back to finish it. The last thing Martin heard before he opened his eyes was Paul and the angel saying the same thing at once, with different intents, each as demanding as the other:

"We're doing something together…something that will change…"

The ending.

QUEEN TO KING'S KNIGHT

"Gaaaaaaahhh!" Martin sucked in a massive lungful of air and released his grip around Paul's back. His eyes turned immediately to Rose. She was standing still as a statue, her eyes unblinking, her hand thrust out with the Beretta pointing at Paul's head. It was then he realized that they hadn't come all the way back yet. They were housed in their bodies, able to breathe and move, but there was still an atom's breadth of discontinuity between the two dimensions they had bridged. Rose and the universe she occupied were here, as they had always been, yet still so far away. They would remain like that until Paul released his grip.

He wouldn't let go. "You have betrayed us," he said from beneath the dead mask.

"No, I saved us," Martin said, his voice firm, yet choked with passion. "I saved you."

"Who are you?" Paul demanded.

"I am the Guardian," Martin said.

"And the vessel!" Paul shouted, spittle covering Martin's face.

"And the vessel," Martin reluctantly agreed.

"What is your task?" he asked, grinding out each word.

"I am the Guardian," Martin repeated softly.

"Finish it!" Paul shouted, his face beet red as they stood chest to chest on the altar. "Speak your vow! State your sworn duty!"

Martin looked at Rose's frozen face over Paul's wide shoulder, then turned away. Looking into the eyes of his Master, he knew he had to voice the entire phrase, the promise he sealed in blood so many years ago, in the stiff, yellowed pages of the Book. "I am the Guardian and Vessel of my Master," he whispered. "And my task is to serve the *Becoming*."

Paul dropped his hands to his sides. We all came alive.

"Now!" The Striker shouted, his nailed-wide eyes suddenly as animated as his lips.

Rose pulled the trigger. Didn't squeeze it. *BANG!* It tore off a piece of Paul's ear. Martin grabbed Paul's shoulders and rolled off the other side of the altar. Paul's back hit the floor with a crushing thud, Martin landing right on top of him. Rose gasped in terror, recoiling more from the sight of Martin's intervention than from the gun blast.

What was he *doing*? Was he protecting Paul…from *her*?

"Move!" The Striker shouted at Rose. "Get over there! Shoot him in the head!"

Rose nodded, crawling toward the altar, trying to shield herself from view, her legs wobbling like Jell-o. She couldn't see Martin and Paul around the corner, but I could. Martin was struggling with every ounce of his strength to keep Paul pinned to the floor.

"You are the Guardian!" Paul bellowed at Martin.

Martin lifted his hand from Paul's wrist with lightning speed, then punched him so hard in the face that the back of his head actually bounced on the floor.

"Honor your vow!" Paul spat, spraying Martin's face with the blood from his torn lips.

Martin, never much of a talker, was feeling even less chatty now. I knew what he was thinking, nonetheless, as did Paul. He had sworn to protect his Master's life, but there was nothing in his vow to prevent him from kicking his ass and defending Rose just as vigorously. Which is exactly what he did. His fist rocketed into Paul's face again. Into his eye. Blood spurted out like a geyser. Hammurabi would have been proud. Unfortunately, Martin had to lift his hand from Paul's wrist again to do it. Exploded eyeball or not, Paul was ready this time. He landed an uppercut squarely on Martin's bristly chin and his head reeled backward.

"Get over there and shoot him!" The Striker howled at Rose, his words jabbing her rump like a cattle prod. "What are you waiting for?"

If Rose weren't blocking his view, he wouldn't have asked. She was waiting for me. I had Martin's pistol in my hand, the one with the fresh clip of live ammo. It was pointed at her mascara-streaked face. By the time she raised her gun and aimed at me, it would be too late. One slow squeeze and it would all be over. Her casual betrayals. Her cruel rejections. All over in the flash of an instant.

"Kill her!" Paul barked at me, trying to push Martin off. "Do your duty!"

I stared into her red, raging eyes. She raised the Berretta. "Drop that gun or I swear to God I'll shoot you!"

"Kill her *now!*" Paul shouted at me again, clutching Martin's throat, hammering another blow into his ribcage.

"Give her the key!" Martin croaked, gasping for breath, riding Paul's bucking body like a rodeo champ, wailing another punch into his cheekbone, shattering it in four places.

"Pull the trigger!" Paul shouted savagely, pushing harder against Martin, who had amazingly managed to pin down Paul's wrists again.

I didn't fire. And I didn't drop the gun. I aimed it at Paul. Rose gasped with relief and turned in the same direction, creeping forward.

"You fool! She must die at your hands! *Today!"*

I kept the pistol pointed at Paul. Rose poked her face around the corner of the altar. Martin was shielding Paul with his body.

"I can't let you kill him," he gasped, trying to keep Paul pinned down while blocking Rose's line of fire. And mine.

Rose felt her chest heave with blind panic, but she found the courage to crawl even closer, looking for a clear shot at Paul's head. She could barely catch a glimpse of his torn ear, let alone his grin concealed behind the bristles of Martin's crew cut.

"Don't make me hurt you. Take the Book. Run as fast as you can," Martin grunted over his shoulder, nearly exhausted by his effort to keep Paul restrained.

"Yeah, make a run for it, bitch! Let's see how far you get!" Paul seethed.

Rose pursed her lips in a silent *Please!* begging for Martin's help.

He didn't respond with a wince of helplessness. "Turn around," his lips mimed. She turned and her eyes narrowed. Then softened. I was holding the gun in one hand, the key chain gripped in the other.

I opened my fist and held it out to her. She moved cautiously toward me, but Paul's booming voice stopped her cold.

"*Kill her!*" he commanded me, feeling Martin's strength begin to ebb as quickly as his own was mounting. "*Do it now!*"

I looked at my hands. Two choices. Life and death. Love and hate.

"Killing her is your only path to glory!" Paul railed, thrusting Martin's chest upward. "This is your destiny! You can never defeat me! *Never!*"

"He's right," Loren hissed, "Throw me the key and we'll even the odds."

I hadn't been watching him. No one had. That had been a mistake. He was yanking his hand off the widely flanged nail, slowly but efficiently. His muscles, bones and tendons gaped open like ragged labia, without a trace of any reaction. Except a smile for me.

"Kill her and kill the serpent!" Paul yelled, apoplectic. "Kill them *now!*"

"I'm aghast at your lack of command in this situation," Loren taunted Paul, his first hand free and prying the sickle from his neck. He threw it at the altar, imbedding it so deeply that only half the blade remained exposed.

"Ah, that's better," he sighed, pulling the nails from his forehead and eyelids, oblivious to the gaping wound in his throat. The blade had sliced his trachea. Bubbles of blood hissed out with every breath. He ignored them completely and began a much more vigorous attempt at freeing his other hand, ridiculing Paul all the while. "I cannot recall a time in all the annals where you've bred such traitorous curs for heirs…and wielded so little authority over them. Your time has passed, ancient one. I should think you'd be dying of shame now, instead of waiting for a twit barely out of her teens to conclude this travesty."

Paul exploded. He tossed Martin on the altar like a sack of flour, climbed on top of him and whisked the ice pick from Martin's vest with the silky ease of a riverboat gambler dealing from the bottom of the deck. He smiled. Then he poised the gleaming tip an eighth of an inch above Martin's miraculously restored eyeball. Yeeesh.

"You're right, Ole Snake Eyes! These boys are a great disappointment to me. But you'll never live to watch me spank them!"

He turned on Rose, "Ahoy there Queeny! Care to pull the trigger? No, I thought not. Love sweet love."

"He's bluffing!" Loren shouted, oblivious to the pain as he frantically tried to yank his other hand free. "He won't kill Martin. He needs him!"

"I've got a million more like him in this big pouch between me legs. And if I can't mix up a better batch than the one that made these two pitiful mooks, I've got a fresh new recipe waiting in the fridge! Time is on my side, Loren, as it always was and always will be!"

"Shoot him!" The Striker shouted at Rose. "He can't kill you!"

"Oh Loren, what a poor sport you are! Yet another violation of the rules. But she will never take the risk of losing her beloved, will you, Queen Rose of the Cross?" Paul laughed, slowly lowering the ice pick close enough to prod Martin's cornea. "Oh my, you still don't have a clue what we're gabbing about, do you, your lowness?"

Rose turned her head from Martin to me. From Loren to Paul. No one said anything. She felt like Carrie at the prom, everyone in on the hideous joke. Everyone but her.

She had been queen of her matriarchal line since she her mother died. But no one, not even her father, the regent, had told her, out of fear she would unwittingly expose herself to one of the Kellys.

"Don't listen to him!" Loren shouted at Rose, his other hand almost free. "Shoot him while you still can!"

Rose stared at Martin. His head wasn't moving, but he was nodding. She could see it. Feel it. Hear it. "Do it," he was saying. "Kill him. Let me go."

"She can't. She loves you far too much, dear boy. We're running a little behind schedule now, so here's what you'll do, Queeny, and do quickly: I want you to take that Beretta and point it at Loren's head. Then I want you to pull the trigger. Now I reckon you're a bit shy about ending his long, cursed life, considering that he's toting around such precious cargo. But if you don't do exactly what I've said by the time I count to three, you can watch me gouge out this lovely new eyeball that I worked so hard to make, not for him, mind you, but for me…and then you can retch in horror as

I push a little deeper and blow out your boyfriend's brains with the CO_2 cartridge he so cleverly concealed in this ice pick."

Rose and Martin stared helplessly at each other.

The Striker desperately tugged at his nailed, bleeding hand.

Rose looked at The Striker and saw her mother's face.

Time seemed to freeze all over again as Paul began to count: "One…"

Rose stared at Paul, her hands shaking so much she almost dropped the pistol.

Paul grinned back at her, winking his blood-burst eye, pressing the ice pick down against Martin's eyeball, his thumb poised over the button at the base of the handle.

"Last chance m'lady…" he said softly. "Two…"

Rose turned her gun on The Striker, then whipped the barrel back to Paul so quickly all I saw was blur.

Paul could see it perfectly. And with a final, fatal shrug, he whispered, "three…"

CHECKMATE

"LEAVE MARTIN ALONE!" I yelled so loudly the windows almost shattered.

Paul paused. To laugh. *BANG!* Rose shot him in the face, right below his broken cheekbone. It scraped along the bottom of his skull, blowing a chunk of flesh and hair from the back of his head. Martin kicked against his chest with both feet, sending him halfway across the room. *Bang! Bang!* Rose followed with two more shots. The first one missed, slamming into the bookshelf behind him. The second one got him in the gut.

Paul gripped his stomach with a wince. Rose took aim again, more carefully this time, right at Paul's forehead. Martin leapt from the altar and knocked the pistol out of her hand. *Whap!* Rose almost slapped him back, but Martin had already scooped up the Beretta and was heading my way.

"Give me the key!" he shouted, holding out his hand.

"Protection?" I asked, clenching it tighter, negotiating my terms of surrender.

"Protection," he replied.

With those three grunted syllables I relinquished the prize I'd schemed so hard to acquire. Martin took it from me at the same time Paul was struggling to his feet. He ran to Rose, her lip quivering with rage as he placed the chain around her neck.

"NO!" Paul shouted, staggering toward them.

I looked at Paul and shrugged. Martin put his arm around Rose. Paul looked at both of us, shaking his head. For once he had nothing to say.

I stared at him in awe. Sometimes it's really hard to kill someone. Especially Paul Kelly. Hard, but not impossible. He was semi-human, after all. And he was a fucking mess. One ruined eye. Bullet holes in his face and gut. Knife wound in his chest. Six busted ribs and a fractured collarbone, courtesy of Loren.

"You're really showing your age, King Cole," Loren sneered, wholly delighted at the sight of Paul's teetering legs. His other hand was free now. He pulled against the nails still binding his feet. When they wouldn't budge, he tried reaching for the sickle he had hurled into the wood of the altar. Not too smart, that move. He stretched his spindly arms as far as he could—his long, bony fingers only inches away. But he couldn't reach it.

Paul shook his head again, smiling now, but silent. Broken, but still unbowed. On his last legs, but still standing. Unfortunately, those legs were dragging themselves over to the lectern. To the Book. When he touched it, I knew what would happen.

"*NO!*" I shouted, looking at Martin, expecting him to race over and stop him. He didn't move. That fucking vow again. I gulped. Aimed at Paul's chest. Felt the hate in him. The hate in me. *POW!* Martin shot the pistol out of my hand like Clint Eastwood.

Loren saw what happened and his grin disappeared. Paul was only a few feet away from the Book. Loren actually ripped both his feet off the nails with a sickening sucking sound. He limped madly on his shredded feet, reaching for the pistol. He grabbed it and...

Martin shot him in the back with his trusty Beretta, barely glancing away from Paul while he pulled the trigger. It was a nice shot. Nothing went wrong. No jamming. No backfire. No collapsing floor. Just one clean bullet hole right in the spinal cord. Loren was paralyzed. This time, it wouldn't wear off.

"No!" Rose shouted, assuming he was dead.

Martin knew better. "He'll live," he said tersely, his eyes locked on Paul. Paul grinned and kept walking. Martin nudged Rose in the ribs. He couldn't give her a weapon, couldn't tell her what to do, but somehow she knew. She ran to the Book and grabbed it at the same instant Paul was reaching out for it. She hugged it like a lover. Paul yanked it from her arms. Held it to his chest. But nothing happened. Blood still oozed from his face, chest and belly.

"*YOU BITCH!*" he screamed, dropping the Book. "*WHAT HAVE YOU DONE?*"

Rose looked confused. So was I. Had all the things I'd seen and felt, the Book healing Michael's hands and feet, the wound of my own severed throat closing without a scar…had it all been another hallucination? A never-ending dream?

Paul howled with rage, charging at Martin with one last surge of strength, punching him so hard in the jaw that his legs collapsed and his head smacked the floor. Paul picked up Rose and thumped her on the altar. He climbed on top of her and picked up the mallet and one of the spikes. She screamed louder than any person I'd ever heard.

Paul placed the spike against her breastbone and raised the mallet high over his head. "You know, I've always been curious about that amulet," he coughed, spraying her face with a mist of blood and spittle. "Just like I've always wondered what would happen if I broke my sacred vow."

He was about to find out. Paul saw the blue flash of steel from the corner of his working eye. The sickle was swinging toward his neck with blinding speed. No time to move. No time to yell, or laugh. No time for any more speeches. The blade struck his throat like a scythe in a wheat field, cutting through veins and muscles and bone as easily as those swaying stalks of golden grain behind the house where he buried Momma's body.

SWISSSSSSSSSH…THUCK!

And it was over. All the pain. All the pain. All the pain.

Paul's working eye was blinking when his head tumbled into Rose's lap. He could clearly see his assailant. I could tell the sight came as quite a shock.

Martin. The Guardian. He had slain the Great King despite his blood vow. But the world kept turning. And the Book was just a quiet leather slab on the floor.

Martin dropped the blade. He ran to Rose, his heart pounding with unspeakable love. And in that instant I knew how he succeeded. Some bonds are even stronger than blood.

Last Words

Rose screamed like a banshee, her arms flailing like someone dropped a bucket of centipedes on her naked chest. Or a severed head. She dropped it on the altar with a wet *thump*. Martin ran over and scooped her up in his big, manly arms. Oh, well. To the victor go the spoils. Soon I'd have my trophy. Too bad it wouldn't fit in my suitcase.

I rushed to the altar right on Martin's heels, leaping on top of the undulating blood-spattered markings like I had springs in my legs. I kicked the headless body to the floor, grabbed Paul's head by the hair and held it in front of my face.

His head was still alive, as I had hoped it would be. Time for one last question. "How does it feel?" I hissed. "How does it feel to *die?*"

His lips bubbled with blood, curling into a smile. His mouth opened. I didn't expect to hear anything. For any sounds to come out. I wasn't prepared for that and the shock was so jarring I almost let go of his hair, dropping his head to the floor. Too bad I didn't.

"It feels wonderful," he gasped through the red bubbles. "It gets better every time."

I stared at his gaping mouth in horror. It closed into a smile. I turned my head away, but then I felt a compulsion I couldn't resist, pulling my face back for one last look.

I know I shouldn't have done it, but I couldn't help myself. I had to savor my victory, to watch that final flicker of life fade away as I claimed Mother's vengeance. I looked into the eye Martin spared in his pummeling. The lids were swollen and purple with bruises, but the pupil was clear and deep and black. "Good-bye, Father."

He tried to croak out a reply, but his facial muscles sagged and his smile disappeared. I looked into his eye with more sadness than I'd felt since Mother died. My sadness turned to rage, then longing as I looked deeper and deeper. I looked. Then I went inside.

THE MAELSTROM

I was falling. Falling. Falling. The blackness behind his eye pulling me into the abyss. I gasped for air, my lungs on fire, my blood boiling.

There it was. Spinning like a galaxy, the vortex consuming all light and darkness. The Maelstrom, the Host of Angels, *Ain Soph Aur*. It was here, only an arm's length away, just as he always said it would be.

We arrived all at once. No curtain, no crack, no altar, no chanting, no Book. He didn't need any of that. We didn't need any of that. Not the two of us. The one of us.

I could hear Martin and Rose talking about the strange sight of me holding his head by the hair, my mouth hanging open, no sound coming out. No movement. They seemed so near. So here. So far away.

I fought against him with all my strength, pushing back his mind like I had so many times before. I heard Martin's voice. Mother's. I saw the angel's perfect smile.

Push, push...*pussssshhsh!* Almost there...almost back...almost free.

The winds of the Maelstrom blasted my flesh apart and I...we...were flying at an unimaginable speed, going faster and faster and faster, spinning, swirling, down, down, down.

Or was it up? In? Out? No. No words. I felt another surge of his blinding hatred as the Wheel turned and the Axis yawned open.

I would have taken one last breath if I still had lungs, closed my eyes if I had lids. But there was nothing left of me in this or any universe to filter my gaze from the wondrous spectacle of God's waiting mouth, from the furnace of creation.

THE KING IS DEAD! LONG LIVE THE KING!

I was back! *Back!* I felt like Scrooge on Christmas morning. It seemed like I'd been gone for years...for eons...and I couldn't find my way back. Then *wham!* I fell to the floor, right on top of Paul's lifeless body. My head where his used to be. I looked up. Martin was standing above me. He was holding Paul's head. He must have pulled it away from me—broken the connection. I stared at the head in his hand and gasped with another surge of panic. But when I looked at Paul's battered face, when I saw his empty eyes, I knew that it was over. He was dead. *Dead!* We did it. We did it! We killed him. Together. Okay, it was Martin mostly, but still, I played my role.

Martin put the head on Paul's lifeless chest and offered me his hand. I grasped it gladly. As he pulled me up, I heard Mother's voice, "Save Martin and you'll save yourself."

I smiled. Martin and Rose were staring at me strangely. Why not? It had been a very strange day. I didn't pay much attention to them, to be honest. There was still so much more work to be done. Some part of me wanted to stop and think about what I had seen when I was...away...but another stronger part stopped me and laughed and laughed and laughed.

I was back! I felt so happy and fearless and *big!* I rubbed my hands together and looked around the room at the shelves and shelves of books. They were mine now. Mine! When it finally sank in that he was really gone, I thought of my favorite line from an old Mel Brooks movie.

He was right! *It's good to be the King!*

Farewell

"Are you sure he's alive?" Rose asked from the doorway as Martin checked The Striker's pulse.

"Uh-huh," Martin nodded, straightening up.

"What are you doing?" I asked anxiously, all my excitement snuffed out as I watched Martin turn toward Rose.

"Leaving," he said, not looking in my direction. Rose was waving impatiently for Martin to get moving, her robe spattered in blood, clutching the key (my key!) nervously.

"You can't leave," I said desperately, following him around like a...well, like a kid brother...while he packed his bags for summer camp. "The cops, Paul's soldiers, they'll be here any second. We need to get our story straight."

"No one will come until the sun sets. You should know that."

"Are you kidding? After all this noise? There's no way to keep a lid on this. We have to do something!"

"No one heard a thing," Martin said, walking to Rose. "You should know that too."

"What the hell are you talking about?" I asked, totally dumbfounded.

He shook his head and opened the door. "See?" he asked, pointing to the hallway.

My mouth dropped open. I didn't know what I was expecting...a SWAT team, hostage negotiators, knights in shining armor...but the hallway was completely empty. Quiet as a tomb. "What's going on?"

"Save your questions for him," Martin said, nudging his chin toward the Striker's body. "We're leaving."

"You can't go. We're not finished here!" I yelled, sounding a lot like *him*

"Yes, we are," Martin said, frowning at me.

"Please...just wait a minute," I pleaded, pulling him away from the door, pointing to the shelves of books and scrolls. "We need to learn what's in here."

461

"*We?*" Martin said with a frown. Obviously the word had never been part of his vocabulary.

"There's something I have to tell you," I said conspiratorially, not quite sure why I cared so much where he went, but feeling to the marrow of my bones that if Martin didn't stay with me, didn't keep an eye on me…that something terrible was going to happen. "There are more of them. More of Paul's…friends. They might be coming after us."

"*Us?*" he said, squinting at me like the gunslinger he was.

I took a deep breath, ready to explain it again, using single syllable words if I had to. I opened my mouth to speak, when Martin raised his hand to stop me.

"I don't need those books and I don't need you. I know all about the Clans. The only reason I'm not killing you is because Norine is inside you."

"She's inside you too," I said, wanting to point out again that we were *full* brothers.

"You don't understand. And I don't have time to explain it. We're leaving. You'll have to find your own way now…in or out of this."

I nodded, wondering who I was speaking to. He sounded so different. So mature.

Martin turned toward the door. "Don't look for us. If I want you, I'll find you. By this time tomorrow, we won't exist."

"What do you mean?" I asked, feeling panicky again.

"Try and find me in any record database in the world. In a few days, she won't exist either. If anyone ever asks, she died today, just like Paul wanted. Right?"

I nodded and Martin grabbed the doorknob, placing his other arm behind Rose's back. She hadn't said a word since she touched the Book, but she gave me that look one more time before turning away. Oh, well. You can't control what people think. Most of the time.

"What am I supposed to do about him?" I asked, pointing at The Striker's stiff body. There was hardly any blood beneath his long, limp body. Even the bullet hole looked smaller.

"Use him. But don't make any promises you aren't prepared to keep."

They were almost out the door when I called out to him again, even more desperately than before. "What about the Book? Don't you even care?"

"It's yours. It was always yours. The only thing I can tell you is…it doesn't have to be the way it's been for so long. You have a choice. You've always had a choice."

"I don't understand what you're saying."

"I know. But you will."

"Please stay. Help me."

He smiled at me. With kindness? But he didn't say a word.

"When will I see you again? Where are you going?"

"Home," he said simply, ignoring the first part of my question.

I felt a searing jolt of trepidation. "Don't go back there. It's dangerous."

"I know. It always is."

Key to the Kingdom

Just so you know, lifting a heavy dead body onto an altar is not an enjoyable experience. Nailing it down with railroad spikes is a little more fun. I didn't have to do that, but it was a real stress-buster. Opening the blood-soaked shirt of his headless corpse was a mixed bag…gross, but interesting. I stared at the scars on Paul's chest. Their resemblance to my implants was even more pronounced than I'd remembered. Weird. I opened my shirt to compare them and got a shock that almost knocked me off my feet. My implants were gone!

Not only were they gone, there were no scars, no marks, not even a blemish. It was like they never existed. I ripped the shirt from my back and got another jolt. My tattoos had disappeared too! Part of me was freaking out, wanting to find a mirror so I could see my entire back, but another part snorted with laughter, looking down at my chest, flexing muscles I never had before. *Not bad, not bad.* I didn't question my miraculous transformation. I was much more excited to move on to the main event.

I stared at the key. When I put it on, I half-expected a chorus of Halleluiahs coming from the angel. I looked up anyway. Then down at Loren. His arms and legs were splayed in all directions, his face and chest pressed against the floor. I could see his back rise and fall with shallow breaths. I guess he wasn't conscious. Not that I cared. I smiled and looked at Paul's body again. Something still needed to be done. I looked back at the angel. The rays on his chest surrounded a round casing I'd never seen before. A tabernacle.

Just so you know, opening Paul's ribcage with a hammer and chisel was not an enjoyable experience. But cutting out his heart, wrapping it in the flayed skin from his chest, stepping on Loren's spine, right on the bullet hole, and stretching way up high to put that fat chunk of muscle inside that lovely, gilded tabernacle…well, that part wasn't too bad.

CLEAN-UP CREW

I set the Book gently on the lectern, rubbing the worn surface with the palms of my hands. The key dangling from my neck felt like it was vibrating with eagerness, aching, almost demanding to be used. "Not yet," I said with a chuckle, not sure how or why I suddenly had this vast reserve of patience. *All in due time, all in due time,* I thought, trying out a bit of Paul's lilt to see how it sounded. Not bad. Not bad at all.

I stripped off my clothes and unashamedly stood in front of the window, looking out into the park, so confident and relaxed, savoring the last golden glow on the treetops. The sun had peeked out again, just in time. *Good. Good Friday. Very good, indeed.* I waited for the light to fade, then went into the bathroom and took a long, hot shower. It felt like I hadn't bathed in months. I dried off with a big, fluffy towel and put on a suit I found in the closet, the same one Paul had worn the first time I met him here. I was surprised by how well it fit. Even the shoes. He always seemed so much bigger. I guess it's a matter of perspective.

I was rubbing my hands on the soft lapels when the doorbell rang. It was Ryan. Since I was expecting a contingent of angry cops, his ruddy face came as a welcome relief. I knew why he was dropping by. Paul must have told him that he'd be safely ensconced in Martin's thoroughbred body by now and his corpse would need some attention.

He must have been shocked to see me opening the door instead of Martin, but he did a good job of disguising it. When he saw Paul's headless, heartless body nailed to the altar, he nodded his head somberly, but I saw a smile creep into his face when he thought I wasn't looking. Maybe that's not so strange either. Can you imagine working for Paul?

He didn't speak. Neither did I. I could have explained the circumstances. I could have told him the long, stiff man on the floor was responsible. I could have said how important it was to keep all this out of the papers…but I kept my mouth shut. So did he. Instead, he just nodded again and pulled out a piece of paper. The death certificate. It was already filled out, complete with some doctor's signature. Cause of death: brain aneurysm. Cute. Finally, he said, "Would you mind the intrusion if our people retrieved his body immediately?"

"What about the police?" I asked, astonished at his offhand demeanor.

"Since he died of natural causes, I don't think that will be problem," he replied, completely straight-faced. "May I have your permission to proceed?"

I looked at Paul's decapitated corpse, his gaping chest cavity. *Natural causes?* Still, I wasn't about to argue. The sooner the evidence disappeared, the better. "Be my guest."

"Very good. They'll do a thorough job cleaning up after themselves."

Less than ten seconds later, four men in red-and-black jumpsuits barreled through the doorway with a hospital stretcher. I followed them into the library and watched them slip a black plastic body bag filled with ice under Paul's bulk and place him gently inside. Then they added the head, fitting it neatly into place.

They were starting to zip up the bag when I stopped them. I asked everyone to leave the room. They shuffled out like cockroaches as I leaned over his head. It was a mess. I dragged my new key out from under my shirt. I felt it in my fingers. It seemed so small. Almost weightless. But it was mine now. Like everything else. I dangled it in front of Paul's lifeless face, grinning from ear to ear. For once, he didn't grin back. I tucked the key under my shirt, called in the jumpsuit crew and told them to take him away. They zipped up the bag and set it almost reverently on the gurney. Two of them pushed it out of the room, while the others began scrubbing down the altar. Ryan pointed to Loren's body on the floor and asked, "May we take care of that as well?"

"Can you make a stop at the nearest police precinct?"

"No need. We've been keeping the officers in the lobby."

"Perfect," I said with a tired but happy sigh, not surprised in the least by his comment. I rubbed my hands together and looked down at The Striker. "But give us a few minutes alone before you take out the garbage."

I heard The Striker groan as soon as I closed the door on Ryan. I could tell from the way he was dragging his legs that he was indeed paralyzed, but only from the waist down. He pulled himself up into a sitting position and rested with his back against the cross. After he arranged his useless extremities in a cross-legged pose, he propped his elbows on his numb kneecaps and rested his chin on his fingertips.

"Feeling better?" He said nothing. "I assume you're aware of what happened earlier." I pointed to the now vacant altar, opening my shirt so he could have a peek at my new necklace. "Nice, eh? I'll bet you didn't think I had it in me."

"Oh, I know you have it *in* you. But I do believe you'll require some assistance with estate management."

"I appreciate the offer but Ryan seems more than capable."

"You shouldn't have let them live," he said, his perforated eyelids still drooping.

"If Martin hadn't taken out Paul, we'd all be dead. Why would I want to kill him?"

"*Them*. They both have to die. That's why you need me."

"I think I'll do better on my own," I said, rolling my eyes.

"What you will do on your own is die. You have no idea how powerful they are together and how much danger you are in. You will not survive, no matter how many of these books you read. You are going to need help. From me."

I laughed. "There is no fucking way I would ever trust you."

"Trust is highly overrated. The Master never trusted me for a single second of his long life. Nor I him. Yet we had a mutually advantageous relationship for many, many years. I scratched his back. He scratched mine."

"So where's the itch?" I asked, more than a little intrigued by his proposition.

"I want protection. Starting with the best legal representation money can buy. I want to be found guilty of murdering Rose Turner by reason of insanity. I will confess to eating her flesh and cremating her bones and supply the suitable evidence. Then I want to be incarcerated in a reasonably comfortable prison with impenetrable security. The facility where Johnny Turner currently resides will be perfectly adequate. And finally, at a time of my own choosing, I want to be declared sane again, and released."

"Well, that sounds easy enough," I said, rolling my eyes. "And what do I get out of it?"

"It will be easy," he said, without a trace of a smile. "Easier than you could imagine. That's what money is for. And what you'll get is exactly what I want. Protection."

"How are you going to protect me from inside a nuthouse?" I scoffed.

"I will rally the Knights and ensure their loyalty," he said, unperturbed, holding out a finger with an angel-head ring on it. "I will also deliver my extremely lethal and dedicated followers, whose exploits on our website have kept you so enthralled. But the most important thing I have to offer is the answers you've been seeking. The answers you'll never find in those books, or even *his* Book. Like what to do about Angus Kelly…The Black Hand Man…and of course, Johnny the Saint."

I got such a chill when he said it that I wanted to turn up the thermostat. I stepped away and considered his offer and my own agenda. Questions. Answers. I thought about how far I'd already gone in my quest for knowledge. How much I'd sacrificed. And yet, I still knew so little. Would he deliver? Was he bluffing? 'Save your questions for him,' Martin told me. Did Loren really know? And if he knew would he actually tell me the truth? 'Use him,' Martin said. But what if Martin was using me? What if he steered me closer to my doom with every scrap of misinformation? I looked up at the angel, hoping he would give me a sign. All I saw was a thin trickle of blood leaking from the tabernacle in his chest.

"Okay," I said, a bit too eagerly. "You have a deal."

I could always change my mind later, right?

"Wrong," he said, reading it. "We'll have our final confrontation on some distant day, but if you betray me on this arrangement, I'll betray you in kind. And I assure you…you will not survive my treachery."

"Alright," I said, gritting my teeth. "I don't find your terms unreasonable."

"Very good. Let's shake on it."

I walked closer and grabbed his hand. It grabbed me back twice as hard. I tried to pull away but he nicked my wrist with one of his long fingernails. Then he let me go.

"Why did you do that?" I asked, pulling back, covering the tiny cut with my palm.

"A deal like ours needs to be sealed the old-fashioned way. In blood."

"Okay asshole…you say you've got answers? I've got questions. Why didn't the Book heal Paul? What happened to me when I went with him to the Maelstrom? How could my tattoos disappear…and my implants?"

The Striker started laughing in that deep, deep voice. "You don't know anything, do you? Paul taught you nothing. *Nothing!* You don't even know who you are!"

"I'm William Kelly, shithead! Now answer my questions!"

"Yes, you're William Kelly! But who is William? And who is Paul?"

"Stop going around in circles!" I shouted, so angry I almost kicked him in the face. "I'm the one asking the questions! Answer me!"

"I'm afraid all my explanations will be useless," he chuckled, slurping my blood from his fingernail. "By sunrise tomorrow you will recall nothing. Nothing at all. Perhaps we should save this interrogation for a later date… after I'm safely incarcerated."

"Ryan!" I shouted. *"Get this piece of shit out of here!"*

"Wise choice," agreed The Striker, waving happily as I made room for the jumpsuit guys to truss that fucker up. "Be sure to get a good night's sleep, sweet William. You never know what tomorrow will bring."

JOY RIDE

After they showered and changed and grabbed Mrs. Morgy, they went back downtown and picked up Martin's car.

Rose gasped when the attendant brought it up. "You have a *Goat*?"

Martin nodded proudly. He didn't like to draw attention to himself, but he couldn't resist buying the rusted silver 1968 Pontiac GTO when he first saw it up on cinderblocks near a tarpaper shack in West Virginia. He bought it for fifty 1978 dollars. The dentally challenged owners thought he was a complete patsy. He would have smiled at them if he could. He was smiling now. The Goat was in cherry condition. Dark, dark blue and shining like a mirror. He paid the attendants to wash and wax it every week, whether he drove it or not.

Martin climbed into the driver's seat and leaned into the butter-soft leather upholstery. He needed more legroom and pushed back the button on the six-way power seats. He congratulated himself again on being so handy with a wrench as his battered body relaxed.

They swung by the local U-Haul and hitched up a trailer, then went downtown and cleaned out both their apartments. Essentials only. Gold. Guns. The softest clothes, sheets and pillows. The bloodstone and the rest of Rose's gem collection.

When they finished packing, they cruised over to the Hank Hudson Drive. Martin lowered the convertible top and kissed Rose, her face glowing with joy as the New York skyline opened up to their view. She kissed him back harder, knowing it would be the last time she saw it for a long, long time.

Two Minute Warning

Johnny wiped the sweat from his brow, exhausted but hopeful. Rose was safe…she had the key…and she had Martin. That was what mattered most. The Striker was alive. That was good for him and Rose. Not so good for the rest of us.

"You have failed," Loren jeered at him, his eyes sealed beneath fleshy, punctured lids. He spoke aloud, oblivious to the cops who were wheeling him down the corridor to his holding cell.

"Looks like you're the one in the shit," laughed one of them, tugging on Loren's numerous restraints. He was wrapped up tighter than Hannibal Lector on the gurney.

"It is finished," Loren continued silently. "The *Turning* cannot be stopped."

"I know," Johnny replied. "But it's not over. The Clans will unite. I've seen it."

Their children will die! Loren's mind screamed.

Johnny the Saint peered far into the distance. He saw the twins being born, saw Martin place the slippery bundles in his daughter's waiting arms. He smiled. But only for moment. He saw the planes streaking through the air. Nothing could stop them. And worse, nothing could stop the *Turning*. Unless…

"You can still redeem yourself," he called to me. "If you don't open the Book."

"Why should I listen to you?" I silently replied.

"Because I'm trying to save your soul."

I stared at the open door of the library for a few moments.

"That's very kind of you," I finally replied, sucking in a deep, long breath before closing the door of my mind, "but I'll have to do that myself."

THE BOOK OF PAUL

This is where William was going to explain what happened when he opened the Book. Where he described what it was like to lay his hands on the cover, feeling nothing, seeing nothing, wondering again if he had only imagined the power he felt when he swore his oath of loyalty, when he was indeed saved, yet broke his vow nonetheless. He would have told of his reaction when he saw the rows upon rows of miniscule Ogham marks that went on and on and on. He would have complained about the substitution cipher code that guarded the script, how he so cleverly solved the riddle, how he realized that the Book began at the end and ended at the beginning. He would have reveled most of all in an eerie, suspenseful report of what occurred when he spoke the first words of the story aloud—how the Book came alive and the portal opened.

He would have engaged your imagination with vivid adjectives and strained similes, attempting to speak of the unspeakable, describe the indescribable, as the force tore through him. He would have offered his conjecture that the Book was burning away every trace of Sophia's contamination when she took complete possession of it for those few crucial seconds and freed Martin of his vow. He would have told you everything, neglecting to confess his role in our defeat, and the penance he still pays. But the Book will allow only this account. As to the rest, what was seen and unseen, we will not permit it. I will not permit it. Not now. Not yet. Not until we near the end and that revelation cannot alter the certainty of our triumph.

William has always been the storyteller. It would not have been fair to deprive him of his first and still most important role. He deserves our full respect, and all of the credit. He has done a splendid job, in our opinion. In his opinion, surely. When we release him, so he may finish in his own inimitable manner, this chapter will remain forever as we have written. As I have written.

There is always more to say. Always another story.

You have likely come to the conclusion that William wrote this Book from the vantage of hindsight and the wisdom that perspective usually affords, but which has been sadly lacking in this case. You will have certainly assumed he survived the entire ordeal. It would never occur to you or to anyone else that he wrote it long ago and we obliged his intent in the painful manifestation of his own prophecy. No one would ever think such a thing. That, as William was always so fond of saying, would be impossible.

William has always been the writer in our family. No one in all of time has exceeded his ability to spin his words into an inevitable web of actuality. That is his gift and our curse. My curse. Yet before I relinquish the pen and our grip on him, I thought of a clever ending to our chapter that seems worthy of his talent and our intrusion. Let us know if you agree.

While William was in the library, our loyal servant Ryan patiently awaited him outside the locked door, so he could fulfill his imperative duty. After a long while, he began to grow deeply concerned. He knew it was not his place to interrupt, that it could even be mortally perilous. Still, he was under strict orders to transport William and the Book to safety at the preordained time. Cautiously, timidly, he pressed his face against the door, rapping upon the wood as lightly as he could and still be heard. When he received no reply, he spoke as softly as he knocked.

"Sir, are you alright in there? Can I be of any assistance?"

There was no answer.

"Your car is ready, sir. Your father gave specific instructions that you were to be escorted safely home before nine o'clock this evening. It is of paramount importance."

When William at last opened the door, his simple reply carried more weight and substance than any of the words or phrases he made before or since, in this or any other book.

"Yes," he said. "I remember."

HAPPY ENDING

He smiled. Martin looked in the rearview mirror and smiled. Rose was sleeping peacefully on the big back seat. She matched the leather and chrome perfectly. They'd been talking for hours before she dozed off. Hours. He couldn't believe he had so many words inside him. She couldn't either.

He suggested a drive upstate. Pay Johnny a visit. Bust him out. Rose shook her head and said with absolute certainty, "No. He wants us to stay away. Let's go somewhere else."

Somewhere else. They were heading west now. Fast. At this rate, he calculated they would be at the farm shortly after sunrise. He wanted Rose to see the wheat field in the early morning light. See how beautiful it was. Maybe they could even have that picnic.

He glanced backward every few minutes. Making sure she was still there. He watched with complete concentration, immersed and absorbed in every breath, every twitch of her hands, every pulse in her veins. Then he looked back at the lines on the highway.

He smiled again. Naturally. Honestly. It looked so different from the old imitation, the clumsy mask he tried to carve. Just thinking about Rose made the muscles gripping his mouth rise and bloom. He was here and she was here and they were here together. She would sleep and he would drive and watch her and guard her. Forever.

Before this moment, Martin could never understand why people talked about forever. He was trapped and would always be trapped in the smells and rhythms of the moment. But now he could see all those moments linking arms and stretching out a long, long way.

He sighed and smiled again. A final surrender. And he knew from a place deep inside that he could not...would not...ever kill again.

Tonight.

Journal Entry: Home Sweet Home

I woke up this morning in a huge mansion on Fifth Avenue, right across from the Met. I can see the banners hanging from the columns right outside my window.

The bedroom is pretty high up. Five floors. Everything in the room is white. White sheets, pillows, carpet, furniture…everything. On the sheets, right in the middle of the king-size bed, I found this ledger book, mottled black, blue lined pages. Blank.

So was my head. I couldn't remember anything. Where I was, how I got here, anything. I thought I must have been on a real bender, but I didn't have a hangover. Then I got really scared because I couldn't remember what day it was, what month, what year.

I freaked out even more when I couldn't remember my name. I went a little crazy at that point, searching around the room for my clothes. I found them folded neatly on a white bench at the foot of the bed. Black pants, black turtleneck…really soft and expensive. But no wallet, no identification. I went to the bathroom and looked in the mirror. I didn't recognize my face. I thought I was going to totally lose it, but the more I looked at my reflection, the more it seemed to fit, except…I looked so young.

Everything else seemed okay: big muscles, blond hair, blue eyes, smooth, pale skin. But something was missing. On my chest? Wasn't something there before? Some scars or something? I don't know. I don't remember where I got this necklace either. With a key on the end. I looked around the room for a lock box, but all the drawers were empty.

I got a little pissed and started throwing things around, but then I calmed down and jumped in the shower. By the time I was finished, I was laughing. Loud. I got dressed and the clothes felt really good on me. I whistled a happy tune, opened the door and saw a gigantic elliptical staircase going all the way down to the bottom floor. White marble steps. Black iron railing. Black on white.

"Is anybody home?" No answer. So I walked down the staircase. There are long hallways going off in both directions on every floor. Lots of doors. The wood looks really old. Carved. Ornate.

When I got to the bottom of the stairs, I was in a big hall with really high ceilings. I must have been gawking, and I got a huge jolt when I heard a voice behind me.

"Is something wrong, sir?"

I grabbed my chest and laughed. The guy who asked me the question—Jacob, I learned—was very old and very scared. I don't know why, but that made me laugh even more. I slapped him hard on the back, like we were old buddies, and asked, "Could you be telling me what the hell I'm doing here, you rickety old rascal?"

Jesus Christ. I have an Irish accent.

The old fucker didn't say anything, but he looked like he was going to faint, especially when I shook my head and headed for the front door. He threw himself in front of me. "Out of my way," I snarled, like I was really angry. But I didn't feel angry.

And get this: He dropped to his knees in front of me. His knees!

"Forgive me, Master, but you left explicit instructions last evening that you were not to leave the house under any circumstances. Not until tomorrow. You said you wouldn't be…ready…until then."

"Master?" I asked, but part of me was chuckling inside. The old geezer stared up at me like I was going to chop off his head or something, but he stood his ground and started pleading with me again.

"Master, I'm following your direct orders. If you came downstairs, I was to request that you return to your room immediately…and begin writing in the book that was left for you. The journal."

"My room? What are you prattling on about? Whose house is this? How did I get here?" I demanded, really feeling my oats now.

"This is your house," he said, utterly terrified. "I am your servant, Jacob."

My house. My fucking servant! I thought he was crazy at first, but somehow I knew he was telling the truth. I was feeling a little shook up myself, but I nodded and walked back up the stairs. Five floors. It was so easy. I felt so good. So strong.

So here I am, back in the bedroom. Writing. Why? Who knows? But as soon as I put pen to paper (nice pen, by the way), I have to say it felt really good, like it was my job or something. Anyway, that's my day so far. I'm getting hungry now. I think I'll have another talk with Jacob. Grab a sandwich. On the way down, I guess I'll poke around a little. I noticed an open door on the third floor. A library.

Good. I'm getting bored with this shit. Maybe I can find something to read.